W9-AZV-443

WE MEASURE THE EARTH WITH OUR BODIES

WE
MEASURE
THE EARTH
WITH OUR
BODIES

WE
MEASURE
THE EARTH
WITH OUR
BODIES

A NOVEL

TSERING YANGZOM LAMA

BLOOMSBURY PUBLISHING

NEW YORK • LONDON • OXFORD • NEW DELHI • SYDNEY

BLOOMSBURY PUBLISHING
Bloomsbury Publishing Inc.
1385 Broadway, New York, NY 10018, USA

BLOOMSBURY, BLOOMSBURY PUBLISHING, and the Diana logo
are trademarks of Bloomsbury Publishing Plc

First published in the United States 2022

Copyright © Tsering Yangzom Lama, 2022

All rights reserved. No part of this publication may be reproduced or transmitted
in any form or by any means, electronic or mechanical, including photocopying,
recording, or any information storage or retrieval system, without prior permission in
writing from the publishers.

This book contains verses from the sixth chapter of Taksham Nuden Dorje's revelation of
Yeshe Tsogyal's life story. Translation by Holly Gayley in *Inseparable across Lifetimes*
(Shambhala Publications, 2019), 24, used with permission.

ISBN: HB: 978-1-63557-641-2; EBOOK: 978-1-63557-642-9

LIBRARY OF CONGRESS CATALOGING-IN-PUBLICATION DATA IS AVAILABLE

2 4 6 8 10 9 7 5 3 1

Typeset by Westchester Publishing Services
Printed and bound in the U.S.A.

To find out more about our authors and books visit www.bloomsbury.com and sign up
for our newsletters.

Bloomsbury books may be purchased for business or promotional use. For information
on bulk purchases please contact Macmillan Corporate and Premium Sales Department at
specialmarkets@macmillan.com.

to my mother and my late father,
to all my relations across time and space,
to every soul who has known, lost, and sought home.

Throughout the whole land of Tibet
there are countless places where I practiced.
There is not a handful or bit of earth
that has not been blessed by me.

Successively, in the future, the signs of truth
will be revealed, extracted one by one as treasures.
In an inconceivable number of little places,
filled with my hand- and footprints in rock,
are placed mantras, seed syllables, and statues,
left behind as the basis for faith in the future
with aspirations to benefit those connected with me.

—PROPHECY OF YOGINI, YESHE TSOGYAL, EIGHTH CENTURY

CONTENTS

I: DAUGHTERS

    Lhamo, 1960   3
    Dolma, 2012   79

II: SISTERS

    Lhamo, 1973   133
    Tenkyi, 2012   179

III: LOVERS

    Lhamo, 1984   227
    Samphel, 2012   263

IV: SELF

    Dolma, 2012   301

    Acknowledgments   347

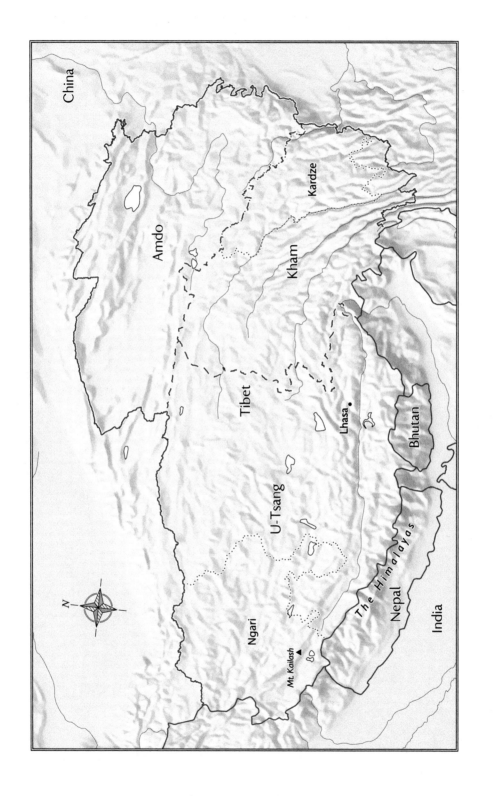

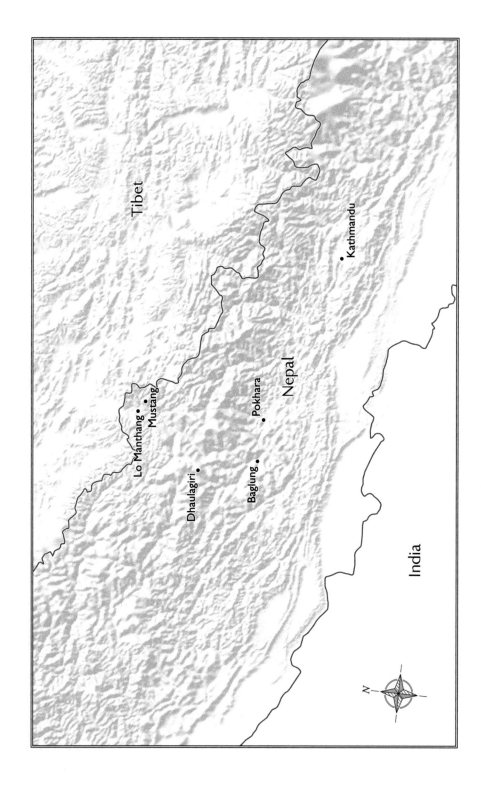

PART I

Daughters

LHAMO

I

Border of Western Tibet and Nepal

Spring 1960

AMA was an oracle. The realization came to my mother late in life, when her monthly bleedings stopped and something else opened inside. Some in our village called it an affliction. They said there was a crack in her mind that left her open to spirits who would consume her. But Ama insisted it was a blessing to lend her body to the gods and allow them to speak through her. In time, everyone would listen, and the words of an otherwise ordinary woman would lead us through the coming troubles.

It wasn't just my mother who had changed. Packs of wolves and rats swept through our valley. Next, there was an earthquake that tore a jagged line through our village monastery. Then, just as I was learning to speak, there came news that invaders had crossed our border, entering our land as two enormous snakes. In the distant town of Kardze, people watched them cross the river in long lines and burrow into the highlands. They wished to be called the People's Liberation Army, but we knew them as the Gyami, a people from the lowlands to the east.

In the years that followed, rumors came like crows, even traveling as far west as our village. Although I was just a young girl, many of the rumors landed in my ears before anyone else in my family. My source was Lhaksam, my oldest friend. He worked as a servant to a traveling merchant who traded in gossip as much as iron pots and pans. In our free moments, Lhaksam and I wandered in the pastures with my little sister

Tenkyi hanging on my back or flopping around in the grass. In those hills, Lhaksam told me the most shocking stories. Gyami soldiers had seized farmland in the east, and many of our people were now starving. *No grain, no salt, no meat or even butter.* I walked around in a daze after hearing this, unable to imagine life without butter. Lhaksam said that although it was quiet in our region, a resistance raged in the east, in places where iron birds circled the skies and bullets big and small rained down on entire towns, smashing bodies as if they were nothing but effigies made of dough, where rooftops were torn apart and no one could tell whether they had found the remains of a loved one or that of a stranger. But I did not tell my family these things. I never repeated them to anyone.

Then, last spring, our village heard of a terrifying ruse: a plan to lead the Precious One into the dragon's home. Hearing about this trap, thousands of our people in Lhasa gathered outside the summer palace, forming a protective circle with their bodies. Even as the soldiers neared and the scent of gunpowder swirled in the air, our people refused to leave. To prevent a massacre, the Precious One disguised himself as a commoner and fled south by night to another country. So did the great Nechung Oracle, who had divined their escape route through the mountains. When the foreign troops learned that our leader had slipped away, they pierced the crowd with bullets and lined the streets with corpses.

After the Precious One left, the sun was erased from our skies. Flowers refused to bloom, and our yaks made no milk. In that darkness, every family in our village wondered if it was time to leave, to follow our leader to the lowlands until the day when it would be safe to return. Others recited a bleak, ancient prophecy: *When the iron bird flies and horses run on wheels, the People of Snows will be scattered like ants across the face of the earth.*

It was that day, nearly ten years after revealing that the gods had spoken to her, when Ama said to us, "Now is the time. I must give my body to the spirits."

Sitting on the kitchen floor beside my sister, I watched my father's face in the hearth's glow. Pala remained still as we chewed on strips of dried meat that Ama had cured over the winter. I could see that our father was clearly picturing everything that would change for us, but after a long while, he frowned, showing all of his new wrinkles at once, and nodded in agreement. By morning, our entire village had heard that Ama would begin the rites for instructing the gods. She would finally call them down to her.

IT MADE SENSE when they said Tenkyi was too young to watch the initiation. She was barely ten, but I couldn't believe it when Pala also ushered me out of the room. While at least twenty people from our village filed into the kitchen, many of them patting Tenkyi and me on our cheeks and heads as if to cheer us up, the two of us were forced to wait in the hallway. Even Lhaksam managed to slip in, though not without flashing a huge grin in my direction. I stood there chewing my nails until the prayers began. Then I realized what I needed to do. Taking Tenkyi outside, I ordered my sister to gather our sheep along the hills and bring them all back, a task that would take at least an hour even with our dog Diksen's help. Thankfully, my sister was somewhat obedient this time. She went off to search for the sheep, and I rushed back home to watch the ceremony through a slit in the wooden door.

Over a thick huddle of bodies, I saw Ama seated on the ground with her head down. Beside her stood a teacher monk and his young assistant, who looked frightened to perform a task like this when he typically spent his days carrying milk and water up to the monastery.

"If you are a god," said the elderly monk as he faced my mother, "take this apron."

The assistant produced an apron and tied it around my mother's waist. Ama continued to gaze at the floor as her body trembled.

"If you are a god, then take this drum and bell."

The assistant placed these instruments in Ama's hands.

"Come to this woman, speak to us! Stay not at the mountaintop but come to us."

Ama began to shake and whisper in a birdlike voice. The assistant placed a heavy embroidered cape around her shoulders, then a five-pointed crown on her head. Despite the weight of the regalia, Ama hopped up on her feet and began to rock side to side. The assistant moved away, his eyes wide with fear, but the teacher monk called him back.

"Take this golden drink," he said, holding out a bowl of beer.

Putting down her instruments, my mother took the bowl, offered it to the sky, and drank the beer in one gulp like a man. Then she danced, spinning to the left and right, dipping and jerking her head. The teacher monk leaned in, pushed my mother's shoulders down to keep her still, and spoke into her ear. She shook like a startled horse and uttered a language I could not understand. Was this the language of the gods? Hearing my mother's words, the teacher monk nodded and reached into a bowl of rice. With a graceful flick, he tossed a handful of grains onto the drum held flat in his hand. It sounded like a rain shower and still echoes in my head.

"It is dangerous to call the gods," he told the audience. "We must ensure that we have not called a malicious spirit by mistake."

The teacher monk explained that if an evil spirit entered her body, there would be chaos for Ama and everyone who sought her help. On the other hand, if part of my mother's consciousness remained in her body when a spirit entered, she would become half god and half human, and then we could not trust her words. Hearing this, I started to shake. If the gods never left my mother's body, she would never be herself again. Why would Pala agree to this? Yet it was already far too late to stop. The teacher said that it was time for the test. Ama must be able to say, without looking, exactly how many grains of rice had landed on the drum. She also needed to know the meaning of this number. What it prophesied. Pressing my face into the door, I strained to learn the outcome.

I had my answer when the elderly monk slowly knelt and prostrated himself before my mother. A wave of prayers rose from the crowd as they, too, lowered to the floor. Only I remained standing, peering through the crack, trying in vain to catch a glimpse of my mother's face. Then my chest felt heavy like wet clay, and I was drawn facedown to the floor of frozen mud, my palms pressed above my head, my lips moving rapidly in prayer as breath spread between my ribs.

WORD TRAVELED ACROSS the western plains. Visitors came to see my mother—a little wary and curious, bowing and speaking in hushed tones like they did at a monastery. Even my father's old friend, Choesang, arrived at our door with his ailing son behind his legs.

"Everything has changed," Pala said. "But to me, she's still just my Yangchen."

"Yes, that must also be true," Choesang replied, tidying his worn sleeves as he settled in and waited for his son's turn with Ama.

In the days that followed, Pala fetched two servants to help with the visitors. Tenkyi and I watched them float around the house with tea and food and ceremonial objects for the divinations while parched, weary horses milled about the courtyard and waited for their masters to be healed. How many hundreds came in that strange time, in the year before we fled the highlands? How many came knocking on our wooden door, sweeping in the dust with their foreign robes, leaving their scent long into the evening? Even now, so far from home, I can close my eyes and remember the peculiar silk brocade designs on their sleeves and collars. I can picture the red gown worn by a distant warlord's wife, that thin, white-haired woman who had come to ask if her child's marriage was well fated. She said her own marriage had been an unhappy one, and whatever answer Ama gave, the woman returned again to ask if she should make a pilgrimage to Lhasa despite ill health and invading forces. Just as Tenkyi and I had grown used to her visits, the summer and fall passed without any sight of her. There came rumors that she had fallen down a well—or was called to its bottom by a demon spirit. Now, it seems more likely that the Gyami had imprisoned her.

Then there were the visitors who came to ask about the health of their herds, or whether they should search at home or in the hills for a lost turquoise. Some came with ailments like melancholy and restlessness. They said only Ama could name the source of their sorrows. Only she could banish the evil from their bodies. Yes, that is what they said.

IT WASN'T LONG after Ama's initiation that the snake entered our village. A row of dark trucks, rattling the earth and sending up clouds of dust. Still, the foreigners didn't seem as frightening as I had imagined. I had almost expected to see horns sticking out of their heads. But they were just young men and women who insisted that they had not come to hurt us. All they wanted was to gather everyone and have a conversation. We were required to do as they said, so Tenkyi and I walked to the village square as Diksen followed closely along. The crowd was thick, but we slipped through to the first row.

"We have heard about the oracles in your region," said the head soldier, his country's words translated by a former salt merchant who was now working for the invaders.

"It's time to get to the bottom of these rumors," the merchant translated, though his Lhasa dialect was hard for us to understand.

As the head soldier gave his orders, I noticed how handsome he was, even as he moved his head in a jerking manner. He couldn't have been more than twenty-five years old.

Two soldiers led three women into the circle. Ama was in the group. Right away, I pulled Tenkyi close so she wouldn't cry out. We watched as the women headed to the center of the square and were instructed to stand in a line. Ama kept her gaze toward the hills while the other women looked into the crowd as though silently requesting help. People murmured and shifted in agitation. Even Diksen began to growl beneath his shaggy bangs, so I nudged him twice with my leg to quiet him.

"If the powers of these so-called oracles are indeed real," the merchant said, "if these superstitions have any basis, these women will surely pass a simple test."

A soldier carried a large bowl of water into the middle of the crowd. He walked around the circle, showing the contents of the bowl. Inside, there were several small stones within the water. All but one of the stones were ordinary. That one stone was a bright red coral.

"Red as the star on my hat," the soldier said, pointing at his head with a smile.

A few people smiled and laughed nervously in return. The soldiers went to the first woman in line and tied a blindfold around her eyes. I told myself there was nothing to fear. This test was not unlike the ones Ama faced during her initiation. She would surely find the coral among the pebbles.

But just as the soldiers covered Ama's eyes, Pala walked over, picked up Tenkyi in his arms, and took me by the hand. "Don't make any noise," he said. We slipped away quietly, helped by a few people who covered us.

Back at home, Pala ushered us through the door, though he remained outside. Even as he tried to sound steady, his voice was tense, as though trying to swallow flies caught in his throat. "Lhamo, take your little sister to bed," he managed to say before heading back on the road toward the village square.

Once we could no longer hear his footsteps, I led my sister to our bed, pulled the blankets over our heads, and began to tell stories about the mischievous hero Aku Tonpa until Tenkyi fell asleep.

Late that evening, the yak bells announced my parents' return. Peering into their room, I watched with secret relief as Ama put away her regalia and instruments in a wooden trunk. In the days that followed, I learned what had happened from pieces of conversation. All three women had failed the test, and they were now forbidden from practicing divinations or healing again. For several weeks, the house was quiet, and no one came with requests. But slowly, people in our village began knock at our doors at night, followed by visitors from farther away. It seemed everyone had agreed that the Gyami test was rigged.

"These soldiers have been doing tests across the entire region," they said.

"I heard the devils failed every medium they encountered."

"We've had oracles in this region for eight hundred years."

"From time immemorial! Even before the Buddha's teachings came to this land."

"Nothing and no one can stop our gods from speaking to us."

But I was finished with divinations. I had seen my father's face as he led us away from the village square. I had imagined my mother's severed hands falling onto our roof. Whenever a ritual took place in the middle of the night, I left the house with Diksen, and we wandered by moonlight into the hills. Even in daylight, I stayed away from our house, choosing to watch the soldiers in their peculiar labors instead.

One afternoon, I heard some thumping above my head. I went onto the roof and saw soldiers attaching boxes to the poles where we normally hung prayer flags. Our flags had been tossed aside, thrown in the corner of the roof even though they were lined with sacred text that should never touch the ground. I quickly gathered the soiled prayer flags so that we could dispose of them properly in a fire ceremony. One of the soldiers came near me and knelt down. He looked young, perhaps just a few years older than me. I pointed up and asked what the boxes were for. He replied in a tongue that was sharp and nasal. When I didn't understand, he tried again, cupping his hands around his mouth this time and moving his lips as if he were shouting. I shook my head and laughed. At this, the soldier recoiled in disgust before standing up and walking away. I will never forget his face. A near perfect square. His hair fell in soft wisps down to his eyebrows, the sides cut close to the scalp, his appearance meticulously controlled.

It must have been the next morning when a strange, high-pitched music blared from those boxes, hour after hour, broken only by long speeches. Ama paced in the kitchen, pressing her ears closed, and Diksen wouldn't stop barking. Eventually, Tenkyi and I led him to the animal stables so he could hide his furry black head in the hay. Sitting there with our hands resting on Diksen's trembling back, I thought about the day Ama was tested by the soldiers. I wondered if she had seen us in the crowd, if she knew how frightened we had been. Did she look to the hills that day because that is where the gods reside, or because she couldn't face us?

SOON IT WAS too dangerous to continue the divinations, even in secret. The soldiers were becoming brash. They called themselves our leaders and enlisted one male child from every family to become a soldier or laborer for the army. Our way of life, they said, was nothing but savage.

One night, a voice from the noisy boxes on our rooftops ordered everyone to the monastery. When we arrived before the prayer hall, the monks were already standing outside in a line. There were even some nuns who must have been brought down from the convent in the hills. Before them, there was a box of iron tools, sickles and hammers.

"You will smash every statue inside," the head soldier shouted. Our monastery had hundreds of statues, some so small that they could fit in my palm, while the largest was a three-story gold statue of Guru Rinpoche containing precious stones.

"They will make bullets of the statues," Lhaksam whispered.

"Don't lie. How?" I asked.

"They melt the statues and use the metal to make bullets, Lhamo. Then they will kill us with our own gods."

The nuns and monks made their way to the front and refused. Some wailed in protest, while others knelt on the ground, pressed their hands before them, and began to chant prayers for the liberation of all beings. The army commander gave a signal, and one by one, the soldiers began striking the monks and nuns with their guns. Each blow made a wet cracking sound as the defenders of our monastery crumpled to the ground. They fell so easily. I wondered why our people had only monks and nuns, but not an army.

The next morning, we were called to the monastery again. The soldiers had now recruited beggars to destroy the holy relics. One volunteered to tackle the three-story Guru Rinpoche statue, but before he could begin, he covered the statue's face with a bedsheet. Then, without a word, he struck it with an ax several times, but his weak arms barely chipped the metal. It took him nearly a week to completely destroy the statue, but by the end, he had found hundreds of precious pellets of turquoise, coral, and even the rare dzi stone stored inside. They celebrated him as a proletarian hero and gifted him a landowner's house, but he quickly descended into madness, laughing and pounding his own head constantly as he roamed around our valley with his precious stone necklaces.

Lhaksam said the troubles of our village were not unique. He had heard of a whole village near Shigatse that attempted to escape together. Two thousand soldiers went in search of one hundred people. The villagers dropped their belongings to gain speed. They hid in caves and drank raindrops. Still, they were captured and imprisoned.

"Will you try to escape again?" the interrogator asked.

"No," the people replied. Then they repeated the lines they were instructed to speak: "This is the most wonderful country in the world and you are our benevolent liberators."

"Good. You must remain here and tell everyone about our leniency."

"We will remain," they promised.

A few months later, the entire village fled again, carrying nothing this time. All but two survived the journey to India.

Even our sky was changing. Sheets lined with unfamiliar script fell from above. The pages were pasted on our doors, strung on enormous banners across rooftops, and handed out in little red booklets. We learned that the foreigner's language was made of whole words, not letters. Each word was made of sharp lines layered one over the other with edges that formed an invisible box. An ornate but rapid script, its direction was different from ours, running up and down instead of left to right. In the privacy of our home, when the servants were away, Ama tore the flyers and fed them into the oven. I had never seen anyone treat written text like that. We would not dream of stepping over a page inscribed with letters, much less ripping it to shreds. Until then, everything written had been holy.

"They came to submerge our senses," Ama said.

"Isn't it time to stop the divinations?" I asked.

"That was just a game. They were playing with us. In five years, they will arrest and kill people like me. Our monasteries will be reduced to less than ten across our land. Even the Jokhang will be ransacked. And our own people will take part in this destruction."

"Like the beggar who went mad?" I asked, but Ama must not have heard me.

"They will not be satisfied with our land alone. They want to possess our minds."

Something came over me. With my whole body tight as a fist, I went up to my mother and said I would kill the soldiers if they ever harmed our family. I said I would slit their throats myself.

"No," Ama replied. "You can't do that."

"What should I do?"

"Lift your chin," she said. "Crane your neck. Show them you're not afraid."

Tears pooled in my eyes as I contemplated my self-sacrifice. I secretly worried that I would be a coward. I also worried that my blood would be the color of their flag, which now flew over every house and even our monastery. Let my blood be white, I prayed. Let it be the color of the gods, white like the khata scarves of our people. But I had seen that everyone's blood is the same color. When it flows, when it merges, blood is nameless.

THE DAY CAME when Ama's younger brother, Ashang Migmar, turned up suddenly at our door with a small number of his sheep and yaks. It must have been four or five years since we had last seen our uncle. He lived with our grandparents in the grasslands a week's journey by horse to the northwest. Each time we reunited, our visits were planned months ahead around horse festivals, the lunar new year, or big religious ceremonies. And although Ashang was not a wealthy nomad, he made sure our gatherings were stocked with good cheese, meat, and bricks of tea—all of which we enjoyed while he regaled us with songs and stories that we would dream of hearing for months beforehand.

But on that day, Ashang Migmar walked into our kitchen without a word or a smile. Not even an embrace. He went straight to Ama and began to share the news of our grandparents. He said that he and Popo, our grandfather, had gone to gather salt. While they were there, the Gyami had taken control of the region, claiming the salt for themselves and bombing the sacred rock of the guardian of the salt.

"In the dust and smoke, Father and I saw something glimmer. At first, I thought it was a fire. But then it began moving through the rubble, and through the dust, we saw a golden horse emerge, galloping along the plain, moving faster than anything I had ever seen."

"Dayay Tsakha," Ama whispered.

"I wouldn't have believed my own eyes, except that we both saw the golden horse hurtling across the horizon. The next moment, the horse began to lift off the ground and take flight, rising above the wreckage and up to the skies. Even the Gyami soldiers couldn't catch him. Then he vanished, and before our very eyes, the salt plains transformed in a flash. As if all of its life force had been lost, it became gray and sullen and dead. Now there's no salt left. Tell me, Sister, who are we without our salt?"

After the bombing, Popo told a few trusted people about what he and Ashang had witnessed, causing everyone who heard the story to weep. But someone must have cried false tears because the next day, our grandfather was taken away. Ashang waited outside the Gyami barracks for a week with Momo, our grandmother. They begged the officials to forgive a foolish old man with bad eyesight. But Popo never returned, and Momo died after refusing to eat for twelve days as she pleaded with the officers.

"Where are Momo and Popo now?" Tenkyi asked.

"Say no more," Ama said to Ashang. "Not in front of the girls."

Ashang turned, surprised to see Tenkyi and me. The expression on his face made me think of an empty walnut shell.

"Girls, take Ashang's animals to the hills," Pala said. "Make sure they're well fed before nightfall."

"I want to hear the rest of the story," Tenkyi sulked.

"Stop it," I snapped. If only she'd been quiet, we could have listened in. Now I would have to leave the kitchen with Tenkyi. Still, I moved as slowly as I could, lingering by the door to gather our slings in case of wolves, which had come in larger packs lately.

Just as we stepped outside, I heard Pala's voice in the kitchen. "The serpent has coiled around our necks," he said. "We should leave."

When Tenkyi and I returned at dusk, a dozen people from our village were gathered in the kitchen. There were several conversations taking place at once.

"We should all head north."

"North, did you say?"

"That's right. I heard the troops haven't gone there."

"But the Precious One went south. It only makes sense to follow him if we leave."

"My family won't leave. Not now, not ever," said our neighbor Au Rignam, Lhaksam's master.

"It's just for a little while, until we get help."

"No one is coming to help," replied Au Rignam. "Can't you see that? Ten years, the godless invaders have been slowly eating our country. They took such small bites that we didn't even notice until our limbs were gone."

"You want to stay until they take our minds too?"

"Let's take up arms! We are not cowards!"

"We cannot kill our enemies. We should do what our ancestors have done. Bury our things safely in the earth and leave until this madness ends. This war, like every war, will end."

Ama stood up quietly at that. She remained standing, and I could tell she was preparing to address the crowd. One by one, people saw Ama and fell silent. "It's no small matter to leave," she said, her voice, steady and familiar. "Our homes are here. Our gods are here, in our mountains and rivers that we know so well. We are tied to this land and this land is tied to us, in every way possible. But one thing has become clear to me. The destruction will not end, not for many years. Meanwhile, our doorway to escape will shrink and shrink, until only a few souls will manage to cross the border each year, like the final raindrops after a storm. This is why my family will leave tomorrow night. If you want to come with us, pack your belongings now. Be ready to walk when the moon is blanketed by clouds. The spirits have given me the path."

2

Mustang, Nepal

Winter 1961

No one would admit this, but I think we have found our temporary home. After months of living in caves and snowbanks, foraging for berries and drinking from mountain streams, we have descended to the desert lowlands. Here, people look and sound a little like us, though they call themselves by different names. Here, we found a valley dotted with many others who fled from other parts of Ngari and U-Tsang. Our group of eighteen families, nearly half our village, huddles together beside a mighty river, making a new village with fabric and sticks. We pitch Ashang's yak-hair tent and build a proper hearth. We find occasional work laboring in the fields before the frost arrives. And we wait, day after day, to return home. Home, which is north of here, just beyond the mountains we have crossed. This is the direction Ama stares in silence, looking through me as if I were nothing but the horizon. I watch my mother now more than ever before, and I often wonder what she's thinking. Is she looking for signs of our return? Preparing for another divination? Or is she seeking answers to the same questions that haunt the rest of us: Where are our gods? Have they left their ancient homes in the mountains and lakes to walk with us, or are we truly alone in this new earth?

It's late morning now, and I have just returned to our camp with firewood in my arms. Soon, walls of sand will whip this land speechless, and it will be impossible to even open our eyes. When the wind rages like this, when it's so loud we can't speak or hear each other, I think about home. I think about Lhaksam, who remained behind with what remained of his master's family. I think about Diksen, who would not stop barking. Fearing this would draw unwanted attention, Pala tied Diksen to a rock and left him behind. Tenkyi had been asleep when this happened. When she found out, she cried that Gyami soldiers had killed every dog in Lhasa. She said shooting Diksen would have been more compassionate than leaving him to starve. I felt the same grief as my sister, but I couldn't cry. Even now, standing in this wind that can hide the sound of my weeping, my tears collect inside me, unable to fall out.

As I enter our tent, I spot a long lump on the floor against one wall. Tenkyi is still asleep nearby. She has been in bed most days because she can't keep food down. I walk over to the other sleeping body, and Pala's face comes into view. His eyes are open, just staring at the sloped ceiling. Footsteps come and go outside, crunching the earth. Ama and Ashang must be foraging for food, and at this hour, Pala should also be off in search of supplies. He tends to go farther than any of us on his walks, gathering firewood, water, and sometimes news. Pala doesn't like to depend on rumors. When too many days pass without information, he hikes up the ridges to other encampments closer to the plateau to see what he can learn about the battles raging there. How are our fighters faring against the invaders? Are they hungry like us? Sometimes Pala returns home with stories of the Chushi Gangdruk fighters and their powers. He says Gyami weapons can't kill our men. Bullets simply bounce off their bodies because of their blessed amulets. These stories make everyone in our group smile, though we smile less as the months pass. Has my father heard some bad news?

"Pala, what's the matter?" I whisper. He says nothing, so I ask again.

"Is she asleep?" he asks.

My sister is exhaling shallow, rapid breaths as though locked in a dream where she's running. She has been feverish and having nightmares.

"Lhamo, help me with my boots," Pala says.

By itself, the request would not normally worry me, but there was something strange in his expression just after he spoke. As if he had failed in some great task. I hesitate for a moment before I lift my father's blanket. The cloth tip of his boot is soft and worn thin between my fingers. I raise his foot, expecting the boot to come off easily, but it doesn't move. I will need to use some force. When I tug, Pala presses his eyes shut and looks away, sucking the air through his teeth. Tightening my grip, I twist the cloth, pull once more, and the boot is finally free.

"What is it?" he asks.

I can say nothing.

"Is the flesh black?"

So he knows. I pull up the blanket to cover the ugliness. Why did he make me look? But of course, I had to. Hunching down, I lift the blanket again and peer inside its mouth. Pala's toes are the darkest—purple and black, as if charred by fire—while the center of his foot is bruised yellow and red, covered with swollen blisters. But near his ankle, the skin is normal, perfect brown. For days, Pala has been complaining about his boots. He said there must be holes in the cloth because his feet were so cold, but no one could find any.

"Ama," I manage to say as my mouth fills with thick, salty fluid. "I'll get Ama."

Pala clutches my wrist. His grip is so gentle. "No. Check the other one."

The right foot is even worse, nearly all of it blackened. Blood pumps inside my ears and presses against my temples. Rubbing my hands, I prepare to heat my father's feet, but I am stopped in place by a small patch of blackened skin rising above his big toe, separated from the flesh. Extending a finger, I lightly graze the skin. Like a dry leaf. I touch his toe again, this time pressing a little.

"Does that hurt?" No reply and his eyes are closed. I ask the question again.

"Does what hurt?" he asks.

Hunching my body to form a warm chamber, I lift my father's feet by the still-brown heels, place them onto my lap, and begin to blow on the skin. The wind picks up and the tent stretches out, then in again, as if trying to take flight. Could the spirits just lift us with one gust, and take us back into the highlands?

"There you are," Ama says, ducking into the tent. A shawl is wrapped tightly around her head, leaving only a slit for her to see through, and she's holding something in her apron. Unwrapping the shawl, Ama goes to Tenkyi, checks her fever, and places an apple on the ground beside her. "I found work in an orchard today!" she says, beaming as she hands me an apple. "Go on, there will be more. Now that the season's almost over, they need extra hands."

I lift the fruit to my teeth. Its skin pierces with a pop. After months of eating leafy shrubs, small game, and whatever barley we could barter for, a fresh apple tastes like something from another life. Closing my mouth, I let my teeth bite down fully, but a staggering pain shoots through my body and I spit out the apple's flesh. On the ground, beside Pala's fingers, the gnawed piece of fruit sits covered in blood. Something small and hard lingers in my mouth. I open my burning jaw and let it fall into my palm. A brown tooth drops, followed by a trail of red-streaked saliva.

Tonguing my mouth, I discover a hollow space so tender I dare not touch it. I pick up the tooth and close my fist around it. And still my stomach moans for more. As the apple's fluid fills the painful gap and coats my tongue, I slip and let myself remember butter, cheese, dumplings, all of which we may never have again. In my hands, I hold two things: a dead tooth and an apple that I cannot eat.

Without another thought, I toss the tooth back into my mouth and swallow the jagged thing. It slides down my throat, and I taste the acrid mix of blood and fruit with grains of sand.

When I turn back, Ama is staring at Pala's feet, stunned for a moment. Then, as if jolted awake, she moves me aside and takes his feet into her lap. "Lhamo, go find some juniper and sage," she says. "We need to start a fire." Humming a prayer, she presses her cheek on his toes. I watch my father whisper something. To my deep relief, Ama gives him a gentle smile and replies, "Shhh. Better soon."

Suddenly, it's as though my mother were back to her old self. Propelled by a secret list of tasks and prayers that only she understands, performing healings no one else can.

FOR SIX DAYS, Ama has done nothing but take care of Pala. She has pressed his blackened skin with barley dough, circled incense around his body, fed him the last of our blessed herbs, and prayed most of the day, trying to call the gods down to her. I have kept myself busy, as well. Leaving at first light, I set off to hunt for game with my sling. I wander the hills, looking for firewood, juniper, and sage. And I care for my little sister, trying to bring down her fever and stop her chills. Ashang Migmar worries that I will wear myself out. But I cannot stop. Whether our fate is good or bad, I see that a thread ties each of us to one another. When Tenkyi has nightmares, when Pala thrashes in pain, I can feel a force draw me to the earth. When Ama is strong, I can feel my own chest expand, my gaze pulling outward. This is why I cannot stop. I cannot stop because Pala says that he feels better. Thanks to Ama's efforts, he senses recovery. Still, I cannot stop because he remains in bed, unable to walk.

But this morning, Ama took Pala's knife, stood in the sun, and cut off her hair. Tenkyi pulled on Ama's arm and begged her to stop, but I knew that she wouldn't listen to us. As her plaits dropped to the ground, turquoise and coral stones woven years ago tapped the earth like fallen chestnuts. Ama told me to help her pull the stones out. We could barter them for food, she said. As we worked through her hair, I saw my mother clearly for the first time, like a stranger would. Her scalp was rough and uneven. Loose hairs stuck to her thin shoulders. In that moment, I recalled a story Lhaksam once shared about another oracle from a nearby village. She had long gray hair to her stomach and lived all alone in a house built into a cave way up in the mountains. Lhaksam said she was a woman of loose morals. All manner of men visited her when they were tired of their wives, traveling to her home with a lantern. His eyes darted before he leaned in and whispered that she accepted everyone into her bed. Even ghosts and demons. *Ever see a star moving in the east, past the monastery? That's a ghost walking with a lantern to the woman's house.* Now I wonder if my mother has become wild in another way, if she has crossed some threshold and entered a path that cannot be retraced.

When we finished pulling the stones out, Ama rushed into the tent with her hair. Pala woke to the commotion. Stuffing the strands into his boots, she said a prayer and turned to him.

"So you may be warm again and heal."

Seeing Ama's bare scalp, my father was quiet. Then he began to cry. Finally, Pala admitted he could no longer feel his feet. He had lost all sensation days ago.

TONIGHT, PO DHONDUP has come to our tent again to help Pala. I wonder what he could possibly offer, this man who arrived here alone a month ago. The day he joined our group, I even thought he might be a ghost. He had no family, no yaks, no sheep. Nothing to trade or sell for food. Who else but a ghost would travel like that?

Ever since Pala became ill and Ama occupied with his recovery, my uncle and Po Dhondup have grown close like brothers as they search for odd jobs among the locals. It's strange to think that only a month ago, my parents felt so sorry for Po Dhondup that they told him to camp with us. Now, if not for his help, we might have even less to eat. Our fortunes seem to change from day to day.

"I should have brought this to you long ago," Po Dhondup says, standing before us with a silk bundle in his hands. The last time he spoke like this, he told us the story of his dead family. Though he will no longer speak their names, Po Dhondup had three children and a wife who starved after the Gyami forced their village to plant rice instead of barley. He spoke slowly that night, and with great difficulty, as if each word cut a nick into his heart. But now it seems he has more to say about his past.

"After my family perished, I wandered from village to village, a man half-dead." He pauses to steady his voice and looks ahead as if peering through the tent walls.

"Go on, Dhondup," Ashang Migmar says.

Po Dhondup straightens his posture, making himself completely still before he continues. In the stream of light pouring down from the tent's center, I see how long his plaits fall when they're not tucked away. Almost as long as Ashang Migmar's.

"Chasing my family's ghosts, I rode across our vast country, along three rivers and five mountain ranges. For two years I rode, and in that time aged twenty years, my hair turning white, my skin loosening from its bones. Finally, on the edge of death, I came to a village in ruins. The homes had been looted and the monastery was nothing but rubble, murals hammered from the walls, thangkas and scriptures burned, earthen statues smashed while the metal ones had been taken. Seeking a place to lie down and die, I found a courtyard where I hoped to enter the bardo in prayer. In a small clearing under a gray sky, I waited for the God of Death. Then something caught the light, sparkling under a pile of fallen pillars. With the last of my strength, I pushed the wooden rubble away. Hidden inside a perfect chamber of air, there was a little statue of a Saint I did not recognize. Somehow, this ku was untouched. He looked up at the sky just as I had done a moment earlier. I marveled at the only survivor of this village. Amid all the destruction, this mudstone Saint had survived. All was not lost, I realized. I felt that I had to carry on, if only to bring the statue into someone's care, away from the foreigners' path. That is how I found the strength to carry on to the lowlands."

Tenkyi is clinging to my back now, the way she would when she was smaller, her ribs expanding and contracting against my spine. She whispers in my ear, "Go closer, Big Sister, so we can see the ku."

"Alright, dear," I say, relieved that she has the energy to ask me for something. We press against Ashang's shoulder to get a better view.

Po Dhondup kneels on the ground before Pala and places the silk bundle before him. "I no longer have a family. I have fulfilled my reason for living, but you must survive. This is why I want to pass this Saint's ku into your care. I sense this is where he should be."

Slowly, Po Dhondup unties the layers of silk. He pulls apart the knots, which are stiff enough to be wooden. After three layers of silk fall away, a small statue comes into view as prayers leave our lips. A thin, almost skeletal figure. Naked but for his loincloth, even the gold pigment on his body has nearly worn away. Seated, he looks up at the sky with a pained expression.

"He looks like a madman, not a saint," Tenkyi whispers.

I try to hide the disappointment on my face. It's true, he doesn't seem like a deity. He is not beautiful or inspiring. His expression is not wise or calm or loving. Instead, he seems a lot like us. Hungry, lost.

"This ku was made from the earth of our homeland," Po Dhondup says. "Many lifetimes ago, I think. The rest of his story is unknown to me, lost in the dust of our upheaval. I don't even know his name."

Ama moves forward, closer to the ku. As she presses her palms together in prayer, her eyes pool with tears. "I know this ku. I prayed before him many years ago," she says. "I was around Tenkyi's age. That's when I had the first break from my mind. Do you remember, Brother?"

Ashang Migmar nods. "We thought you would die."

"Each night, I was tossed in a river of nightmares and visions I couldn't understand. During the days, I lost control of my body and bled through every dress. Our father searched high and low for someone to heal me, but no one could help. Then one day, a high monk was riding through our valley, and our father tracked him down by horse and pleaded with him to come see what was causing my misery. Right away, the high monk recognized that the spirits called to me. He said my symptoms were a sign of god sickness. He said the spirits had chosen me as their medium. The monk also believed that of all the spirits calling to me, the one who called the most was Targo, a god who lived in a mountain to the north. This explained why I wanted to run in that direction at all hours."

"Our grandmother too," Ashang says. "She was a medium for Targo. And her mother before her, back and back for many generations. Our father never heard the spirits, but now the link had been restored."

"Will we have a break from our minds, Big Sister?" Tenkyi whispers.

"No, no," I reply, wondering why Ama had never shared this part of her childhood before. "Not us. It's just a story."

But really, I have no way of knowing. Is Tenkyi suffering from god sickness? Am I? We have enough nightmares, enough aches and dark visions that flash and tease us. Yes, our bodies and minds have been our enemies for many months. But we are so far from the holy mountains and lakes of home, and every move we make takes us farther yet.

"Still, I resisted that fate," Ama says. "Even as a little girl, I knew that being a vessel for the gods would not be an easy life. I wanted to marry and have children and live as an ordinary woman."

Ama recalls that the high monk needed to find a way to heal her god sickness or else she would have died within days. That was when the high monk brought out the Saint's ku, the very one Po Dhondup now offers to us. The high monk explained to Ama that this was no ordinary statue. Just days before he came to her aid, the monk's dreams had been visited by an unfamiliar Saint, who directed him to a nearby cave where a ku was hidden. The Saint also told the high monk that the ku did not belong to him or anyone else. It would appear and disappear depending on who needed it, and the high monk must respect that. For now, it would be in his care. Following the Saint's instructions, he retrieved the ku and carried it with him on his travels.

"For three days, the high monk read prayers day and night as I gazed up at the ku. I was tied down at the worst times, locked inside when necessary. Until finally, the spirits took their leave."

Po Dhondup gazes at my mother, his eyes wide and watery. Placing the ku in her hands, he manages to say, "So this is why I have carried on."

Beginning her prayers, Ama touches the Saint to Pala's forehead and each shoulder, then his back and chest. "I regret one thing," she says. "I never asked the high monk for the Saint's name."

I wonder why we need his name when his story is enough. What matters is that he is here with us. This precious ku, made of earth alone, yet capable of surviving so many years, so much destruction. If he comes to those who need him, in the times when they need him, there could be no family more fortunate.

3

Dhaulagiri, Nepal

Spring 1961

To the west, a faint orange light signals the day's end. This is a relief to me, for everywhere we go, we seem to move without making progress, caught inside this heavy mist that leaves our clothes and skin damp. What's more, our steps are guided only by rumors now. Food and medicine, someone told us, await in a place called Baglung. Is this true? Is it even a real place? To find our way there, we have resorted to tracing a river that has been at our side since Mustang. All this because Ama says the gods don't speak to her anymore. It isn't clear to me if she can no longer summon them, or if she just refuses to try. The only certainty is that we cannot remain in one place for long, now that we have parted from the rest of our village. We have to keep moving, constantly checking our surroundings, always in fear that we could be robbed by bandits at any turn.

Ama pauses ahead, scanning the surrounding hills. "Let's stop here for the night," she says.

Ashang Migmar nods and drops his bags. Without a word, he and Po Dhondup enter the forest to gather firewood to keep us warm while we sleep in the open. While Tenkyi looks for berries, I begin a fire with a few sticks nearby. Pala's instructions ring in my mind as I pull out a pinch of his tinder (*Start with less than you think you need*), build a little pile of sticks, and make a spark with his flint (*Keep the flint and tinder dry*). Then

I tuck the flint back in the leather pouch that Pala had decorated with silver studs and blue thread. These were his favorite colors, and this pouch was the last thing he gave to me. As I pump my father's sheepskin sack, the fire grows with each gust of air.

After Pala's death, something must have changed for Ama. She scattered our group, telling people who had fled with us to continue on their own. Despite their pleas, she would not pull out her leopard skin or don her five-pointed hat. She would not sing to the gods. She even lost her patience when an elderly man named Po Damjor begged for a divination.

"Can't you see," she scolded him, "that we are no longer home? Isn't it enough that I led you through the mountains?"

"You're the most powerful medium in our region," he cried. "You can fly across the sky, ride on the backs of wild animals, muster physical strength no ordinary human can. How can you abandon us now?"

"Our home is far away. The spirits are far away," she said, trailing off.

In tears, Po Damjor cursed my mother, trying to shame her for turning away from her duties. But Ama was intent on one task: finding a pure burial site for Pala. She climbed six hills and examined a dozen caves before finding a place without any other burials. It was a small cave on a red hill that faced in the direction of our village, so that Pala may be reborn there.

Ashang and Po Dhondup carried my father's body on their shoulders, climbing up a steep cliff, while Ama led the way. Tenkyi and I stayed behind in the valley. We watched the procession grow smaller and smaller. We listened to Ama's drumming and prayer songs echo against the cliffs. Even once we could no longer see them, Tenkyi and I stood and listened to Ama's voice grow faint. We listened until all we heard was wind.

THE AIR CHANGES, a gray quiet settles around us, and snow begins to fall.

"Come here, my girls," Ama says from her seat on a boulder. The Saint's ku sits before her, the only devotional object Ama takes out nowadays. Her five-pointed crown, her mirror, even her leopard skin are nowhere to be seen.

"One minute," I reply, stoking the fire. Once the flames begin to crackle on their own, I walk to Tenkyi and Ama. Taking my little sister's hand, I stare at my mother, who seems so different now. Her hair is cropped short like a nun's, but patchy and rough. A few locks drape over her face, while the scalp is exposed in other places. Since Pala's death, Ama's hair has also gone gray. Even Tenkyi has noticed the changes, how Ama stares at the sky or pebbles, as if carefully remembering the arrangement of the world. Now she stares at us in the same way, her eyes traveling over our faces. I feel a sharp pain in my chest.

"Ama, look at us," I say. I want to shake her, but instead, I grasp at her thighs, digging my face into her legs. How thin she has become.

Pushing my hair back, Ama says, "Now, now, what's the use in being sad?"

I feel my mother's warm breath on my face. Everything is cold except for my mother. Reaching into the chest pocket of her dress, Ama pulls out a small metal plate. The mirror from her divination ceremonies. In this round plate, my mother has seen the deities who speak through her. Within its metal face, she has seen so many visions. Omens of death or danger, like someone picking red flowers, or dressed in a red cloak, or sinking into the ground, or riding naked on a donkey. It has shown her good omens too, like someone drinking sweet-tasting water or clad in iron armor, riding a tiger on a mountainous ascent.

She hands the mirror to me. "Lhamo, keep this safe."

"We don't know how to use it," I say, waving the mirror away.

Tenkyi reaches out and takes it in her small hands, turning it around and flashing light in our eyes. I take the mirror from her and lay it face-down on my lap.

"You can look," Ama says.

"No," I reply. "Tell me what you see when you look."

"I see the Targo Mountain and the river that flows from it. I still see them, even though I cannot go there anymore."

"Can you hear the gods?" I ask.

"I can feel Targo. Other gods too. But they cannot speak, and that is painful to me."

I realize that I have never heard my mother express her sorrow so plainly.

"I saw two girls," Tenkyi says, turning the mirror up again.

Two strange creatures look up at us, their faces lashed by black sand, blistered by wind. I am as disconnected from them as I would be any villager who crosses our path. I think about how Tenkyi, Lhaksam, and I used to play back home. I think of the day, two summers ago, when we pretended to be oracles. We shook and sobbed and pretended to speak in the language of gods. We divined each other's fortunes and healed each other's aches and pains. How easy it seemed then.

"Put it away," I tell Tenkyi.

"Look at this beautiful place," Ama laughs softly. "These familiar mountains, gleaming against the blue-black sky. This river, which will always be beside you, in which all of humanity swims. Under your body, there are sacred channels in the earth. Do you feel them?"

We place our palms together on the boulder. I press hard and feel only the pulse of my own body, which now seems like a burden. How easy it once was to keep our hearts beating day after day. We once believed that our lives would continue on and on, like the hills of our valley, our parents always in the corners of our eyes, looking after us no matter what. But Pala is gone and Ama is shrinking. Whatever food she gathers, she gives to Tenkyi and me. In her ravaged body, her mangled hair, even her years as a vessel for the gods, she has laid herself out like a field to sustain others. But when she needs it most, her body is failing her, and I can do nothing.

I DREAM OF water. Trickling in the crevices between rocks, setting off small streams of their own, leading turn by turn back to our village. Then in the next breath, I wake. The sky is a deep blue with faint streaks of pink. On the same boulder where she gave us the mirror, Ama sits before the Saint's ku, her back erect, her white hair luminescent against the snow and moon. With cropped hair and a gaunt figure, my mother doesn't look like a woman, or a man. In fact, I now see that she looks like the Saint.

"Ama," I say, but my lips produce no sound.

I try to get up, but my body will not move. A great weight presses down on my back. It's my sister. Tenkyi's face is buried against my side, and her arm rests like a tree branch across my spine. Her hot breath spreads on my ribs, and her heartbeat seems to match my own, as if she had taken over my body. I can't even turn my neck. It makes no sense. My little sister is no heavier than a small goat.

Ama sees my struggle. She holds my gaze and speaks to me without speech. She wants me to know something. *This is what you will do: Carry your sister on your back, as though she were a part of your body. Keep her alive, as though your own life depends on it. She will travel farther than any of us. And one day, she will throw a rope across the oceans. At great personal cost, she will pull all that remains of our family to the other shore. But for now, you must carry her. Do you understand?*

A rope across the oceans? I understand nothing my mother tells me. I open my mouth to speak, but already, I know that no sound will come. Now Ama stares at the horizon as her lips move rapidly in prayer. Her skin, her clothes, her hair—everything has turned gray and white. The world itself is gray and white. The wind picks up, erasing all sound, and it is as if we had been transported to the top of a mountain. Suddenly, Ama's limbs begin to soften at their edges and fade like a sand mandala. This is a dream, I tell myself, but as soon as the thought leaves my mind, Ama dissolves. As if she had been nothing but an idea. As if her body, from which I emerged, from which came a sweet smell of baked barley wheat, and into which I nestled on so many nights, had been nothing but a short and vivid dream that she finally dismantled and dispelled.

WHEN I WAKE in the morning, I hear the sound of rocks tapping each other. Ashang and Po Dhondup are nearby, placing rocks on a part of the riverbank. I know what is underneath those rocks. I know this before I even stand and walk over. Ashang and Po Dhondup must have worked through the night to bury her. The ground froze overnight, so they couldn't dig deep, and bits of Ama's dress push out above the rocks. I move two stones out of the way and see some of her hair, a bit of her skin. Leaning in, I move another stone. The pale skin of her hand is not as gray as it had been in my dream. There are mottled patches and veins of red, purple, and blue. I remove two more stones. I see that her gray hair, too, is streaked with strands of black, red, and brown. My mother was not just an idea. She was made of a body, and a body is not simple or plain. It has its own will and its own mysteries. When it gives up, no song, no prayer can bring it back.

4

Pokhara, Nepal

Summer 1962

B Y sundown, they tell us, we will reach our sixth and final camp. Five rented buses have driven our group as far as the roads and riverbank would allow, and now we are on foot, walking in a deep river gorge, our steps and sightlines hemmed in by an endless procession of hills. The trail is narrow, so we walk in a long, slow line, all four hundred of us gathered from various border towns. Ahead, Ashang Migmar and Po Dhondup carry our possessions, their heavy sheepskin coats hanging from their waists, while I carry Tenkyi on my back. Like so many in our group, my little sister is unwell and too weak to walk. At least she's still with us. In Baglung, we heard that our aunt, Shumo Yangsel, and her husband had been there for several weeks before our arrival. They had begged for food on the side of the main road, telling anyone who passed by that their children were waiting in the mountains for help. Ashang thinks Shumo's sons must not have survived the journey out. He wants to find her, his little sister, and keeps asking the two foreign aid workers who rented the buses about her. But they don't know anything about Shumo's whereabouts. All they can tell us is that we're heading to the camp, our *new home*, they call it. A message passing slowly, in pieces, from their tongues to ours.

But where are they leading us? I had thought in Mustang that we had reached the lowlands, but here, with this heavy air, we can hardly breathe.

It frightens me to think that the earth could keep falling down and down like this. Meanwhile, the sun grows hotter in each place we go, as if to light us all on fire. Yet in the corner of my eyes, behind these dark hills, I can see a line of mountains, white and silver, even more luminous than the sun. As I take these steps, I think of home, where we don't have roads. Where we walk any place we wish, across the grassy plains, along the wide gentle hills.

Half a day has passed without food or water. We have become a silent line of bodies that traces the unceasing river to our right. My lower lip cracks and bleeds from thirst, and as I lick its rough surface, I peer down over the edge at a river that taunts me with its waters. If I go down for a drink, I doubt I could manage to climb back up this cliff.

Finally, at sunset, we hear foreign chatter. The aid workers ascend a small hilltop and pull out some papers. Then they drop their bags and move out of view.

"This must be it!" someone shouts behind me.

Gripping onto bunches of grass, we clamber up the hill to see the land. Even Tenkyi is on her feet now, walking to the top of the ridge. As we look out on a small clearing of hard earth and few trees, I clutch her hand.

Ashang kneels and rubs the soil with his fingers. "Nothing will grow here," he says. "With this kind of earth, the milk will be thin. The butter will be pale." How, he wonders, can we raise animals, or have any measure of space in this narrow plot of rocks? How, he whispers, can he call himself a nomad? A nomad would never pitch his tent on such barren land.

But no one says a word to the foreigners. We hear that they have paid the Nepali government for this bit of earth. They have also made promises to local villagers to give them water pumps and more so that our group of four hundred or so *refugees*, as we're now called, can stay here. On this hilltop, we must make a new life.

OUR FIRST SEASON passes quickly. Four makeshift funerals by the river, two supply drops of grain, a medicine run, and the gradual construction of thirty shacks with thatched-grass walls and bamboo roofs. In the lowlands, each of us learns our new role. Children collect firewood, carry water from the river, and forage for nuts and berries, while the adults learn to build huts and till the land. But everyone sings throughout the day. Tenkyi and I have learned many new songs that we perform for Ashang in the evenings. As I watch our uncle smile and clap for our performances, I can see that he is a kind man who will care for us. For food, we are rationed a handful of rice a day and some pills the foreigners pass out every so often. It is a blessing to have something to eat each day. In exchange for this help, they say we must not beg or look for work outside the camp.

Despite this separation, we have had three tense arguments with local villagers—those sharp-nosed people in pale, gauzy dress who live in houses with doors so small you have to bend down and step up at the same time to enter. The villagers want more compensation for the quarry we have dug. They're still waiting for the water pumps they were promised.

I keep a tally of these events, knowing that we may have to move again, that the food could run out, that tomorrow, it could be Tenkyi or Ashang who does not wake. I keep a tally of our nightmares too. At least once a week, someone in the camp will cry out in the middle of the night. They've seen their dead children at the door. Or they've heard the rumbling of iron birds circling the sky. Some just yearn for a carefree summer day in the pastures back home. When Tenkyi begins to moan and stir beside me, I wake myself and watch her face in the pall of the moonlight. I watch her eyes flicker beneath their lids, seeing things unknowable to me. When her face seizes in pain, just as her mind cracks itself awake, I pull her back to me. In tears, she tells me about a woman with a face shrouded in darkness. A woman whose mouth is locked, who grits her teeth and shakes with rage.

I have nightmares of my own, circling my body like monstrous dogs. When they come for me, they show Ama calling out from the border, still alive under a bed of rocks, begging us to come back for her. They show my father's blackened skin spreading outward, covering my hands, my face, and finally enveloping the sky.

I must learn how to wake myself, to swallow the cries and be as still and mute as the boulders outside our hut. I must focus on the boulders, picture myself among them, and make myself become like them. This isn't easy for me. Sometimes I need to press my palms against my gaping mouth. Sometimes I must dig so deep with my fingernails that in the morning, there are small cuts on my face, which I cover with mud or hide under my hair.

AT THE CAMP meeting, the elders say more people will come here. Tenkyi and I huddle in the back, listening in.

"There are still a hundred families at the border from every clan. Bhompa, Bawa, and even Khampas from the far east."

"Some will keep waiting for the day when they can return home. They'll stay there as long as they can."

"But once they're forced to slaughter the last of their yaks and sheep, they'll be like us."

"No choice but to come south."

I try to imagine how there could be space for a hundred more families in this narrow wedge of land between the river and the hill overlooking us. Already, we can hardly stretch our arms without hitting each other.

"What about the Chushi Gangdruk at the border?"

"I heard they don't even have bullets. Isn't that right?"

"What can you expect when they're living in shelters made of juniper branches and sleeping on pillows of stone?"

"It's important that we all pray for them."

"Can't defeat the Gyami with prayers. Bullets and bombs, that's what they need."

"We should ask the queen of England for help." Everyone falls quiet. We wait for the man, whose name is Pema Lhakpa, to say more. He has two bullet wounds in his right leg. "She was here a few months ago. Her nation is very wealthy and important. The king of Nepal even gathered three hundred elephants to greet her. She went on a hunt with those elephants and shot a tiger and an enormous horned beast that we don't have in our country—"

"Poor thing, why would she do that?"

"Must be to pass the time. They don't eat those animals or even wear their pelts."

There's a flurry of laughter.

"She must not have a religion."

"I heard she dresses in very plain clothes. One of the villagers saw her in a simple yellow dress around town."

"How strange, a queen who shoots animals and dresses poorly."

"Do you think anyone ate the meat?" Tenkyi asks me, scratching the sores on her ribs.

"Would you dare eat tiger meat?" I ask, smirking. "What if the other tigers found out and came looking for you?" I pull her hand away to scratch around the sores for her so she won't bleed. At least the ones on her legs are healing.

Pema Lhakpa shakes his head, losing his temper. "Forget about the tiger! The point is they can spare a few bullets, can't they? For the righteous fight to regain our country and save our people? I would go myself if I didn't have this useless leg!"

"Enough of this foolishness," Ashang Migmar says. "We live on one cup of rice a day, and instead of figuring out how to make anything grow in this lifeless soil, you're talking about bullets and bombs. We're losing our way. That is very clear. We need a religious teacher."

Ashang explains that the camp leaders have sent an urgent request to Kathmandu. We are pleading for a teacher to live among us, to guide us in prayers and bring solace to our souls. The trouble is, we do not know which teachers survived the destruction of their monasteries, and which of those survivors managed to escape into exile. We also don't know whether any of the teachers would come and live with us on this isolated hilltop where the crops will not grow. But if one would come, he could hold the right prayer ceremonies and our crops might even flourish.

"At least we have the Nameless Saint," I whisper to Tenkyi. She sighs, leaning against me. This is the name people in our camp have given him, or maybe it's just the name we accepted after a while. In either case, our ku has been visited by every soul here. We take the Saint's ku to the ill, to bless our water, and to watch over prayers. Before any long journey, we request the ku to be placed on our heads and backs. Some simply want to look at the Saint, to contemplate the face of our camp's protector and spend time in his presence. And the ones who have died here, each took their final breath beside him. The way Ama did on her last night.

I KEEP HEARING rumors of bananas in the lower valley. Wanting to give Tenkyi something sweet, I sneak away to spend the afternoon searching for them. When I reach the banana trees, I'm astonished to realize that a single leaf is the size of a person. Passing between the trunks, feeling their rough, furry bark as the wind lifts and shakes the leaves, I feel as though I were surrounded by people reborn as banana leaves. Some droop down to the ground as if in mourning. Others arch high above me, as if preparing to take flight. Imagine what Ama and Pala would say if they could see these strange beings. And the bright red flowers dotting the hills, perched like eager faces above the bushes. Back home, our flowers stayed close to the earth, sheltering from the cold, shy and delicate. But these red flowers look almost cheerful, gazing up at the mountains above the hills. When they stare at that white and silver streak in the horizon, they don't see a constant reminder of a faraway home. They don't wish to take flight like these banana leaves.

I search every tree, but none is bearing fruit. With a sickle hanging unused from my father's belt, I return at sunset empty-handed. Outside our hut, Ashang is seated with a group of other stonebreakers. Covered in white powder, they look like a gathering of ghosts. Out of everyone in the camp, my uncle breaks the most stones each day. He rises at dawn, drinks some old tea or water if there is none, wraps his plaits around his head, and leaves for the quarry. When he returns at sunset, we know to leave him in silence until he has rested. Tonight, he seems in good spirits.

"Does anyone know the love story of the river here?" Ashang asks his dusty companions. My uncle has resumed his old role as a storyteller. "The story is about the river beside this camp," he continues. "Here, they call it by a different name, but the river begins in our country."

I take a seat, and Mo Yutok, our neighbor, extends her blankets over my crossed legs. It's as if my uncle were speaking to the river itself, which seems to grow louder, encouraging him to tell its story. The crickets and frogs have also raised their night songs. Even the fireflies have come to show their lightning dance. Meanwhile, the sun slips behind the tabletop hill above our camp, and we're all washed in a pink light. I wrap my arms around my body and rub my skin to build some heat. There are times when I can see the beauty in this place. When the rice fields in the valley become a mirror for the sky, or when a flute song echoes from the hills.

"A long, long time ago, there was a princess and a poor boy. They met while wandering the plains and fell in love at first sight. But her family would not accept the boy, so they sent her to the far corner of the country, so far away it took months to travel there by horse, so far away she didn't know how to return home. Separated, the princess and the poor boy passed through the years, secretly longing for each other. Then, in their old age, they died at the same moment and with the same wish: to embrace the other in the next life. To embrace in a way that no man could break. And so, in the next life, the princess was reborn as this river, and the poor boy was reborn as the hill range that cradles the river without end. An embrace that no man could break. In the end, they had their wish."

"Poor things," someone sighs, tossing a few sticks into the fire.

"I love romantic stories, don't you?" asks Mo Yutok as she covers my knees with her shawl again.

Ashang stands and continues the story as he circles the fire. "But soon, the place will have Gyami names. Every mountain, lake, and grassland of home will be renamed."

This can't be part of the love story.

"Will the love remain the same with foreign names?" he asks, shaking his head. "With words that mean nothing to our ears?"

Ashang should just tell the stories as they're meant to be told instead of changing them to match his mood. It's as if he can't help himself. My uncle has something to say about the name of the mountain here, too, which the locals call Machapuchare, for its sharply pointed angles that resemble a fishtail. This doesn't sit well with my uncle. He thinks it's profane to call a mountain by anything but a deity's name.

He often says to Tenkyi and me that we have fallen to a place that his heart can't settle into. But *this* is the last year away from home, he insists. Once the leaders of America learn about what's happening to our people, they will help us. We will get our country back. We just have to wait a

36

few more months. At camp meetings, he argues that there's no point in building a school. No need to plant grains that won't yield for another year. We just need enough to survive for the time being.

Ashang keeps his bags packed. He keeps count of the days we've been away. And as if to keep inventory, Ashang tells Tenkyi and me about the objects that await our return, the things he and Pala buried in the earth, at the base of a hill in our valley. This is our inheritance, safe underground at a depth of two men's height, between three boulders shaped like heads. He promises us that this place will be simple to find, even if Tenkyi and I return without him. One good day, he promises, when things go back to normal, we will return. And all the things we didn't want to risk losing in the escape will be in the earth, waiting for us. The gold statues of deities, the silver offering bowls, the prayer books, the thangka paintings, the animal skins. They will be there, safe and unaware of the madness that occurred above. One quiet day, we will walk back to the elevated land of our home, kneel down, and dig. And our lives will reemerge, unsullied by the bloodshed and sadness of the world. And the Bhomi, the People of the Snows, will live again as we have for thousands of years.

But I've had enough of Ashang's new stories. To return on the trail where my parents lie would be just as awful as remaining here forever. I push myself up, hang my sickle on a pole, and go back inside our hut.

THE NEXT MORNING, my task is to weave a fence for the goats. Our crops failed again, so we're building more animal enclosures. As I tie a row of bamboo sticks, I hear someone call my name.

"Wai, Lhamo," Bhu Tsering says, kicking up the dust as he nears.

"Wai!" I say. "You're back."

"Just barely," he laughs. "I was sleeping on a hill last night and nearly slid off all the way into my next life!"

We have a good chuckle, but I'm relieved that he has returned safely from his trip to the capital to buy medical supplies. Though he's cheerful, he looks tired, with his cracked lips and matted, oily hair. At least two people from our camp have died from the long journey between here and Kathmandu. Nyima Dolkar starved to death when she could not find anyone to give her food along the route, while Mo Tenzom succumbed to the bite of a rabid dog.

"This is for your uncle," Bhu Tsering says, holding out a small envelope decorated with an elegant script I'm unable to read.

"Who sent it?" I ask.

"Yangsel. Your relative. Pass it on to your uncle, will you?"

I nod and slip the letter into the chest pocket of my dress. I saw Shumo Yangsel and her family many years ago at a summer horse festival. Tenkyi was just a toddler then. So was one of Shumo's sons. The two little ones cried for half a day, feeding screams to each other until we had had enough. We wrapped them both in sheepskin and stuck them in sacks on either side of a yak to wander the pastures, finally lulling the children to sleep. We never saw Shumo after that day. What does she look like now? Does she resemble my mother?

Behind the latrines, I open the envelope and stare at the script for a long while, but I can recognize only a few words. Shumo Yangsel must have enlisted the help of someone literate in the Kathmandu settlement.

All night, the letter lies hidden against my chest as I wonder what it says. Have other relatives fled to this country? Or is it now safe to return? I need to know before I give the letter to Ashang, though he can't read the script either. Only the schoolteacher Gen Lobsang can. At daybreak, I scrub my face, tie a red ribbon around my hair, and head to his hut.

"Acha! Acha Lhamo!"

It's my sister. The little owl must have sighted me from across the field. I try to send her back home, but she follows me all the way to the teacher's hut. We quietly approach the doorway and stand there, our ears against the curtain, checking for sounds of movement inside.

"Who is it?" he asks from inside.

With a low, quiet voice, I say, "Genla, it's Lhamo. I received a letter from our aunt yesterday but I can't read it—"

Gen Lobsang swings open the curtain and ushers us in. As my eyes adjust to the darkness, I see that his face is also freshly scrubbed. "It's a big day, girls. A new teacher is coming from America."

"You said America?" Tenkyi asks, as if she had any idea where that is.

I hold up the letter and say, "Our uncle would like you to read this for us, if you can spare a little time."

"Have a seat then," he says.

The three of us sit on the floor. I notice that Gen Lobsang is building a mud stove in the corner. As a former monk, he must be skilled in cooking. Every monk must prepare meals for his monastery. They must also learn to read, write poetry, play instruments, dance cham, do their own laundry, and pray for the liberation of all sentient beings. That is why Gen Lobsang is the most learned man here. Once the camp is in a better state, Ashang says I can join his classes. Tenkyi has already learned how to read at least ten words from Gen's lessons.

With the letter held out directly before him, Gen reads slowly, repeating important words. The letter says that neither of Shumo Yangsel's sons survived the journey to Nepal. It says Shumo has learned that her brother Migmar is now raising the daughters of their late sister. Considering the hardships of doing this alone, my aunt wonders if he would send one of the girls to live in the capital with Shumo and her husband.

"The elder daughter must be practically a woman by now," Gen reads, "so we have the little one in mind."

I take the letter from Gen's hand before he reads any further. My voice shakes as I ask him to keep this between us, just for a little while. Gen Lobsang gives a slight nod, though I don't know if he means he will keep this quiet. There is no choice but to hope he does.

Tenkyi, meanwhile, asks about the camp in Kathmandu: How many children live there, and whether they have more books. Without wasting another minute, I usher my sister out toward the field. "Don't tell Ashang about the letter either," I tell her.

"Why not?" she asks, freeing her hand from mine.

"Here, sit." I pull up a clover stem from the ground and chew on it so I can think and calm myself. "Because Ashang can't read."

Tenkyi begins to make herself a white crown of clover blossoms to place on her knotted hair. Her thumbnails are too short to weave them, so I press my nail into the stems and thread the clovers in a small circle. "Ashang will be embarrassed," I explain, pleased with my reasoning, "if we see that he can't read the letter. I'll give it to him later."

Tenkyi stares at me unconvinced. Then she drops her gaze to her belly.

"What's the matter?"

"You're lying. You're leaving me."

I hoist her up and place her on my lap, holding her close, though not so tightly that it will worry her. "Never. Not even if I die," I say. "Now go and show off your crown. Go on, I have to start work now."

"Make a crown for yourself too."

"Alright," I say, forcing a smile.

Tenkyi runs off in the direction of the tabletop hill, shouting, "I want a necklace and bracelets too!"

Lying on the grass, I stare at the cloudless sky above, Tenkyi's half-finished necklace sliding from my fingers. A group of women sings nearby as they dig up the earth. I can hardly hear them over the wind, the river, and the late croons of the roosters, but parts of the old melody reach me now and then. Ama hovers somewhere within them, so faint I cannot hear her voice so much as feel her humming body. Nowadays, I cannot even see her clearly. Not as a face with distinct lines and shadows, but only fragments. Like the leaves of a tree. A tree too large to be seen.

A shower of clovers floats down. Tenkyi's palms hover in the air as she breaks into giggles. I take in my sister's happy face above me. Her cheeks have regained their fullness, but three of her front teeth are missing, the rest are black with rot. She's eleven this year, but she hasn't grown since we left home. Neither have I, truth be told. By now, I should have begun my monthly bleedings. That's what the nurse who came to measure our bodies said to me. If Tenkyi and I grow in strange, stunted ways, I can live with that. But if we have to face what Ama did in her childhood when the gods called to her and her body and mind failed, who could help us here? We may be in trouble already with the spirits that circle us in our nightmares. Only Ama could tell us what to do. She could chant the right prayers, bless us with the Nameless Saint, and free us of our sickness. Shumo Yangsel's letter, sharp and rigid, presses flat against my chest. Could she help? But if Tenkyi goes to Shumo, she might never come back. And if I go, my sister would be left all alone.

"What's that?" Tenkyi asks, squinting. In the distance, a thin line of dust travels along the riverbank. I shield my forehead from the sun, waiting until the form comes into focus.

"A car is coming!" I shout, getting up and running toward the river.

By the time the white jeep reaches the camp, dozens of us are walking alongside it and peering in. When the driver stops, the crowd moves aside to let Gen Lobsang approach. This must be the American teacher, I think. My first American sighting. The man who steps out has skin as black as a crow. I nearly fall to the ground.

"Say Tashi Delek to Teacher Mark," Gen Lobsang shouts, but we have become mute.

"Teacher Mark," Gen Lobsang repeats.

Teacher Mark stands against the red cross on the car door. As his eyes travel across our group and the camp, his expression changes. For just a moment, he looks at us as if it were our skin that's strange. I turn around to check what worries him so, but all I see are children who wear clothes that are too big, dresses and shirts inherited from our parents and relatives. My own dress is Ama's. Ashang Migmar cut it with a quick tear, then folded it vertically in the back along my spine before cinching it in at the waist with Pala's red sash. Wearing a dead parent's clothing brings you blessings. Teacher Mark might not know this.

He steps forward with an easy, handsome smile and shakes hands with Gen Lobsang, then Au Rinzin, who likes to be among the first to greet visitors, then Mo Pelkyi, who just happens to be standing nearby with an empty hand because her squeaky prayer wheel is out of commission. However odd we might seem to him, one by one, Teacher Mark greets all of us with his hands folded before him. Moving through the crowd, he talks with the men of the camp as they lead him toward the administrative hut. Meanwhile, people whisper what Gen Lobsang translated of Teacher Mark's words: *He says he didn't realize the conditions of our camp. He says he has failed. He says he will try to gather more supplies for us.*

Tenkyi appears in my sightline. Her eyes have grown larger than I knew possible, and her mouth is stretched in a gaping smile. With her missing teeth, she could pass for a village fool, I think. She's staring at the back of Teacher Mark's head, observing his every step, trying to hear his words even though we don't know his tongue and at least a dozen people stand between us. But her expression, this curiosity. I can hear her questions to Gen Lobsang already: How many kinds of people are there in the world? And how big is the world? And when can I see it? Now I know the truth. If I tell Ashang about the letter, Tenkyi will leave to be with Shumo, a smile across her little face. She will sail from this hill to the capital, and even farther perhaps. This is my sister's nature. But I want to tell her: In the next life, yes, we can both go wherever we please. In the next life, we will be free and safe and happy. We will grow under our parents' gaze like small trees until we are strong women, able to decide our fates. And when our parents are old and frail, we will watch over them until they enter the bardo, and when they enter the bardo, we will light a million butter lamps so they can see the path through the in-between. And when they reach the shores of their fates, we will know that we have done the most important thing anyone can do for their beloved. We will have cared for their souls and then let them go. But that was not our path in this life. I press my hand on my chest and hear the paper crackle. Shumo's letter is still there. And there it must remain, until I find another way.

5

Pokhara, Nepal

Tsemo Seymakar Tibetan Refugee Settlement
Fall 1962

S OMEHOW, I have been named the best and fastest rope weaver in the camp. My handiwork holds together all kinds of buildings here, from the new outhouses to the administrative hut, which also serves as our clinic. Today I'm tasked with making ropes for the school where Tenkyi will soon study. Most people like to work together, but I prefer to weave alone at the edge of camp, with my legs dangling over the river. Left in peace, I enter a kind of lovely trance and hardly notice the effort of weaving, needing only to give a few short glances at my fingers to put a new blade of grass in line or to tighten a stubborn knot.

Two crows have appeared, circling above my head, speaking to each other. What, I wonder, do they say? How do I appear to them? Alone on this small patch of arid hilltop. A girl who's thin and dirty, with hair so matted it could break a comb. And look at my dress: fraying at the hems and pocked with holes. But it's my solitary nature that singles me out. Even the people here worry about me. I can almost hear them say, *There's that girl again, staring into the valley, body tight as a rock, talking to herself.* They tell Ashang Migmar to watch me, to have me checked out by someone, though they can never say who is able to help me in this strange land. My uncle, meanwhile, suggests I go somewhere farther out so people will not be troubled by the sight of a girl sitting alone.

But I have something they don't know about. A secret letter. With each breath I take, the paper moves with my chest like a hard and brittle shell. Months have passed since Shumo's letter fell into my hands, and though it's not a lie to say that camp life has been full of distractions, the longer I stay silent, the more the letter weighs on me. Still, it is surprisingly easy to continue saying nothing, doing nothing with it. Not destroying the thing, not handing it over to my uncle. Another secret: I find myself wondering about Shumo these days. Does she have my mother's voice or her laugh? It's almost worth going to the capital just to find out.

More crows drift by, joining the circle above me. I wave my arms and try to shoo them away. To this, the crows freeze in place, then swing down to the river. I know these dark birds well. They're going to the banks to search for carrion. Once our morning prayers end, they'll soar back up to the camp and pick at the offerings scattered here and there. This is their casual freedom. For two-legged animals like us, so fixed to the ground, no path is so easy. Is this why we still wait for a religious teacher to come?

I hear Tenkyi in the field behind me, somewhere along the newest row of grass huts. She's reciting the English alphabet, and although I don't know the letters myself, I can tell that she sounds clear and confident. Like a bell, her voice rises with each utterance above the rhythmic hammering of the quarry workers. Nowadays, we have two outdoor classes for the children: one for Tibetan, taught by Gen Lobsang, and one for English, taught by Teacher Mark and the camp's newest resident, Teacher Amy, a pale woman with hair like a field of barley. Most days, I overhear bits and pieces of their lessons as I work. Once, I spent an afternoon watching the men carry broad, thin sheets of wood from town. They propped the sheets against boulders and painted them, layer after layer, with a coat of black so deep and pure it looked like a portal to the night. The next day, the teachers took small pellets of white powder and scratched English symbols onto the sheets, still leaning on the boulders.

Teacher Mark now responds to my sister in English. The only word I can make out is "good," which he repeats. My little sister must be bright. From the start of classes, she has brought as much focus and determination to her lessons as the adults do to digging latrines, building huts, and planting grains on our infertile patch of land.

"My older girl," Ashang often says, for we are his children now, "tries very hard. But Tenkyi is the smart one. She got her mother's mind."

"What kind of mind did I get?" I once asked.

He squinted for a moment, then let out a big laugh. I couldn't help but copy him and chuckle along. We had not laughed together, just the two of us, before that moment, and I felt as though we shared something important. After the moment passed and we were quiet again, I waited to see if he would answer my question. He didn't. Ashang carried on digging a ditch, and I was left to gather the crops.

Still, I wonder: What else did I fail to inherit from my mother? What else passed over me and landed only in my sister? Some parts are clear: Tenkyi has Ama's round and rosy cheeks, whereas I have Pala's plain, narrow face, which makes me look lowly and boyish. But then there are the parts neither Tenkyi nor I have. Ama's low, hazy voice. The warm bready sweetness of her skin. All of a sudden, her face flashes before me, so complete she could be right here on this hill. I squeeze my eyes shut and stay perfectly still, but she's already gone. A fleeting sight, barely the length of an inhalation. And yet she feels nearer to me now than in her final years. Now, I could even ask her the questions I was too afraid to speak then. How, Ama, did we end up here? Where are our gods? Tell me. *Speak!*

My half-finished rope sails into the gorge. I shake in place, clutching my fists. Down on the rocky riverbank, it lies twisted like an abandoned snake skin. Tucking the torn hem of my mother's dress into my father's belt, I scale down the gorge, taking care not to step on any nettles or sharp rocks. The soles of my feet are still healing from the last time I lost my grip and slid down the cliff.

The river is busier than it seemed from above. Water buffalo have settled along this stretch, and farther up toward the hills, two village women are washing clothes at a small pool. Ashang said the camp's river begins in our country. I pause inside this thought, imagining a long, winding thread home. All kinds of things are carried by a river, especially small objects. If I searched with my hands, would I find a coin from home in the silt? What if I were a fish? I could swim back unseen by the Gyami soldiers. If everyone in the camp became fish, we could all flop into the river at once and move our fins upstream in unison. We could change the direction of the river itself.

While I'm down here, I might as well forage some wild grass for rope. But as I tug at an untouched patch of grass, something catches my eye. Two figures on the horizon, treading the rocky banks and heading in the direction of the camp. They're too far away for me to see their faces, but one is a boy and the other is a grown man. Whoever they are, they don't hold hands, or even walk close to each other. And my eyes keep returning to the boy. As I watch him slowly come nearer to me, a strange sensation ripples through my body—a wave of happiness I cannot explain.

"Wai!" I shout, but the wind scatters my voice. I'll have to wait for them to come closer. By the height of the sun, I know it is nearly time to return for our daily cup of rice. But I want to wait a little while, just until I can see who they are. Squatting, I tear up blades of grass and pause every so often to check on the two figures. Their progress seems slow. At times, it looks like they're getting bigger. Other times, it's as if they were standing still.

When their faces come into view, I recognize the tall one as Po Dhondup. So he's finally back. It's been nearly a month since he left for Kathmandu, where his brother-in-law was rumored to live at one of the camps. But who is the boy?

"Lhamo," Po Dhondup says, breathing with difficulty as he approaches me.

"Tai' Delek," I say, leaning in to touch foreheads with him. I cock my chin in the boy's direction and casually ask, "Who is he?"

"My sister's son," Po Dhondup says. "His name is Samphel."

I lean in to touch the boy's greasy forehead, but he ignores me. Instead, his eyes travel up to the grass huts at the edge of the camp. Up close, he is older than I had assumed from afar. We could even be the same age because we stand nose to nose, like a mirror image, filling the same space and casting the same shadow. His journey must have been as difficult as any of ours. We will need to wash and mend his clothes. His skin is beaten red and black by rashes. But his face. How unusual. Ever so slightly off balance, one eye turning up and an eyebrow brushing up along with it. The other eye has no slope at all. His lips also move asymmetrically, as if only half of him wished to speak. Beneath the pale dust, his lips are deep red. If he licked them once, I'm sure they would come alive on his otherwise muted canvas. I feel a brief and freeing weightlessness, then I shiver just once—as if someone had grabbed me by the shoulders and tried to wake me.

"Did we meet in Mustang, at the border with your uncle?" I ask.

Po Dhondup replies wearily that this is impossible. The boy lived with his father, but his mother remained behind in our country. She's with her other family, a husband and four children, still living in their old village.

"The husband has joined sides with the Gyami," Po Dhondup says. "He's a running dog, probably wearing a red star cap and thrashing his own people right now. The boy was born out of wedlock."

Po Dhondup picks up the bags and heads toward his place. "I need to rest. Lhamo, look after him for a while."

"Sure, Popo. Rest up," I shout. Now that Samphel and I can talk with ease, I resume my questions as we head into the camp. "How old are you?"

"Don't know." His voice is light and quiet. It crackles like a bent feather.

"What's your birth animal?"

"A cow, I think."

I almost burst out laughing. "You mean an ox? A cow! So that means . . . you're thirteen. I'm a year older." I wait for his reaction upon hearing my age. When he gives none, I add, "The Swiss aid workers didn't believe that I was fourteen because I'm so small."

"You're not so small," he says, straightening his back. "All those Enjis are giants. They must have lots of food."

"Do they eat like cows?" I figured we would both break into laughter, but he's straight-faced. I notice something tucked under his arm. It looks like a deflated ball, the kind our teachers bring out on sunny days. "Where were you staying before?" I ask.

"Jawalakhel camp," he says, adding, "I'll be going back soon."

So he's from Shumo's camp in the capital.

"You know, you're lucky. This is a good camp. We have a machine that can push air into that ball."

"It's got a hole," he pauses. "But my father will patch it when I'm back."

I say nothing. If Po Dhondup has brought him here, his father has either died or abandoned Samphel. In either case, no point dredging it up. "I have some thread so I can patch up the ball for you," I say. "Then we can kick it around in the field ahead. See there, where the children are?"

As we cross the field, the lessons are ending. Some of the children line up to embrace Teacher Mark, while others go straight to work carrying rocks to the middle of the camp, where a schoolhouse is being built. I spot Tenkyi collecting stones.

"Who's he?" she asks, giving Samphel a smile.

"Po Dhondup's nephew," I say. "From Shumo's camp."

"Are you here for a visit?"

The thought of visiting a camp, as if on holiday—where does my sister come up with these ideas?

"Do you want to hear something funny?" Tenkyi asks. "A boy from our camp named Hring-hring is telling everyone that he's going to ride in an airplane soon." I tell Samphel that Hring-hring is our nickname for a boy who likes to run through the camp with his arms outstretched, making airplane sounds. The elders scold him for imitating the noise of the invaders' iron birds, but we just call him Hring-hring to tease him.

I lift a pair of large rocks and ask Samphel to place one more on top. He takes the smallest one nearby and rests it gently between the two in my arms. Laughing, I tell him he can pick something a little larger. The schoolhouse will never be finished otherwise. Once he adds another to my load, he insists on gathering some for himself, even as Tenkyi and I object that he should rest after his long journey. He smiles for the first time, then heaves and lifts the biggest rock in the pile—one that he could barely reach his arms around.

As we shuffle over to the site of the schoolhouse, Samphel tells us about his best friends back in his camp, a pair of brothers named Polo and Golok whose father etches prayers into rocks for money. I don't know why he's talking about earning money, but at least he's more at ease now. On our way, we pass some other children heading in the other direction, some of whom stop to help us carry our loads. We end up walking sideways with arms outstretched to share the load. How fun, Tenkyi cries, as others pair up and take our lead.

6

A WEEK has passed since Samphel's arrival, and he continues to accompany us through our daily routines. When work ends at dusk and everyone returns home to say their prayers, Samphel, Tenkyi, and I wander the camp together, pretending that we're the only people in the world. It's a moonless night, the warmest in weeks, and the fireflies are out in full force, gliding like flickering stars just above our reach. We move together between the silhouettes of fences and huts. Goat bells clink, roosters cluck, and footsteps shuffle around us as people gather outside for small talk. Bhu Tsering says the teachers are starting a bonfire by the river, so everyone should gather a bit of wood if they'd like to join. The three of us decide to head there at once, our metal plates in tow in case someone has milk to spare. We walk toward the gorge, our footsteps slow, our hands stretched before us, and we find some dry sticks along the way. At the edge of the gorge, I lead Samphel and Tenkyi along a safe path to make our way down to the river bank.

At the bonfire, we find a dozen or so camp dwellers already gathered with Gen Lobsang, Teacher Mark, and Teacher Amy, who is tuning her guitar. I motion to Tenkyi and Samphel to sit on a broad, flat stone, while I squat down beside them, tiny streams of cool water running between my feet and under my hips. I move a little closer to the fire and extend my hands. The world beyond us is dark and overflowing with insects, but the mountains loom above. Their peaks seem closer when the hills disappear at night. As firewood snaps and shifts, it releases a sweet, comforting fragrance that covers the smell of our exhausted bodies.

Teacher Amy starts to strum. "This is a new song," she says, in her slow, steady Tibetan.

"Wai," Samphel says, surprised by her fluency. Teacher Amy is improving each week. Soon she'll be able to read more complex words than most of us can.

"It's the biggest song in America," she says. "It asks when peace will come to the world."

"That's right, a good question," whisper a few people.

I look at everyone sitting around the fire. How ragged and tired we seem. Like old prayer flags strung across a hillside, the colors have been stripped from our bodies over many hard days. What would peace do for us? Would it make us new again? Would it stitch us back together?

Teacher Amy begins to sing with a low, gentle voice, closing her eyes and swaying her head from side to side. Her red sweater is the most colorful piece of clothing around. Everyone's attention is fixed on her, and her hair glowing in the firelight. Teacher Mark gazes at Teacher Amy too, though he's not smiling. He's watching her as if he knew her. As if he had heard the stories that she does not tell anyone else. Is that how love looks from the outside? Like adoration mixed with secret pain?

When the song ends, Teacher Mark takes the guitar. "This is a song written by a blind black man. It's about missing the place where you're from," he says.

My feet sting from the cold water, and my scalp itches. I move to a dry spot and find a twig to work through my knotted hair as the repetitive, sorrowful tune begins. The song moves in phrases, hesitates, then tracks back and repeats. People around the fire look down at their feet; others gaze at Teacher Mark as though they might understand the words if they watch his face carefully. I catch a few words here and there, but they don't amount to anything. I wonder about Teacher Mark's home. What does he miss from home? What kinds of hills and flowers and gods do they have in his country?

Samphel leans in. "It sounds like someone crying."

"Their music is like that," I tell him.

"They have endless songs," Tenkyi says.

As the song ends, Ashang Migmar and Po Dhondup appear, walking up to the fire. Everyone shuffles to make space for them.

"Tell us a story, Migmar," Bhu Tsering says to my uncle.

"A story?" Ashang nods. His braids and shoulders are covered with a fine layer of stone dust. "How about the story of our camp's Saint?"

"Yes, my nephew here doesn't know the story," Po Dhondup says. "I've brought the Nameless Saint here for this reason."

Across the fire, Po Dhondup looks strangely frail. He still hasn't recovered from the journey. He's even struggling to undo the knots on the small silk bundle in his lap.

"Have you ever had a dream that returns to you over and over?" Ashang Migmar begins. "A dream that repeats across time, linking years of your life? Have you described this dream, gone through everything you saw and heard and felt, recounted it in great detail to a friend or a neighbor, and then heard the other person say, 'I *know* this dream! This was also my dream'? That is the story of this statue. Made from the earth. Many lifetimes ago. A ku of the Nameless Saint."

I've never heard Ashang tell it like this. Settling into a free seat, I steal glances at Samphel, who's listening intently. What does he think of the story? I wonder. Does it move him in the same way it moves all of us? He seems to be taking in every word, yet his face reveals nothing of his mind. I could stare at him all night and still not discover a single thing about him. Po Dhondup gets up and walks around the bonfire, tapping the base of the Saint on each bowed head, one by one.

"So much of the story is unknown to us. For now, it is scattered just like we are. What we know is this: Here is a statue of a Saint that disappears and reappears, as if by its own will. When the time is right, the Saint comes to those who need protection. Men like our Po Dhondup, here. How this man has suffered—" My uncle pauses as his voice cracks.

"The Nameless Saint protects our camp," Tenkyi whispers to Samphel. "Now that you're here, you'll be alright. Just think to yourself: Everything will be okay. Remember that especially at night, when your mind wanders to bad places. Remember that the Saint is here on our hill."

Although she doesn't know it, my sister comforts me with her sense of safety, wholeness, rightness. We are here together. Maybe that is the peace we can know.

But now, as I hear about Po Dhondup's journey from village to village searching for his family's ghosts, I think our journey home could not be half as difficult. We could leave tonight, walk back to the highlands. We're well enough to try it. We could sustain ourselves on birds and mountain herbs, hide in caves, pressing on until we find our village and our house again. But Pala and Ama would not be there. Maybe someone else would be living in our house, Gyami soldiers or people who fled another village seeking safety. Maybe our house is now only rubble like the monastery where Po found the Saint. We could take that rubble and start again. We could rebuild our house, stone by stone, with a kitchen just like we remember, our bedroom facing the small lake where a water god lives, a room for Ashang, and another for our parents across the hall, with a window overlooking the village. But the stones would not be in the same place, the earth would not settle in the same way. We don't even know if our parents' ghosts would return and live with us.

But Teacher Mark and Teacher Amy? Their homes are still intact. Their countries have not been captured. And one day, sooner or later, they will return to the places they came from. Their families will be waiting to wrap around them in a long, joyful embrace. For a little while, Teacher Mark and Teacher Amy will remember us, and maybe they will even continue to live here in their minds. But then, the current of their old lives will pull them in. Slowly, surely, our camp will fade in their minds, and we will seem like a distant dream, our names just shy of their tongues. But we will still be here. Yes, we will still be in this valley, singing songs of home, gazing up at the mountains and trying in vain to recall our dead parents, their faces and voices, while the winds of time erase them a little more each day.

I reach into the collar of my dress and pull out the letter, this awful piece of folded paper. This blade I've held close for two months, even though it wants to cut my sister from me. The truth is, I'm afraid. I have always been a coward. From the day my mother told me to stick my neck out to our enemies, I have known this to be true. I am a small, frightened person. But in this one thing, I will not be afraid. It is the only thing Ama asked of me on her final night. I will watch after my sister. I cannot allow her to be taken away.

Sliding forward onto a rock, as close to the flames as I can bear, I pull the letter out of my dress and toss it into the fire. No one seems to notice. With the stick I used to scratch my head a moment ago, I push the letter deeper into the chamber of the fire. The envelope curls into itself like a new moon, burning bright before disappearing. Regret stings my chest, even as it feels naked without the letter. I've lost my chance to see my mother's sister. The last woman who might resemble Ama. But it's done. At least Tenkyi and I won't be separated.

People are now discussing which song to sing. Someone wants to do a roof-flattening song, but Bhu Tsering points out that they can't do the dance, not without the wooden pole with the rock affixed to the end. They could thump the earth with their feet and move slowly in a line, snaking around for hours even, but without the right tools, it just wouldn't feel right.

I get up and start to head back to the camp. Tenkyi and Samphel follow. I have no desire to hear those familiar songs anymore. It's hard enough when people sing as they work during the day. With daylight, at least I know where I am. But at night, I could be fooled into forgetting everything that's happened. I could think that I'm in our village again. I could spend hours looking for my parents.

On our walk home, Tenkyi asks if Samphel can stay with us tonight. It'll be more fun for him than his uncle's hut, she reasons, and she has a point. Po Dhondup's place is mostly full of adults.

"Yes, he should stay with us," I say.

Without the letter, I feel almost euphoric. Countless stars stretch across the sky; each one feels friendly tonight.

"You know," I say to Samphel, "the Nameless Saint is really your family's statue."

"Is it worth a lot?" he asks.

I am taken aback, unsure of how to answer such a strange question.

"No, it's not his! It's the camp's," Tenkyi cries.

"Be quiet. His uncle will pass it on to Samphel one day."

Later, as I prepare our cot, Tenkyi instructs Samphel to lie on his back while she and I lie on either side, facing him.

"We've got a few ghosts in our camp. We must always be vigilant," she explains.

My little sister believes that whenever two backs face each other, a ghost can slip unseen into the rift. I've gotten into the habit of sleeping on the right, facing Tenkyi, and if I ever turn in the other direction,

I am usually woken by a tug on my shoulder, prompting me to turn toward her.

Samphel lies with his arms pressed tightly against his sides. His body is as stiff as a log, even when a mouse grazes our toes. I push the rodent away and tuck the blanket under our feet.

"You can spread out a little more," I tell him.

"I'm used to sleeping like this," he says, explaining that he shares a bed with his father and always lies right up against the wall. This way, when his father comes home late at night, stinking of alcohol, Samphel can turn and smell the grass wall instead.

"That makes perfect sense," Tenkyi says.

Lying side by side, we listen to the rain and feel drops of cool water slip through the roof onto our shivering skin. Farther down the hut, someone is snoring. Maybe it's Gyurme or his father. Tenkyi reaches across Samphel's chest and clutches my arm with her cold fingers. Letting out a sigh, she begins reciting simple prayers she knows by heart. In the darkness, I take in Samphel's scent. So different. I try to put my finger on it. Like old paper. Or is it Kathmandu on his skin? Closing my eyes, I picture walking along the capital's alleys and boulevards with him.

"Wai," Tenkyi nudges me. "Ashang isn't home."

She's right. His bed is empty, the blanket still folded up neatly at the end. Near his pillow, I see the shape of Ashang's prayer wheel propped against the wall. The bonfire has been quiet for some time, and no one is breaking stones anymore. I look up and down the long room. A dozen souls asleep in two long rows.

"Stay here." I get up and place the blankets over my sister and Samphel. As I step into the courtyard, Tenkyi orders me not to go out in the night alone.

"It's the ghost season," she whispers.

"You say that about every season," I reply and carry on, somewhat worried as my hands stretch out before me, expecting to feel the door.

A thick mist has come into the camp. I stand still and try to detect any sound of Ashang. Nothing. Just the constant noise of crickets and other insects over the rushing river. I hold my breath and listen carefully. There's a faint mumbling, followed by a few coughs. It's coming from Mo Yutok's hut. I walk over into the pitch-black with my hands before me, uttering a prayer to Guru Rinpoche, pleading not to run into any ghosts. I decide to close my eyes, just in case. When my fingers come up against the rough wall, I stop in place and listen.

"She has dreams of her dead sons. She says it is unbearable to be the one who survived." It's Ashang's voice.

"Poor thing," Mo Yutok says.

"How can I refuse? The camp in the capital has a proper school already."

"Yes, I heard that too. The girls will cry on the day they separate, but you know, they're young. They can forget things, unlike us."

"I went to Gen Lobsang to have him read my sister's letter. He told me he already read the same letter a few months ago. To Lhamo and Tenkyi, he said."

"That can't be. He said that? That can't be . . ." Mo Yutok's voice fades.

"They have never lied to me before."

I cover my mouth with my hands to keep quiet and walk back slowly in the dark. Shumo had written again. Ashang knows. He might even know that I hid her first letter from him. And now Tenkyi will go away. It's all my fault. Had I taken the first letter to Ashang, he might have said no to Shumo. From the sounds of it, the second letter was more desperate than the first, which said nothing about her nightmares or unceasing sorrow.

Back inside the hut, Tenkyi is asleep with her arm draped over Samphel, their faces turned toward each other. In this light, they appear even younger. I envy their closeness. I envy their aloofness. Wake up, little sister, I want to say. Don't you know what is coming? Wake up so we can cry together.

I lie down at the edge of the bed and peer up at our thatched roof. A small mouse is moving up there, crunching the dried grass. Maybe it's the same one from earlier. The sky must have cleared because now specks of moonlight pierce the roof. I must do something to keep my sister here. If I don't, our family will be broken forever. Ama under rocks, Pala in a cave, me on this hill, and Tenkyi in the city. Has this always been our family's fate? To begin together in a few years of happiness only to break into so many shards? Reaching out my hand in the dark again, I hold my sister's wrist. This wrist—this small meeting of bone and skin. It is made of our mother and father, their bones, their skin. When I hold my sister's wrist, I hold the echoes of their wrists. My hand travels up Tenkyi's cool, damp arm, her flesh filling my palm and fingers. This too is theirs. Although I no longer have their faces, at any time, I can squeeze this arm. I can kiss these cheeks. I can smell this hair. And by caring for my sister, I can keep caring for my parents. No force, no person can take this from me. It is as simple as that.

7

IN the morning, I almost expect to see Pala on the other side of the room, and Ama shuffling around outside, humming prayers as she tends to our yaks. Then my mind travels further. We could be reborn as birds, our whole family. We would get to do things over. It's possible that Ama knew everything that would happen and secretly moved Pala's consciousness into a pigeon's body, the way the great guru Marpa did for his son.

That old story. I still remember it. Marpa's son had fallen off his horse and cracked open his skull. As the son lay dying, Marpa moved his son's consciousness into the body of a pigeon that had just died nearby. The bird then flew across the mountains to India, where it found the body of a young boy about to be cremated. Once again, Marpa moved his son's consciousness, this time from the pigeon to the Indian boy. The boy woke up on his funeral pyre just before it was ignited. He rose and walked away, embarking across the mountains in search of his father. Ashang would often tell this story. How slowly, how wrenchingly he delivered the tragedy and rebirths of that tale. But now, when people request the story, Ashang refuses, saying it will do no good for anyone in our camp to hear it.

When I turn to rise from bed, Pala isn't here and Ama isn't in the courtyard. Neither are Tenkyi and Samphel. I tie my father's belt around my waist and walk to the cistern tap, where I rinse my face and mouth. Roosters flap their wings in brief agitated bursts as a man shouts, "Hurry hurry!" Then Hring-hring runs by the hut, heading toward the center of the camp. I tighten the tap and follow the little fool, still walking in the daze of my dream until a large crowd appears at the main road.

"Po Dhondup's dead," Bhu Tsering tells me, as he sits slumped against a stone wall. Three children are crying nearby. "I found him with his head in a bucket of soapy water."

"What? What are you saying?"

"Maybe his heart gave out," he replies, shaking his head.

Hring-hring whispers to me, "I heard his face is so swollen from the water it's almost unrecognizable."

"Shut up," I say. "Don't you know when to be quiet?"

Standing at the edge of the crowd, I struggle to make sense of what Bhu Tsering and Hring-hring have just told me. Could they really mean the same Po Dhondup? He just completed a long journey. If you survive a trip like that, you ought to be able to breathe a sigh of relief at the end. It's only right. Besides, Po Dhondup was alright a few hours ago, sitting across the fire, carrying the ku of the Nameless Saint from person to person. He can't be dead.

Now I catch a glimpse of Ashang Migmar speaking to the crowd of people. It takes a moment for me to realize my uncle is organizing the death rituals. So it is true. Po Dhondup is gone. I feel myself slip into someplace damp and airless.

Listening in, I learn that Ashang will take the body to Kathmandu, where Po Dhondup's brother-in-law lives. That must be Samphel's father. Their camp has several monks who can perform the proper rituals. It isn't surprising that my uncle would volunteer to take care of his friend's funeral. Some part of me thinks he needs to do this, not just for Po Dhondup, but for Pala and Ama.

But how will he manage such a feat? Already, someone is collecting donations for butter lamps and prayers, but now there's the question of how Ashang could even transport a corpse all the way to Kathmandu. Buses and jeeps drive by the camp's main road, making pickups a few times a day. But no vehicle would take a corpse. It would just be bad for business.

"We can disguise the body as a living person. An ailing relative," Ashang says.

"But how will you move him?" Pema Lhakpa asks.

"I'll carry him on my back."

A flurry of prayers comes from our mouths. Our only hope is to encounter a driver who doesn't ask too many questions. Ashang spots me in the crowd and calls out.

"Lhamo, get the boy and his things."

"The boy?"

"The one the deceased brought here last week . . . Samphel."

"But he just got here," I say, unable to think of a better answer. I try to explain that Samphel is a bastard and an orphan, but my uncle won't listen.

"Lhamo," he says, as I begin to walk away. "Bring your sister too. With her things."

BACK AT OUR hut, my hands shake so much I'm barely able to grasp my clothes. Mo Yutok comes by, sweeping the courtyard.

"Momo, have you seen Tenkyi?" I ask.

Mo Yutok comes over and wipes the tears on my face. "I saw a group of children lying in the field by the school construction site. I bet Tenkyi's there," she says, adding the old refrain, "Don't cry. It hurts your parents' souls."

She must not know about Po Dhondup. No point in upsetting her, I think. Eventually, the news will come to her, and hopefully by then, the body will be long gone. Mo Yutok lost her husband and daughter in the journey over the mountains. Now only her granddaughter remains by her side.

I run as fast as I can to the field. Sure enough, Tenkyi is at the clearing, leading a group of children in a tight pack as they stare at the ground.

"What are you doing? I've been calling your name!"

"Counting the ant mounds. What are we at now?"

"Twelve," Pemba replies.

"No, it's thirteen," Tenkyi corrects him.

Gripping her hand, I lead my sister to a boulder heated by the sun.

"Put your face on this surface. Your hands too."

"What? Why?"

"Don't argue with me. Hurry or they'll take you far away."

Tenkyi squints in pain, for I have said the words I should never say unless I really mean them. She lies on the rock and places her cheek and palms flat on the burning stone. Before long, she begins to cry, her teardrops falling briefly onto the hard surface before they vanish. I lean over, hold her hands, and press my forehead to hers. The heat is searing, and I'm surprised that my sister has endured this long.

At the main road, Ashang is pacing back and forth in the center of a crowd. Samphel is crouched on the ground, holding his busted football and weathered backpack. Someone must have found him.

"Don't say anything," I tell Tenkyi. "I'll do the talking."

We take a few steps forward, but suddenly, two men lift Po Dhondup's corpse and place it on my uncle's back. Someone else begins to wrap a shawl around Ashang's torso to keep the load fixed in place.

"What's that on Ashang's back?" Tenkyi asks, stepping back. "Is that Po Dhondup?"

"Don't use his name now that he's dead," I whisper. Seeing Tenkyi's wide, frightened eyes, I squeeze her hand and say gently, "Just call him the deceased or Samphel's uncle."

"Look at your girl's face!" says one of the men.

"Let me see." Ashang waves us over. "Why is her face red?" he asks.

"She's sick again," I reply, my voice faint and trembling.

With the weight of the corpse bearing down on him, my uncle can barely move. He stares at us for a long while, but doesn't say anything. He knows what I've done, I'm sure of it. I lower my gaze to the ground, praying that I don't cry again. If a single teardrop falls onto my dusty toes, we're done for.

"Ashang Migmar, this plan will never work!" says someone in the crowd.

"We should carry the body to the bus station in town."

"You're right. Migmar can't manage like this! There's no way!"

"If we carry the body on foot, it will take half a day or longer."

"It is downhill part of the way."

"That's right, we took Dickyi to the hospital like this before. If we have six men, we will manage."

"Dickyi was alive, you fool! Think about a corpse in the sun."

"Then Migmar still has to take a bus all the way to the capital."

"Kunchok khen! What will we do? It could be days before a jeep comes."

Slumped against a low stone wall, Ashang looks me in the eye. "Lhamo, you'll come then. I need your help."

Just then, there's a rumbling noise from up the hill. A bus sways side to side on the dirt road, its metal innards screeching. I know this patchy pink and blue bus, which passes our camp every so often. Today, it's decorated with a splash of dry vomit fanned across its side. Villagers sit inside, wrapped in shawls, holding bags on their laps and clinging to the rusted metal bars of the seats before them. Some cover their faces so they don't have to look down into the gorge.

Tenkyi embraces me, and I motion her to step back, behind the crowd. Things will be alright, I try to tell her. We will be back soon. She's shouting into my chest, but I just pat her on the cheek. Now I've gripped her arm too hard. Poor thing, she looks worse than ever. My throat feels like it's filling with sand.

"Coming or what?" the driver shouts through the doorless entry, his thin body bouncing on the seat as the motor shakes, his sandaled foot straining to hold the brake pedal down.

Ashang, Samphel, and I board the bus and take two empty rows, right behind the driver. Sitting sideways, Ashang slides Po Dhondup's body against the window and faces the aisle, slumping with exhaustion as the arms remain clasped around his shoulders. Samphel and I take the row behind them. I cover Po Dhondup's head with my shawl so no one, not even Samphel, can see the swollen face.

The bus driver looks up at the small mirror above him and catches my gaze.

"He knows, I swear it," Samphel whispers.

"Be quiet," Ashang says, turning back. "It's just because we're foreign."

We stay perfectly still and mute, staring at the front windshield, breathing uneasily. The driver releases the brake, and the bus moves again. A gust of wind blows through the windows, and the shawl slips off the deceased's head. I cover him again and try to rest his head against the seat, but the neck has gone stiff. Sliding my hand under the face, I pull it toward the seat as a cold nose and lips press against my wrist. I notice the deceased's right hand resting on Ashang's shoulder, as though he were still alive. How long his fingernails look.

Something tickles my neck. When I turn, a row of small, pudgy fingers wiggle before my nose. Two infants extend their hands toward the corpse, their eyes thickly lined in black kohl to ward off evil spirits, making them look slightly demonic. They smile as I try to swat their fingers away, while their mothers are so motion sick they barely notice.

"Shhh," I say, pointing their attention to the gorge.

All around us, the bus is packed with even more children. Their parents and grandparents cover their faces or sleep while the children all seem to stare at the corpse's head. One tug from a baby and we're done for. I throw the end of the shawl over my shoulder, covering the deceased's face from another angle.

As the bus rattles down the hill and turns around a sharp bend, I realize the camp is already gone. Our grass-thatched huts, our small group, they all disappeared so easily behind a hill, as if they had never existed at all.

EIGHT HOURS LATER, we reach a dusty clearing in Kathmandu crowded with buses and travelers. Ashang waits under a tree with the body still strapped to his back, while Samphel and I go off in search of water.

"We used to live in tents nearby," Samphel tells me. "In a big field where the military does their exercises. We didn't have a tent at first. But my father managed to get us a tarp." Samphel moves easily through the city streets, leading us to an old stone fountain.

"Do you know the capital by heart?"

"Some of it. Over that way is the royal palace. The king lives there. He's a descendant of a god. That's why he took pity on us and let us live in his country."

"Long may he live. Which god?"

Samphel shrugs. "One of their gods."

"The one with the elephant head?"

He laughs. "Maybe. I haven't seen the king's face."

Following Samphel's lead, we press to the front, place our heads beneath the tap, and drink. When people try to push us away, we elbow them back and quickly fill a bottle for Ashang. My uncle drinks all of it without speaking. The corpse releases a putrid smell now. Flies are dancing around us, tickling our knees and faces, as if we were all just pieces of meat on a butcher's stand. Will anyone take us to Samphel's camp, with this stench attached to us?

To my surprise, as soon as Samphel calls for a rickshaw, drivers swarm around us, each offering to take us for a better rate, patting our shoulders, tugging at our arms. Samphel haggles because he speaks the most Nepali, settling on an older man so thin he makes our bus driver look portly. As Ashang gets up, pressing his hand against a tree trunk, the driver glances at our cargo but says nothing. The corpse's forehead is the only part of his face that's visible, but how strange it looks. So pale and smoothed of its many wrinkles, as if he had become a baby.

Ashang and the corpse take the seat, which is deep enough that they can both sit facing forward. Samphel and I sit on the floor, our feet dangling over the road. We set off driving, and the flies are left behind. What a relief to be free of them! As the driver pedals, his hairy legs brush up against our backs and tickle us. When he stands to peddle up a hill and his butt nearly touches our heads, Samphel looks at me and fails to stifle his laughter.

THE CAMP IS on the outskirts of the city. Like ours, it has a single dusty road leading to its mouth. But this is the only point of similarity. If our camp sits like a buffalo sunning on a hill, revealing everything, Samphel's camp is like a forest. It can be known only if you step inside and walk along its many alleys. With every door we pass, I know that any could be Shumo Yangsel's.

"Here," Samphel says, stopping outside a low building with a row of identical, numbered green doors. He knocks and shouts, "Pala!"

The home is padlocked from the outside, and the curtains are drawn tight.

"Pala!" he repeats as he runs around the corner.

Ashang, the corpse, and I sit on the ground, and people begin to gather. So do the camp's flies, which seem larger and more abundant, with the many stagnant gutters nearby.

"Au Tsepa hasn't been home for months," says a man wearing a straw hat.

"He went off to India," adds an elderly woman carrying a load of old newspapers. "Was that his son?"

"Poor thing," mutters another.

"We came from far away to bring this body to his family," Ashang says to the crowd as two flies move about his forehead. "Now it seems the brother is gone. Yet here I carry his relative's abandoned shell on my back. Our fate in this land is such . . ."

Prayers flutter from a dozen lips.

"Kunchok khen!"

"Jowo Rinpoche . . ."

Ashang begins fidgeting beside me. He tries to get up, but the weight of the body on his back is too much. Suddenly, many hands reach out to assist him. The corpse's arms and legs are clenched so tightly around my uncle, I step away to give people enough space to help.

"Mmm," the corpse says.

"What was that?" asks one of the men, freezing in place.

"He moaned," another man says in disbelief.

Everyone holds still, waiting to see if Po Dhondup will moan again.

"The body must be releasing some air," Ashang says. "He's dead, believe me."

Once my uncle is finally unburdened, he slumps against the building, his clothes covered in sweat. We can finally see Po Dhondup's face and body, but his face is unrecognizable without its wrinkles. At least twenty years have been wiped away. Was this how he looked as a younger man, before his days of wandering alone across our country? Now it dawns on me that my uncle didn't bring the Saint's ku here. Did he simply forget, or could this mean that Samphel will return to our camp?

"His feet!" someone cries.

Po Dhondup's feet have turned deep purple-red. So have his hands. All the blood must have drained downward. My father's darkened feet flash in my mind, and my eyelids grows heavy. But there's no time for us to stand still. We must find a place to keep the body.

It seems like everyone from the camp wants to help. A crowd carries Po Dhondup to a metal basin in the handicraft factory, storing his body in a cool room where the wool is dyed and washed. Soon, a monk comes running, his sandals barely hanging on as they slap against the ground. While Ashang goes around town to buy butter and wicks, and to borrow items we can't afford for the ceremony, Samphel and I stay with the body and the monk. Butter lamps must burn day and night to help Po Dhondup see his path through the in-between, so the two of us are charged with the unending job of cleaning, refilling, and replacing the butter lamps.

While we work, the monk begins reciting from *The Book of the Dead* to guide Po Dhondup's soul, which is presently experiencing the trials of the bardo. As he reads from the block of worn scripture, the monk sounds a little like my Pala. I close my eyes and feel soothed.

"O nobly born, what is called death has come now," he chants. "You are leaving this world, but you are not the only one. It comes to all of us. Do not cling, in fondness and weakness, to this life. Even if you cling, you cannot stay here."

Hearing the monk's recitation, I think of the words my uncle said so often on our journey over the mountains: *We could not even light a candle for them.* Now as I see the rites my parents should have received, I realize what he had meant. Ama and Pala needed a caretaker like this monk, someone to help them along the dark and disorienting path through the in-between, to make sure they reached the other side of their fates. But in the time of their deaths, we could offer them nothing—not even the light of a single candle.

Now a new thought comes to me: If this monk can help Po Dhondup in his passage, he must know the fate of others who have died. Could he tell me where my parents went? Are they now back in our home village, or have they been reborn close to us, in this new country? I will wait for the right moment to ask him.

SAMPHEL'S HOUSE STAYS locked, and Shumo Yangsel is also away. So Ashang, Samphel, and I have to sleep in a drafty dormitory where orphans and other travelers take shelter. Each day, we begin work before dawn and finish in the late evening, sleeping only as long as the largest candle can last. There's no time to raise my questions with the monk. No time to even properly rinse my face or hands, which have blackened from the butter lamps.

On the third day of the ritual, I finally work up the courage to approach the monk. Walking into the storage room with a fresh butter lamp, I linger. Po Dhondup's corpse is positioned like the Buddha when he left the earth realm. His body is propped on his right side, a blanket covering all but the tip of his head. Sitting beside the body, the monk chants and sways back and forth.

"O noble one, listen without wavering. On this third day, the yellow light dawns. This is the purity of the element earth. Now, from the yellow southern Buddha-land of Shrimat, the yellow Lord Ratnasambhava appears seated on a fine horse, carrying a precious wish-granting gem."

I reach out to replace one of the dying butter lamps on the table by the monk, lifting the hem of my dress over my mouth so that my breath won't defile it. Meanwhile, the monk takes a bit of butter from a plate with his fingers and dabs it onto the top of Po's head. The door creaks behind me. It's Samphel bringing some tea. The monk turns the page of the prayers and continues chanting. His second and third fingers are much shorter than the rest. It's rumored that Gyami soldiers chopped them off.

"Under the influence of pride, you panic and are terrified by that brilliant, energetic yellow light, and you flee it. You feel a liking for that soft blue light of the human realms and you approach it."

The monk pauses and takes the tea.

"Will the deceased find liberation?" I ask, wiping the table to remain longer.

He takes a sip of tea and shakes his head. "If he has faults like anger or attachment, or if he's afraid and doesn't listen, he will not find liberation."

"So he'll be stuck in the bardo?" Samphel asks, walking in.

"He will be reborn. Hopefully in a pure land," he says. "But it's too soon to know."

I wonder if Po will come back as a water buffalo. He spent more time soaking in the river than anyone else in the camp.

"What about Lhamo's parents?" Samphel motions to me.

"Are they sick?" asks the monk, tossing a handful of uncooked rice on the body.

"They died," I say, pulling my gaze from Samphel.

"Poor thing. Many have died . . ." the monk says, trailing off.

"So you can't tell us if they were reborn, or what?"

The monk shakes his head and turns the page.

"My father lost his feet," I say, wringing my rag. "My mother died by a river."

But the monk carries on his prayer.

"Come on," Samphel says to the monk, "couldn't you find out? Is it in that scripture?"

"Stop it," I tell him.

"Where's your uncle?" the monk says at last. "I don't have time to talk to children."

I decide to leave the room. Outside, the sun has already set, and a few stars are visible in the purple sky. Each day seems to pass faster than the one before. Already two years have gone by since Ama's death, yet in moments like this, I feel as if I were still lying on that riverbank. Kneeling on the ground, I hide my face in my palms and wish for the release of tears. Then someone wraps their arms around me. It's Samphel. I'm surprised by how he embraces me. Not like Tenkyi, who grasps at my body, demanding attention, food, safety. No, he holds me as though he needs nothing from me. I lower my chin and rest it on the cool nook of his arm. No one has comforted me like this in years. In the places where our bodies press together, I feel my heart beat echo. Then without a word, Samphel stands and runs away, leaving just as easily as he came. Without his weight on me, I am adrift.

8

WITH five days of prayers remaining, Samphel and I find only brief moments of rest when the tasks of making and cleaning butter lamps wane. I'm in one such blissful break, napping on the porch on a humid morning, when I hear him shout my name and run toward me from the other end of the hallway.

"Lhamo, Lhamo!" Samphel says. "Look." A shining pink treasure dangles between his fingers. A five-rupee note. "The wind blew it straight to me. Like a bird hopping down the road!"

I'm speechless.

"Let's go spend it in the city," he says, smiling. "We can eat until we're fat!"

Without hesitation, I lift myself up from the floor and say, "Yes, we have enough clean lamps for now."

Samphel takes my grease-covered hand, and we set off down the road without telling anyone. It feels wonderful to say yes to him. I want him to ask me more questions so I can say *yes* to every request, so I can spend my life saying *yes* to him. As I run hand in hand with Samphel, leaving the camp for the first time since we arrived, I feel the city surge up like a storm cloud around us. We turn into a bustling alley that leads to a wide, brick-lined market square. On our way in, we walk past a long funeral group led by horn players. Perusing the market stalls, we find ourselves within a wedding procession full of people dancing to heavy drums. We crouch under an awning, find an empty stairway, climb three stories without a sound, and come up to a roof terrace covered in chili peppers drying in the sun.

From there, Samphel takes me to see paved boulevards with imported cars, whitewashed monuments, and official buildings rising like hunched giants in the valley. Walking down the lanes, we hear the king's announcements from trucks decorated in red and gold garlands like brides. The Bagmati River weaves through the city with water so clear that no one can doubt its holy connection to the Ganga. With the right gust of wind, I can smell the rice paddies surrounding the city. When the wind pauses, we can hear the sounds of the cows and goats who wander into the city, unafraid.

Next, Samphel leads me along shaded paths and steep stairs toward the Swayambhunath Stupa. When we reach the apex of the hill, we stand below the great white dome and marvel at the many temples that surround it. Circling the stupa, we take blessed cookies given out by pilgrims before sitting down to a meal served by wealthy temple patrons seeking merit. Bellies full, we walk down through the forest and see a thousand monkeys swinging from branch to branch. We lie down on a bed of pine needles, looking up at the canopy against the sky before we fall asleep, facing each other.

When I wake, for a moment I've forgotten everything—my name, my face, my sister, my village, my parents. My limbs are weightless, and my blood floats like air.

"Is this heaven?" I ask.

"Maybe," Samphel says, putting his hand on mine. "I think it is."

A smile spreads across my face as the sky rearranges its clouds. It occurs to me that the sky does this, day and night, whether we notice or not. The earth, too, rearranges itself, and all of us on it. Why don't we let it? Why can't we float along as easily as the clouds? I close my eyes and see the world within my eyelids. The trees sway in the wind. The ants weave through the earth. And Samphel lies beside me. The world remains unchanged, yet now it is mine. I have become its navel. A heat builds in my center, and I am hollowed of everything I have forgotten. I am nothing but heat. The sun grows between my legs, gathering strength as I cup it with my hands. A warm well without end. Beating with a rhythm so familiar, I realize my heart must have traveled south. Its warmth intensifies. My body lifts from the ground. I feel pine needles rise below me, sticking to my clothes. Everything is gone. Gone beyond everything. I want to laugh. Who knew all this could come from me? I see myself clearly. A god and a demon at once. Perhaps I finally know how it felt to be Ama.

WHEN THE SUN finally sets, Samphel and I return to the camp. We walk through the alleys and speculate about the scolding to come. But when we spot Ashang in the courtyard, he's smiling and rolling a rosary as he sits on a wicker stool. Across from him, there's an elderly woman turning a heavy prayer wheel whose cracked wooden base rests on her thigh. Rising slowly from her seat, the old woman waits for us. As we near, I sink into the ground a little with each step, realizing that I'm looking at my mother.

"Just like her," Shumo Yangsel says with a sigh, as if reading my mind, before reaching out with her bony hands. "She looks just the same."

I give her my hands and lean in to touch foreheads. Her skin feels dry and delicate. I close my eyes. I have just seen my mother's thin lips and nose. Shumo holds me in the embrace for a while, reciting a prayer for my long life. I grip her back, wishing she would hold me tighter. She reminds me of bread and old wood.

"Do you remember me?" she asks, leaning back.

I nod, looking over at Samphel, who knows nothing about my aunt's letters. I don't want him to think badly of me.

"Liar," Shumo says and laughs. "But very pretty. Just like my sister. Come on then."

Shumo and Ashang must now know that I hid her first letter. I steal glances at Samphel, wanting him to leave so he doesn't see them scold me. But Ashang says nothing. He just puts away the stools, gathers his things, and tells us we're heading to Shumo's house. We walk in silence for a long while, turning down new alleys that lead us farther into the camp. How far does the place extend? As we pass through an arched passageway, we see the world darken and the sky narrow into a stream of light. I wish Samphel would take me by the hand and lead me back into the city's bright and lively boulevards, but he moves impassively now, even as he takes furtive glances. Just as I can no longer tell one green door from the next, Shumo Yangsel gestures to her home.

"Bhuchung's gone to look for work," she says of her husband, inviting us into a lifeless room with two beds on opposing walls. "He'll be back in a week or so."

One corner is stacked from floor to ceiling with tin suitcases and old newspapers. Another corner is piled with cans, some cut up and twisted into shapes like dogs or windmills. Shumo says her husband makes these toys to sell around the city.

"Around Boudhanath, Bhuchung can get two rupees a piece."

Shumo says her husband is also looking into the musk business. She explains that it's risky to bring the pods across the border into Nepal, so people are now hiding the pods inside disks of dung, pressing a thumbprint to mark the right disks.

Samphel listens intently. "How much does each musk pod sell for?" he asks. "Where do the deer live? Who buys the musk?"

Now that he has held five rupees, he has found a taste for money.

Shumo rises, pressing on a table for stability. "How about some butter tea? I'll go pick up some butter."

"Water or black tea will do, sister," Ashang says. "No need to use butter."

Shumo will not hear of this. She pulls a small change purse from the prayer altar, digs out some coins, and clutches them in her fist. Just as she's about to walk out, she pauses and opens a wooden box by her bed.

"There they are!" she says, before approaching Samphel and me with two pieces of candy pressed between her thumb and index fingers. The candies shake slightly. We take them in our palms, unwrap them, and open our mouths almost in unison. Have I ever tasted anything at once so perfectly sweet, salty, and creamy before? It's a kind of torture. Shumo watches us with a smile. As the sweet nectar melts on my tongue, the words *I burned your letter* fill my mouth and nearly spill out. But I say nothing.

Shumo returns with a small package of butter wrapped in a torn piece of newspaper. The tea she makes is rich and frothy. As the last of the day's sun filters through the yellow curtains, there is a nice glow inside. How different is a home with a mother to run it, even an empty home. Tenkyi could be happy here. Maybe her nightmares would stop. Without me and Ashang as constant reminders of the past, maybe she could start over.

"Boy, run and check on the butter lamps," Ashang says to Samphel. "Must be time to light some fresh ones."

"I'll be right back," Samphel says, holding my gaze.

I give him a faint smile and watch him leave. For a long time after that, Ashang and Shumo speak quietly across the room. Every so often, they fall silent and watch the shadows on the floor change as the sun sets.

"I'll tell you something," Shumo says, a little louder. "I should have stayed . . . died in our village instead . . . scraps of meat along the way." She shakes her head and turns to me. "You really remind me of your mother when she was your age. We all suffered because of her illness."

"Yes," I say, unsure of what Shumo means. I peer outside, wondering when Samphel will return.

"I was married and gone by the time she recovered."

"People in our village would go to our sister instead of the monastery for help," Ashang adds. "Isn't that something?"

Shumo nods. "Hmm . . . I heard she was highly regarded. I have never visited a medium. To tell you the truth, my Bhuchung thinks these old traditions are just superstition."

"Nearly half our village followed the escape route she divined."

"Tell me, Brother, are the two girls like Sister in any way? Other than their physical resemblance?"

"The younger one is very intelligent. Sometimes she has nightmares," Ashang says. "But no, they haven't had any trouble."

"They say those things are passed down through parent to child. It must have skipped our mother, but she was prone to moods, wasn't she? Then again, I'm not sure about this whole business." Shumo hesitates before leaning in and whispering to Ashang, "They say the children of a dead oracle can be possessed by their parents."

"Do they?" Ashang asks, somehow unmoved.

"Keep an eye, Brother. I heard rumors about our grandmother too. Who knows how far back it goes?"

Shumo's words have left me speechless. It's as if she had casually pulled back a rug on the ground, revealing a secret, winding tunnel without end. And just as easily, she drops the rug back as the conversation turns to her husband's health.

It's well into the night by the time Ashang and I finally head back to the orphanage. Samphel is waiting for us in the courtyard, sitting slumped against a wall and staring at his kneecaps. I'm so relieved to see him that I barely notice the commotion at the gates of the dormitory. A young man runs in, and then we hear someone sobbing. A familiar dread comes through me as I sense something terrible drawing nearer to us with each step we take.

"The cook found a child lying dead in the dormitory," Samphel says. "No one noticed until midday."

The girl's body is now cooling in the same tub that contained Po Dhondup's body. They have washed her mattress and laid it outside against a wall to dry. Nearby, people keep their eyes to the ground and speak in low voices as they arrange the orphan's rites and rituals.

As Samphel falls asleep, his nose whistling a little, I stare up at the lines of newspaper script covering the ceiling. A sea of black scratches beyond my comprehension. In the corner of the dormitory, a little boy is coughing and thumping his chest from a top bunk. He's trying to swallow each cough, but I can see his body convulsing. It is a terrible thing to fight another person, but it's worse to battle with your own body. After watching my mother shake and jump in her trances, I had asked her many times: *How does it feel to be in a trance?* One day, she finally answered.

I see the gods in the mirror. I see colors, like a rainbow. The mirror grows larger and larger. The world becomes so bright. There is a growing fire. It enters my body. Everyone in the room blurs and shrinks. Their eyes gleam like stars at night. But their voices become smaller and smaller, while the mirror expands until it fills the whole room. Then everything is black. And I am gone.

Shumo worries that Tenkyi and I will be like our mother. But she doesn't know that we are already battling with ourselves. If she sees this, if she realizes how we struggle, perhaps it will frighten her and she will not want us. I could sit on this bed, imagine a five-pointed crown on my head, then chant and hiss and shake like a madwoman. I could do and say whatever I please, until I disappear from everyone's view. Maybe then would I be free to live as I want.

9

Six men carry Po Dhondup's body through a marshy path to the stream beside the camp, where a Nepali boy waits by the pyre he has built with scrap wood and sticks. The boy stands next to a cow, now unburdened of its load, and the two move together to the side as we approach. As the cloth-wrapped body is placed on the pyre, hundreds of small branches crack under its weight. The men leave right away, returning to the camp instead of staying for the ceremony.

Now it's just Ashang, Samphel, the boy who built the pyre, his obedient cow, and me. Across the stream, an older Nepali man stands looking toward us, a goat grazing at his side.

Ashang lights a piece of wood and places it in Samphel's hand. "Family should light it," he says.

Samphel turns to me and says, "I can't."

I place my hand on his shoulder. "Circle the pyre three times, then light it."

He shakes his head, his face crooked with pain. Po Dhondup's face was the closest Samphel ever came to seeing his mother. I try to picture her—a woman with doe-eyes and gaunt cheeks—but then I stop myself, fearing that this image might replace my own mother's face.

"Come," I say, taking Samphel's hand and leading him to the pyre. We walk slowly around Po Dhondup's body. The white cloth is thin, revealing the tinge of his skin and the faint impression of his face.

"Your mother looks like your uncle? That means we must remember him. Look, your uncle had deep-set eyes. His nose was broad and flat, like a bird in flight. His chin was small. His lips were thin. He loved to swim in the river by our camp, right alongside the buffalo. Someone told me he used to sing in a traveling opera. I didn't believe them then because he rarely even spoke. But looking at his chest now, he seems like he could really sing. His hands, they were the hands of an artist. The tips of his fingers were almost translucent. You could see sunlight through them when he wove rope. Your uncle was not a farmer or a nomad like the people from my family. We labored with the earth, with animals. Your uncle came from merchants, so that means your mother also came from such a family. You got your right eyebrow from her, the wild one that gives your face its light. Your uncle had a hint of that too. You see?"

Samphel looks at me. There is something indefinable in him, in the air around him, in his expressions, and in all the inexpressible details of his face. I feel like a tree when it clamps into the earth, turns its roots inward, and knows it will remain there for a thousand years. Together, we dip the flame into a crevice among the sticks and hold it there until a column of thick smoke begins to rise.

WE RETURN TO Shumo's house after the funeral and find her seated outside in a small band of sunlight, trying to thread a needle. On the ground beside her is a pile of old clothing she is mending for the local tailor. I watch my aunt squint as she struggles to catch the needle's eye. When she sees us, Shumo sets down her work and begins to serve the tea and pak she has already prepared.

After we eat lunch, I insist that Shumo rest and let me gather the dirty dishes. Balancing the plates, pots, and cups on my arms, I head outside into the cool afternoon. At the tap, I crouch down on the ground, pump a basin full of water, gather a small mound of grainy powder soap, and scrub away. It is a peaceful hour. There are clouds at the perimeter of the sky. A breeze passes through the camp, carrying Po's ashes off into the hills. He will be alright now. The monks were diligent with the prayers. We kept the butter lamps burning and the oil as clean as we could manage, no dirt or bugs. We did as well for Po as we would have wished to do for Ama or Pala. We can return home knowing this, at least. Shumo hasn't mentioned anything about me staying here in Kathmandu. And because

Samphel's father isn't here, it's clear he must come back with us as well, right? I smile at the thought of us returning to the camp. Samphel and I would tell Tenkyi all about our day wandering the city with five rupees to spend. He and I would wander the hills behind the camp in the same way. I would say *yes* to him anytime he asked to go somewhere. He would take my hand whenever he felt like it.

Back at my aunt's, a silence falls as soon as I approach the door. Something happened while I was away. Ashang looks over from his seat and motions me over. Shumo turns away and tends to something on her kitchen shelf. Meanwhile, Samphel is asleep in the corner.

"What is it?" I say, remaining at the door, water dripping off the dishes and down my legs. "I don't want to drag mud into the house."

"Your aunt is all alone these days," Ashang says. "You will stay here with her."

"What about Tenkyi?" I ask, picturing her alone at the camp, awaiting my return.

"You'll see her again. Won't she, Sister?"

"Of course. For the new year celebrations, you should visit her then."

"Losar is eight months away," I say.

They give me no answer.

Ashang and Samphel return to the dormitory for the night. At dawn, they will set off on foot to the city center and catch a bus back to Pokhara. I must stay here.

LATER THAT NIGHT, I take Shumo's husband's bed, which is pushed against the window facing the alley. Shumo sleeps on the other side of the room, snoring lightly with her back to me. Outside, stray dogs begin barking. The sound carries so far in the valley that distant dogs return their call, causing one man to shout at them to be quiet. I listen to the city's creatures. Dogs, crickets, and frogs who own the city at night. I think about Tenkyi. Does she sense what has happened? Is she having nightmares? Who will help her when I am so far away?

All of a sudden, my throat begins to close and I can only take short gasps of air. I call out to Shumo, but she remains asleep. I try again, but she can't hear me at all. It's as if some demon had fallen on my chest. Is it even my aunt on that bed? The dogs bark so loud that their sounds echo inside the room. And the cries of a hundred frogs filter in through the walls. What weight sits on my chest? Is it the city? Or night itself? I want nothing more than daylight. I close my eyes and think of the Nameless Saint. I try to pray the way my mother taught me. If nothing else, prayers could drown out the noises that surround me. But I cannot gather enough air to finish a single line. Something wants me to die. Why shouldn't I just die? In the dark, a needle of light flashes, but when I open my eyes, it's gone. I close my eyes again, find the tiny seed of light, and pull it closer.

Ama is in the light. My mother is here, the size of a drop of rain. I try to bring her closer. But she remains small. A tiny vision in perfect clarity. Just like on the day she died, she has short, gray hair. Her limbs are sticks. She is unadorned. No cloak of leopard skin, not a single piece of coral around her neck.

"Hello, flower," Ama says.

I'm pulled through a tunnel. I'm a child again. "Ama, where did you go? Why did you leave me?"

"I'm here."

My mother does not move. She just stands, letting me look at her as much as I need to.

"I don't know how to live without you."

Ama smiles. "You used to cling to my dress and follow me into every room. When your father was away, you filled my life. You reminded me of my own parents and helped me know them again. Even though we have parted, take heart. Our love is no less than what other parents and children have after fifty years together."

But this is not enough time. Nowhere near enough.

"Stay here, Ama. Let me show you to Tenkyi. I promise to find a way. Stay, and if you need a home, fill the whites of my eyes. I will keep you safe there."

I tense my body, try to make myself into tight fibers of strong rope. My ears buzz, then the entire surface of my skin vibrates. I need more and more air. My toes want to kick at something. I need a release.

Why don't I let myself kick out? Why don't I do as I please?

Like a madwoman, I will let my hair fall.

I will shake and hiss and dance.

I will frighten everyone with what I contain inside, all that I have kept hidden. And no one will have a say. They will just watch in awe as I do whatever I want.

My body spasms, just once. A moment of pleasure, as if I had shaken something off my skin. Then the urge returns and another spasm comes. I let my body do what it needs to do. Now my mother is gone. I open my eyes, hoping this is the end, yet the spasms keep coming. Now I see another pinprick of light. There's a little girl inside. She looks like me, but she is not me. I want to speak to her and know her name, but someone is shouting in my ears.

It's Shumo, bent over me with wild eyes. Her lips move but her voice grows faint, as if she were very far away. Now she's gone again. The front door is open. I cannot stop the spasms. Nausea rises through me in waves. Is it my time? Do the gods speak to me? One after another, they try to shake me awake. Are you there, Ama? Under my eyelids, as you have always been?

I hear Shumo's prayers once more. Footsteps pace around me as Ashang's face appears above.

"She'll go home—" my uncle says. "Help me lift her up."

Samphel runs up and reaches for me. "She can barely breathe," he cries.

I'm so happy to feel his hands under my shoulders. The little girl in the puncture of light. She looks just like Samphel. Can he see her too? She's ours, I want to say, and she is willing herself into existence. If I could speak, I would tell him what this little girl means, that we have a life ahead of us. A life from which other lives will spring. I try to smile, but another twitch stops me. A blanket takes flight. Then a great weight falls on my limbs.

DOLMA

I

Toronto, Canada

2012

THE street lamp emits a sickly yellow glow that filters into our basement window the same way it does every night. It's just enough light for me to find a clean shirt without waking my aunt in the next room. She's asleep at the kitchen table, her head bobbing above a dinner plate, her mouth slightly open. She must have returned from another double shift while I was napping. In the shadows, Shumo Tenkyi's face is all ridges and slopes, and she's so still and thin. I owe her everything, yet I cannot bear the sight of her frailty, the weariness she wears so nakedly across her face.

My aunt brought me here—or I should say *pulled* me here, for that would be the closest approximation of our word—with my first plane ticket and my first passport. "Don't be too clever when they check your papers," she instructed over the phone before I left for Tribhuvan Airport. "Say nothing unless they ask you." Throughout my two-day journey, I pictured a disastrous arrival in Toronto. I imagined being turned away just after landing (it happened to a cousin of a friend) and shuffled into a holding cell, where I'd wait until I could be returned to Nepal. Even after the border agent stamped my passport and I picked up my suitcase, I expected someone to turn me back. It was only once I was in this apartment that I unclenched my teeth and let my eyes relax and lose focus.

Then a new unhappiness set in, a new understanding that I'm still circling after five years in this country. My aunt was in pain and so very alone. Her state had been unknown to our family and neglected for years. Sometimes she cries and cries and cannot tell me why. Sometimes she stops on the sidewalk and laughs so loudly everyone on the street turns to look. Most of her struggles, her strange behaviors, remain private between the two of us. A stove left burning. Days where she only drinks water, or when she turns off all the lamps and keeps the curtains drawn because light makes her head pound, her joints ache. She tells me that even her eyes fail her on some days.

Was this country the cause? I often wondered this in the early days, as I roamed my new neighborhood, along streets named King and Queen though they were lined with low-income high-rises full of black-haired foreigners like ourselves. Would my aunt be cured if I could make us wealthy, comfortable? Or if we became true Canadians with those embossed navy passports? But it soon dawned on me that paperwork alone wouldn't be enough to make us belong. We wore our difference on our bodies, not just in our dark hair and brown skin but in our posture, the slower, foreign rhythm of our steps. Amid the squat brick storefronts of Parkdale, Shumo Tenkyi and I walked with our necks pressed down by some invisible force, our line of sight hemmed in by the endless web of streetcar cables above us. Along the side streets, we found our forgotten neighbors from Nepal. They now lived in houses cut into apartments, which were once halfway houses and before that, the summer holiday homes of the wealthy. Nearby, just past the Gardiner Expressway, the gray expanse of Lake Ontario sent a winter draft we could not shake. And everywhere in the air, there was the distinct feeling that our corner of this city was not the Western world—not the one we once imagined or the one we would ever describe to our relatives in the camp. Some triumphantly call this place "Little Tibet." But to me, this place is the camp built anew. A copy of a copy of home. Another temporary stop in an endless journey.

When I saw my mother last, at the gates of the airport in Kathmandu, she said to me, "This is your life. You must take your happiness into your own hands now." Yet even now, I feel my life has not begun. Neither has my aunt's, nor my mother's, nor that of anyone in our camp. What surrounds us is temporary, a placeholder for what will come someday. For what must come. This is why I don't keep a diary or collect photographs like other girls my age. I want no record of this time.

I have plans to move out. Despite what it will do to my aunt, my mother, and Po Migmar, I must leave this place. This much is clear to me. Yet, even though I make five hundred dollars a week from working at the sandwich shop between classes, I haven't been approved for any of the apartments I've applied for. So I have a new plan. Tonight, I will go to a party that I have been invited to by my professor. An event put on by his friends, he said. There, I will impress Professor Wallace with my academic seriousness, and with his guidance and support, I will gain entry to a graduate program. A living stipend will follow, and I will begin a new life, a real one. A life of the mind.

Standing at the mirror between our shared bedroom and the kitchen, I carefully check my shirt and jeans for stains and tears. Then I notice something in the kitchen. A line of ants moving above the counter. They're heading to the kitchen sink for scraps of old meals. For weeks I've worked around these ants, carefully filling my coffee mug and turning off the tap right away, washing my dishes with a thin stream of water in corners of the sink where they had not congregated, and watching as they scurried out from the other end. But after inadvertently rinsing a dozen ants down the drain the other day, I went straight to the hardware store.

The shopkeeper was a devout Muslim who closed his doors several times a day for his prayers. I waited outside until he finished and rolled up his small, ornate rug. Inside, he had a glass display lined with insecticides and traps for cockroaches, bedbugs, mice, and other vermin. The man shook his head when I asked about ants. He saw no reason to resort to poison. They were at most, he said, a little disturbing. I nodded, showing appreciation for the fact that he had just finished praying and probably didn't want to aid in the killing of harmless creatures. I didn't want to kill them either. If that had been my objective, I would have turned on the faucet full blast. I just wanted to keep the ants away from my sink, to get them to leave my home, to stop having their lives in my hands. Did I know where they were coming from? he asked. I had not looked for their pathway, but I assumed it was somewhere behind the backsplash. The man came around the counter and led me into one of the narrow aisles. He presented me with a tube of paste that would harden over small holes. It was $1.99, water-resistant, and would solve the ant problem once and for all, he was certain of that.

Now I'm digging under the sink for that unused tube. Once I find it, I blow gently until the ants scatter and clear the hole in the backsplash. I squeeze some white paste and press it down with my index finger. But as I wait for it to dry, it dawns on me that the ants before me will now have to stay in the apartment. They will be cut off, probably forever, from the rest of their group now traveling inside the walls. Just like that, I've severed their ties. An act at once so meaningless to me and world-changing to them. I stand there for a long while, wondering if I should wipe off the still-wet paste, reopen the cavity, and try again when there are fewer ants in the apartment. This is the kind of project my Ama wouldn't hesitate to reverse midway. She would instead carry the ants, group by group, out into the front yard on a sheet of paper.

But as soon as I finish, a small hole appears in the middle of the hardening paste. They're breaking through. As if on cue, one ant wriggles out and scurries onto the counter, traveling quickly toward the sinkhole where fragments of old rice have collected. I almost want to laugh.

"Where are you going?"

It's Shumo Tenkyi, blinking her dark eyes slowly.

"School," I stammer.

"At this hour? It's already dark." She looks at me as if trying to figure out if I'm telling the truth. I should have left while she was asleep instead of fussing with the ants.

Pulling on my coat, I tell her, "I need a book at the library. Look, your dinner's gone cold. Do you want me to heat it up—"

"No," she says abruptly. "Just be careful out there. It's raining and some of the street lamps aren't working."

"I'll be back in a couple of hours," I reply and head out.

After locking the door behind me, I run up the stairs to street level. Despite the rain, it's a relief to be away from my aunt, moving farther with each step. I hop onto the streetcar at Queen Street and sit facing east toward downtown. But as the row of bars and restaurants pass by in a glowing stream, a clot of sorrow twists in my chest. Despite what my aunt may think, I am still capable of feeling shame for lying to my family. Yet lies were what got me to this country. Two simple ones set up my life in Canada: that I was seventeen when I landed at Pearson International Airport, and that Shumo Tenkyi was my mother. Shumo often says that these were not really lies but approximations—for she had raised me from the time I lived in Kathmandu, had she not? She also said that to live in a country as fine as this one, you must have either good fortune or a good story. And everyone knows, she said, that you can't tell a good story without inventing a few details.

With time, the stories compounded, until the girl I was in Nepal fell away without a sound, like some discarded skin. Even my name has changed. The Canadian tongue struggles with our names, so they give us new ones. Often it happens during our first moments on this soil, when a border agent scans our strange, laminated documents and speaks our name anew. From that moment on, I was no longer *Doh-ma*, a short, soft name spoken with the deepest recesses of the throat and ending with the sound we utter from our first breath: *ma*. Instead, I became *Dol-mah*, a name that lurches at each syllable and ends as if to ask: Is that really you?

I've reached the address of the party, a red-brick mansion in Rosedale. Who will I need to become here? With all my weight, I push the iron gate open and step toward the hedges that line the curving driveway. At least twenty cars crowd around me, and as I walk between them, my feet begin to warm for the first time in an hour. The driveway must be heated. From inside, hundreds of voices seep out of every crevice, rising out of the chimneys and into the cloudy autumn sky. Professor Wallace is in there, I tell myself. He invited me. I just need the courage to walk in.

Something irritates my head. A few raindrops fall around me. I want to scratch at my scalp, but I won't allow myself to do it anywhere outside my home, not even here. In some unspoken part of myself, I believe that the moment I do, the lice of my childhood will return. In the camp, lice were not a secret or a source of shame. Once a week, I would sit in the sun with the other children, our heads lathered with oil, waiting for our elders to pull a metal-edged comb through our hair. It was thought that the longer we waited in the sun, the more effective this process would be, so I insisted on always being the last to have my hair combed. I savored the sensation of metal scraping my scalp again and again, pulling out the lice and their eggs. Once that was finished, the women picked through our hair slowly, trying to find the white lice eggs that were too small to be caught by the comb. My mother and the older women found this task difficult because their hands were rough and stiff from working for so many years. So the younger women took on the duty of snapping the eggs with their thin, nimble fingers, making our heads bob forward with each kill. I secretly relished the high-pitched popping sound, even as the women muttered prayers for each dead louse.

When I moved to the capital at age eleven to attend the British School, I lived with Shumo Tenkyi, who had just become the new teacher at a Tibetan school. She took to her duties with relish and seldom had time to tend to my lice. At the British School, my classmates were immaculate. They rarely scratched their bodies in the classroom and never wore the same clothes two days in a row. I knew I had to take things into my own hands, so I came up with various remedies. I tried slathering my hair with petrol; I tried wearing lice shampoo all day until my head hurt; I tried suffocating the lice by wrapping my hair in a plastic bag. When my remedies failed, I taught myself not to scratch my head more than once an hour, even if the pain was excruciating, even if I could feel them biting into my scalp.

One afternoon, I was taking an after-school class in square dancing. I was eager to enroll in these free programs and often signed up for one thing after another—harmonica, karate, ping-pong, gymnastics. I lapped them all up, though I never showed any special talent in these activities. The dance class was popular with the girls, and I was hopeful of making friends. As the teacher stood in the middle of the circle directing everyone to the moves and changes of direction—vine to the left! vine to the right!—I followed along happily. There was something so pleasing about knowing exactly what to do, and in knowing that I always had a partner.

In the middle of a country song, I felt the familiar prickling. It quickly grew more intense, as if a tiny ice pick had burrowed into my scalp. In the freedom of the loud room, and in the chaos of spinning bodies, I scratched my head, quickly, just once. In that single swipe of my fingernails, something caught—this had never happened before. I could feel it wedged under my middle fingernail, and I knew instantly what this meant. I brought my hand down. There it was, the black thing, legs wriggling. The thought of a creature caught in my fingernail was at once so horrifying and incredible. Most of all, it was shameful. This was the truth of my roots, the camp where I was born, the story of my life. Squirming between my fingernail and my fleshy fingertip, the creature looked up at me. The next thought was even more terrifying. Had anyone caught sight of the thing? When I checked, everyone was still dancing. I must have paused for no more than a few seconds. I flicked the louse into the air and continued dancing, still in a daze.

The next day, the principal called me into his office after school. I walked to his door, certain that someone had seen me with the louse and informed the highest authorities of my new school. Would I be smacked with a ruler? Would they take away the scholarship my aunt worked for years to secure? I prayed that he would hit me a few times and let me off easy. Was forgiveness even possible for someone so clearly beneath the school? Entering his office, I held back my tears and awaited my fate, but the principal simply inspected his glasses and told me that I'd been chosen to receive tutelage from an expert. I cried on the spot. This was worse than I had imagined. The thing I had feared most, that people at my new school would notice how behind I was, had come true. In vain, I'd hoped that if I remained silent, kept my head down, and spent my free hours reciting the lessons out loud, I would eventually absorb their meaning and appear equal to my wealthy foreign classmates. My new tutor's name was Mr. Henri Giroux, the principal said, adding that his fees had been taken care of. This was a gift I should cherish and take seriously.

Henri lived on the outskirts of the city, and I would need to take a series of buses to attend my lessons. Though the house that Henri and Mariana rented was modest from the outside, I was stunned when I walked into his study and saw that every wall was lined with books. I had never imagined that anyone could acquire thousands of books, much less read them, in one lifetime. At first, Henri simply perused his bookshelves, pulled something out, and told me to read in a wicker armchair opposite his desk, which faced the foothills. As I read, I traced the words with my index finger and tried not to make a sound. Though I had been taught in the camp's primary school to absorb texts by speaking each word, in the British School my classmates read silently unless asked otherwise. So I would press my lips shut as I read, though sometimes I couldn't help myself. A word would slip out, and upon hearing my mangled pronunciation, Henri would correct me before carrying on with his work. At the end of the visits, he inevitably turned from his desk and asked me what I had learned. I would piece together what little I had understood and make up the rest, and Henri would sit there nodding, correcting nothing. Sometimes he even praised me.

Almost immediately, I started speaking like Henri. I adopted a French accent, making a tongue for myself that had traces of British, Nepali, and French intonations. For some time, my classmates and even a few of the teachers mocked my speech. But after a year or so, everyone seemed to forget. They even appeared to respect me more. I had learned to read silently, and when I did speak, I sounded just like Henri.

Now, as I stand before a slick, black door, preparing to speak with the worldly and wealthy of this city, I can only hope that I won't let my mentor down. After knocking and waiting for some time, I turn the giant brass knob and find the door unlocked. Inside, I stand in an ornate oak room covered with hexagonal carvings in every direction. Ahead, an oversized staircase curves downward, almost fully concealing a man hunched over a piano. He's playing a gentle, lilting melody that matches his expression.

A woman approaches me on my right, asking if she can take my coat. She's a brown-skinned Asian like me. I hand her my ragged wool coat, and she disappears into a deep closet. Smiling as she emerges, she asks if I'm the new babysitter.

The question confuses and startles me at the same time. I respond that I'm not a babysitter. I'm here for the party. Her smile vanishes, and she cocks her chin toward the hallway, telling me that I can go in. I wonder if I should say anything else, in a softer tone this time, but it's clear that she just wants me to move on.

I do as I'm told, walking farther into the aura of money as ambient heat rises from the floor and travels through my body. Down the hallway, a gentle new tune comes from nowhere in particular. This is the kind of house, I think, that's suddenly decorated a day before Christmas and then cleaned up right after—seemingly by no one, without any effort.

The next room is mercifully empty. I edge up to a large mirror to assess my reflection. What a poor sight I am. My face is flushed red and my hair is soaked from the rain, yet it goes beyond these details. I have never been the great beauty my mother was in her youth. Even my father had admirers of his own. So instead, I did what my father told me long ago: accept my ordinary looks and learn to speak English. *Learn it so perfectly that even white people are struck dumb.* What then, Father?

The living room is teeming, every inch of floor and furniture occupied. In the center, powder-blue sofas and white armchairs are burdened with guests, while the wood floor chirps faintly with footsteps. It reminds me of a description I once read of the imperial palace in Kyoto. Nightingale floors, they called them, for the guards would walk across them in specific rhythms. But if the floor sang a new tune, it meant that there was an intruder. What sound would signal the guards here? Or is it already clear that I don't belong? Everyone in this pale crowd is either over fifty, with an air of confidence that speaks to their wealth and power, or they're young, beautiful artists in their twenties, dressed with hope and hunger. Amid the faces, I search without success for my teacher. Then my eyes fall on a statue of a bronze Buddha—Thai, it seems, from the pointed spire of hair and the sleekness of his body. There's something comical about his presence in the room, standing far off in the corner, overlooked by everyone, his right hand raised in the mudra of bestowing protection.

A silver tray of drinks pauses before me just long enough for me to pick up a glass of red wine. Drink in hand, I return to the hallway, slowly taking in the house, its many Persian rugs and vitrines of ceramics. A two-story library appears to my right, covered in warm oak shelves and green velvet curtains that gather at the floor. I cannot help but step inside. My eyes soar up and down the columns of books. *Traditional Hopi Painting. Four Thousand Years of Nigerian Art. The Joys of Collecting Pre-Columbian Art. Artifacts of Asia's Last Nomads. Journey into Romanian Folk Art.*

I'm reminded of Professor Wallace's passing comment about the hosts of this party: "The Cabrinis are great admirers of Asian culture." I didn't ask him what he meant by Asian culture, or their admiration for that matter. This was a week ago, during my first one-on-one meeting with the professor—with any professor in Canada—and I was nervous. He had written to me over the summer break after receiving my term project on Nepal and the fallout of the long civil war between the Maoist insurgency and the Royalists.

At our meeting, he shared that he had been to Nepal and Tibet. I did not hide my delight in hearing this and asked him to tell me more. As he described circumambulating the holy site of Mount Kailash, I realized that he must have guessed my background correctly based on my name. What's more, he was speaking of the place where my mother and aunt were born, in the far west of a country I've never seen. Still, I didn't share this detail. Instead, I asked what it was like at the holy mountain. Professor Wallace recalled the strong winds, the treeless landscape, thousands upon thousands of prayer flags woven together along the mountain pass. He described the frost on the squat bushes of yellow and red flowers, and the golden light on the mountain at dawn as pilgrims began their prostrations, lying on the ground in supplication for their sins. He described how the pilgrims would stretch their arms forward, mark the earth with their fingers, stand up, walk to that mark, and lie down again. For weeks, he said, they circled the mountain in this manner until they completed their symbolic act of death and rebirth.

Of course, I knew about prostrations. They were part of our daily rituals at home, in the morning and again at sundown. In the camp, we often heard stories of people who made long journeys with prostrations. I remember the story of one pilgrim who had even traveled across all of Tibet, from east to west, lying down and rising, over and over until he reached the yearly Kalachakra prayers in India. My mother and aunt listened in awe, sighing that the pilgrim was fortunate to perform this act of devotion and earn so much merit. But the awe I felt was different. The idea alone was staggering. To measure the earth with my body, to know our country with my own skin. It seemed like the only way to fathom such a land. Yet I did not know if I would ever glimpse a meter of Tibet with my eyes. And so, as the professor spoke of Kailash, I was silent. I wanted to hear everything. I wanted to know if he had seen a village on a small lake near two wide sloping hills. These were the only details my mother offered when I asked where she was born.

But then Professor Wallace asked me about myself, and I let the conversation move on naturally. He wished to know if I would travel to Tibet someday and what I planned to study at the university. To both questions I answered that I did not know, but I was certain that getting a visa to my country would be much harder for me as a Tibetan in exile than it had been for him. To the second question, I also had an answer, but I lost my nerve. Only Henri knows of my singular, ardent wish to become a scholar.

Sitting at his desk, his youthful features darkened by the bright sky behind him, Professor Wallace struck me as a soft-spoken and somber person. After dedicating so many years to reaching the highest level of education, he seemed somewhat disappointed by his teaching post, his light-starved office shared with an octogenarian economist. I answered all of his questions about my family, not mentioning my lost, broken father or the complicated story of my move to Canada. Professor Wallace then praised my term project and said that I had potential. This was the kind of encouragement I could believe in, both conservative and open-ended.

That night, after our meeting, I dreamt of walking the mountain passes he had described. Between me and the night sky, Mount Kailash glowed as if lit from within. To so many, it was the navel of the world, home to the divine, an unscalable pyramid with a mythic scar down its side. From its base, I saw the veins of the Indus River, the mighty Yarlung, and even the river that flows before our camp in Pokhara. As I walked the ancient, footworn path in the twilight, I realized that I had been endowed with all the knowledge of the mountain and the land. I knew the story of each saint, pilgrim, and beggar who had laid their body on the rocky trail encircling the mountain. I knew the name of every blossom they admired, the songs of the lonesome birds that have lived in this valley through the ages, the faithful patterns of breath from the sky in each season, and the eternal sorrows of the rivers splitting into streams around me. I understood this place completely, as though I had always been there. As though I had never been anywhere else.

When I woke up, I felt something harden inside me. I wrote to Professor Wallace right away and shared my intention to study the history and literature of my country. Typing as quickly as I could, I asked for guidance on how I could become an academic like him. Sensing I might lose my nerve, I sent it off immediately. He wrote back two days later, inviting me to this party with the offer to make some introductions. Yet there is no sign of him tonight.

As I return to the hallway, a large group passes by like a steamship. At the helm is an elderly woman, impossibly thin, with long silver hair. The others, mostly young, glide behind her toward a light-filled room at the end of the hallway. Was this woman with silver hair a Cabrini? I follow them into a vast, two-story kitchen with French doors leading to the garden. People drape over a massive kitchen island, copper pots dangling just above their heads. Others gather on an enclosed porch, washed with a strange pink light. Here and there, silk-white kites hang from the coffered walnut ceiling, fluttering like sails. Is this house meant to feel like a dream-scape? Is this how the wealthy prefer it?

On the far side of the kitchen, I notice another brown Asian woman. She sits before a dormant fireplace so large you could step into its mouth without hunching. Hands folded in her lap, she smiles and listens to an older white man with a shock of snowy hair. With her high cheekbones and earthen skin, she could almost be Tibetan. I find her beautiful and familiar in a way I cannot name, as though she were a lost memory.

"That's one of our new acquisitions," says a young blonde woman to my right.

"Sorry?"

She nods to a large painting a few inches away. "Do you like it?"

The canvas depicts an austere young couple on either side of a little boy. All three are painted in black, white, and gray. Across their chests, a thin red line rises and falls, disjointed at times. The trio is placed against a mottled background, the kind used for family portraits.

"It's beautiful," I admit, gazing at the giant, melancholic faces.

"Elise Sandberg," she says, extending her hand. "I'm building the collection for Martha."

"Tenzin Dolma," I say, wondering how old she is. With her cherub cheeks and tidy bangs, she looks about twenty, but she's dressed like a nun—black turtleneck, long skirt, and tights. The only distinguishing part of her outfit is a necklace with a flat stone the size and color of a lemon resting on her collarbone. It looks like the necklaces my mother sells to tourists at Phewa Lake, except five or six times larger.

Trying to place me, Elise asks if I'm an artist. I shake my head and she laughs. "You haven't talked to anyone, not even Martha. For a minute, I thought you might be a baby curator with that infinite stare."

I explain that Professor Wallace invited me. She frowns briefly and says that she doesn't know anyone by that name. A pretty brown woman joins us, embracing and kissing Elise on both cheeks. She introduces herself as Dia. Her upper-class Indian accent reminds me of my classmates at the British School. It is a well-traveled voice, layered with a deep, self-possessed tenor.

Elise pivots back to the glum family and begins to share her view of the piece. It acts, she says with a practiced eloquence, as a counterpoint to the cynical realism of other Chinese artists. She calls it a perfect convergence of art, family, and the Sino-Western relational sphere. Dia says nothing but considers the painting, adjusting her intricate Kashmiri shawl slung across her chest and cascading down to the floor. Another man joins in and asks Elise about a new triptych of fragmented Chinese calligraphy near the kitchen. The three of them move toward the paintings without inviting me to join.

It's just as well. My phone is buzzing. I pull it out of my back pocket and see that it's my mother. I consider ignoring it, but this is an unusual time for her. Ama tends to call me during her evenings, my midmornings. It's now eight here, which means it's nearly six in the morning at the camp. A busy hour of prayers, breakfast, and preparations for the day's labor. So now, my paranoia demands that I answer. What if something has happened to her, or to Po Migmar?

I turn to face the corner. "Hello? Ama?"

"Dolma. Dolma. Is it you?"

There's honking in the background.

"Yes, it's me. Where are you? It's so loud."

"What's that? Where are you?" Ama asks, cutting out momentarily. When the line returns, she asks it again: Where are you? A simple question about this specific moment. Yet it's not simple. Our lives need translation that we're incapable of. How can I tell her that I'm in a house like this?

But this question is always the starting point. We need to locate each other, to know or imagine the place the other stands or lies or sits. If I'm eating, she wants to know what I'm eating and if it's any good. If I haven't eaten yet, she asks what I'm going to eat. These are expressible matters, the things we can say to each other. Plain, simple, routine. All the rest cannot be said—all the moments in the days that make up our lives apart, all the small disappointments, frustrations, hopes, memories, and sorrows.

Each passage in a book that I have to rewrite by hand because it stirs something in me so large I must repeat it like a prayer. Each pattern my mother weaves in a friendship bracelet that comes together just as she'd hoped. The past my mother returns to when she goes quiet, the one I can never know. The new streets I walk along, which she might never see.

"I'm at a friend's house, Ama. You?"

"Lakeside, by Raja's store."

I picture my mother walking before Raja's old camera shop, her backpack full of friendship bracelets, imitation stone necklaces slung around her wrists and hanging from her rough, work-worn hands. Like so many Tibetans and Nepalis who sell their wares along roads at Phewa Lake, my mother approaches tourists gently with her rehearsed English phrases. Years ago, when she was young and beautiful, rumors say a few foreigners had even tried to woo her. Now, they would view her as an old woman. Another brown face among many brown faces who linger by open air restaurants and cafés, hoping to make a sale before they're shooed away by the staff for bothering their patrons.

"How's business?" I ask.

"The yellow-heads have gone back to their countries for the winter," she says, "but I sold yak bone earrings yesterday to an Israeli boy. He wanted to get a present for his mother." She sighs. I know she's thinking that soon, the boy will be reunited with his mother.

How I wish we still had our shop, the one she opened during "the good years," a rented storefront between an English bookstore and a souvenir shop. She was the only woman in the camp to run her own shop. I boasted to children and adults alike that my mother now sat through her days, on her own stool under the shade of a roof, with a cabinet full of wares. When we sat behind the display case, we had a view of Phewa Lake with its small temple island in the middle, and the mountains beyond. How we loved to watch the mist rise from the lake's surface in the quiet morning hours, when the tourists were asleep and the only sounds came from the temple's ringing bells. But the shop had only been a brief dream. Civil unrest in the late nineties kept most foreigners away, and, in time, we could no longer afford the rent. Even now, with peace reinstated, the shores of Phewa Lake are often deserted.

"Did you eat dinner?"

"Yes," I reply. "Did you get your RC renewed yet?"

"Soon enough. I need to go to Kathmandu to apply."

Every year around this time, my mother has to renew her Refugee Card for another twelve months. Even though she's lived in Nepal for fifty years, her RC card is the only thing that allows her to stay. With the rules changing constantly and the trips back and forth to the capital, the renewal is a source of constant stress. And yet, it's better to have that card than not to have it, which is the fate of any Tibetan born in Nepal after 1989. The camp has dozens of these paperless kids—unclaimed by any nation, and considered nonentities, even though they have their whole lives ahead of them. Somehow, they have to find a way to study, work, and try to get to the West, where they might someday become a full citizen. But even with the RC, it's been impossible to get my mother to Canada. Twice, we've applied for her visa. Twice, she has taken the three-day bus ride to the Canadian consulate in Delhi, only to return empty-handed.

"How's your aunt?" Ama asks. "Is she looking well?"

I don't know what to say.

"Should I request prayers at the monastery?"

The other day, Phurbu from the community center called me while I was in class. He told me that my aunt was crying on Queen Street and that I must go home to her. When I asked how he got my number, he replied wistfully that my aunt had become a laughingstock, that she'd changed ever since she came to Canada. I told him that people also said Shumo Tenkyi changed long before Toronto. They said she hadn't been the same since her time in Delhi. Then he asked me blankly: "Why don't you help her? It's up to you." I replied that I would take care of things. But what I wanted to tell Phurbu and every other person in Parkdale is that this is nothing new. All I've ever known of my aunt is a woman whose mind dances and flares in sudden bursts, a woman who moves and thinks as unpredictably as a firecracker.

"Tell me," my mother pleads.

My aunt is eating my life, I want to say. I have to get away.

"Dolma, are you there?"

"Maybe," I finally admit. "Yes, some prayers."

Silence.

"Ama?"

"I'll go to the monastery tomorrow," she says, her voice almost inaudible above the street noise.

My mother and I end the call expressing the usual pleas and promises to each other—to eat well, to dress warm, to not worry about the other. I'm relieved that it ends this way. The last time we spoke, this ritual was broken. As we said goodbye, Ama's voice became as thin as a bird's and she began to cry. With my own voice failing, I begged her to stop crying. She said, "It's worse than death, this separation." After she hung up, I stood with the phone in my hand for a long time, thinking of my mother's words, unable to move. It was a shock to hear her grief. It rattled me for days.

From my earliest memory, it has always been the two of us, without air for anyone else, not even my father. In the mornings, we prepared for our days together, me putting on my school uniform while Ama donned her long chupa. Next, she oiled and plaited my hair in two braids, before doing the same to her own hair. Then we'd leave for Phewa Lake together, carrying two thermoses, two lunches, two backpacks—books in one, friendship bracelets and imitation stone jewelry in the other. At the end of the day, we'd sit hunched before a kerosene lamp as she made more jewelry to sell and I studied for school. When it was time for bed, Ama lifted her blanket and I entered the warm chamber between her arms. As she said her prayers, I burrowed in her bosom and suckled my thumb as I slipped into a dream.

Back then, we took turns promising never to stray far from each other for long.

But in the end, it was my mother who sent me to Kathmandu to study at the British School, and then farther still to Canada. All this has left our family fractured and indebted for decades to come. And for what? The promise of a future on which I have yet to deliver.

2

C LINK clink clink."
  The woman with long silver hair, who is indeed Martha Cabrini, begins her toast at the kitchen island. She has dark red lipstick on her thin lips and kohl applied messily around her eyes. Her skin is iridescent and loose on her delicate frame. Heavy rings and bangles swirl and clang as she gesticulates with nearly every word.

"Many of you know that I've always been a collector, whether of art or experience. It's what I do. Rob prefers real estate, but I invest in art and democracy. But the thing is, Rob's a tiny bit younger than me."

Some people laugh at what must be a familiar joke. A twinge flashes across Martha's face. "Well, these things become clearer as you mature. Anyhow, with our foundation, Rob and I want to make art accessible to everyone because in the end, it's not about . . . money, it's about *access*. Really and truly, that is what matters."

The speech stretches on as she explains that this year, the family is sponsoring a dissident Burmese artist, the beautiful woman by the fireplace. Martha says the artist will stay in Toronto for the next six months, "living in her artistic practice," before she continues to New York and Belgium for artist residencies. People seem to tighten the circle around Martha and the Burmese artist, locked in blissful smiles. Martha spills some wine as she speaks. She laughs and everyone laughs with her. I get the feeling this speech is rehashing Martha's most well-used lines. The room is getting warm, and everyone's faces are flushed red. Past the crowd, through the tall windows, branches thrash in the winter wind, and I catch glimpses of an endless hedge maze in the garden. How would I describe this place in Tibetan? Do the words for an artist residency or an art collector even exist in our language?

"Dolma! Over here!"

It's Professor Wallace, waving at me from the dining room.

He introduces me to his companions, all of them academics from the university: Dave Fleming, a Sanskritist, Lena Kingsley, an economist, and to her side, Aaron Horowitz, an anthropologist. As we shake hands, I recognize Horowitz. His name and photograph pop up occasionally on campus event posters: mostly talks on Himalayan-language preservation and nomadic communities.

"We were just talking about Lhasa," Professor Wallace tells me. "There's a music shop in the Barkhor run by a man named Lhundup Dorjee—"

"Gone," Horowitz says, shaking his head. "I'm sure of it. If it's not, it will be razed any day like the rest of Old Lhasa."

I recall Horowitz's name lining Henri's bookshelf. He's an all-around expert on Central Asia, his niche carved out many decades ago. Somewhere he must have a photo of himself, a young blond European standing on a mountaintop with a notepad and a pink nose. With his sallow, plain face full of wrinkles, and the glass of whiskey between his fingers, Horowitz has a grimness that's fundamentally likable.

Professor Wallace is momentarily distraught about the music shop. But Horowitz, seemingly oblivious, keeps going: "The state is making way for new buildings, which will be built in the image of the old. This is just part of a plan to sanitize Old Lhasa while maintaining the so-called traditional qualities of the minority culture. Chinese tourists don't want the real gritty thing. They want something palatable, a version of a place they have heard about, but it has to be easy, romantic, simple. Fixed and dead— like in a museum."

"Like the Potala Palace now," I offer.

Everyone looks at me expectantly.

"On a busy day," I continue, "five thousand Chinese tourists visit the winter home of the Dalai Lama, which has been emptied of its ancient artifacts and all but a handful of monks who clean and maintain the grounds. His throne is still there, but in his place sits a blanket contorted roughly in the shape of a person. It's an image of unspeakable sorrow for my people."

"Well, yes," Horowitz shrugs. "This is the way now. And the locals reenact the scripts written by others, whether Chinese or Westerners. Just look at the town dubbed 'Shangri-La' in Dechen county. A holiday destination to fulfill Chinese fantasies of Tibet. The twist is that it's named for a utopia literally invented by a bloke from Lancaster who never even left England."

"Ah, *Lost Horizon!*" Professor Wallace shakes his head. "I'm embarrassed to admit I read that novel ten times. The spine eventually gave up and fell apart into pieces."

"Tibet is now mimetic of itself," Horowitz sighs.

The comment doesn't sit well with me, but I hold back. The myth and name of Shangri-La were Westernized, but the idea of a hidden valley of peace—whether as Shambhala or beyul—has deep roots in Tibetan culture.

"Speaking of the Potala, did you hear about the dealer who filled an entire room there with statues?" asks Fleming, the middle-aged Sanskritist. "He was an antiques dealer. After a long career of *gathering* artifacts from across Tibet and making obscene amounts of money, one day he was suddenly struck with a profound debilitating guilt. He realized that he had sold his country's treasures to fill his pockets. To atone, he shuttered his business and donated dozens and dozens of gold and silver statues to the Potala."

Fleming tells the story with unexpected relish—stretching it out over five long minutes, his eyes wide, searching for excitement in his audience like an entertainer at a children's party. I admit that I was rapt, but now that it's over, I feel ashamed. The story of this antiques dealer had contained so many personal and national tragedies, so much loss, and yet I had savored it as I would a ghost story.

"Maybe he's the one who sold Martha her latest piece from Tibet," Horowitz says.

"Did you see it?" Fleming asks, leaning in. "I hear the statue is absolutely exquisite."

I want to ask about the statue, but Professor Wallace interjects. "Dolma wrote a paper on Nepal, about the civil war, for my class. It was really strong."

"Wonderful!" Kingsley says. "The civil war has been tragic for the country, especially the poorest. Although I'm sure you could tell me a lot more."

"She's one of my finest writers," Professor Wallace beams.

"Excellent!" Fleming says, laughing. "I wish you'd come and teach my students how to formulate a sentence, Dolma. In fact, I could use a lesson!"

Their eager lines of praise rise and fall within the length of a few seconds. I've come to recognize this as something of a local custom—to express enthusiasm and agreement without real interest. A kind of polite but unyielding distance that saturates so many interactions. But now, their raised eyebrows and tight-lipped smiles fill me with a new sadness, clarifying where I stand in their eyes. Theirs isn't the gaze of a mentor upon a student but a fixed asymmetry. They look at me as though I am a child whom they can tolerate at the table as long as I know my place. For years, I've sensed this violent but hidden truth—that beyond the welcome smiles of this country lies a vast and impenetrable wall: a national self-regard that insists on a mythic goodness. This is a nation that gives and gives to the less fortunate and asks nothing in return. Nothing, that is, but our grateful acquiescence to their silent expectations.

I must speak. That is all I can do. I must speak now and make a path for myself with my words. Clearing my throat, I find an opening line.

"I left Nepal just as the civil war was ending in 2006, so I have personal knowledge of it, but I'm primarily a student of ancient history."

"Say more," Horowitz commands.

"She's interested in graduate school, eventually," Professor Wallace says with an encouraging smile.

I hesitate and consider my words.

"Yes, I've been studying under Henri Giroux in Nepal for some time. Do you know him? We had been researching the autobiographies of women in the Himalayas mostly. Saints and nuns."

"Giroux . . ." Fleming squints and shakes his head.

"Yes, I know Henri," Horowitz replies, nodding with new interest.

"He's written extensively on termas," I say, proudly.

"Treasure texts," Horowitz says. "The story goes that these texts were hidden in Tibet around a thousand years ago by Guru Padmasambhava, the legendary carrier of Buddhism from India."

"Except it was Yeshi Tsogyal, his Tibetan consort, who did a lot of the work of hiding the texts—she rarely gets credit for that," I add, correcting him as gently as Henri would. "The termas don't have to be actual texts, either. They can be mind termas, which means they're like psychic treasures. Hidden in caves, lakes, temples, trees, and rocks, even a person's mind, just waiting to reemerge when the teachings are needed."

"It's such a beautiful idea," Professor Wallace says, smiling.

"It is, but also a frustrating one," I say, expressing two positions at once, just as Henri tends to do. "It's as if time stopped for Tibet long ago. New texts are just discoveries of old ones. Our masters are forever reincarnations. Everything is rooted and sourced back to India—which seeded some of the greatest philosophies of Tibet—"

Horowitz interjects: "Termas were a useful tool for the Buddhist Empire. Whenever a new treasure text is *discovered*, the practitioner claims a direct transmission from Guru Padmasambhava, calls it a treasure text, and *poof*, it is legitimate—an unbroken lineage. The canon can keep growing."

Listening to Horowitz continue, I see that he's nothing like Henri. If my mentor were here, he would talk about termas in the same way he does reincarnations—neither skeptical nor believing, simply holding a space between. For Henri, there's no hierarchy, no need for comparison between the Western worldview and that of Tibet. No choice to be made. For as long as I can remember, I've wanted to move through the world in the same way as this kindly old scholar. I even dreamed as a child that he and his wife, Mariana, might ask me to move in with them and join their family. What I wouldn't give to be in his study again, to face the foothills at the edge of the valley and to read the books he chose for me, for my mind's development. What I wouldn't give to see him chuckle! How I miss trying to delight him with my thoughts. How I miss the packages he used to send to me from Nepal. Before opening one of his letters, I would hold the envelope to my nose and find that somehow, even a slim stack of paper beaten by weeks of travel could still hold the scent of home, of freshly baked bricks, of wilting, sun-drenched marigolds, of stray dogs with fleas in orbit. And most of all, the scent of his library. Nothing smells like that here.

But it has been a long time since his last letter. Henri has had a difficult year, with his pancreatic infection and his daughter's divorce. But there's at least one more book in him, if he could just have one season of good health. Nowadays, when I think of Henri, my mind turns to the monk's prayer calling to his teacher: Ah Lama khyenno; ah Lama khyenno. Oh Teacher, think of me; Teacher, think of me. To lose your teacher, to be parted from him, is a moment of utter trauma. The mere thought of such a loss would bring a monk to tears.

My mother has never understood my relationship with Henri in these terms. Perhaps she hasn't understood much about me at all. But Henri and I are afflicted by the same need for the past. When we read, it is to fill our bellies. Each book we read reveals more days we've missed, more painfully exquisite sights we can only imagine, more stories that serrate our hearts and strip the present world of sound and color. And yet, every time I sit to work, even as a quiet elation washes through me, a calm I can only access in these moments, I hear my mother ask: Why do you read a saint's story with a pencil in hand? Their stories are meant to inspire you, to help you understand your own suffering and guide you through example. Why do you spend your days dismantling these texts, seeking the human in the gods?

But I am not looking for the human in the gods. I don't want to lock these saints to the mundane. Far from it. I want to be close to them, closer than even prayer can bring me. I want to be near to these saints in their time, in their world. My mother never speaks of her past, her life in Tibet. But I am in love with the past—all of it. I want to be in the Yarlung Valley a thousand years ago, watching a dead king as he is placed on a copper throne and sealed into his tomb while mourners cut off their hair, paint their faces red, and lacerate their bodies. I want to be in the vast region of western Tibet called Ngari, where my family comes from, in the time before it was even Tibet, when it was a kingdom called Zhangzhung. They had another language and a culture that was closer to Persian. When Po Migmar said our tongue was older than people knew, was that what he meant? Yet even an answer from him wouldn't satisfy me. Because I want to hear the original tongue itself. I want to live through all of it, to see the long dead come alive, to have their worlds open to me. But my mother? For her the past was obliterated long ago. It is less than a flickering shadow of a flame.

"Have you ever felt a cool pocket of air around you?" I ask the professors, repeating Henri's words. "You don't know it's there until you touch it, but it's always there. All you have to do is hold out your hand. That's what it's like to receive a terma. To lay a hand on a rock and recognize verses of metaphysics. To grind an herb and discover a moment of wisdom that unleashes entire teachings. Or to look up at the sky and see a symbol right there that unlocks a transmission from a thousand years ago. Imagine how that feels. To come up against something so ancient, which was left there just for you. All the termas discovered in Tibet are still there, reburied for the next generation as instructed by Guru Padmasambhava. There could be many thousands more that haven't even been unearthed. Just waiting there . . ."

"Ian, we should introduce Dolma to Tim," Kingsley says, glancing at Fleming. "He should hear about her research interests."

"Tim directs the Tibetan studies program," Professor Wallace whispers in my ear.

All I've ever wanted flashes before me, like a distant, shimmering planet. It is only a possibility, and I must move carefully. But there it is. I see it.

"I would love that," I reply. "Thank you."

"What color is this drink?" Horowitz asks, holding up his glass of whiskey. "Doesn't it look a little pale?"

The conversation turns to colors and perceptual encoding. Professor Wallace shares that he recently came across a paper by a researcher from Stanford on the role of adaptive necessities in determining what is visible to different creatures. The transparency of water for us is, in a sense, a kind of blindness, which arises out of a necessity to see only what is essential to our survival. So when we look at water, we see only the fish, while other creatures see much more. Horowitz then launches into a series of questions about wavelengths, most of which Professor Wallace can't answer, since he had read the paper for pleasure.

The professors keep talking, laughing, and chewing away on canapés that have come around. I realize I'm smiling as I listen to everyone banter and take playful jabs at one another. I am standing here, with them. Henri will be happy to know this. All these years I've worried that he must think poorly of me, academically aimless in Canada, showing no signs that his years of mentorship would amount to anything tangible. Now it seems there might be hope for me yet.

I'm also struck by the idea that we need a kind of blindness to see what matters. But how do I determine which mysteries to leave alone and which ones to pursue? Look at this house, filled with gathered artifacts from around the world. Somewhere here, there is a statue from Tibet. What treasure has Martha Cabrini purchased from my country?

I spot Elise moving with determination down the hallway. If she's growing the family's art collection, she would have been involved with purchasing the Tibetan statue. And if the piece is as Fleming described it, *absolutely exquisite*, I must at least try to view it. Leaning toward Professor Wallace, I excuse myself and follow Elise as she heads to the stairs. When I reach the landing, I grip the banister and hesitate. Elise must have sensed me, because she stops and turns. "Hello again."

"Sorry," I say, climbing briskly to catch up. "I was just looking for the bathroom—"

"It's no problem!" she replies instinctively before cocking her head to the side and giving me a strange look. "Wait, are you Burmese?"

"No."

Elise stares at me, swaying and smiling. I realize that she's waiting for me to tell her my ethnicity. She also seems to be drunk.

"Tibetan."

"Come with me," she says, pulling me by the hand.

We wind upward to the third floor and enter the first door. This is where Elise runs the family's art estate, she explains, doing the day-to-day bookkeeping, consulting with art advisers, fielding thinly veiled calls from the scavengers at Sotheby's and Christie's about the health of the Cabrini family. Unlike the main floor, this space is a complete mess. Two large mahogany desks are littered with bills, catalogs, and empty coffee cups. Even the marble fireplace is filled with crumpled paper, and old ash fans out across the floor.

Elise says she has an intern, but he never leaves Martha's side. "You probably saw him orbiting her downstairs. He was hired to help with this mess, but he hasn't been up here for weeks." She laughs it off and slips behind the main desk. I notice a small dusting of white powder on the surface.

"Want some?" she asks.

I look around. "Will someone see?"

She scoffs. "No. Rob thinks cameras are . . . *indiscreet*. Can't imagine why he wouldn't want them around!" Elise takes a business card, scrapes the remaining powder into a line, and motions for me to take it. I could use a pick-me-up.

"Thanks," I say. When I stand up, she's looking at me with a goofy grin, bouncing in place.

"You're not going to believe this," she says, flinging open a floor-to-ceiling cabinet to reveal an imposing safe. "Actually, hold on." She slides past me, locks the office door, and hurries back. Slowly, with intense focus, Elise presses six buttons on the safe and turns the latch. It doesn't open. She tries again, but no luck. I'm beginning to wonder if she has mistaken me for someone else.

"The fucker changed it," she mumbles, and opens a drawer in the desk with a Post-it note sitting on a pile of papers. "There you are."

Holding up the note, she presses a new set of numbers, turns the latch, and pulls open the heavy door. I still can't see what's inside, but she's putting on a pair of white gloves.

"This is our latest acquisition," she says, ducking behind the door. When Elise reemerges, she places a wooden box on a stack of old newspapers. Working with extreme care, she pries the lid open with a nearby letter opener and pulls out a smaller box surrounded in bubble wrap.

"Were you born there, in Tibet?" she asks, slowly unwrapping the plastic.

My eyes are locked on her hands. "No."

"But you've been there," she states.

"No," I repeat.

"Really?" The plastic wrapping is stuck, and she needs to unhook it carefully. Her right hand is visibly shaking as she lifts the box. Both of us hold our breath as she fidgets with the last layer. Sighing, Elise pauses for another sniff at the desk before continuing.

"One day, maybe," I reply, trying to sound genial. I end up sounding more hopeful about the prospect than I intended.

Elise nods. "My boyfriend Harvey went to Lhasa two years ago. He did the Potala, Jokhang, the whole thing. I'm hoping to go soon with Martha, actually. You know, she had a meeting with the Dalai Lama."

"That's great. I hope you both get in."

"Thanks! We should all get lunch sometime."

Elise opens the lid. A black velvet mouth opens up at me.

"From central Tibet. Fifteenth century."

I step closer and see a tiny brown face in the dark, gazing skyward. Elise dips her white-gloved hands inside the box and carefully places the statue down. It's a little man, naked and emaciated, kneeling on a lotus flower. He peers up with his mouth open, his eyes squinting at the sky. It doesn't look like any statue I've ever seen. Completely unadorned except for a faded layer of gilding. And his expression puzzles me. It is not the calm, muted smile of most Buddhist deities. It's not even the fearsome snarl of a wrathful god. No, his expression is completely singular, perhaps even deliberately illegible. This is a being seized either by devastating sorrow or blinding confusion, or perhaps even ecstatic revelation.

"You're sure this is from Tibet?"

"Oh, without a doubt. We believe he's a Mahasiddha."

A Mahasiddha. Those saints on the edges of society. Half-mad mystics who can shrink to the size of atoms, converse with animals, lie with lepers. Which one is this—Naropa? Tilopa? Someone outside the legendary eight-four? I can't tell. The table creaks under my weight. I'm afraid to stand too close, but I don't want to allow any distance between us. Somehow, I am drawn to the ground, as if I must bow. Never before has this impulse come to me. I wonder if Ama would recognize him. Or Po Migmar. He knows the life stories of a hundred saints.

He looks different to each person. Po Migmar's voice echoes in my mind.

Tell me more, I said. My favorite phrase as a child.

It's in his expression. It's impossible to describe or picture. You just have to see him for yourself. In a way, he looks like any one of us. A saint made of earth, wearing a human face.

Every single hair on my neck stands on end. A saint with a human face. Not a serene, beautiful god's face, but a face like Po Migmar's, like so many men in our camp. The Nameless Saint.

"Tell me more about him," I say to Elise, taking another step forward, my waist pushing against the desk.

"Well, he's at least six hundred years old. Twelve centimeters tall, five centimeters wide, three deep." Elise moves the statue back slightly, away from the edge of the table.

"So small . . ." I whisper. "What is he made of?"

"Mudstone. That's just gold pigment on top."

Earth. Tears pool in my eyes. It is just as Po Migmar said. I didn't believe his stories of the Saint. I thought they were just like all the others Po Migmar told about love affairs between mountains and rivers, about ghosts and snake gods. The fantasies of an old man who still wears his hair in plaits, who still waits for the day he can return to the pastures of his youth. But to this day, Po Migmar speaks of the Nameless Saint's return. Of course, it was real. *One day, when he reveals himself to us again, we will know his full story.*

And here he is. Our camp's lost Saint. So humble, so precious. Looking up with teeth bared, eyes wide, as if struggling to speak. I almost want to laugh because right here on this cluttered oak table, in this object, is our entire history, the whole of our civilization. Nameless Saint, you once sat in the sun of my ancestors' time. You heard the rain in my mother's village. You endured earthquakes, wars, and all the small dramas of day-to-day life. You heard songs that are now forgotten, gazed at kings whose bodies are now flowers. I have never been so close to it all.

But how did you survive all those years with this body made of earth? These last sixty years of exile, were they hard on you, as well? Do you miss that land which made your body? Do you speak of it to anyone who will listen? Or do you also find—like so many I know—that this is a loss too big to speak aloud?

"Where did you find him?" I ask, blinking back my emotions.

Elise is already primed with a response. "I can't tell you much, obviously, but it was a really special case. We actually acquired the piece directly from the dealer in Nepal. You have no idea how difficult it was to negotiate, with the power cuts and labor strikes. Everything took twice as long. But so worth it. There's so little coming out of Tibet these days."

I think of Fleming's story about the reformed antiquities dealer and feel slightly nauseated. "How did the dealer get it?"

Elise shrugs. "Just *look* at the detail on his ribs. You can see each indentation in the ribcage. That caught Martha's attention right away."

"You don't know how the dealer got the statue?" I ask.

"We verified the provenance, but I can't give specifics."

"Was it taken legally? By the dealer, I mean."

Elise looks up and holds my gaze. "I thought you'd like to see the statue," she sighs. Her eyes are intensely green, like two deep eddies in a river.

She wants me to thank her, I realize. "Thank you for showing this to me."

"I can share one special detail, a folktale of sorts. Apparently, some people believe this statue comes and goes on its own. As if by magic. Isn't that fascinating? Martha loves that."

"That's an interesting story," I reply. "I wonder how the dealer obtained something so important to a community."

"This statue will be loaned to the National Gallery in Ottawa. There's even talk about it touring the West."

"Wouldn't the galleries want to know its history?"

Elise gives a tight-lipped smile and begins to pack up the statue. "You're new to this world, Dolma. Museums exist because of people like Martha. Collectors like her support artists and galleries, and then the public also benefits. See how that works?" she asks. "You should be glad we got to it first, honestly."

I look back toward the safe. "Can I take a photograph?"

"I'm afraid not. Definitely not."

"Okay, sorry."

She's holding the camp's Saint in her hands, and here I am defaulting to the usual apologies, as though she can kick me out of this country.

"No, I'm sorry," Elise says, as if soothing a child she doesn't particularly like.

"It's a great acquisition," I say, using her word. "How much did it cost?"

"You know I can't tell you that," she says.

"Fifty thousand? A hundred?" I say these numbers as if I could gather the sums.

Elise raises one of her eyebrows and smirks. She finishes rewrapping the small box and places it inside the bigger box. Then she slides it into the safe. The metal door is closed, the same buttons pushed, the hatch pulled, and that's that. He's gone. I look down at the stack of garbage on the desk and the floor. How can she leave this mess when there's a six-hundred-year-old Saint's statue within these walls? Behind the desk, I notice an opened wooden crate with a crumpled piece of paper lying on its surface. The sheet features some text I cannot decipher from this distance as well as a watermark of a familiar Buddhist symbol: the endless knot. The endless knot signifies, among other things, the interconnectedness of all phenomena. This is the shipping notice from the company in Nepal that has stolen and sold our Nameless Saint.

3

I follow Elise downstairs but cannot bring myself to rejoin the party. As she approaches the nearest group and begins chirping, I gather my things from the coat closet. When I reach the gates, I notice the girl with the Kashmiri shawl walking a few steps ahead, a fine layer of frost on the road glistening darkly around her silhouette.

"Dia!" I say.

She turns and waits for me to catch up before asking where I'm headed.

"Parkdale," I tell her, though as soon as the words leave my lips, I realize I have no wish to return to my aunt right now. When I see Shumo next, I will have to decide whether to tell her about the Saint or let the matter pass in silence.

Dia suggests a nightcap somewhere nearby. She knows a good place. I accept the invitation if only to delay the decision I must make. We head south on foot, mostly in silence but exchanging periodic small talk as we hustle through the cold. Bloor Street West is empty at this hour. The department stores are closed, and everyone has retreated indoors. We walk by the Royal Ontario Museum, looking at the enormous glass and aluminum shards that jut out from the original stone building. Dia tells me she hated the addition at first, as many others did, but now she's warmed to its boldness and wishes to see more like it around the city. I watch our reflections appear in brief flashes on the glass as Dia reveals bits and pieces about herself. She was born in Delhi, though she never learned Hindi formally—something to do with attending an international school. Then her father was transferred to a UNHCR post on the Thai-Burmese border, where her family still lives. Dia's past sounds as though it were exotic but refined, marked by pretty homes nestled in lush gardens.

But I'm quietly distracted. I keep thinking about the Nameless Saint. I could make a quick call to my mother, but what then? Beyond telling her about the ku's reappearance, there's not much I can do.

We walk down Devonshire through the university. As we pass the brightly lit football field, I notice a group of girls doing drills against a black sky, their figures gamine even in their winter track clothes. As three girls sprint back and forth, the rest cheer and shout encouragement, their voices echoing in the distance. Past the field, we walk in darkness as a few stars appear overhead. The path is flanked by stately redbrick buildings, each one the home of a different discipline.

"I go here," I say softly, momentarily dazed by this fact.

Dia asks what I'm studying. An hour ago, I thought I knew.

"Just taking a few courses," I reply.

I recall how Fleming relayed the story of the smuggler as the rest of us drank it up like gossip. I replay Elise's story of the Saint, a *folktale*, she called it. A charming but ridiculous bit of trivia to decorate their purchase. And wasn't I ridiculous too, staring dumbly while she placed our ku back in the safe?

Now that I think about it, I don't really know how Henri would have responded either. It's possible that he would have seen the statue just as they did—as a cultural artifact that belongs in a museum, where experts can study it. He might have joined the professors in dissecting the Saint's aesthetic qualities. Still, I have a persistent thought that this puny conversation among Tibet scholars does not matter. The world has forgotten us. To the vast majority, we do not matter. How else could they pass around our gods as possessions, display them in the sterile confines of museums and private collections, as though we were already long gone?

Dia and I turn onto Queen's Park Crescent as the CN Tower appears in the distance, its peak washed in red. Crossing a small overpass beside the Ontario Legislative Building, Dia answers a call from a colleague who has lost his wallet in the Cabrinis' garden. A taxi passes, filling the quiet street with an old Hindi tune. I know this song. "A mirror or a heart," the voice sings, "in the end it breaks." Humming to myself, I remember a tin shack by Phewa Lake where I would watch Indian movies after school.

Dropping a few coins, I would find a spot on a wooden bench and let my sandals sink into the mud floor. There, in a hot and airless room, I sang along to a hundred Hindi love songs. How quickly I abandoned it all after moving to Canada. When I pass the Indian stores in Parkdale, I no longer recognize the latest movie posters or even most of the actors. I am often surprised by how much I have changed. Perhaps this is what it means to be free.

We duck into the first bar that isn't packed with televisions. Settling into a booth, I sip my beer while Dia spends half the time scrolling through her work emails. Every so often, she widens her eyes before typing short, furious replies. To be engaged in pressing work makes her appealing. Dia says she works for a global prodemocracy group run by a wealthy family. She lives to advocate for others, to spread herself across many causes. When a Kenyan microfinance project failed to launch, she decided to focus her attention on politically sensitive culture and art from Southeast Asia. In a few years, I imagine she will move on to another cause. Though I admire her, I also feel the urge to shake her somehow.

"Elise took me into her office earlier," I say.

"What for?" Dia asks, laughing.

"She showed me the statue they just acquired. It's very old. From the fifteenth century." I pause, wondering why I'm sharing this. Do I want Dia, this professional fighter with institutional backing, to give me a clear and righteous verdict, to insist that I stand up against injustice and reclaim what's rightfully mine? I sense that she has enough courage for the both of us.

"Okay, so what's it like?" Dia asks, swaying side to side to the music.

"It was small. A Tibetan mystic without a name." I pause because I don't want to tell her the camp's stories. I don't yet trust her not to laugh. "Elise wouldn't tell me about its history."

"What are you worried about?"

"Just that there was so little information about the statue, who it belonged to, how the antiques dealer got hold of it. I *did* see the company's logo, I think."

"Oh, the Cabrinis wouldn't buy from illegitimate sources if that's what you're implying," Dia says. "They're good people. They really love—okay this sounds dumb—but they really love Asian culture. They're big supporters of all kinds of democracy and cultural initiatives."

"But how do you buy anything from Tibet legitimately?" I ask, confused by her reaction. "The people have no control over their policies, much less their priceless artifacts."

"I get that."

"The statue will never, ever make its way back," I say, suddenly unsure if I mean back to Tibet or to our camp.

"Dolma, I get it. I'm with you," she says, leaning in. "But really, how do you think the British Museum got its treasures? They stole them. They literally sawed off pieces of the Parthenon to transport them back to England. At least this statue is intact." She waves the waitress over.

"If I can prove that the statue belongs to someone else, or a group of people, do you think they would return it?" I ask.

"Let's get another drink, hmm? On me this time. Oh, hold on," she says, scrolling through her phone. "Elise says she's at an after-party."

"Let's go," I say.

THE CONDOMINIUM IS right by Lake Ontario. It belongs to the white-haired man who accompanied the Burmese artist at the Cabrini house, though now he's nowhere to be seen. In the kitchen and hallway, a handful of people remain scattered in small groups, bleary-eyed and speaking quietly with their heads tilted to the side. The counters and tables, meanwhile, are covered with half-emptied glasses and decimated trays of food. It looks like the end of a pretty good party.

A svelte, neatly dressed man gives Dia a kiss on the cheek.

"This is Friedrich," Dia says. "He works in logistics for aid distribution. Friedrich, this is Dolma, my new friend."

"Nice to meet you," I say.

"A pleasure," Friedrich replies with a soft German accent. Next to his button-down shirt and polished shoes, Dia looks starkly bohemian with her long curly hair, colorful scarf, and globally sourced jewelry.

After a short, polite exchange, Dia and Friedrich excuse themselves and head toward the kitchen. I wander into the living room and sit on an empty sofa, facing a wall of glass that overlooks the lake. Before me, a gray-black sky melds almost indiscernibly with the dark water. Somewhere in the distance, past a cluster of flickering lights, is Niagara Falls and America, or *Ari*, as Shumo Tenkyi calls it wistfully. Ari, Ari, Ari. We used to speak of this country in the camp as if it were just over the hills. As if it were the answer to every question. Then, when Shumo Tenkyi applied to move here with the help of her friend, a country called Canada entered our dreams. The distances we've traveled. The distances we dream of. For those of us who cannot return home, all the world is a dream.

Scanning the room, I see no sign of Elise, Professor Wallace, or his friends among the few scattered guests. On a far wall, a projector plays a series of spliced videos: Japanese schoolchildren dancing; angels sitting on heavenly clouds; a vulva opening and closing; Krishna revealing the world spinning in his throat; a nun ringing a church bell with the weight of her whole body; an aerial shot of antelope fleeing a predator; children mesmerized by a Ouija board; orthodox Jews praying before the Western Wall; machines whirling in an enormous factory; Charlie Chaplin making potatoes dance on two forks.

Behind me, a group gossips about one organization that has surreptitiously gotten hold of another organization's donor list.

"What a coup," a man says. A roar of laughter.

I stand and head for the balcony, which wraps around the building. The eastern edge of the city stretches out below me, the highway whirring forty stories down as thousands of lights pass through its black arteries.

Looking up again, I see Horowitz smoking nearby. He smiles, appearing somewhat weary, and I ask if he's seen Professor Wallace. Horowitz shakes his head and turns back toward the lake. "He never stays long at these things." Reaching for another cigarette, he gestures with the pack and I motion to decline, disappointed to have missed the chance to speak with Professor Wallace. Tomorrow, I could try to visit him and somehow broach the topic of the statue.

"Do you know *Black Narcissus*?" Horowitz asks.

"The old movie?" Henri had a videotape copy that he played for me one afternoon, calling it a masterwork of Western filmmaking.

"A clip was playing inside," he nods. "The shot of the nun ringing the bell just to break the silence of the mountains. That kind of height can do strange things to a person," he says, looking down at the highway. "Being so far from the earth."

"I have a vivid memory of the opening scenes," I say. "That imagined village in the Himalayas."

"Yes," Horowitz laughs softly. "Not much better than *Lost Horizon*."

I smile. "Actually, I was impressed by *Black Narcissus* at first. The houses and costumes had looked so familiar. I wasn't used to seeing any of it in Western movies. But no, you're right. All the actors were in brown- and yellowface, playing silent and ignorant natives. And when they did speak, they emitted this awful tongue of invented grunts."

Sitting in Henri's chair, I had felt washed in shame, imagining that this was our image in the West. It all seemed like a horrible misunderstanding—as though someone far away had tossed together a dozen fabricated characteristics from India, Nepal, China, and Tibet, picked randomly across centuries of history, shook them around in a box, and let the pieces fall out. Yet the senselessness of the images flashing before me didn't even seem to matter for the film, because the locals were only a backdrop. The story's focus was a group of Anglican nuns who had taken up residence in an abandoned palace and former harem. Over the course of the film, the nuns are exposed to native influences and become possessed by erotic desire.

"But you prefer it to *Lost Horizon*," Horowitz asserts.

"Well, it's interesting that the Anglican nuns don't view their new home as a utopian escape. They're alienated in the foreign land, and that feels truer, even if it's a racist portrayal. But ultimately, they fail in their colonial project and flee. So what changed between those two movies?"

"Two world wars and the decline of the British Empire," he replies. "Where did you go to school in Nepal?"

"The British School. Do you know it?"

"I know it very well. What do your parents do? Carpet business?"

I take a sip of my drink. Horowitz is trying to figure out if I belong to one of the prominent entrepreneurial Tibetan families in Kathmandu. "My mother makes trinkets and sells them to tourists. My father cooks and delivers meals to offices."

"How did they manage the school fees?"

"They didn't. I snuck in and out every day."

I can tell that Horowitz is confused. But why should my life be legible to him? I didn't ask where his parents live, how they raised him, or how they paid for his books and school fees. "Actually, I have something to ask you. Do you know much about the market for Tibetan artifacts?"

"You'll have to be more specific," he smiles.

"Is there a process for recovering artifacts that have been taken illegally?"

"What does it mean for an artifact to be taken illegally?"

"Well, if it's not sold freely by the owner."

"Does anyone sell their artifacts freely?"

"You know what I mean."

"Do you know how many pieces of Indigenous art were sold to museums in the 1960s and 70s in this country? Masks, regalia, serving bowls. All sold freely. Because their way of life wasn't going to continue, or because their owners simply wanted the money. Something tells me you wouldn't be happy with that either."

He thinks I'm completely naive, that I don't know how the world works. I rephrase my question. "What if something was stolen? Just basic theft?"

"Sure, governments have tried to retrieve stolen artifacts: the Indians, Greeks, Egyptians, even West Africans have pursued things that were taken centuries ago. But you know, this happens everywhere. Even the most important pieces of French royal furniture are in British museums. I say, thank goodness, otherwise they might have ended up in a revolutionary bonfire."

"You could retroactively justify so many crimes with that reasoning. What about appeals by smaller groups of people?"

He's silent for some time. "I recently came upon the ongoing case of a Buddha statue said to be a thousand years old. Villagers in eastern China had been protecting the statue for decades, ferrying it from house to house, even burying it during the Cultural Revolution. Apparently, their religious teacher was mummified inside the statue. Then poof, it disappeared in 1995. Just wait, one day it will turn up in some museum."

"What if there's no government to make a claim? What if it's a group of refugees, for instance?"

"Something tells me," he says with a chuckle, "that refugees have more important things to worry about."

I pull back. This man doesn't understand anything outside his own terms. Power, survival, domination—these are the bricks of his mind.

I wonder what he would think if he stumbled on one of our camp's water prayer ceremonies, when we line up in pairs along the riverbank to bless palmfuls of water for the benefit of all sentient beings. Would he find us to be well-meaning but foolish? It doesn't matter. He has given me a kernel of hope. There is a precedent for how we can recover the Saint's statue.

I take a last sip of my drink. The clouds in the distance are lit faintly by planes, their flashing lights giving the appearance of a lightning storm. Perhaps it is a good thing, the *right* thing, that Horowitz doesn't understand the people of my camp, for this is a man who treats knowledge as acquisition, understanding as control.

"Not a single star in the sky. What a waste," he says, continuing to scan the horizon as though he might still find one.

"What led you to study Tibet?" I ask.

"I went to India, to Varanasi, on a fellowship in the late seventies. A series of accidents led me to Lhasa, which was opening up at the time. Traveling around the country, I realized that in the West we fundamentally misunderstood Tibet."

"How do you mean?"

"Insofar as notions of pre-occupation Tibet. We think of Tibet in romantic terms rather the realities of a feudal theocracy, or the noble but difficult lives of nomads."

"Is it better today? Millions of nomads have been forced from their traditional pastures and resettled in camps, where their lives are sedentary, depressed, and impoverished. A lot like what happened to Indigenous peoples here."

"Well, there's no denying that Chinese rule is problematic in certain senses, but we have to be realistic about the past as well. Do these stories of a peaceful, humane, independent Tibet help the cause? There's no denying that many monasteries extracted heavy taxes."

"This justifies a violent occupation?"

"Dolma, I have lived in Tibet for several years at a time studying the nomadic life. It is a *difficult* life."

"My parents and grandparents were nomads. They fled with nothing. They—"

"I don't want to diminish the suffering of your parents. But I'm a historian. I'm interested in the whole of Tibet."

"The whole of Tibet wasn't a feudal theocracy," I reply, my ears burning. "That's well-established and it wasn't the same as feudalism in Europe. There was relative freedom, even for those bonded to the land. But that's all beside the point because if other countries could modernize on their own, isn't that also our right? You spoke earlier about Tibetans aping back what the Chinese and Westerners expect of us, but I think you underestimate the agency of six million people. Just because it looks like someone is performing an identity scripted by Westerners or the Chinese, or you see a restaurant named Shangri-La in Toronto, doesn't mean it's a performance for your benefit, or that it even means the same thing to us. People can recite the language of oppressors for a different purpose—"

"There's no need to get upset," says Horowitz, his voice deepening. "I can express a view that you disagree with and vice versa."

"But you are an expert speaking about a colonized country. Can't you see how much power you have to shape the discourse? Much more than any Tibetan. To the academy, to the wider public outside my community, you are seen as the objective, enlightened arbiter of truth."

Horowitz leans in, speaking quietly. "Dolma, what power do you think I have? I haven't been granted a visa to Tibet since 2007, not one academic you met tonight has. We're not some unified group of monsters out to oppress you. We're also not freedom fighters. We're scholars. If you have a different perspective, I welcome that. You'll have to make your case like everyone else, regardless of your background."

He makes it sound so simple, as if anyone could have the same platform just by choosing to speak.

"Professor Horowitz, I want to be a scholar. All my life, I've wanted to study my people. Our history, ideas, and literature. But I've never known how to make it happen. How can I study Tibet without access to it? So I'm left with one narrow corridor: I must find a way to do it in the West, within your world."

"And I hope you do."

"I know some scholars bow deeper than others before the Chinese state, but ultimately, you and your colleagues can choose to be silent on many things. You can draw a veil over the politics, call the occupation by another name, or ignore it completely, studying only the pieces of us that risk nothing for you. But the occupation doesn't begin and end on the edges of my country. It lives in the words you select when you write about us. The very fact that you can even make such decisions belies your distance from Tibetans. Because your fate isn't tied to ours. Our history doesn't live in your family. This doesn't hurt you in the same way—"

I stop to regain my composure. What is happening to me? I am humiliated by my weakness. Horowitz places his hand on my shoulder. Blinking back the tears, I shrug him off and step to the side.

"Dolma, I can't know what you feel inside. But you can't know what's in my heart, either. I have spent my whole life on this work."

I say nothing, and he leans over the railing, his saggy, pilling corduroy jacket hanging down. It is the first time I have noticed his clothes, how everything fits too large—as though he had shrunk from his former self. Under his wispy, wayward mop, Horowitz frowns in silence, seemingly unaware of my gaze, his eyes intent on the empty glass in his hand.

I turn to face the dark expanse. It's already morning at the camp. The sun rose hours ago. By now, people will have finished their morning rituals of tending to their altars and washing up at the cistern taps. I can see them moving around the small hilltop. The women are arranging their wares in a long row along the camp's main road, waiting for tourists who visit throughout the day to see what a Tibetan refugee settlement looks like. The young boys are working at a small juice factory established by an American couple to provide employment. The young girls are cooking lunch, which they will sell from their kitchens—spicy potatoes, cold rice noodles, dry flattened rice. At the primary school, children are reciting the Tibetan alphabet at the top of their lungs, sitting on long wooden benches made smooth and shiny over the years. Popo Migmar is at the old folks center, rolling a rosary and talking to his friends about necessary repairs around the camp, though he can no longer make them. And my mother is at Phewa Lake, walking up and down the main road, wearing a baseball cap to cover her face from the sun, her hair plaited as always in two braids. I can almost see the stoop where Ama likes to rest, the concrete wall by the water where she stops to eat her lunch.

None of them knows about the Saint's fate. No one but me.

4

THE day the starving leopard came to our camp, I had stayed home
from school with a fever while Ama set off for our shop long before
sunrise. I was deep asleep when our neighbor Mo Yutok woke me with
a grave face and led me outside as quickly as she could. We rushed down
the footpaths to her home, and she lifted me onto her rooftop, where there
were several other children whose parents had gone to work. Standing
on her tin roof, I saw a bewildering sight. Everyone from our camp was
on their rooftops, scanning the ground in fear. Mo Yutok said that Bhu
Tsering was the first one to spot the animal, drinking at dawn from a puddle
beneath the cistern tap. But it was Gen Lobsang who alerted everyone
after coming within a few meters of the leopard right outside the school.
Now it seemed the creature was hiding among the houses.

When the leopard finally appeared up the road, I studied her intently
as she roamed the dirt path. Each footstep soft and soundless. A tail that
hinted at her thoughts, extending to caress a hanging plant, then curling
back again and sitting suspended like an inhalation. And her belly—
luscious and empty. She was looking for something, searching left and
right with pale marble eyes. Her skin was spotted gold, her mouth slightly
open and crested with silver whiskers. Have I ever seen anything so beautiful since that day? Why don't they build altars for leopards?

Then she rounded the corner and approached our house. Slowing her
steps, she paced back and forth. I stood on the tips of my toes and stretched
every muscle in my body to see her. She lingered at our kitchen window,
barely moving. It looked as though she were smelling our walls and

listening for voices. She came to us, I whispered. She came to see us. Wasn't my grandmother born in the year of the tiger? Somehow this detail, shared once by Po Migmar, still clings to the walls of my mind.

The leopard heard some noise down the path and carried on, disappearing from view, just as a fair-skinned man climbed onto Mo's roof. He was dressed in a silk shirt and pressed pants. His hands were smooth and plump, not rough and wrinkled like the hands in our camp. His shoes were polished black as his hair. I knew right away that this was the richest man I had ever seen outside of Indian movies.

"Who's that, Momo?" I asked.

"His name is Samphel la. He's your Amala's friend."

To my eight-year-old self, it was unfathomable that my mother would know someone so wealthy.

"They were sweethearts," Mo Yutok said with a smile. "But that's ancient history."

A certain glow formed around him. Against the sunlight, his hair floated gently in the air. His silk shirt rose and sank with the wind. I moved closer to get a better look. Sitting on a bucket of soil, I fell into a pleasant daydream, imagining that my mother was just like the heroine of an Indian movie. A girl from a poor family who caught the eye of a rich boy.

Eventually, the man must have noticed me examining him with a goofy look on my face, for he gave a startled look. Unable to hold back my laughter, I smiled and told him that I was his sweetheart's daughter. But he did not reply with joyful surprise. Instead, he turned and walked off to another corner of the roof, seemingly troubled by something. I could see the truth. He didn't want to talk with me because I was poor.

A rumble echoed against the valley. It was a police jeep heaving slowly up the road. Hearing the cheers and applause from the other rooftops, I set my disappointment aside and joined in. There were even a few villagers hollering with joy from the hill above the camp. The jeep lurched to a stop, and four policemen wearing motorcycle helmets hopped out. Someone on Po Rithar's roof pointed and made fun of one policeman for wearing flip-flops. As it turned out, he was the chief of the station. Reaching into the jeep, the chief pulled out a broken side mirror with a long handle, which looked as though he'd torn it off an old truck.

"Be calm, all of you," the police chief shouted. "I'm in charge now. Point me toward the beast."

"By the field!" someone shouted from the ridge.

"There! There!"

She was running across the middle of the camp. From a distance, she looked so diminished, like an unfed street dog. Everyone began to shout. "Go go! There there!" But the police stayed outside the field, on the other side of the gate. The chief policeman slipped the mirror through a small opening, rotating and maneuvering the clumsy device. After a minute, he nodded. They flung the rusty gate open and began firing into the field, breaking a few windows in the camp's handicraft factory. Then everything went quiet.

I stood behind Mo Yutok, whimpering that the leopard had come to see us. But Mo Yutok must not have heard my words because she kept telling me not to cry. Then she offered the hem of her wool dress for me to blow my nose. We all waited outside a long time to see the leopard again. The sun burned my face and left my cheeks raw for days afterward. Eventually, we all climbed down from the roofs and gathered along the narrow space of the camp's only road. Though we were moving in confusion, the crowd was as thick and tightly banded as a rug.

Then she appeared, carried like a queen by the policemen, her limp body cradled between two men's arms.

"Go on, touch it," the police chief beamed. "The beast can't hurt you now."

Dozens of hands reached out. Some managed to touch her pelt, others pulled back at the last moment. As the leopard floated by, I unfolded my arms and stretched as far as I could, desperate to brush against even a single hair. I was convinced that if I touched her, the leopard would know it was me, and she would not be afraid. And even in her slumber, she would know that we had met. But I could see nothing, feel nothing against my grasping fingertips. Sinking deeper into the crowd, I worried that I had missed my chance. Then Mo Yutok lifted me, and I reached out again, finally meeting the leopard with my hand. She was rough and warm. I realized that her heart was still beating, and tears rolled down my cheeks, landing in the dirt.

Two years later, during my usual lunch hour spent in the library of the British School, I saw her again. Leaning over the desk, with my face hovering just a few inches above the encyclopedia, I carefully studied the pictures. *Old friend.* She had not been an ordinary leopard, whose spots would have been small, even circles. Hers were large and varied, like darkened clouds or borders outlined on a map. She had a long tail, the same length as her torso, which arched up as her head aimed low. She was a clouded leopard, a species believed to be extinct in Nepal for over a century. And yet she had lived in secret amid the hills of our camp.

On that day, we did not know how rare she was. Even after she was taken away, everyone stayed inside. Mo Yutok made butter tea and bread for the rich man and me, peering out her windows every so often and praying that the beast would not return. We even missed the sundown prayers. But just before dark, the three of us went to the rich man's dark-blue jeep. While the outside was as muddy as any vehicle that drove to our camp, inside it was spotless, smelling almost sweet. Mo Yutok climbed into the passenger seat and marveled at the seat covers made of wooden balls strung on wire. She kept running her hands up and down the seat, her jade bangles clicking as she proclaimed that her back had never felt so good. As we drove away, the rich man rolled down all the windows at once. In the back of the car, I sat up on my knees and craned my head and arms out the window. Spreading my arms like a bird, letting my hair blow in the breeze, I watched the hills and the river become a blur.

I thought he might take us to a roadside tea shop for a meal, but the man drove to the center of Pokhara. On a busy lane lined with department stores and gated hotels, he parked before a grand restaurant and led us inside. And though I never stepped foot in the restaurant again, nor could I begin to guess its name, I was mesmerized. The dining room had high ceilings, pure white columns, and a pair of clay elephants flanking the kitchen. Smartly dressed waiters stood at attention, gliding over to our table as soon as the rich man raised a finger. I don't remember the many dishes we ate, but I know this was where I had my first taste of watermelon juice. I could not believe that someone had taken a real watermelon, squeezed out every drop, and put it in a tall glass. Such a thing seemed unimaginable.

After dinner, I walked out onto the street, feeling proud to be seen leaving that restaurant. Though I was stuffed with food, I felt somehow weightless as the car sped away. Since we were not far from Phewa Lake, the rich man dropped me off at Ama's shop before taking Mo Yutok back to the camp. As I hopped out and waved goodbye, his eyes were fixed on our storefront.

"Do you want to come inside?" I asked, imagining a happy reunion.

He seemed to consider it briefly, then shook his head. "I better head back."

"Don't mention any of this to your mother," Mo Yutok warned as the car pulled away. "Just tell her that I brought you here, okay?"

"I swear on my life!" I shouted over the engine noise, but I forgot my promise the instant I walked into the store.

My mother was in the back, where we kept a mattress and stove for occasional overnight stays. She was cutting the fat off a piece of beef while a broth simmered on the gas burner. I ran up and grabbed the hem of her dress, spinning myself into the fabric until I was pressed right up against her body. Breathless, I told her about the fearsome leopard who circled our house, possibly twice, before the police shot her. Then I told Ama about the rich man, his wooden seat covers, and the restaurant with watermelon juice. My mother put down her cleaver and became very still.

"Imagine if you'd married him," I sighed.

Ama shouted a sharp curse. I stood frozen inside her dress. After a moment, she returned to cutting the meat.

"Don't ever speak to him again," she said.

"Never ever," I promised, my body pressed against the one person in the world I would need forever.

But I could not forget him, and because we did not speak of him directly, he came to mean so many things. Like smoke that would never escape, the rich man surrounded us. Each time someone talked about the leopard, he was there. Each time Mo Yutok would visit, I wished I could ask about him. And each time someone remarked on my mother's childhood, I pictured her lost sweetheart. Ama had dug a trench between us, and in her silence, it widened into a rift that I still fear we cannot bridge.

5

A T sunrise, I walk to the bathtub and turn on the tap. Easing into the pool of hot water, I let myself go weightless below the neck. My lips, nose, and eyes slip underwater. I feel every muscle in my body as I lift myself back up. Dressing myself slowly in the dark, I see only a small part of what's before me. It's as though I were looking through a pinhole. In that light, I see my worn clothes on the floor. In that light, I see the Saint sitting inside a box on the other side of the city. Just two streetcar rides away, or two hours if I walk. And if I prostrate? I could kneel, lay my body on the cold floor, touch my forehead to this cracked linoleum, rise, and then take another step. Progressing one length of my body at a time, I could move across the city, my skin flush against the skin of this country. Could I know this place then? Could I be known in return?

My aunt is up. I can hear her moving on the mattress.

"Shumo Tenkyi," I say, walking into the main room. "I have something important to tell you."

She mumbles as she makes the bed. How small she is, just like my mother. Even standing upright, she barely reaches my shoulders. I watch as she folds her blanket, and I'm filled with tenderness. I want to tell her everything.

"I saw the Nameless Saint that went missing," I say. "I saw the ku from our camp."

My aunt repeats the words, pondering their meaning.

I kneel on her mattress, holding her gaze. "I know it sounds unbelievable."

"The ku disappeared years ago."

"I didn't believe it either."

"You're not serious."

I begin to laugh. "I swear it. I saw the ku at a rich family's house. They had bought it from a dealer in Nepal who must have stolen it years ago. But it was the Saint. He was just as Po Migmar described. Made of simple mudstone but with a strange, powerful expression."

Shumo Tenkyi sits on the edge of the mattress, staring at her knees. I kneel on the ground and place my hands on her little kneecaps. They don't even fill my palms.

"The Saint was protecting us," she mumbles. "I have to tell my mother."

I shake my head. "Do you mean my mother? Please, Shumo. What should we do?"

She says nothing at first, then looks at me and nods. "We should ask someone important . . . Gyaltsen la. He'll know what to do. I'll call and ask him to come for breakfast."

"Right," I say, but it seems unlikely that a former bureaucrat in the exile government would be useful in this matter, or any matter, really. But admittedly, I have paid so little attention to the people my aunt knows here that I must put my doubts aside. "Do you really think he'll come?"

"For a home-cooked meal?" She grins. "The poor man is always eating McDonald's."

Shumo phones the former minister, who says he will be here in fifteen minutes. My aunt is at her best when she acts out of a sense of duty. Whether it's going to the community meetings to help with a candlelight vigil or working to send money back to my mother and Po Migmar, when she knows her purpose, she's able to sit inside a task.

We get to work making a meal to butter up the former minister. I pull out some dough from the fridge and begin to warm and massage it, while Shumo starts boiling a pot of potatoes. On the next burner, she gets the butter tea started. I dust the counter with flour, rip off a small mound of dough, make a smooth ball in my palm, and flatten it with a rolling pin. Placing the dough on a pan, I turn and flip and press its edges with a tea towel until flatbread rises like a balloon. Next, I open a can of chickpeas.

Shumo has already whisked eggs in a bowl and is now chopping red onion and coriander.

"We haven't cooked together in a long time," she says.

"It's beginning to smell like the camp at sunrise," I reply.

"People used to stop by all the time, without warning. Just like the rain. We never used our latches. Sometimes in the morning, just before I open my eyes, I think I'm back there."

She closes her eyes. I do the same. The Nameless Saint flashes in the dark, then floats across the camp, held up by a hundred hands just like the clouded leopard.

There's a knock. Then another. My aunt wipes her hands and goes to the door. A soft male voice greets her in formal Tibetan. Shuffling around the small kitchen, I step back to make room for the man to enter and take off his glasses, which have fogged in an instant. While my aunt lets out a string of formal speech, I give him as much space as I can without stepping into the bedroom. The man is short, round, probably in his fifties. He wears a beaten gray parka and shoes that aren't warm enough for the winter. She introduces him as Gyaltsen la.

"Is this the famous niece with the French accent?" the man asks with wide eyes. He takes my hand delicately. "I've been so curious to hear one of our own sounding like a French person."

I can't tell if the man is mocking me, but his handshake is oddly soft, the kind I imagine royalty give their subjects. There's also the way he replied to the mention of my name, as if he had been waiting to meet me for a long time. Is this how he reacts to every introduction?

"A small offering," he says, extending a plastic bag full of oranges to my aunt.

"There's no need, Gyaltsen la. How embarrassing," Shumo Tenkyi says, taking the oranges. "I've only cooked a humble meal. I'm such a poor cook."

"You should learn, Tenkyi! No wonder you're unmarried. I've always loved to cook but never found the time myself. Anyhow, I could not possibly come empty-handed to visit your house for the first time."

I follow them into the other room, carrying the flatbread and omelets. The former minister sits assertively on my mattress, right in front of the

TV, while Shumo Tenkyi kneels on the floor and pours him butter tea from a thermos. I try to catch her eyes to see if I should broach the topic now, but she quickly heads back into the kitchen for the dishes of potatoes and chickpeas. As I serve the man breakfast, I find myself falling into old habits—bending down, making myself small, just the way I was taught.

"That's enough," he says, flipping through TV stations with the remote.

"Just a little more," I say, with a softened voice as I add more food, stopping only when he insists he'd had enough again. This is the custom. Then I take a seat on the floor instead of the mattress, waiting for him to eat before I fix myself a plate. As the rising sun brings brighter light into the bedroom, I can see that he has a colorless, almost soot-like skin tone.

It turns out that Gyaltsen la arrived in Toronto only two months ago. His wife and son are still in India, waiting until he gets permanent residency in order to sponsor their visas. I'm a little stunned by his cheerful tone as he tells us this. Does he know that this separation could last years? There must be hundreds of people on this street alone who have been away from their families for over a decade. But Gyaltsen la seems blissfully unconcerned with what's ahead of him. Instead, he tells us the story of his arrival.

"I didn't sleep a wink," he says, "through the *entire* twenty-eight-hour journey from Delhi to Toronto."

"Why not, Gyaltsen la?" my aunt asks.

"I didn't want to miss the great big world! How often do you get to pass over the earth at such speed and comfort? But then, just before the plane landed, somewhere over the eastern edge of Canada, I finally gave in to my exhaustion. Any man would have succumbed to sleep much earlier. Well, it was only when the plane's wheels hit the tarmac, thrusting my body back into the seat, that I awoke. Can you believe that? I missed the most important view, the aerial perspective of my new country!"

I imagine him, blinking in silence as he peered out the tiny window at a gray expanse of sky, ground, and buildings. Terrified in that moment, just as I had been, and my aunt before me.

"So, I walked off the plane, passed through the immigration office after a few hours of questioning, and went straight to the taxi station as my friend instructed. I had stowed my friend's address like a prayer in my internal jacket pocket, and truth be told, it was a little damp after my time in the immigration office, but I carefully unfolded it and showed it to my driver. I thought I was finally safe to relax. But as the taxi flew down the enormous Canadian highways, the meter ticked higher and higher, and I began to sweat, converting each new dollar amount to rupees, seeing a week's salary flash before me. I almost asked to be let out on the side of the road so I could walk the rest of the way."

We laugh because Shumo and I still mentally convert the cost of many of our purchases into rupees.

"Gyaltsen la," I say, clearing my throat. "Given your experience with the exile administration, I'm wondering if you can answer a question."

"Ask me," he says, gesturing with an open palm.

"As you know, our sacred objects have been stolen since the occupation began, whether by smugglers or by governments."

"Stolen, burned, smashed, turned to bullets and building materials. Gyami soldiers even built toilets from our prayer stones."

"Tut-tut," Shumo says, "poor fools."

The former minister folds his arms as he nods.

"But a small number of our treasures made it out, perhaps smaller than the number of souls. Just like us, they spread to all corners of the world. Now they live in universities, museums, and private collections, even here in Canada." I tell him that this kind of theft has happened to many nations, but now, some countries are trying to get their stolen treasures back, even hundreds of years after they were taken. The Greeks, for instance, are demanding the British Museum return the Parthenon's marbles, which were looted over two hundred years ago. The Egyptians have made the same demands of British and German museums. Dozens of other countries have as well. Some have even succeeded. In 2010, an American university returned objects taken a hundred years ago from Machu Picchu—

"An American university, did you say? Ari people are very good. Very good," Gyaltsen la says. "Without them, we Tibetans would be long forgotten in the world, plunged into darkness, wiped from all history books. Of course, any good fortune we have is because of His Holiness, who is the sun to our world. Who would even *look* at our lot if not for His Holiness? India too. They have been very good to us. Would any rich nation do half as much as the Indians have done for us? And now, Canada. What a nation! When I open my wallet, everything I need is here: medical card, social insurance card, phone numbers of various social welfare offices that will care for me as . . . one of their own."

"If we Tibetans were to launch a similar campaign . . ." I offer.

"Take this case to the International Court of Justice or the United Nations?" he asks.

"Yes, how would we do that? If we wanted to have an object returned, hypothetically?"

He sits forward and rips off a piece of flatbread.

"Gyaltsen la, if you could tell me the names of the right people in Dharamsala, I would do the work . . ."

He tucks a bundle of chickpeas into the flatbread, dips it in chili sauce, and starts nodding as he chews. "I know the person you need to speak to. He's the minister of foreign affairs. If you mention my name, he will meet you in a heartbeat."

"Wonderful," I exclaim, almost laughing. "I don't know how to thank you."

"Oh, but he's not in Dharamsala right now. He's traveling through the south of India for the next three months. Even so, he is about to be replaced, and we don't know by whom. The elections will take a few months and then there's the matter of settling the new cabinet, budget, and agenda. Of course, taking care of the welfare of a hundred and thirty thousand souls in exile is no small matter either, not to mention those inside Tibet who look to us for hope. But in about eighteen or twenty months from now, you could reach out to the secretaries and request a meeting. Do you have a Greenbook? I'm assuming you've been paying your yearly dues to the exile administration?"

Eighteen or twenty months from now. I'm too stunned to find my words.

"Yes, Gyaltsen la," Shumo says, softly. "We're not wealthy but we pay every year."

"Eighteen months from now? Surely I could speak to someone sooner? Perhaps someone else?"

"You're speaking to me!" he says, slapping his thigh. He smiles. "But you know, you should really practice your Tibetan first and foremost. It's very poor. That is your duty as a young person. If you don't speak your language well, who are you? What use is your fancy English education and French accent?"

The conversation moves on to the next community protest, at which Gyaltsen la is eager to speak about the history of the Tibetan people and our righteous struggle. Shumo Tenkyi has been active in these gatherings herself, making and handing out tea, helping to transport placards, even reading some of her poetry. But now Gyaltsen la wants to know why he hasn't seen me at the Chinese consulate or Queen's Park.

"I'm not much of a protestor," I say.

"What? I've never heard such a thing. Protesting isn't an identity! It's our most important duty as Tibetans who live in freedom."

"My niece splits her time between school and a job. She goes to demonstrations when she can," my aunt says with an apologetic smile.

"There was no such thing as splitting time when we were young. Everything was full-time. Full-time begging, full-time struggling. Imagine if we had sat around licking our wounds instead of getting our hands dirty. Would we have built half the schools and monasteries in exile we have today? You must get up and do something now, while you can. If I could have studied for even a year or two . . . can you imagine?" he asks, looking at Shumo Tenkyi. "They said I was the most intelligent Tibetan they ever met, the Indian ministers did."

Eventually I promise, without much conviction, to attend the next rally. Shaking his head, the former minister eats a second plate and continues flapping his mouth, but I can't hear anything else he says.

I am too full of dread. It's clear that my life has changed forever. The Nameless Saint has come to me and braided our fates together. Whether I find a way to bring him back to our camp or do nothing, I will never be able to move on from him. A swell of anger rises in my chest. Why did I have to be the one to see the ku? I should have stayed downstairs with the professors. Then my life would have continued on in its rightful course. My concerns would have remained the same as before: gaining entry to graduate school, becoming a scholar, moving out of this dark apartment. But now, all of that seems impossible. The Saint will not let me go.

I look at Gyaltsen la, still chewing and talking at us. He parrots the narrative I've heard many times about our people. It is the story of a good and just people who have fallen into a period of darkness, a people who must struggle as one body, for as long as it takes to regain our home. This story echoes in the cave of our misery. It repeats and repeats, drowning out all of our other stories, edging out anything that isn't about nationhood. A single sound, day after day. I am tired of it.

But to his other point—this imperative to act, to do something while I can—what if this foolish man is right? How long can I carry on floating through my life, telling myself that everything around me is insignificant, a momentary blip before my true life begins? There are the lies I've told others, but what about the ones I tell myself?

The numbers repeat in my head. Six simple digits. It is ludicrous that the Nameless Saint is locked away, separated from us because of those numbers. At this very moment, he stares upward, trapped in a nesting doll of wood and metal boxes, dreaming of his skies and the ones who speak his ancient story. I can hear him as I hear the ants. He calls to me.

PART II

Sisters

LHAMO

I

Pokhara, Nepal

Tsemo Seymakar Tibetan Refugee Settlement
1973

THIS is how the edges of our camp harden. We begin with the administrative building, pulling down the rotten grass-thatched walls,
digging straight lines for a rocky foundation beneath the soil, mixing
and slapping mortar with small sheets of metal in our palms. Climbing
onto the roof, I see my old ropes still holding the bamboo together. It
gives me no pleasure to cut the still-tight braids with my sickle, throw the
dead, fraying grass into the gorge, and watch them float down for the goats
and cows to pick through. From the flat hill overlooking our camp, I see
the men lay down new roofs of corrugated tin sheets, putting in place
small, metal lakes that shine in the light. The sun multiplies before me and
is never the same. Then the monsoon comes and the rain, too, has changed.
Against our tin roofs, the rain is no longer soft, wet taps from the sky, slipping onto our skin at all hours. Now the rain is made of nails—raging,
threatening, but never breaking through. People now say with pride: Our
camp makes noise in the rain. We have no country, but we have a sound.

   In the same breath, we wonder: Why did we survive and not our kin?
What separates us from the ones who were caught, who starved, who
were lost in the mountains, who did not endure the last winter, that last
season of illness or melancholy? When I look around, I know the truth:
Nothing at all separates us. We are not the strongest, smartest, or even

the ones who wanted to live the most. It can only be the Saint, the ancient ku that, through a series of karmic outcomes we cannot fathom, came to reside in our camp, amid our group of orphans and childless parents. This small figurine is precious because of all who have held him, wearing away at his gold patina and earthen body. On his form, we can see traces of the devoted touch of so many people and places beyond our reach. The traces of my mother wrapping silk scarves around the ku, my father's faint and final breaths, the unrelenting winds of the border, the shells that pounded a village into dust, my grandfather's wrinkled temple. And how many before, and how many before that? Here, for eleven years, the Saint has been carried from house to house to watch over our sick, our newly born, our betrothed: to enter into our dreams so we emerge with lost memories and premonitions. But Ashang Migmar doesn't like to call the ku the Nameless Saint. Ashang says we must find out his identity. We must take the ku to a place where learned people can tell us his name. Maybe we need to go all the way to Dharamsala, the seat of the exile administration and the home of the Precious One.

But it won't be enough to have his name. After we know it, Ashang will want to offer the ku to a monastery rather than keep the Saint here in such poor circumstances. Some have shared this worry privately, but none would dare oppose my uncle's decision. For who could deny that the ku should be in a grander place? Still, I cannot accept this. The Saint must remain here, where he chose to come. If the Saint belongs anywhere else, it is with Samphel, whose uncle was chosen as the ku's last keeper. And someday, Samphel may return.

I still think about him from time to time. That mysterious bliss that bloomed within my body when he first appeared along the river. How free I felt beside him. And how tethered I felt to him, as well. All these years later, I still struggle to conjure any memory of the capital without him. I think about the little girl too. The one who appeared to me when I fell sick. Yet all of that seems to fade by daylight. The day after Samphel and I were separated, on the bus ride back to this camp, I wove in and out of consciousness. While my Ashang prayed over me, I felt my clothes soak with sweat and my vision blur so much I thought I was going blind. We reached the camp at dusk, and Ashang carried me in, just as he had carried Po Dhondup's corpse out. He laid me down, covered me with his coat, and ran out for help. The hut was quiet, dark, and unsettled in a way I couldn't name. I sensed a presence in the corner just beyond my sightline.

"Hello?" I croaked, trying in vain to crane my neck. The figure took a step toward me, bare feet rubbing faintly on the mud floor. "Are you the girl from my vision?" I asked. "Come closer."

"Acha Lhamo," she said. It was Tenkyi. I had, for once, forgotten all about her.

Mo Yutok flew in just then with a group of women. They circled my bed, murmuring prayers, and ferried off Tenkyi to live with another family in the camp until I was well again. For six days, the women dressed me, bathed my body with cold wet cloths, and fed me a broth full of buffalo fat. Chanting prayers, they drew plumes of juniper smoke around my limbs and against my chest and back—they even blew the smoke down my throat. When I needed to relieve my bowels, they suspended me over the edge of the gorge in the rain and hummed songs from home. I bled for the first time floating in their arms above the river.

"Her time has come," they whispered and wiped me with leaves that remained behind on the ground, so darkly red, I could see nothing of the green underneath.

"What does the blood mean?" I asked. "Am I dying?"

"It means you can give birth," Mo Yutok said. "Even though you're still a child."

"I'm going to have a daughter," I told her. "I saw my future, just like my mother used to."

"Listen carefully, Lhamo," Mo Yutok said, laying me down. "If you hear the spirits call for you, don't reply. It's dangerous. We are too far from our land. The teachers who helped your mother are dead or beyond our reach. We can't know which spirits are speaking to you. All of that is behind us. Do you understand?"

Mo Yutok's hand was like a warm crinkled newspaper. I wished she would lie down and wrap herself around me. If only she were my mother, I could tuck my hand into her shirt and feel the soft warm skin beating above her heart. I could hold her loose nipple between my fingers and fall asleep the way I used to as a little girl. But Mo Yutok had her own losses and ghosts to tend to. Her daughter and husband were dead, and she was raising her only grandchild, who bore the same name as her dead daughter.

"We could all go mad if we let ourselves," Mo said. "But you've survived, so you need to keep living. That's all there is."

2

A new man has arrived, and word is traveling from house to house like a hungry crow. Yet hardly anyone has seen his face. The only souls outside at the time of his arrival were the roosters, the goats, and Tenkyi. She happened to be coming back from the river with laundry when she sighted the tall stranger walking alone on the dusty road leading up to the camp. She ran straight to the carpet factory, a basin of wet clothes dripping from her waist, to tell us all about her good fortune.

"Tell me exactly what he looks like," Dawa says, turning so forcefully I'm nearly thrown off our seat of suspended lumber two meters above the ground.

"He's so beautiful," Tenkyi says.

I adjust myself and weave the last of this line on my side before hammering down the wool. "How's it look from down there?" I ask my sister.

But Tenkyi is still thinking about the stranger. "Oh shit, I forgot to ask his name," she laughs, her face flushed red.

I want to reach down and tell her to calm herself, but I'm also curious.

"I wonder who he'll marry," Dawa sighs. She takes the hammer from me and roughly pushes down the layer we've just finished. I cut out the long metal needle in the carpet, trim the extra wool, and begin the next line. The loom stretches up before our noses, a wall of hundreds of taut strings running from the ceiling to the ground. With my left hand clawed into the strings, I place the needle to start a new line and weave the wool thread repeatedly around the strings, tying it down at each loop. This carpet will have the eight lucky symbols, my most complicated design yet. Among the two dozen women weaving here, many of them work on smaller rugs on their own, but Dawa and I usually ask to work together on the larger projects. That way, we can talk and pass the time together.

It's been a good season for carpet orders. The hundred rupees I earn from this rug will pay for Ashang's eye examination and new glasses. When this work dries up, I'll go back to pickling and brewing barley wine. I've recently learned how to make spicy mango pickles, just like the locals, so there are at least a dozen orders every month.

But Tashi Tamding, I soon learn, is not the kind to work with his hands. He is a different kind of beast, one whose beauty and confidence and fearlessness lead to various kinds of ecstasy and turmoil for everyone in the camp. *If only he wasn't so good looking!* The words are uttered so often, it prompts children to echo the phrase in high-pitched squeals. Going with the fashion of the day, Tashi wears brown pants that narrow at the knees and flare out over his boots. His shoulder-length hair is loose and curly. Eyebrows thick, a big nose, full lips. And his voice. He speaks in a low, lazy voice, as if what comes out of his mouth were the humming of his body. The impression he gives (and not just to Tenkyi) is that he has nothing to worry about. He's part of something bigger, like a mountain or the goddamn sky. Listening to him, I feel, despite myself, that the humming of his body is really the humming of my own body. What is it about him? The power of Tashi Tamding's mischievous smile and boisterous laugh— head thrown back, eyes squinting, feet thumping the ground—is felt almost instantly by the men, women, and children in the small camp where he has come to live.

Only a week later, during the quiet hour before I prepare dinner, I catch sight of my sister ambling down the hillside with a big smile. As I beat our musty blankets and rugs against a boulder, I notice Tashi reclining on the grass, facing the mountains with his elbows propped like an Indian film hero. And Tenkyi could be a heroine, with her gauzy pink blouse and dress with yellow flowers. Her long hair is swept over one shoulder, and the wind presses the fabric against her slim body. I'm struck by my sister's beauty—her silhouette in the sun, her deep black hair. Ama used to lift my hands to her cheeks and marvel at their softness. But while my hands have become rough, Tenkyi's still feel like rose petals. She has the unmarred palms and fingers of a student.

When Tashi sees my sister, he remains lying on the grass, but as she draws close, he clasps the hem of her dress and says something I cannot hear. She kneels on the ground beside him and accepts a white flower that he twirls between his fingers. They gaze out over the valley, watching the clouds pass below them.

I take a few more swings with a heavy rug, slapping it against the boulder and setting off a billowing cloud of dust. Coughing as I wave at the air, I check on my sister and Tashi. Still there, seated with their backs facing me. What words they exchange, what my sister feels for him, I do not know. Have they kissed? Have they held each other? Will Tenkyi surpass me even in this? I know there are others in the camp who wonder about this as well. I turn twenty-three this year, which means everyone is anxious to see me paired with a boy. When will I find a sweetheart? they ask. If not someone from our camp, they say, there are other camps in this country—two in Pokhara now, and of course the one in the capital city.

Yet I do not feel alone. In my dreams, I often notice the little girl beside me, just to my left. Edging up to her, I can see that she is reading something. As her dark eyes scan a script that is incomprehensible to me, she looks so peaceful. Her mind is alive and free of the past. Her mind is clear like spring water. She has never laid eyes on her grandparents, our village, our mountains or lakes. She does not know all that we have lost and what it means to leave your dead parents on a trail you will never cross again. I have decided that this is a good thing. And although I cannot speak with her, I know the little girl wants to live more than I have ever wanted to. She wants to live, and she is willing me to act, to bring her into this world. She wants me to find a way back to my beloved.

But then, I hear a new voice in the dark. It is my mother. She is singing an old melody. Her lyrics are unfamiliar, belonging to a tongue I cannot understand. Could it be the language of the gods, or could it be the language of my unborn child? Still, I hear my mother and I want to go to her. But I know that I must not. Instead, I must follow Mo Yutok's advice from all those years ago, to ignore the spirits' calls. Her words have kept me within this world. With tears rolling down my face, I turn my back to Ama's voice and compel my legs to run away from my mother and toward the little girl. But then the girl moves ever farther into the darkness, and I do what I must: I keep walking in search of the child. Walking until I can no longer hear my mother's voice.

Dreams are one thing, but I lose courage in daylight. It's already been ten years, and I don't know how Samphel feels about me, or if he remembers me at all. Besides, what can I even say to him? That I have not forgotten him, that I think about him every day? Do I tell him that I stand in the place where we first spoke to each other, and remember every word we said?

A year ago, I asked Tenkyi to write a letter for me. Because I was too embarrassed to write Samphel directly, I had the letter addressed to Shumo Yangsel in the hope that she would ask him to read it to her. The letter said that I was feeling much better and had not experienced any more of the violent trembling of my final night in her home, all those years ago. The letter asked if I could come for a visit during the new year celebrations, in case Shumo needed some help around the house. Near the end, it asked how Samphel was doing and whether his father had ever returned from India. For sixty-five days, the letter sat written and ready, tucked inside a folded dress in my drawer until I heard that Pasang Gyari was leaving for the capital to visit his sister. I walked to his house and presented him with two parcels of dried meat and butter, one for Pasang's sister, the other for my aunt. This offering touched him, and he agreed to deliver my letter as soon as he reached the camp, but with the warning that he wouldn't return to our camp for many months. Shumo would have to find someone else to send a reply. I wasn't worried about this. Samphel would find a way, I told myself. He might even come back himself. I stayed until Pasang tucked my letter into his bag and set off along the dirt path.

But the new year came and went without a word. Then I learned that Pasang had decided to carry on to northern India to find his niece, who had turned up alone at an orphanage after fleeing the Gyami army. It wasn't clear to me if he had even stopped at Shumo's camp. So, there it was. A pebble cast into the mist without a sound. And I continue to linger in this place.

As I fold up the blankets and rugs, Tashi and my sister begin walking side by side, taking shy glances at each other. A few fireflies sparkle around the two of them, while nearby a couple of wandering goats graze a patch of flowers. The sun has begun to set behind the hills, casting a pinkish light over everything. I notice how at ease Tenkyi and Tashi seem being in silence with each other, their silhouettes merging into one, but what I feel isn't envy. Rather, I wonder if this is how Samphel and I would walk together. In some secret and cherished part of my mind, I imagine it's the two of us who are ambling down the hill together. We don't need to say anything because we are still so young and we have all the time in the world.

3

I T must be the season of men on the move. Gen Lobsang, who had been away for official camp business in India, has just returned. But instead of going home to rest, he has come directly and with great urgency to our courtyard.

"Lhamo, where is your sister?" he asks.

"What's the matter, Genla?" I ask, rising from my stool.

Gen Lobsang drops his bags on the ground, catching his breath. This startles a couple of roosters by my feet, sending them into brief flights. Mo Yutok, too, is awakened beside me. She had been asleep against her house with a rosary dangling from her fingertips. I notice that Genla's face is streaked with sweat and his shirt is soaked as well. Setting down the rough wool I had been combing between two paddles, I offer him my stool. "You must be tired," I say. "I'll bring you some tea."

"Yes, but where's your sister?" he asks once more.

"There's a mouse in our rafters again," Tenkyi says, emerging from the doorway with a ladle of lentil soup. "Taste this," she says to me.

Gen Lobsang pulls out an envelope from his shirt pocket. As he holds it out to Tenkyi, he wears a look of deep contentment I have never before seen on his face. Even his white hair seems to glow in the sun. Tenkyi passes me the ladle, wipes her hands, and begins reading the letter.

"What's this about?" Mo Yutok asks, rising to peek at the letter though she cannot read.

"Tenkyi has a seat to study in Delhi," Gen Lobsang announces. "Where's Migmar?"

"Did you say she already has a seat?" I ask. "When did she apply?"

"Yes, your sister has been offered a seat at the big school," he nods proudly. "Where only the best and brightest go after they finish their SLC exams."

"What a wonder!" Mo Yutok says. "They wouldn't let the rest of us in, would they?"

Genla laughs. "She's the first from our camp, but she won't be the last."

Tenkyi looks up from the letter. "I didn't think it was possible," she says, almost without emotion.

Gen Lobsang sighs and takes the stool. "Lhamo, I'll have that cup of tea now."

Mo Yutok sits down as well. "So our girls are leaving us," she says.

"Just the younger one. Lhamo will stay here."

"Where would I go?" I mumble.

"That's good," Mo Yutok says. "Your uncle needs you."

I turn to my sister. "What about teaching at the school in our camp? Wasn't that the plan?"

But Tenkyi must not have heard me, because she's now caught up in a conversation with Gen Lobsang about the issue of her fees.

"It won't be easy," he says. "Nothing is. But I'll write to the exile government for guidance."

"But why so far away?" I ask. "Isn't there a college in Kathmandu she can attend?"

"Not for us. Not without citizenship," Tenkyi says. "Weren't you going to get tea for Genla?"

I head inside to pour some tea. It's clear why my sister didn't tell me any of this. She's long been imagining a life beyond our camp, a future whose shape is outside my comprehension. Whereas I had to leave school and begin working after three years of classes, Tenkyi has always been special—chosen by our mother, gifted with the same mind, one that instantly captures everything that matters. Meanwhile, the rest of us carry on half asleep, retaining hardly anything. The other day, she recited fourteen different bird calls she had been learning. Even in daylight, she can tell me where dozens of constellations sit hidden in the skies. And when tourists come to our camp to see how refugees live, Tenkyi is the one we send to sell our crafts. Her English surpassed Gen Lobsang's years ago, and with no one to teach her, she has resorted to memorizing English-language programs on the radio and reciting them for practice.

I doubt Tenkyi knows how much I love it when she reads to me. This private ritual of ours in the evenings. Before I prepare dinner, I make sure the kerosene lamp is full for my sister. Tenkyi then sits before the lamp and, while I cook, reads through an English book line by line, translating it for me. Slowly, she tells me stories of orphans who suffer abuse and of entire peoples killed by invaders. It's never long before tears flow down our cheeks and we shake our heads in wonder and dismay at the world.

But of course, this isn't enough for my sister's remarkable mind. She wants to read effortlessly in that foreign tongue without interruption, without needing to slow down for me. Like a bird forced to walk in the dirt, she is desperate to take flight. Meanwhile, my body is trained for the earth. At the end of each day, I lay my head against a pillow and feel my feet vibrate in pain. My fingers also sting, recalling the motions of weaving and scrubbing, and my eyes burn, wanting to look at nothing. There is no time to study, to hear stories of other countries, to learn ideas about trees, animals, and the histories of other people. Only in my sleep can I rest or let my mind soar beyond this hill.

Two years ago, when the camp's new school was completed, before the opening ceremony prayers, I swept and wiped down the classrooms. I took my broom between the rows of benches and tables, along the walls, into the corners of the roof. With a cloth, I polished the tables, benches, and windows. Unable to contain my pleasure and longing, I sat down on the low bench, imagined a book open before me, and fantasized about reading without effort, the world open and clear to me. If I had been able to study as my sister had, both of us might be preparing for the big school right now.

Maybe I had just cleared some space by moving to the side, as a small tree might for a newer tree—one with greater promise. Maybe I had helped my sister become something. Still, I am stubborn like my sister. I am determined to take my life, my happiness, into my own hands. Like Tenkyi, I must at least try.

AT DUSK, WHEN the camp is quiet with dinner preparations, I slip away and walk to Gen Lobsang's house with a warm bundle of flatbread.

"Genla," I whisper outside his door. "It's Lhamo. I've made some balep for you."

Genla comes to the door and pushes the curtain aside. "Oh, it's Amdo-style. My favorite," he says, staring at the thick loaf. "I just made some tea. Come on in."

Slipping off my sandals, I duck past the curtain and take a seat on a stool. Genla pours a cup for me and then tops off his own cup. As he tears a piece of the loaf, I decide to ask my question before I lose the nerve.

"Genla, could I go to school too? With my sister, I mean."

He is silent for some time as he looks at me in confusion.

"I'm not clever like Tenkyi, I know—"

"I always thought you were so intelligent," he says, softly.

"If I could study with you for a few months—"

"It's too late for that, Lhamo. Far too late."

"Of course," I nod. "You're right. I am ignorant." As tears pool in my eyes, I rise to leave. "Please forget my stupid questions."

"Wait, Lhamo. Just wait for a minute." His eyes are searching for something. "You're a young woman. Of course, you should be curious about the world. My mother is elderly and she lives more or less alone in the Kathmandu camp. I've tried to bring her here, but she refuses. Would you go and check up on her? I could give you some pocket money, and you'll be able to explore the capital city and meet other young people."

"Genla, you mean the Jawalakhel camp?" I ask. "Would I return before Tenkyi leaves?"

He returns my smile, taken aback. "Yes, of course. It would only be for a month or so. Are you willing?"

This is my chance to visit Samphel's camp on my own terms. I fold my hands and nod. Gen Lobsang tells me that I'm the most responsible young woman in the camp and would undoubtedly take good care of his aging mother. Mama is in the midst of preparing for a move, he explains, so if I could go there immediately and help arrange the shift from one apartment to another, that would be especially helpful. But I shouldn't speak with Gen Lobsang's brother. He is a "fallen man" and can't be trusted with a young woman like me. This makes me laugh. I'm not worried about Gen Lobsang's brother or his advances. Samphel will be there.

"I'll even arrange for a flight," Genla says.

"A bus ticket would be helpful," I reply, having no desire to be flung into the air.

Genla explains that plane tickets are cheap. Flights within the country are still a new concept to the locals, so the airline companies can't charge too much. Besides, with a plane, a trip that takes a whole day by road will take less than an hour. I am about to insist on a bus, but then a thought comes to me: Imagine telling Samphel about my journey to Kathmandu. Imagine telling him: I floated through the sky to see you. I became a bird to be with you.

"I will take the plane ticket," I say.

I PULL THE window cover all the way down and press my head against the cool wall of the plane. Still, my limbs tell me we have reached an unholy height. A minute ago, how minuscule the village houses looked upon the hills. Would our camp seem so small? Was this how the Gyami soldiers saw us from above? The plane dips suddenly, and prayers rise from the fourteen seats in this metal tube. I pray to the Nameless Saint first, before Guru Rinpoche or anyone else. His face is clearest before me. His gaze is most near.

"Bring me back to Samphel in one piece," I whisper, as earnestly as I have prayed for anything. "And make me pretty in his eyes."

When the plane finally lands, slamming onto the runway, there's a round of tearful applause.

Outside the airport, taxi drivers encircle me, promising the best rates. I walk past them and down the hill to the main road outside the airport, where Gen Lobsang told me I can hail a bicycle rickshaw. The rickshaw driver swerves through the streets, nearly flinging me out at several turns. There's frightening, chaotic energy in every direction of the city, on the verge of overflowing. The roads are teeming with new cars, while new houses have sprung from every bit of free earth. And who knows, another hundred houses could be trembling just below the surface, about to break into the sunlight. Everything is in motion here—the gills of the dead fish being fanned, the row of women smoking and grilling corn, the children playing with stones and rubber bands, the bells and prayers and harmonium music rising from a thousand temples. And every so often, there are lanky, fair-skinned foreigners wandering the roads dressed like Hindu ascetics with cameras looped around their necks. Yet I am the outsider. It's as if everything in the city is huddled tightly, locked in a conversation I cannot yet understand. Not until Samphel is by my side again.

At sundown, I finally reach the dirt road to the Jawalakhel camp, but something twists in my stomach. He's just a few steps away, and now I wonder: What if he's indifferent to me? After all, Samphel has always had a certain coldness within him. It greeted me the first time we met, and some part of me thinks that had I not felt that vague and inexplicable pull toward him on that day, we might have remained more or less strangers, even as we lived side by side. I wipe some strands from my face and realize that my skin is coated with dust. It's even in my teeth. Up the hill, abutting a field of rice paddies, I see a line of Nepali people at a water pump and ask the rickshaw driver to let me off. Splashing myself and scrubbing quickly, I clean my face and arms. Then I dunk my head under the thin, frigid stream, comb my hair back, and braid it neatly. As I walk down the road to the camp, my entire body shaking, I'm at once so happy and afraid.

This camp has grown just like the city around it. There are more homes built of stone and brick now, though some people still live in tin shacks that lean on each other to stay up. There's also a new row of shops selling grain, vegetables, and stationery. People sit in front of shops, turning their prayer wheels, smoking cigarettes or sipping on tea, watching me with curiosity. I stare back, wondering if Samphel is among them. A row of small children appears, walking hand in hand before me, probably on their way home from school. As I follow them deeper into the camp, I realize that these children are so young they must have been born in this country. One by one, they separate from the group and enter their homes, or stop at the garbage mound to pee.

Shumo Yangsel's alley is overgrown with moss, and I can barely read the numbers above the doors. At house fifteen, a water pipe drips rhythmically and the cement wall is coated with brown and green slime. By the door, there's a thin, gray dog lying under the awning with five newborn puppies suckling, their eyes barely open. How small and beaten Shumo's door appears, as if it had been battered by a hundred rainstorms.

"Who are you looking for?"

It's a woman on the second floor, several apartments over, leaning out of her window.

"Shumo Yangsel, my aunt."

"She went to Dharamsala, on pilgrimage. See the padlock?"

Somehow, I had missed the brass padlock. "When will she be back?"

"Don't you know the whereabouts of your own aunt? She went two months ago to seek an audience with His Holiness before she dies. She has such luck! Not all of us can leave like that, right?"

"What about the boy?"

The woman is distracted by something inside. She turns around and slips away. I step out into the alley and try to look up into the second-floor window to see if she will come back.

Down the lane, there's a small, smartly dressed Tibetan man walking from door to door with a long ledger's notebook. He doesn't knock on the doors or talk to anyone. He just observes each home, writes something down, and moves on. Approaching Shumo's house, he keeps his gaze on the walls, scanning with an efficient concentration. His eyes run down the length of Shumo's front door, pause briefly at the dogs, then up to the overhang. Ignoring me, he peeks into the window, but the yellow curtains are closed and held flat with something from the inside so that not even a sliver of Shumo's home is visible. Still, he stares for a long while at the window shutters and glass panes.

"Do you work for the camp?" I ask.

He says nothing, continues scribbling in his book.

"This is my aunt's house. Do you know where she is? Or Samphel? He's about twenty-five now?"

He flips to a page in the front of his book. "Yangsel doesn't have a son. All children are deceased."

I lean in to check the records. The man is startled and jumps back. He stares at my face as he tucks the notebook into his bag. "Think carefully before you do something like that," he says, disappearing into another alley.

"The boy left years ago," says the woman from upstairs. "Samphel. Yangsel's adopted boy, right? Very quiet but clever in surprising ways. It's a shame about his father. Poor thing. Sometimes we'd hear him crying at night for his parents. You can hear everyone's business in these crowded houses. I know so much it hurts my head."

"Where did he go?"

"He went to join a new monastery in the Indian jungle."

"Are you sure?"

She says she has the best memory in her family, and besides, she needs to leave now. She isn't one to nose around in people's business, but the boy has definitely gone to a monastery somewhere in the south of India.

"Go talk to the shopkeeper at the end of the lane if you don't believe me," she adds. "He helped arrange the whole thing, since his cousin heads the monastery. They had a falling out years ago but anyway, he still sent the boy there—the boy had just the right temperament for the contemplative life. Like I said, I'm not the kind to stick my nose in people's business. Go to the store yourself."

I sit down on a ledge facing Shumo's door. Some part of me still expects Samphel to open the door and greet me, though I know this is impossible. And yet, I cannot believe that he's a monk either. The boy I know would never last in such a place.

4

As promised, I care for Gen Lobsang's mother, Mo Sakya. But things are not exactly as Gen Lobsang described. She has no intention of moving, and her younger son has gone to join the sweater business in India. I'm also surprised to see that Mo Sakya is an energetic and social woman, who enjoys puttering around her camp to gossip, help with little tasks, and join in any prayer sessions. But she's lost her sight in one eye completely and the other is failing as well. So it seems my trip here was not pointless after all.

"We make a fine pair!" she often says, holding my face close so she can see me.

Mo Sakya shared that some people thought her condition could be permanent snow blindness. When she was escaping Tibet, she had been separated from her sons for several days, trapped in a blizzard. After that, she never recovered her sight. At the same time, I think she's well into her eighties and so her eyes are probably just aging. People say all sorts of things to be kind, especially to someone so vibrant. Sometimes, when I see her chanting prayers by memory or vigorously polishing her prayer bowls, I can clearly picture Mo Sakya as a young woman.

Since my arrival, she has relaxed and even branched out in her interests. She has taken up smoking and drinking in private. I don't see anything wrong with this old woman forming new habits. She's fortunate enough to have her own home, so who's to stop her? For my part, I make sure there's always a pitcher of barley beer in the kitchen and a new pot fermenting in a cool, dark corner. Whether Mo Sakya knows it or not, I too am experiencing a new freedom in her house. Without anyone in my family around, I have found a solitude I never knew before—independence, even.

Still, I'm tethered to Samphel. Even as my hopes of seeing him dwindle, I experience a growing intensity of feeling for him. It's as if I could sense his residual heat in this cramped and confusing camp. In the damp alley walls, along the narrow night sky hemmed between the rooftops of the camp, I feel the same longing to leave that he must have felt. And the time we shared here years ago seems to enlarge in my mind. Those memories swell, flecked with the shimmering gold of nostalgia. Why did we always run from place to place back then? Did we somehow know we would have so little time together?

At night, I dream of the Indian jungle where he lives. I crawl on hands and knees through thickets below a canopy of banana leaves so dense no light can pass through. There are no mountains where Samphel lives, I am told. Just the steaming earth beneath your feet, the unrelenting sun above. I also dream of our past—our day of wandering the capital, resting on that hill in Swayambhu. In my dream, he's sitting up, taller and with broad shoulders, while I lie in the grass beside him. But I can't see his face. Then something strange happens. He takes a razor and begins to shave his head, as every monk must. Tufts of black hair fall on me as I ask him to stop, but he ignores me and continues shaving his hair.

Despite myself, one evening as I prepare our dinner, I begin telling Mo Sakya everything I feel.

"Wait for him," she says.

"He's a monk now."

"Monks don't always stay monks. My son used to be one."

"Gen Lobsang? I heard that long ago, but I still find it hard to picture him as a monk."

"Right up until he was twenty. That's why he can cook. He can also paint thangkas very well."

It pleases me to think Samphel will be like Gen Lobsang, well-mannered and worldly.

"I had a sweetheart once," Mo Sakya adds, smiling at the wall to my right. "You don't just give them up. People say you can't love deeply when you're a child, but I look around and it's really the grown men and women who cannot love. Wait a little while. He'll come back."

I let out a laugh. This is all I've wanted to hear.

"Come close," Mo Sakya says.

I stop cutting potatoes and go to her, letting her hold my face to her milky eyes.

"I can see your mother in you."

"You knew her?"

"I heard she died suddenly. Something went quiet that winter. I took a different path, but I went to your mother once, long ago. I used to have a searing pain right here," she says, guiding my hand to her spine.

"I didn't know . . ."

"She healed my back. And you look so much like her," Mo Sakya says, scanning my face with her moist and trembling eyes.

"Which parts?" I ask.

"I'm looking at her again," she says, her eyes now darting across my face. "We women have to hide our strength. But not your mother. She refused to hide her power." Mo Sakya hesitates before speaking again. "Like Thrinley Chodron, the young nun who led a revolt."

"I don't know her."

"Three or four years ago, her group captured and killed many Gyami soldiers before she was finally executed. Like your mother, Thrinley Chodron was also a vessel. She was possessed by Labja Gongmo, the holy bird from the Ling Gesar epic."

I smile in amazement. "I would like to learn more, Mo Sakya. More stories about such women."

Mo Sakya laughs. "Even though I'm half-blind, I remember so much. More than almost anyone else here. Isn't that impressive?" she asks. "But soon I'll be dead and after some time passes, you'll think of me as just a dream."

IN MY THIRD season at Mo Sakya's house, there's still no sight of Shumo Yangsel. But one day a message arrives in my name at the camp's office. It's from Gen Lobsang. He has finally found sponsors for Tenkyi's school fees. She will be leaving the country in a few months and Ashang Migmar wants me to return to the camp. Just like that, I begin preparations to leave.

On my final day with her, I let Mo Sakya hold my face for as long as she needs, both of us silently aware that we'll never see each other again in this lifetime. Then I lead her by the hand to the kitchen corner where the next batch of barley beer is fermenting. I show her where a fresh pack of cigarettes is tucked away. The beer will be ready in four weeks, I tell her.

"One more thing," I say. "If Samphel returns, will you tell him about me? Say that I'll be waiting at my camp?"

"I will tell him everything."

We touch our foreheads. Mo Sakya drapes a white khata scarf around my neck. She says a prayer for a safe journey back, and for my long and healthy life. Then she presses money for the bus home into my hands. Taking one last look at Mo's face, I light a cigarette in my mouth and place it between her lips. I have been happy in this place, I think. She has shown me how a woman can live in happiness alone. Walking down the dusty road, I can still feel her hands on my face.

5

My sister's sponsors are a couple from America's western coast. They have sent us three photographs so we can know the source of our good fortune. In one photo, Mr. and Mrs. Stanley stand with their two grown-up sons who wear smart suits and harried expressions. Behind the family, there's a large indoor tree covered in lights and colorful decorations. Tenkyi and I study the photo closely. The family has curtains made of the same fabric as the sofa: a floral pattern with shades of pink and beige. A light hangs above, made of gold. Leaning against the wall behind them is a narrow, waist-high bag with metal poles poking out. Gen Lobsang explains that this is used to play a sport over a field that spans a distance greater than our camp. There is a second photo, but it's of an empty beach with many large, solitary boulders. We're not sure why they wanted us to have this one. The last photograph is of Mrs. Stanley smiling and standing in a line with other women before their church.

"Why so plain?" Ashang Migmar asks, gazing at the block building behind Mrs. Stanley. "It's nothing like our monasteries back home."

Tenkyi brings out a new frame that she picked up in town. Selecting the photograph of the Stanley family, she pastes it over the stock image of a blond couple. Ashang Migmar drapes our nicest silk khata around the photograph and, praying for the long life of the family, sets the frame on our altar. It sits behind the statue of the Nameless Saint, which has been kept in our house ever since Po Dhondup's death.

Soon, people begin to come over to see the photographs of Tenkyi's sponsors. Young and old, they visit in equal measure to speak with my sister about her future life. They ask questions about America and the family's life there. Tenkyi answers with animated guesses or by embellishing the details in the letters. Because so few of us can read English, her word is as good as law.

"It's as if people think Tenkyi is going to America, not Delhi," I say to my uncle, watching the hubbub.

"You never know," says Pema Dickyi, a teenage girl who worships Tenkyi.

"Wouldn't that be something," my uncle sighs, adding to the growing hopes for my sister—hopes that require much more than the Stanleys have offered. In our minds, Tenkyi is as good as their daughter. We half-expect a future set of photos to include my sister, standing in their American living room between their two sons.

"Do you want that?" I ask my sister. "To go to America?"

She looks at me, surprised by my question. "I want so many things. I want to make lots of money. I want to take us out of our poverty. I want to help our camp, so that we can be happy and know that our lives matter."

"Will that happen if you go to America? Will our lives matter then?"

"Maybe," she says thoughtfully. "But first let me get to Delhi. What about you, Big Sister?"

"What I want isn't important. I have to cook and weave and wash things."

"Come on, what happened in Kathmandu? Did you speak with him, at least?"

I say nothing. I'm embarrassed I told Tenkyi about wanting to see Samphel.

"You didn't tell him," she says. "I bet you just sat quietly in Shumo's house and pretended not to even notice him. Have some courage, Acha."

Her words sting. "I have to go to the handicraft factory," I say. As I head out, Pema resumes the hopeful chatter about my sister's sponsors.

EVER SINCE TENKYI'S departure was announced, Tashi has been visiting us in the weaving room. At times, he's in and out, passing through the wool dyeing room, helping to weigh and sort sacks of rough wool, or packing up carpet orders. Today, he's lingering here among the looms. It's the second time this week. While Dawa and I work, he lounges on a pile of finished rugs, listening in on our conversations and songs, and interjecting occasionally. Something about him scares me. Maybe it's because I now wonder what he thinks of me—how I look compared to my sister. I catch him smirking at me. Is this what men do? When the one they really want decides to leave, do they immediately scan the horizon for the next woman? Tenkyi hasn't even finished packing for Delhi.

"Don't you have work?" I ask.

"Not right now," he says, sitting up, surprised that I've finally said something. He begins tightening a ball of wool. "I already drove into Phewa Tal to pick up the dyes. Rest of the day is for relaxing."

Relaxing all day! I can't help but smile at the idea. Worse, I can feel a laugh coming. Shaking my head, I stare at the incomplete carpet slowly rising from the ground and decide not to say anything else to him. The truth is Tashi does work hard, running errands at all hours for the camp. By learning to drive our camp jeep, Tashi has become one of the most useful men in the community. Beyond the usual supply runs, people seek him out day and night for trips to the hospital, to pick up important visitors and furniture pieces that we could not bring here easily before, like wardrobes and bed frames.

"Tashi, would you do something for me?" I ask, smiling. "Take Tenkyi and me to the photographers."

Photographs have become the new fashion in the camp. Every family either has a portrait or wishes to get one soon. On the day itself, they scrub their faces, comb their hair slick, and dress up in new clothes. Boarding a bus to the studio in town, they pose before painted backdrops, standing upright like trees, some refusing to smile at such a solemn moment while others are unable to contain their pleasure. But the backdrop is just as important. Karma Lhanzom's family chose a landscape of mountains, while Po Nyima had his family pose before an elegant Western-style living room featuring a curved staircase and an ornate gold light fixture. Tenkyi and I haven't decided on our backdrop, but there is no question that we will get our portrait taken before she leaves. And Tashi, ever willing, ever suspect, agrees to drive us to town.

★　★　★

THE NEXT MORNING, Tenkyi and I are in our best outfits as we head to the camp road. Along the way, we stop every so often as different friends call to us from their fences and porches to talk about our plans for the photograph. When we reach the main road, we find Tashi reclining under the peepal tree, arms folded beneath his head, while two boys devotedly wash the camp jeep with rags.

"Nice of you two to dress up for me," he says, smirking at us.

We laugh him off, but as I climb into the jeep, I take a moment to admire my sister. She chose a new pink and black blouse under her blue chupa. Her long hair is clipped at the back of her head and flows down over her shoulders. There she is, I think. Dark bird. Moving through the world, about to set off. Just one photograph to make her big sister happy, and then she'll be gone.

The photograph itself takes no more than five minutes.

"Is that it?" I ask the man operating the machine.

"What did you expect?" he replies, ushering the next group to come forward. "The prints will be ready in a week."

We collect a numbered ticket and head home somewhat disappointed that we can't simply wait a few hours for the photograph. Tenkyi and I had hoped to drive out to the far edge of Phewa Lake for grilled meat. I even put aside some of my earnings so we could feast with abandon. But the photograph will take days to develop, and as it turns out, Tashi has to go to Mugling soon for a pickup job.

On the drive home, the jeep is sweltering from sitting in the sun. As it rattles along the mountain road like an old steel animal, Tenkyi and I discuss whether we chose the right background.

"The living room backdrop was similar to the one in your sponsors' photos," I say wistfully, regretting that we didn't pick it for our photograph. We had settled instead on a landscape of hills and mountains, which was Tenkyi's choice.

"It didn't feel right," she says again, taming her hair in the wind. "I want a photograph that looks like us."

How light her hair appears in the sunlight, her loose ends waving in the air as we're jostled along the dry part of the riverbed. When I see her next, she will be a different person, maybe the kind who could belong in the living room backdrop. And won't I still be frozen in that mountain photograph? I reach out and touch the back of her soft, student's hand against my cheek. She turns and smiles at me. But I cannot bring a smile to my face. Instead, I think to myself, *I have watched you all my life and now I must watch you go.*

IN THE FINAL days before Tenkyi leaves for Delhi, I bury myself in an endless list of preparations. Every day, we recite prayers for her safe journey, to free her of any obstacles. In the evenings, we visit different homes for farewell dinners. And while Ashang gathers loans, school supplies, and bedding for Tenkyi, I help her shop and pack her clothes while trying to understand what she can wear in a place where eggs fry on the sidewalk and rubber sandals melt under people's feet. A place without a mountain in sight. There is a river there, Gen Lobsang promises, though it's not like ours. It's not a quiet place to rest by or wade into during the summer months. Secretly, I'm relieved by this knowledge. Maybe the river and mountains will bring her back.

On the morning of my sister's departure, I rise at dawn, say my prayers, and prepare the dishes I craved while I was away in Kathmandu: flatbread, a thermos of butter tea, some chicken in a curry broth, and fried potatoes.

"Make sure you befriend a group of women on the bus," I tell her as she gets dressed. "If there's anyone of our kind, great, but even Nepali women will help you. Keep your purse in your arms, especially if you fall asleep. Try not to fall asleep, though. You really can't trust anyone, not even our people."

Something taps the tin roof above us. It's a crow hopping around. A second crow lands soon after. *Old friends.* I look up at the rippled metal and wonder what they're thinking, looking down at our commotion. They must see how this camp has changed over the years, how we have changed, even outgrowing this hill. *Soon, my sister will fly away. Free as all of you.*

"I'll write to you once I'm settled," Tenkyi says, her eyes bloodshot. She hasn't slept either, I realize.

Until this moment, I had had no sense that my sister felt anything but elation. Now she looks worn and afraid, like the little girl I carried on my back after our parents died.

"You'll see all kinds of things," I say, smiling. "When you come back, we'll all seem like children."

Tenkyi's face crumples in her hands. But before I can comfort her, she shakes her head and picks up one of the shirts from the pile of clothes she is leaving behind. "I'll take this too," she says, picking up a blouse.

"Good idea," I nod, folding the pale pink fabric. It's a versatile color that will bring out the rosiness of my sister's cheeks. When she returns, will she still have those full cheeks of youth? Forcing a smile, I say, "I bet you'll catch the eyes of a very smart boy wearing this—"

"I'm not going so far just to find a boy."

"Of course," I laugh. "I know you will do much, much more. You will work hard every day. No matter what the world throws at you, you'll keep pushing. And someday, looking back on this time in your life, you'll think: I did something, I became someone. The thought of this makes me so happy."

"If a boy was all that I wanted, I could have married Tashi."

"You're right. Don't be angry with your older sister. I can only see within the limits of this place. Don't be angry with me, alright?"

"Tenkyi!" Someone shouts from outside.

Ashang ducks in. "Tashi is almost here with the jeep," he says. Turning to me, he asks, "Are you sure you don't want to come along to the bus station?"

I shake my head. "What's the sense in me going?"

He looks at me with worry but moves on. I know my uncle is grieving like me, but he can't slow down to feel any of it yet. As we walk outside, Tashi takes the bag from my hand and heads back to the jeep. There's a crowd standing around in our courtyard, khatas hanging from their hands. One by one, they approach Tenkyi, say their prayers for her success and happiness, and place the silk scarves around her neck.

"Come back to us," they say. "We will be praying for you. You are the camp's pride."

When Tenkyi approaches me, I embrace her. "I've packed bread, potatoes, and a thermos of tea in the black bag," I say, speaking slowly to keep my voice as low and steady as I can manage. "Whenever you're afraid, make sure to chant prayers to the Nameless Saint. He protects us.

I will have more prayers done for your safe journey. Don't worry about anything."

Pulling out a khata, I drape it around Tenkyi's neck and tie the ends so it won't float away. "Okay, it's alright, go now," I say and head back inside. From my bed, I hear the engine start as the children shout "Bye-bye" in English. I feel the ground shake as my sister drives away.

6

A week after Tenkyi's departure, the camp drifts back into its familiar rhythms, but I'm slow to resume my life. Even Ashang has noticed that I've been slipping in my chores, the laundry and dishes piling up in the corner. So this morning, I finally decided to take a heaping basin of clothes to the river. I ended up there for most of the afternoon, scrubbing and beating and twisting an endless series of clothes.

When I finally climb back up the gorge with a heavy basin of wet clothes, Dawa waves frantically at me from the cistern tap.

"Lhamo, come here!" she says, eyeing her pot as it slowly fills with water. "Your uncle's meeting with a man at your house. He seems important."

I rest the basin on a brick wall as my hip radiates with pain. "Why would anyone important come to our house?"

"Do you think it's a suitor?" she asks with a grin.

"I better go."

Back at our courtyard, the scene is ordinary. As usual, Mo Yutok is seated outside on a grass mat, squinting as she tries to pick out insects from a tray of rice.

"Leave that for me," I tell her, before whispering, "Who's inside with Ashang?"

"No idea, dear," Mo Yutok says, rising slowly with a hand braced against the wall. "Need a hand to dry those?" she asks, looking at the laundry.

I give her a nod and set the basin down. When I duck inside, my uncle is seated beside a young man in pressed khaki pants and a button-down shirt. On the low table before them, the Nameless Saint sits facing the two men.

"You're back already?" Ashang says.

"I was gone for hours," I reply, before greeting the stranger. "Tashi Delek."

"Well, this is Kesang la from Dharamsala. Serve him some tea, Lhamo. I couldn't find the leaves."

Squatting by the clay basin, I slowly fish out a few cups of water into a pot and light the gas burner. I work as quietly as possible so I can listen to their conversation.

"This ku might be very old," Kesang says. "A hundred years. Maybe older."

"Do you think so?" Ashang asks. "What a blessing."

"Will you stay for lunch?" I ask softly. "We have some mutton."

"Oh no, I must be going soon."

"She'll cook anyway. Stay for a meal," Ashang insists.

As the water reaches a boil, I toss in some tea leaves. Then in another pot, I pour some rice and begin running the grains between my fingers. This batch has a lot of dead insects and even a few large pebbles. I have half a mind to return my bag and Mo Yutok's to the shop.

"You know, Migmar la," Kesang says, speaking deliberately, as though he had been struck by a new and promising thought, "My aunt lives in the capital. She has a friend who might be interested in the ku."

I take a quick glance over my shoulder. My uncle is nodding and staring at the Saint, but he says nothing.

Kesang continues, "He's a devout man. Highly educated, wealthy, and charitable. His shrine room is lined from floor to ceiling with scripture. A statue like this would be very interesting to him."

Ashang stops nodding and gathers his words carefully. "I'm a simple man, Kesang la. I used to be a salt trader. I don't know much about the interests of wealthy people."

"Of course," the man says, backing off gently. I can see his eyes search for another pathway.

But Ashang is unconcerned with Kesang's agenda. "My dream," he says, "has been to uncover the ku's real name. It's important that we should know the Saint we've worshipped all these years. Once that happens, we should offer the ku to a monastery. If you can help me with that, I would be grateful. I've heard you have contacts with some important monasteries."

"Of course, I will ask some people," Kesang says, getting up abruptly. "I really should get going."

The tea water has become a rich, dark broth. I pour some milk in and ask if Kesang la prefers sweet or butter tea. But the man says he won't stay. After a few rounds of customary pleading, my uncle relents and walks him out. I drop two peeled cloves of garlic into a mortar and pick up the pestle. A sharp pain shoots through my wrist. The stone feels heavier than normal. I set the pestle down and stare at the pots before me. A cup of tea that's nearly done, rice that needs to be washed and strained, and mutton softening in a pool of water. My labors have only just begun and then there will be more. Day after day, for years to come, I will grind garlic, make tea, pick insects from rice, wash the clothes. Meanwhile, men will make plans. They will look at our Saints the same way they look at our bodies, and they will decide what to move where, whom to claim, and whom to send away. They will decide who should become learned and who should stay ignorant. I move close to the Nameless Saint. With my hands pressed together, I gaze at him, the details of his form. The hollowed stomach, the lines of his ribs, the sharp angles of his shoulders, elbows, and even his thighs under the indents of a thin loincloth. And his tense expression facing the sky, as if longing for an answer. As if begging the spirits to speak, the way my mother did at the border.

I bend down and look under Ashang's bed. Dust-covered boxes and suitcases crowd the space beneath the frame. In the very back, there is a tin suitcase with my parents' belongings. Ashang has kept the items safe all these years. But I haven't once looked through them. One by one, I drag the boxes out, setting off a cloud of dust and some spiders scurrying around. The tin suitcase glides out, lighter than I had expected. There's rust along the edges where rainwater must have seeped in.

"Wai!" Dawa says, standing at the door. "Where'd the man go? Did you reject him already?"

"Come in quick."

"Wait a minute," she grins as she walks in, "are you packing to leave? I had a feeling you'd get hitched quick when the opportunity struck." Dawa kneels down beside me and fans her blouse, which has wet patches from doing the dishes. "Will you ask him if he has a brother? I doubt my father will ever stop drinking for a minute to find me someone. Maybe I should just put a sign in our window saying that a dutiful and resourceful girl lives here. Please knock. What do you think?"

"Stop it, Dawa. That man wasn't here for me. Ashang brought him here to look at the ku."

"Oh, how boring. Why can't your uncle let that be?"

"Lhamo," Mo Yutok says, peering in from the doorway. "Bhu Tsering has some paint leftover from his fence. He's asking if anyone wants it."

"Which color?" Dawa asks.

"We don't need paint, Momo," I say. "Come in and have some tea later. It's almost ready."

"Yes, come in now," Dawa says, turning to the stove. "I'll take care of the tea. You do whatever it is you're doing, Lhamo."

As Dawa begins fiddling with the salt and butter, Mo Yutok walks in slowly and sits on my bed. "I think it was blue or white paint," she says, eyeing the suitcase before me. "What's in there?"

"My parents' things," I say, placing a hand on the cool surface.

"No kidding," Dawa says, churning the butter tea. "You're lucky. I don't have a single item from my mother."

Mo Yutok gives me a worried look and begins rolling her rosary as she chants a prayer quietly. Unlatching the suitcase, I push the cover up. The hinges creak from rust. Inside, the suitcase is full of clothes that my parents never wore after we left our village. They were too fine to put on while we were fleeing. Fishing around, I see something catch the light. It's a lustrous silk chupa in a shade of brown so deep it's almost black.

"This was my favorite dress from Ama's collection," I say. "She wore it to weddings."

I had once asked if I could have it when I grew up. My mother replied that the dress was old and worn through. She said, *I'll have a nicer one made for you.* At the time, I couldn't imagine a more elegant dress. Even now, where would anyone find this quality of fabric? Who could afford it? I wonder if the dress will fit me. When I lift it from the suitcase, I realize that it's almost weightless. Unfolding it, I find only a small square of fabric.

"Where's the rest?" Dawa asks.

I rifle through the other clothes. All of them are merely fragments of the original. Mo Yutok begins to guess at what might have happened, saying Ashang might have sold them for food, or maybe he just left them behind to lighten the load. Mo Yutok had done the same with her husband's and daughter's clothes. Dawa says her father burned her mother's things along with her corpse because he didn't want a soldier to find them.

I picture my parents' clothes, scattered somewhere in the forests and mountains, flung around by the wind like rags. I press the fabric to my cheeks and eyes. The silk embroidery is cool and rough to the touch. If only dresses could grow like the dandelions outside.

"Here, drink this," Dawa says gently, holding out a cup of tea.

I wave it away and dig through the suitcase some more. Something furry meets my knuckle. My first thought is that it's a dead mouse; they lie hidden in the corners, forgotten until their putrid smell fills the whole room. But digging past the clothes, I find the source. It's Ama's leopard skin. Mo Yutok and Dawa say a flurry of prayers, but I'm too stunned to speak. Already, its weight is too much for me to hold. How did Ama wear this skin? How did she dance with it on her shoulders? I place the pelt on the floor.

The inside of the skin is ragged and so dry it could snap if I'm not careful. The pelt smells about a thousand years old, like wool, butter and a long-sealed room to which there is no door. A faint ringing enters my ears. Murmurs of a prayer only my mother could sing, in a language we did not know. Drums beating to the high-pitched yawp of a leg bone horn, while around me, the ground trembles.

"I need to find her mirror," I say, reaching back again. But the suitcase is empty. I slump back against the bed and look around at the rags surrounding me. Nothing makes sense.

"What about in here?" Dawa asks, unzipping some bags. "We'll find it, Lhamo. Don't worry."

For fifteen years, I have been too afraid to look at Ama's mirror, to see what it revealed about me, what it divined of my future. Yet I always believed that it was here, just under the bed, waiting for me to gain some courage. But now, the awful truth: Just like my mother and her clothes, the mirror is long gone. It cannot tell me the future. It cannot tell me what to do. Wherever I take my life, I must decide this on my own.

I HAVE BEEN uneasy the past few days. I find myself walking aimlessly, forgetting simple things. There aren't any new carpet orders, so even the distraction of weaving isn't available. Walking out of the handicraft factory, I head to the back of the camp to climb the hill. On the way, I notice the door to Tashi's house is wide open. It looks dark inside. I pause before the doorway, wondering if I should close it for him.

"There she is!"

Peering in, I see Tashi on the bed. He's shirtless, lying down with his head leaning against a small window covered with newspapers. In the corner, a round paper lantern turns over a candle, casting a spinning shadow of scripture over the room.

"You should shut the door," I say. "Flies will get in."

"Is that right, darling Lhamo la?"

I stop myself from smiling. Tashi lifts a nearly empty bottle to his lips and takes a long sip.

"So tell me more," he says. "Tell me some news from around the camp. It can't be as boring as it seems."

"My uncle is trying to find the Nameless Saint's identity," I say. "He has help from people in Dharamsala—"

"So what? Will knowing the name get us flushing toilets?"

I burst out laughing. "You really are shameless!"

Tashi drinks the last drops from the bottle, shaking it over his open mouth. Then he rises from the bed and picks up another bottle from the shelf by me. Reaching his arm past my face, he closes the door. The motion is so smooth, the warmth of his arm so near my face, that I lose my breath.

"Have some," he says, holding the bottle to me. "Makes the day go by faster."

When I refuse, he says with a softened voice, "Have a little, Lhamo. I mean, what else have we got? See, you already have that look . . ."

"What look?"

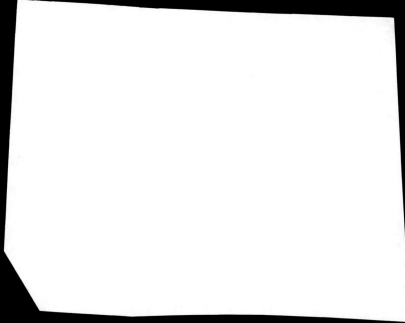

He smirks. "Your sister is off to study. But what about us? I don't want to rot in this place for the rest of my goddamn life."

I take the bottle from him. Its weight is startling. Putting a hand under the base, I breathe in a scent as strong as kerosene. The drink is milky in color, but it tastes bitter and burns my throat.

"Come, sit with me," he says. "I can't bear to be alone right now."

He touches my waist lightly with one hand and pulls me along to the bed. I can smell him now: gasoline and sweat. When we land on the bed, his grip around my waist stiffens. It would be so easy to give in. I could just sit here and forget the day. No one would think to search for me here. Lifting the bottle to my lips, I take another sip, longer this time. As the alcohol settles in my limbs, we begin to talk about nonsense. Tashi tells me about the horse festivals in his mother's town, far to the east of Lhasa.

"Each year," he says, "people gather from great distances for these festivals, preparing to race their horses and show off their finest clothes and jewels. But the young men and women come for a different reason. Can you guess what that is?"

"Don't be stupid."

"To find love. At first, the boys and girls go walking around, figuring out who's good looking, who's fashionable. When a boy sees someone he likes, he sings her a song. If the girl isn't interested, the boy has to move on."

"Poor thing," I say.

"But if she *is* . . ."

"What happens?"

"They make love in the meadows, in a bed of flowers. They make love in their tents. They make love in the rivers. Under the hot summer sun and the bright cloudless night sky."

"Shameless dog!" I say, swatting him.

"Do you know how the boys would get into the girls' tents? With a piece of nice, juicy, fatty meat. They toss it at the guard dog, and when the beast is distracted, the boy goes inside without the parents' knowledge, and they make love."

"Then?"

"Then he leaves before dawn. If the two are still in love, they marry."

"Do you think festivals like that still happen?"

"Not anymore. Of course not. Nowadays, people back home are probably in meetings all day, reciting Mao's words."

I take another sip and pass it back to Tashi, whose eyes are clear and shine even in the faint light of the lantern.

"What will you do?" I ask. "With your life?"

He laughs.

"What's so funny?"

"No, it's just that I have this great new plan. I just forgot! I'm going to start a trekking company with Suraj. We'll take the yellow-haired people up to Everest base camp, set up the tents, hire porters and a cook. There's so much money to be made in trekking."

"You'll be in the mountains a lot."

"For the autumn season, yes, but once winter hits, the Enjis go back to their countries, and I'll just relax until the warm season. I'll build a house in town, rent the lower floors out. That's year-round income."

"That sounds nice," I admit.

"Look at me."

I face him, and he gazes back at me. He's so attractive, I'm perplexed by his face. But now he has a worried expression on his face. "What is it?" I ask.

He hesitates and says, "Nothing." Then he leans forward slowly and places his lips on the side of my neck, then down toward the loose collar of my blouse. It's possible that he has done this very thing to my sister's neck. Still, I let him continue. I want to see what a man will do. He reaches for my blouse, pulls it out of my dress, and runs his hands over my shoulders and across my chest. Kneeling on the bed, he lifts up my dress and rubs my thighs. The way he clutches my arms and waist, the way he grasps at my body, it's as if I could fill some void in him. It is a power I did not know was mine.

A MONTH LATER, Tenkyi's first letter arrives. It is so small that if I press it between my palms, it disappears completely. The paper is thin, almost transparent, and it smells like fermented fruit. Carefully, I open the letter and scan my sister's writing. How fine her script looks these days. Some of what she's written, I can't read on my own. There are words I don't recognize. Bit by bit, though, I read the letter aloud, putting the words together.

> *My dear sister,*
>
> *I've settled into my new life. It took some time before my head . . . Cities make ants of people like you and me. I spent many days and nights here feeling . . . I've made a friend. Her name is Palzom and she comes from a settlement like ours . . . India. She is so very good to me and takes me to see all of the sights I hope to take you to one day. She showed me . . . four hundred years old and to trees . . . shoot water into the sky. All of the grand buildings of this city are lit up at night. Delhi is . . . city . . . modern and moving at a rapid pace toward . . . You could fit five cars side to side on the roads here, and there's never . . . empty. Did you know that all famine has ceased since the Green Revolution? The Indians are remarkable. They gained freedom after two hundred years of foreign rule . . . thanks to . . . and now they're making a country to rival the rest of the world. It . . . hope for our sad fate.*
>
> *How is Uncle's eyesight? . . . fixed in an instant at the hospitals here. When I'm rich . . . buy you Western clothes, then Palzom and I will take you dancing. There's so much I wish you could see. Tell me, how is the camp?*
>
> *Eat well and be good to our uncle,*
>
> *Tenzin Kyinzom*

I don't know what to make of the letter. I can't imagine my sister feeling like an insect. The Green Revolution sounds frightening, and I hope Tenkyi doesn't join its rallies. Although I'm happy she has found a Tibetan friend, I worry that Palzom is taking her deeper into that world.

But when I think about what I will write to my sister, the problem becomes clear. I want to tell Tenkyi about Tashi, but I don't have the words. I don't even understand my own actions.

I have also wondered about Tashi's actions. The moment before he kissed my neck, he had stopped and looked at me, as though I were a complete stranger. As though he had forgotten who was sitting there. But in the days since, he has appeared transparent and simple. He has set his expectations clearly. I am for him. I am his. At first, his desire touched me. I had never known this kind of attention. Still, I can see that what he offers me isn't love. It is something more basic. He offers me his emptiness, a chance to be important, to fill him. When he holds me tight in the darkness of his house, I can feel the hollow of his chest—as if a tunnel has burrowed through his ribs and into my chest. When he sighs into my back, breathing in my smell and rubbing my skin, I imagine I'm made of cold air, that I can slip out from between his fingers.

7

A SHANG Migmar, Mo Yutok, and I sit under an overcast sky that seems so low I might be able to touch it from a nearby hill. Maybe later, I will take an evening walk on my own. For now, I'm preparing dinner in the courtyard while Ashang combs bunches of wool between square metal brushes and Mo Yutok works the spindle.

"The monastery is finally sending monks to our camp," Ashang says. "Six of them."

When the monks arrive, we will hold a week of prayers to bless the site of our future monastery and to remove any obstacles ahead. Everyone will join in the prayers, sitting over four days under a large tent that is being procured from the capital. We will pray for the liberation of all beings, we will express regret for our sins, and we will earn merit for our next lives. Then the monks will accept our precious offerings, and the Nameless Saint shall be packed with great care and transported to India by the monks. There, the greatest scholars who survived the journey into exile will uncover the Saint's true name. In due time, he will no longer be the Nameless Saint.

"Is that why the Saint's statue wasn't on our altar this morning?" I ask.

Ashang nods. "Mm, the ku is in the administrative office for safekeeping."

"So, it is decided," Mo Yutok says, her voice high and mournful.

"Why can't the Saint remain here after the ceremony?" I ask.

"Yes, we've kept the ku safe all these years," Mo Yutok adds, turning the wheel of the spindle with one hand and pulling the raw wool back with the other.

"It's out of our hands now," my uncle says.

"I don't know why you spoke to that man—Kesang—in the first place," I reply, cutting onions against an upright sickle-shaped knife held between my toes.

"But to send the ku so far away, Migmar . . ." Mo Yutok says. "We may never get to pray before the Saint again."

"Kesang did a good job," Ashang says, seemingly trying to convince himself. He pulls a tuft of softened wool from the brush, hands it to Mo, and continues combing the rough strands.

"What about Samphel?" I finally say. "The ku should be his. It belonged to his late uncle."

"Yes, we should keep it here until Samphel comes back," Mo Yutok says with excitement. "Poor child. He's completely orphaned."

"Don't pity him. He's a monk now," Ashang says. "Offering the ku to a monastery is the same as if he'd kept it. Better even."

"Maybe he won't always stay a monk," I suggest.

"Shameless! You can't say such things," Mo Yutok laughs, swatting at me.

Tashi walks up and lies down on the grass mat beside me, dropping his heavy head on my knee. "What are you all talking about?"

"Never mind," I say. I lift my knee so he has to get up, and start cutting potatoes, running them past the blade over and over.

"She's so mean to me," Tashi says. "Ashang, you better give me her hand right away."

"I already checked on the dates," my uncle says. "The astrologer says you're not a harmonious match, so we'll have to get some prayers done. Then we can set an auspicious date for your wedding."

"Are you happy?" Tashi asks me softly.

"Of course she is. Look at her, she's embarrassed now," Mo laughs.

"We need more cabbage," I say, rising. I head to the field behind our courtyard. Squatting among the heads of cabbage and carrot leaves, I look up at the darkening sky where a few stars are faintly visible. Already the night creatures are filling our ears with their songs. I wish for silence. I wish to make the crickets and frogs still, to pause the monks on their way from India, to freeze the moon in place and create an eternity between now and the auspicious date. I wish to hold and move the world the way my uncle and Tashi do, the way my sister does now too. But I can hear Ashang calling me, pulling me back under his roof, until he can pass me on to another man.

BECAUSE TASHI'S PARENTS also died long ago, his uncle has traveled here from the south of India to request our engagement. He comes to our home in his best clothes, with presents of butter, barley, tea bricks, and mutton. I'm not supposed to see the ceremony, so I have to stay out of view. Hiding behind the house, I listen to the endless trail of engagement songs as women prepare dumplings and tea for the day's meals.

I'm reminded of the story Ama would tell about her own engagement. She was fifteen when her parents sent her to visit distant cousins, two days' journey by horse. When Ama returned home, her parents said her wedding would be held the following day. They presented her with a red dress embroidered with gold thread and turquoise jewels for her hair— extravagant gifts from her new family. The hair-washing ceremony would be performed by a woman whose animal year was in sync with my mother's. But Ama refused to marry the boy. She had already found her sweetheart. So, the night before the wedding, she ran away and waited in a cave for her love. She never said whether our father was that love or if he was the husband our grandparents chose.

Now I wonder: What if Samphel arrives just before my wedding? This thought keeps returning to me, like the frog songs that come to this valley night after night.

WHEN MY WEDDING day comes, Ashang has decorated our house with ceremonial scarves and flowers, and there are brand-new prayer flags flying over our roof. There are bowls of fruit, wheat, and rice, served with endless cups of tea and barley wine. Neighbors peer in through the windows and doorway, while the master of ceremonies sings about the rising sun, the blue cuckoo, the thawing lakes. Because a ceremonial pole is tucked into the back of my dress, right against my spine, I am forced to hunch and experience this strange day in a state of isolation, capable only of staring at my lap. My neck, too, is bent with a growing pile of silk scarves. As each wedding guest lays a khata on my neck and utters a prayer for my happiness, I try to identify them by their voice. Meanwhile, I whisper Samphel's name under my breath. Will you come tonight? Or at sunrise, or the day after tomorrow? Even if it is too late, come.

I MOVE INTO Tashi's home, which abuts the hill overlooking our camp. He has rebuilt the walls with new bricks and laid linoleum floors. It still smells of mortar when we move in. As I arrange the kitchen and hang up my pictures, it's apparent that the bricks are coated with tiny blue threads torn from the factory tarp. Tashi and I pick these dancing threads off the walls, collecting them in a bowl of water to keep them from escaping.

"Why didn't your sister come to our wedding?" he asks.

"It's too far. Too much trouble."

"For her older sister's wedding? It's natural for her to be a little jealous," he says. "But she should have come."

I had phoned Tenkyi at her hostel when the wedding date was set. When I told her the news, there was a long silence before she finally said she didn't know I had feelings for Tashi. I replied that feelings had little do with it. Then Tenkyi said something unexpected. She asked if I was certain. What could I say? Say how you feel, Tenkyi replied abruptly. The wedding date has been set, I replied. We've found the most auspicious day according to the astrologer. I wished my sister had said: Come here. You don't have to stay in the camp. The world is a big place. Come and live with me in Delhi.

But she didn't. She only asked about Ashang's health.

There are many stories about bad couples. If their astrological signs don't match, that's one thing; prayers can help with that. But then there are the polluted marriages of people who should not marry—cousins and blood relatives. They would have been punished back home. Sewed up together in an animal skin and tossed into a river. Buried underground alive. Or simply banished.

Tashi and I are not bad in that way. But we are still a bad couple because we don't belong together, and we both know it. How will we be punished?

Or is it just me who must be punished? As far as I can tell, Tashi does care for me. He intends to be a husband to me in the way he can.

Outside, the rain is ending. As my husband breathes shallow little breaths in the dark, I slide out of bed. My nipples are sore, my crotch has been used. It was not my first time lying with him. That's the local custom, not ours. But he did something new this time. He stood me in front of a small mirror, undid my dress, and kissed my breasts while I watched. I guessed then that this desire of his, this optimism, was the aftereffect of the wedding celebrations. With time, his attention will wane and match my own feelings, or they will pull me along into a kind of love. Either is fine. I don't expect a love story to match a Hindi film. I let go of those fantasies years ago.

But I won't let go of everything. There is still something that belongs to me.

From my trunk, I pull out Ama's leopard skin, lay it over my shoulders, and straighten my back against the leaden weight. The kerosene lamp scrapes the table gently as I bring it with me. Outside in the darkness, I turn up the wick, light a match, and slowly walk toward the football field. Frogs sing to each other across my path. A few goat bells ring in the dark. The trees shuffle their leaf-lined branches on the hills across the river gorge. I am the only source of light in this valley. Even the moon is asleep. I think of the oracle Lhaksam spoke of, the one who lived alone in the mountains. I think of the lamps that men and demons carried to her cave. Were they really demons, as Lhaksam said? Or was it just the oracle herself walking at night? Are women even allowed to walk alone in the dark? Are they allowed to take what they want? Tonight, I will.

To the songs of a thousand frogs and goat bells, I weave through the footpaths of the camp. With a kerosene lamp, I walk like a ghost, a light floating in the hills. I am the feared and derided oracle. I am one of her lovers. No man can have what's mine. Not my new husband, not some monks. I reach the narrow administrative building. Bracing myself on the sloping grass, I walk from window to window, until I see the Nameless Saint.

I WAKE EARLY the next morning to scrub the dead skin and sweat from my flesh. With a long panel of cloth tied around my torso, I walk to the cistern tap. Lathering my arms and back, I let the soap and water seep through the fabric. Then I reach up my legs to soap my thighs. Next, I untuck the panel from my chest, open the dress, and stand under the tap to rinse the lather from my body. Once that's finished, I tuck the fabric back tightly around my torso and unfurl my hair to wash it.

The whole process takes about half an hour, partly because I often have to stand back and let others with quicker business use the tap ahead of me. I don't mind this. Bathing is one of my keenest pleasures, though only in the warm months. In the winter, the mountain runoff is cold enough to cause blinding pain after just a few moments. That's when I have to heat a basin of water over the stove, mix it with cold water in a bucket, and wash myself sparingly, cup by cup. This is such a cumbersome process that I avoid washing until my follicles hurt from oil and grime.

Dawa must have seen me from her window, because she comes out of her gate with a half-full basin of laundry. As she soaps the clothes, I wind my wet hair around the top of my head, tuck the end into a bun, and begin to scrub my shoulders. At first, we work quietly, each inside our own mind. Then Dawa pokes my leg, cocks her eyebrows, and says, "Well?"

"Well, what?" I say. "Nothing earth-shattering to share, even if he is the camp hero."

"Hoo hoo!" she laughs. "But did you hear the news? The statue of the Nameless Saint is missing."

"What are you talking about?"

"Nyima went to open the office a few hours ago and couldn't find it. People have been looking high and low for the ku. It's like the Saint just . . . vanished."

"Maybe he has moved on," I say.

"What? Like in the story?" she asks. "Well, the camp is holding prayers every day for the next month in the hope that we will find the statue. I bet Kesang just misplaced it. He didn't seem like the most careful person, between you and me."

"You might be right," I say with a shrug and continue scrubbing my back.

★ ★ ★

FOR A WHILE, Tashi goes to the center of Pokhara regularly to talk to various travel agencies and trekking businesses, speaking to some potential partners about routes and packages they might offer. When he returns at two or three in the morning, he wears the unmistakable scent of other women on his skin. One night, he strips off his clothes and tries to embrace me. I go stiff and shake off his hand. The rejection sets him off.

He shouts, calling me a frigid witch. I tell him to find another woman. In his rage, he slaps me hard across my face, just once. His tears come instantly, but I will not cry. I hate him with everything inside me. Sensing that he will not hit me again, I look up at my husband. I want to smile at him because he's weak, because by hitting me, he has released me. But before I can do anything, he leaves our house and runs off into the camp.

Mo Pema finds him the next morning, lying in a ditch beside a cow decorated in marigolds. She lifts him up like a child and guides him back into my care. We resume our lives. Before long, all mention of Tashi's trekking business ceases. I have become the sole breadwinner. People in the camp inevitably notice and begin to talk. Tashi is a failure, they say. How, they wonder, could he let his new wife work when he squanders it all away at the gambling hall? When Po Tsering hosts a game of cards at his house one night, Tashi heads there with my earnings and loses it all within an hour. But Tashi doesn't accept the loss. He says that Hring-hring changed the rules. The two of them start to argue, and everyone takes Hring-hring's side because Tashi is still a newcomer to the camp by comparison. They let the insults roll. Dawa watches as they call him a leach, a bloodsucker, a drunk. Tashi overturns the small table and walks off, promising never to lay eyes on this wretched camp again.

A month after Tashi disappears, I separate our beds, pushing his into the corner, perpendicular to mine. Under his bed, I store a box with photographs of the wedding along with his clothes and shoes.

Wishing to comfort me, Dawa says that the separation is only temporary. Tashi will be back, she insists. My friend assumes I will simply pull the box of his things out on that day, join our beds again, and resume my life with him. I let her talk. What's the point of explaining it to her? What matters now is that I know how things will go. Now that Tashi is gone, there's no man for me to take care of. I have nothing but time, all of it mine. The house is mine, the money I earn is mine, the quiet nights and the long days are mine.

Nowadays, I often think of the dead pigeon from Marpa's story—the bird he used to transport his son's consciousness into another boy's body. I am that pigeon. I carried Tashi in my body—his desire, his hunger, his rage. Like my mother, I was just a shell, a plaything. Not anymore. My little sister has learned from books, but I have learned from these past years. I want to be independent like Tenkyi, living as I please, without anyone daring to say a word to stop me. Each day, I smile as I picture Tenkyi reading books somewhere in the distant country I have never seen, filling her mind with knowledge. Go and live, Little Sister. And I will too. The things you want for yourself, pursue them without hesitation, without self-doubt. Let no one, no force hold you back. For this freedom, our parents laid their bodies on the mountain paths.

TENKYI

Toronto, Canada

2012

ALL my life, I have wanted to tell you this story. But a story must start at the beginning, and I have almost nothing from the start of my life—not your face and not Pala's. All I have is a few corners of our abandoned house. I erased the rest without intending to. I let them fall away by doing nothing. Instead, I'm cursed with a thousand memories I cannot reach. My sister must remember what you looked like, but Acha Lhamo never answers my questions about the past. If only I could open her mind like a jar—if I could just peer inside and see you once, how real you would become. How real you are struggling to become, even now, from the distance of fifty years.

When I saw you last, you were leaving to gather firewood. In the final minutes of daylight, I watched your back slip away between the trees. With each blink, you grew fainter until there was no shape that resembled you. Then it was morning, and Acha Lhamo said you had died in the night. *Where where?* I asked, craning my neck to scan the snow-dusted riverbank, then searching for you in Acha's eyes. *Gone gone,* she said. I could hear nothing but water flowing down the mountains, along the bank of the river we had followed for months. I told her she was wrong, that you were just picking up branches. *Gone gone,* Acha repeated, her eyes red and large. *Gone beyond gone.*

So much has happened since that day. Dawn after dawn, your eyes did not see. Cities and hills your feet did not trace. My introduction to a thing called an "ocean" you never beheld. I want to show you all of it. I want to tell you about everything you've missed—of my life, of what I have done and what has been done to me, your youngest, the camp's hope, the one nobody speaks of anymore. Even if it is a broken story, I must have you know it. Just tell me that you can hear me.

MY EYES SPRING open in the dark. I am alone here. Even my niece is gone, her bed empty across the room from mine. Where has that girl gone?

And what's this above the television? Two thin, jagged lines stretch across the length of the wall. New cracks in this old house? I feel around for the plastic button, click it, and the lamp flashes on. The lines tremble. Hundreds of ants are making a long passage from the bathroom to the kitchen and back. Two delicate threads in motion. Could this be the most important thing happening in Parkdale?

The alarm clicks on and starts beeping at its usual hour, telling me to prepare for my shift. I reach for my phone while waiting for my eyes to adjust. There's a message from Dolma. *Read the message,* I tell myself. *Stay present for her. She is beginning to look at you like the others used to.*

"I need to speak to you," she wrote at two in the morning. "Be home soon."

Pushing off the layers of blankets, I prop myself up and dig my toes into the rough carpet, which is thin enough that I can feel the cold cement foundation underneath. It's nearly the end of the semester; maybe Dolma's school marks have come through. She is a lucky girl, going to university in this country, in this calm city with its rules and opportunities laid out like its roads—in straight, bright lines for all to see. Yes, she must be doing well in school.

Yet I know my niece. She would not message me about her grades. She would only tell me about them if I asked, after much prodding and insisting. In fact, I sense she hides the world of her education—as though I would be somehow ashamed or saddened to hear about the books that she reads and the classes she attends. Perhaps she thinks that I'll be reminded of the life I once had? That, upon hearing of her studies, I will view my current work as lowly and demeaning by comparison? *No, I want to tell her. I am the one who pays the rent, who keeps you safe. And so my work—whether I'm cleaning rooms or picking through recycling bins—does what any job should: It makes other lives possible. With each bed I dress, each towel I fold, I make possible our life, and your mother's, and Po Migmar's. And do you also not realize that each morning, when you go to the university, and every night, when you return home with your bag stretched by books, your mind alive and searching, that you make my life possible?*

But my niece does not understand this. A number of other possibilities come to mind, each as absurd as the next. She wants to tell me about a boyfriend, perhaps someone she has kept secret from her family until now; she wants me to meet him, which means that she wants me to know *her* more fully. Or she wants to go for a holiday to Niagara Falls, the way I've always suggested: just the two of us, standing amid the mist, sleeping at a beautiful hotel overlooking the Falls. Or another possibility: This is about the Saint, or whatever statue she thinks is the Nameless Saint. The meeting with the former minister will not have satisfied her, and I sense that she will now want to raise the issue with the exile government. I know this because I know the mind of a young woman with intelligence and dreams.

"OK," I type. "C U."

In the bathroom, the faucet handle squeaks as it opens, and the pipes clang as if beaten by a man trapped inside. A quickly warming river runs through my fingers. Here, I can wake slowly from my dream. I can linger among the trees, the faint moon at dawn, the thin dusting of snow. There's always water between my ears. But this is the past. This is not now. Another bad night of little sleep, and my body is getting restless again.

What of the Nameless Saint, though? When I first saw him, he was floating high above me in Ama's fingers, with a strange light dancing on his polished body that was sparsely covered in gold pigment. I stared at the lotus petals rising from the statue's base, the fine ridges of his ribs, arms, and knees. Even though I was feverish, I realized that the light upon his form did not come from the tent's mouth. Rather, the Saint was lit from within. I looked around, and saw that all of us inside these walls were washed in his luminescence. Everyone's faces seemed different—their skin sparkling like sand in the sun, their eyes glimmering like stars.

It was as though the ancient moon were passing through our tent. Ama told us that the Nameless Saint's statue came and went, appeared and disappeared, as if by his own will to visit those who needed him. Through our tears, we smiled in gratitude and relief. We realized then that all along, Ama had been right. Every step she chose, each turn we took, all of it had brought us to the Saint.

Then I thought of my father, still unable to walk, and his feet, which I was not allowed to see. I closed my eyes, exhausted by the colossal waves of sorrow, and let my head drop, swinging here and there. My sister clutched me from behind and held me down. Ama knelt before me, and I watched as she lowered the base of the Saint slowly, until its rough surface tapped my temple, breastbone, and spine. My skin vibrated in those three points. A calm spread through me, and I lost consciousness.

I must have been gone for a long time, because when I opened my eyes, the tent was quiet and dark. The only person around was Pala, asleep under a pile of sheepskin. Did I dream of the Saint? Could my mind conjure such a fantasy? I looked at my hands and my arms, which did not sparkle. I looked at the tent's black walls, which were wearing thin and likely to tear again from the terrible winds of this bleak land. The moon was not inside our tent, and Pala's face was bloodless and loose on his bones, his expression weary even in sleep. Then my eyes glimpsed a dark object. It was the Saint's statue, except now it was dull and lifeless, blending in with our ordinary belongings. Now, it was just a statue of a little man made of earth. Even the flecks of gold that remained on his ribs and stomach did not seem so bright.

After that day, I waited to see the Nameless Saint illuminated again, shining from within. In secret prayers, I begged him to show himself, to make me and my surroundings glow as only he could. Even in my nightmares, I spoke to him over and over. But I didn't know the truth until much later: What dulled the Saint's light was not the land but me. My mind is darkness. My mind eats light.

"Be there in thirty minutes," Dolma writes.

"OK dear." Enough time for me to go to the lake. I must go now, before another minute is wasted. I must go to the water's edge.

★　★　★

ON THE CORNER of Springhurst and King, I spot the usual crowd huddled, shivering in the early-morning dark until the white van comes to take them to the bread factory. No one wants to be seen at this hour. Better to avert my gaze. Still, I can't help but look. Maybe I know someone in the group. What if one of them is from my camp? Wouldn't they be sorry for ignoring me now? The Saint is here in Toronto, and they have no clue. They just carry on with their grim thoughts, going from job to job, their movements netted like the streetcar cables.

Crossing King Street, I head toward the highway overpass. Garbage and seagulls are tossed around in the lake's erratic wind. The downtown skyline appears to my left as a few cars pass here and there beneath my feet. The lake and sky look like soot, but the sun is rising somewhere behind the clouds. Nights fill me with dread. Days are dangerous. This is the only time I feel like myself. I dig my hands down into my pockets and tuck my face into my coat collar.

A few geese waddle by, saying nothing, defecating along the banks. Even in the gray light, I see their black heads hiding their black eyes. The people on the television are right. The earth is not well. I know this because the birds have dwindled. During my first summer in Canada, twelve years ago, the shoreline was full of geese, floating across the water's surface with their necks glistening. One afternoon, sitting on a rock, I watched them until one stopped, turned, and faced me. Pausing in the water, he stared at me for a long while, insisting I return his gaze. I got up and whispered to the floating shadow, "Who are you?"

I have asked many others the same question: perfect fields of grass, cups on the shelves at the Salvation Army, books at the Parkdale Library. To the space between my eyes. To people of long ago in moments caught in my throat. I ask that question because this is a country that gives so much weight to the answer, as if they could measure someone by it. Yet this doesn't mean that they like the answers I give. When I reply that I'm a teacher, or that I read English literature in university, they raise their eyebrows or shake their heads, as though I must be mistaken. Instead, they want to hear that I'm a refugee, someone good who needs their help.

From the cement ledge, my body slides under the railing and drops onto the rocky banks. One small pebble is all I need. But this task is getting harder as we approach the colder months. Crouched down and digging through the wet puddles of rock and sand, pulling up chunks of sediment, I feel like a hunter. My fingers are beginning to sting, but physical pain has never stopped me from doing what I must. I dig and dig. There. A nice flat stone settles into my palm.

A tall white man stops downshore. He and his little gray dog are staring at me. I keep perfectly still, unsure of what to do. The man and his dog are also frozen. The next moment, they turn around and walk back the way they came. Maybe I appear strange, huddled under the dark walkway. Though I wonder: What was that man doing earlier? What did he do during the night? Who can say? If you let them, anyone can make you feel ashamed of your impulses. Sometimes I think that is the true religion of this country.

Pebble in hand, I duck into my nook under the concrete walkway. For a while, I had built the cairn out in the open, but no one would let it stand for more than a day. Now that I have found this little cave—which I've cleared of nearly a hundred beer bottles, takeout containers, and cigarette butts—I can build this tower day after day, one pebble at a time, the way travelers do at mountain passes. The rough concrete ceiling catches my hair, tugging painfully. I bend down, like Ama stoking the oven fire, and hum her songs, though I don't remember the words. Gently, I place my new find on the top. The rock trembles in the wind. Water runs in thin streams around my feet. But the cairn is stable. Closing my eyes, I ask across time and space: "Are you here, Ama?" Something roars across the sky, traveling slowly east. Heat spreads across my brows, and I listen to the faint jingling of sheep bells as my beloved Diksen barks at the sky.

"Ama," I whisper. "I think the Saint has come back."

Silence.

"Ama," I repeat.

Something new comes before me. The lake has turned turquoise, and red cliffs are visible in the distance. To my right sits a two-story mud house. At last, a glimpse of home. But dark clouds roll rapidly over the cliffs, down toward our valley. I know this day.

It was a winter morning, and things were strangely quiet in our house. No animal sounds in the shed downstairs, no voices in the hallway, no creaking steps. Yes, I remember. I was meant to be in the pastures with Pala and Acha Lhamo, learning how to care for the animals. But they were gone, and my boots were in my hand. At the window, I pushed the shutters open. A line of pilgrims moved slowly below, praying and prostrating themselves all the way to the monastery up the hill. The bells went off as the red dots of monks moved around, getting ready for morning prayers. The sun had just risen, and already plumes of juniper smoke climbed skyward from every roof in the village.

Off in the direction of the pastures, the sky was heavy and low. I was worried about another hailstorm. Nothing could be worse than being alone in a storm. Then I heard a voice drifting out of the kitchen. It was my mother singing a prayer. As I went toward her, I swayed to the sound of her voice, which reminded me of grained orange wood—bright, smooth, and delicately rippling. When I reached the kitchen, I dropped my boots to the floor to get my mother's attention.

Ama looked up. "Come," she said, patting her thigh.

Walking in, I covered my smile with my hands. Ama raised me into the empty pocket between her crossed legs. How nice it was to sit against her chest, in the center of her body.

"There might be another hailstorm coming," I said, looking up as her hair fell over my eyes. Why can't I see her face clearly, even now?

"Is that right?" she replied.

"We should pay the Ngakpa the hail tax," I determined brightly.

"He's been paid plenty to keep the hail away. Even so, my dumpling, listen to me carefully. There is a greater storm coming to us. You must prepare yourself. In the same way that we prepare for the winter months, you should begin that work now."

"But you and Pala will be here, right?"

"One day we will die, just like all beings. You must learn how to stand on your own feet, understand? So, I will start teaching you a special meditation today. It's an important lesson, but it can be dangerous if we don't finish it completely. Will you commit to the whole lesson?"

"Did you already teach Acha?" I asked, wondering if my sister had kept this from me.

"Not yet. You are the first," she said with a smile. "So you will fully commit to it?"

It was usually Acha Lhamo who taught me things: how to fill the feed bags, how to flatten and dry the animal dung for the stove, how to weave flowers into crowns and bracelets. But now my mother was bringing me into her secret world. She was teaching me how to be like her.

"I promise," I said.

"Good. We will offer your body to all beings."

I didn't understand why we would offer our bodies.

"It's to free us from desire."

Again, I understood nothing. But I didn't care. I leaned back as she began to chant, her body vibrating against my spine. Up close, she smelled so nice. Like firewood, fresh sweet bread, and cheese cubes. Once this is over, I thought, I'll ask for a cube of dried cheese. I will gnaw on that piece for a week, softening the hard lump little by little in my mouth, sucking in the salty flavor for a few hours, and then tucking it away for the next time.

Ama told me to picture a vibrating, glowing ball of energy inside my body. She said that was the essence of my mind. She wanted me to focus on the ball and visualize it rising up my spine until it shot off into space. At that moment, my mind would split from my body, and I would float above, watching the flesh and bones I had left behind. Then I should visualize cutting my body.

"See yourself cutting off your limbs, flaying your stomach open, pulling out the intestines and, yes, even your heart. Line them up nicely, two eyes, two ears, two lips, ten fingers, ten toes, two nipples, ribs, a tongue, a kidney, the lungs, a stomach, a thick nest of hair, piles and piles of skin. Separate your body into countless pieces until all you see are anonymous parts of a body." Ama reached under the table and pulled out a horn made of knee bone. She took a long inhalation and blew forcefully into the bone. The sound it made was unlike anything I'd heard before. Like a yak's groan, but higher-pitched and airy.

"That sound can be heard throughout all of space, through every dimension including that of enlightened beings, mortals, demons, and gods. Now say: Don't be afraid. We are preparing the white feast. Say: Peh, peh, peh."

I told the beings to come, come, come to me. When I closed my eyes, they approached from across our village, from beyond the hills, under the earth, and down from the sky. My cut-up body took the form of whatever pleased them. For Pasang, the servant, my body was a new horse, as well as a hundred dumplings with a platter of hard cheese. For Pala, my body was enough turquoise so that he would never have to leave our house for months and months again. For the Gyami soldiers, my body was an enormous flock of birds to fly them back to their country, to where their parents awaited. But then I saw they still wanted more, and I became afraid.

"I want them to stop. How can I stop it, Ama?"

"Snap your fingers three times like so." Ama moved her hands in a graceful sequence. First, with her arms held square before her chest—snap. Then arms crossed over—snap. Then square once again—snap.

I copied her motions, and with each sharp sound, the world I knew returned.

"They're gone."

"Yes, it's magic."

"The meal is over," I said. "My body is closed," and Ama howled with laughter.

Yes, it was just as my mother said. This *was* magic. Long ago, our world was full of enchantment. When Ama was alive, when we roamed our pastures and lived beside lakes and mountains filled with gods. Then we crossed over the mountains and magic snagged on the ridges. It slipped off our bodies and we lost our beauty.

But something has shifted. With the emergence of this memory, I have found a way. A little stream to an ocean of memories. Yes, now there is a way. And I know who swung the axe to break open this passageway. It can only be the Nameless Saint—he has crossed the oceans and returned to us.

Still, I am uneasy, for this memory has revealed the source of my life's trouble. An incompleteness long hidden inside. Because we fled soon after that day, Ama and I never finished our lessons. All I learned was the means of giving my body away, of watching as others tore me apart. But life has taught me something else: There is no end to the hunger of the world, and they feast upon those who offer themselves. I must learn to protect myself, but how, Nameless Saint?

2

M Y niece is at the door, clutching her canvas bag stained with coffee and ink.

"Where were you?" she asks. "I kept ringing the bell."

In my childhood home, my dear. In my mother's lap.

"I went for my morning walk," I say. "You have a key."

"Since when do you walk at six in the morning?"

"Did you lose your key again?"

"I must have left it here."

In the kitchen, we throw off our coats and kick our wet boots to the corner. There's a draft in the basement. I pass Dolma a shawl and wrap another one around my shoulders. Not much time now until I need to catch the streetcar to work.

"Sit," I say, taking the kettle. "I'll make us breakfast."

"What are you smiling about?" she asks.

Do I tell her? Do I dare? If I say what the Saint has done, it's doubtful that she would even believe me. And if she doesn't believe me, if she backs away, I will have no one. If she gives me that look—I *know* that look, even if people don't think I do—then I will have thrown away everything, wasted all the years I've been so careful. I cannot go back to how things were in Delhi. The days of no future. When everyone could see just what I was—nothing but a lonely insect. And I cannot go back to the way I was in the days after I returned to the camp, circling the monastery one hundred and eight times, praying to die, praying to be reborn, my feet bleeding on the stones. I must be careful, because this time I may not recover. I must be careful. I must keep setting the alarm, keep going to work and community gatherings, keep saving money for Ashang's eye surgery and Acha's visa to Canada. I must care for my niece. It's up to me. Dolma will be safe and happy, with a future spent not down on her knees, but standing on her feet, unafraid and strong.

"What is it, Shumo?" my niece says.

"Hmm?" I realize I've been cutting onions.

"You were saying something."

"It's nothing." I reach for the eggs. "I'm making omelets."

Dolma turns away. She sits on the chair's edge, her legs shaking under a shawl. There's so much of my sister in the girl. Often, my niece's face hooks me back to our childhood. On nights when I cannot sleep, I check her mattress and find my sister lying there. It was around this age when our paths broke apart; when I left for Delhi and she married Tashi. After that, we each entered a more private world. I want so much to remain close to my niece.

But where was she last night? Where does she really go in the evenings, and what does she do when she's away from me? All those hours working at the quiet sandwich place, what does she think about? Once, I stood outside and watched my niece behind the counter. She was staring at the surface, not even at the register or the trays of vegetables and sliced meat. Just focused on the wooden table. Then I realized that her gaze was dancing across the surface—as though the grains of wood were shifting before her eyes, showing a world visible to no one else. Sometimes I want to push at my niece's stomach, just to get a word out.

She's really not herself today. Her movements are frantic, even as she sits. Her legs are bouncing, and her breathing is shallow. I recognize this bad energy. I hope it is temporary. Now I see that her arms are locked around something. It's that ratty old canvas bag she won't throw away.

"Sit for a minute, Shumo," she says, patting the empty chair.

"Nearly finished." The omelet is done, but I need to make toast.

"I—just come and sit with me, Shumo."

Taking the chair across from her, I place the omelet down and give her a fork.

"Eat," I tell her, pleased with myself.

Dolma takes a bite, then another. Her baby hairs are sticking straight up, forming an electric halo around her face. Her eyes are bloodshot and her pupils are so black, like the mouths of two caves. They seem to grow before me, drawing me in. I pull back and realize why my niece looks so strange. In this light, in her condition, she resembles Palzom, my old friend, my second sister. The one who sheltered me and also forced me into the world. Yes, it's her. The one I cared for and the one I abandoned. Palzom, who is now less than ash.

We met in Delhi, a city with enough souls to match the stars, which in turn faded from view. I was twenty-six that year and believed I had come to fulfill my destiny. But then I realized I had come to Delhi like a mouse before a dark forest of jackals and tigers. And something old and familiar returned to me. The suspicion that I was small and insignificant in the world. That perhaps I was not even whole but a broken, shattered thing; that beneath my skin, something had been severed and lost long ago. This feeling pressed down on me from every angle, even from the hot, softened concrete. I tried to soothe myself with memories of praise Gen Lobsang and Ashang had given me. With recollections of the soft embrace of a sad, beautiful boy named Tashi. With the strange, impenetrable stories of the British writers I was studying at the university. Dickens's orphans, Austen's spinster sisters, and Shakespeare with my dear morose Hamlet.

The Danish prince would flash in my mind as I walked through the campus. A child haunted by the ghost of his father, estranged from the world and clutching the remains of a jester he once knew. There was no other portrayal like this, nothing else that spoke of such wild loneliness. I looked forward to the day when I could recount the story to my sister, though I didn't know if it was possible to translate such lines. *What is he whose grief bears such an emphasis, whose phrase of sorrow conjures the wandering stars and makes them stand like wonder-wounded hearers?* I stared up at the Delhi sky, but I could no longer see the stars. And my memory was failing me. I couldn't remember the constellations, just as I couldn't absorb the texts for my exams. All my life I had insisted on my own greatness. I even let Gen Lobsang carve a path for me to leave the camp. But the university and the city had laid bare my truth. My education was far behind that of my peers. I could feel their pity and derision in the lecture halls, a hundred eyes witnessing my fraudulence. Their gaze followed me as I rushed back to the dorms with my pages slashed by red pen marks. And in all that time, I didn't receive a single letter from my sister, though I had sent her several.

For weeks, in the long, solitary hours after classes, I wandered around the markets of Kamla Nagar. With nowhere else to go and no money to spend, I sat on benches and gazed at the constant traffic of people, glimpsing their joy: the perfect couples walking hand in hand to the cinema, the unbroken families who piled three or four on their motorbikes. I briefly followed a mother's sari flapping in the wind as she drove away on a scooter. I even envied the laborers who crouched together to smoke and slept side by side along the roads. Often, I floated by pockets of college-aged girls, lingering among them as we moved together in a crowd like one. Even children could be openings for a conversation, I learned. When they smiled at me and I smiled back, a parent sometimes would instruct their child to say hello.

It was on one of these afternoons that I met Palzom. The sky had just gone dark, and there was a thrashing sound somewhere in its belly, before an ocean rained down and turned the streets into surging brown rivers. I sought shelter under a storefront awning, squeezing myself shoulder to shoulder with two families and a group of young boys. Other than me, the only other solitary person was a young woman. She looked a little like Pema Dickyi from the camp, a teenage girl who had visited me often to ask about my sponsors before I left for Delhi.

"Make some room, Bhaya," she said to a man, speaking Hindi with a familiar accent.

As the man moved aside, the girl noticed my gaze and smiled as if we were old friends who had planned to meet there. "Are you a Bhopa?" she asked, to which I nodded, too shy to speak. "My name is Palzom," she said, coaxing on the conversation.

Because the rain showed no sign of letting up, we decided to wait it out at a busy tea shop nearby. Palzom was a nursing student who had grown up in one of the Bylakuppe settlements in the south of India. With two years in the city under her belt, Palzom considered herself a veteran of Delhi. She had even taken a succession of secret Indian boyfriends.

This, I suspected, was the source of her confidence. Bohemians, she called them. Carefree men who sought carefree girls.

"But they're not poor. They won't even let me *look* at the bill. By the way, I'm paying for this. I saw your eyes when we walked in."

I nodded again in silence, ashamed that she could tell I was worried about money yet unable to protest her kindness. As she carried on talking, I studied Palzom's deep brown face. She had thick wiry hair cut to her ear lobes, small round ears that stuck out, and lips that were dark purple, almost black on the outer edges. Her voice was loud and monotone. She was impossible to ignore.

Then Palzom reached for my hand and said, "Why don't you come live at my dormitory? There's plenty of space in my room and you could save some money, stop worrying about every meal you eat."

"At the nursing school? Is that allowed?"

She laughed and shook her head at me. "Who will notice? The guards can't tell our kind apart. They'll think we're the same person."

"I'll think about it." Already, I felt certain that Palzom had been brought into my life by some greater force. The rain shower was predestined, as was my routine of wandering those streets in the afternoon. We were fated to meet and relieve each other of our loneliness.

When I returned to my hostel, there was a message from my sister, asking me to call her right away. I fished out my purse and paid for a phone call.

"I just got back. What's the matter? Is it Ashang?"

"He's fine. Everyone's fine," Acha Lhamo said, sounding hesitant and quiet. "I have something to tell you."

I let out a breath and reached into my bag, resting my hand on my copy of *Hamlet*. "Did you get my letters?"

"Yes."

"You didn't reply," I said. I must have sent three or four by then.

"I can't write as well as you. Besides, what can I say? You're the one in the new place. Life here is the same as ever."

That had never stopped my sister from asking someone to draft a letter in the past, not when she wanted to reach Samphel. I considered telling her that even a few lines would have been better than complete silence. Instead, I asked, "What did you want to tell me, then?"

"You remember Tashi? His uncle came to ask for my hand."

I must have been quiet for a long time because she began calling my name to see if the connection had died. I wanted to say, *My Tashi?* Instead, I quipped dryly, "Isn't his uncle a little old for you?"

"It's for Tashi. My hand," she answered.

I watched the ticking hand of the clock. "I can't stay long. This call is expensive."

"Will you come back for the wedding?" she asked, sounding desperate. "They're setting the date as we speak."

I stammered through the rest of the conversation, eventually promising that I would try to return for the wedding—though I knew it would wipe out my allowance from the Stanley family. Even if I could borrow more money, even if I could erase what lingered in my chest for Tashi, something much bigger was stopping me from returning for the wedding. Through that hazy telephone line, I could hear the camp. The small world of chores, the buzzing kerosene lamps, the endless gossiping, and most of all, the impossibility of breaking out. I could hear that entire hilltop, all that it held in, and all that it couldn't hold. Though it was still called a "camp," there was nothing temporary about it, not anymore. And although at least once a day I longed to see my sister and my uncle, I told myself I had managed to break out. I was free, living in a city so infinite, so electric, I should feel a boundless light radiating within myself. How, then, could I return so soon? I had decided that when I did return to the camp, it would be as someone very different, someone who had found her rightful place in the greater world. I would return only as a visitor.

Over the course of three days, I moved into Palzom's dormitory little by little on my own, putting my things in bloated plastic bags, keeping my gaze downward. The slow-moving process only intensified my desire to be in Palzom's world.

My new home was an enormous cement box. Thirty, maybe forty metal bunk beds in four rows, several of them empty except for a thin foam mattress. All around, towels hung from the bars and ladders, suitcases sat crammed under beds, and strings of laundry traveled between bunk frames. Some of the girls welcomed me but most were indifferent, busy with their lives. A few commented on my poor grasp of Hindi, but they did not stick around to say much else. This was a good thing. No one, Palzom assured me, would bother to tell the guards about the new girl if I kept my head down and stayed out of the way.

At night, when only the nurses in white uniforms walked between buildings, Palzom got dressed up. She lined her eyes with kajal, spread a dark red lipstick across her lips, and checked her reflection frequently in a small round mirror hanging from a string off her bunk. Sometimes she asked me how she looked. Other times she did not have time to talk. Then she was off to see her boyfriend, sneaking out through the bushes behind the dormitory, and disappearing until morning.

In my first week, Palzom didn't stay in the dormitory a single night. I had expected her to stay on the third night, or the fourth at least. By the end of the week, I was silently injured. I felt used in some vague way I could not articulate. Why was I even there? To take Palzom's place in the dorm, to fill the void she left? No one knew or cared that I was there— least of all, my new friend. Foolishly, I'd imagined that Palzom would be my companion in the way Acha Lhamo had been. To now have that dream snatched away, to feel so alone in Delhi once again, was a cruel joke.

And then, on my eighth night in the dormitory, Palzom turned to me and said, "Did you want to come along?"

"SHUMO, SHUMO TENKYI."

When I open my eyes, my niece is sitting on the bed, watching over me.

"How long have I been here?" I ask.

"A few minutes. When was the last time you slept?"

"I . . . I should leave for work."

"Wait one second," she says. "I need to show you something."

Dolma's eyes don't frighten me anymore. We are both just tired women. "Okay, show me."

She helps me sit up against the wall. Then she retrieves her canvas bag and pulls out a large bundle wrapped in a plastic dollar-store bag. After gently placing the package on the coffee table, she stares at it as if in shock.

"What is it?" I ask.

Dolma says nothing. All I hear is the crackling of the plastic bag as it settles in place and the hum of the fridge, which sounds like a third person breathing. A car backs up against the window, and we both look up as the room goes dark for a moment. Then Dolma unties the knots in the plastic bag and pushes the bag down, revealing a black box. It sits on the table like a temple, latent with powers.

Something shifts in the air.

"Did you feel that?" I ask, stopping myself before I say anything else. The house creaks around us, and a low, throaty drone travels up through the ground, from my feet to my ribs, to the top of my head. It's as if the house itself were expanding, stretching its skin for whatever Dolma has brought into its walls.

But my niece ignores me. She is in deep concentration. I swallow with some difficulty as Dolma finally unlatches the box and reaches in. She lifts up a small statue and places it on the table. My palms join in prayer before my lips.

Have you ever had a dream that returns to you over and over? Ashang's voice is so clear in my head, he could be in this kitchen. *A dream repeating itself over time, linking years of your life?*

Dolma claps her hands and lets out a little laugh. "It's the Nameless Saint, isn't it?"

I lift the hem of my dress to cover my mouth so I won't defile the holy ku. I gaze at his face as though it were the face of a loved one. His thin nose, sunken eyes, wide-open mouth. Gently in my free palm, I lift him up. He is so much lighter than I remember. I hold the ku to the crown of my niece's head, then tap the base of his lotus seat to her chest and back. She does not react, but perhaps something is stirring inside her. I am about to touch his base to my own head when I stop myself. What if I feel nothing? What if the glowing light fails to show itself? I say a prayer and place the Saint gently on the table.

This mournful, insistent face, flecked with gold. This face of struggle without concealment. Has anyone ever seen an expression like this on another saint? Not in our village monastery, not on our kitchen altars. It's as if he endured for us, for our time. He too traveled over the mountains, first to the border through Po Dhondup's hands, then through the hands of my mother, father, uncle, and now my niece. And now I understand that he brings a message that is really a question: *Does your sorrow look like mine? Do you feel all alone?* Before we can reply, he says, *I have traversed the earth to be with you, to tell you one thing: Just like you, I am in anguish. Like you, my insides twist and jerk, a bird unable to take flight. My body, like yours, is worn through and could snap at any moment. But I will not break because I can endure so much more. I can take your agony, your hunger, your nightmares. I can bear all the misery you have carried since your birth. Through my face and my body, I will reflect your torment back to you. And you will know, finally, that you are not alone.*

"Get a khata," I say.

Dolma retrieves a silk offering scarf from the cabinet, and I help her gently wrap it around the statue's base.

"There . . ." I say. "How did you retrieve him? Did you tell the rich family our story?"

Dolma gives a strange smile before her face contorts in distress. "You can't tell anyone about the statue."

"What are you talking about? Everyone will be so happy."

She says nothing.

"I'll keep it between us. Tell me."

"I took the ku. I saw someone enter the safe code at the party, so I went back for it last night."

I laugh a little because my niece likes to play jokes, or at least she did when she was younger. Once, she came home from her British School and spoke only in a language made of English words broken in half and reordered.

"Come on," I say, checking her expression.

"I couldn't just ask them for it. Do you know how much the Enjis paid for the statue? This is what the family does. They have people who go around the world looking for old things to pluck and bring back."

I start to tell Dolma that she has made a grave error and that her mother will die from worry because now everything has been lost. I start to tell her that it was always my biggest fear that she would be corrupted by drugs or boys or silly friends who go to dance clubs and ink themselves with flippant scribbles, but not like this, not like this—

"Shumo, listen. I saw the paperwork from the company that sold them the statue. It's a company in Nepal with an endless knot in their logo. That's who stole the statue from the camp, Shumo. We just have to figure out which company—"

"Endless knot?"

"Yes, do you know them?"

I thought the scoundrel went out of business years ago. How did Samphel get a hold of the Saint? I will have his head for this. For years, I've shown him kindness solely because of my sister. Poor Acha Lhamo. From the day she met him, some karmic string has tied them together. She could go years without saying his name, and still I knew. Even now, I understand this about her.

But I will tell Dolma nothing about Samphel. The less she knows, the better. I've kept that man away from her and my sister all these years. Once, I nearly let him see Dolma and Lhamo. I even arranged the meeting. I visited his store, informed him of how things would be, and named the place and time. My niece was so young then, with her whole life still ahead of her. And a single factor could determine the trajectory of that life, whether she would be educated or not, rich or poor: Samphel. I figured he could do at least one good thing, and maybe in time, he could even earn a relationship with my sister and niece. But then he threw away that possibility by chasing after a phantom when it was the living who needed him.

"Listen to me, Dolma. Listen carefully. We must put the statue back. Today, before the family notices and the police get involved." I push forward a pad of paper. "Write down their address."

"But the ku doesn't belong to them."

"Write."

"You can't just *go* there, Shumo."

Speaking slowly, I say, "Don't argue with me." For once, I sound strong. Like the teacher I used to be. "Leave the ku with me and forget this ever happened."

3

I head to Queen Street, blood thumping in my head, my limbs like lines of electricity. Even my head is fuzzy because I have the Nameless Saint on my back, against my spine. His ancient body jostles with every step I take, his form warmed by my skin. How can I give him back? Not now. Not yet. I will go to the rich Enjis after my shift. That will give me time to think. Yes, I'll wait a few hours. A little more time with the Saint so I can think.

Of course, there is more to the story. The statue of the Nameless Saint didn't just vanish from the camp like everyone believed, not at first. I know this because I saw him in my sister's hands. For years, she had kept him hidden from everyone, even her family. She only brought him out because I was dying. This was just after I withdrew from the university in Delhi and returned to Nepal. I had left without telling Palzom because, like everyone else, she laughed at me for my failures. She denied it all, but I heard the things she told her boyfriend. Words I can never repeat.

In that time, my mind kept slipping away like a fish between my hands. Ashamed of my state, I returned to the camp in the middle of the night so no one would see. My sister was waiting at her doorway with a blanket. The next day, light stung my skin and blurred my vision, so I closed every window. Because I could not sleep anymore, I sat on the edge of my bed most nights. Then I began to see the ghost of my childhood—the woman with a mouth she could not open, shaking her head and gritting her teeth in rage. She wanted to speak but could not say a word. And yet, sudden sounds of wailing would come to me. I could feel Delhi clinging to my skin, a thick film neither I nor my sister could scrub away. On days I had more energy, I stood before a mirror and picked at my skin, wanting to find the lip of the film. I dug and dug until my skin bled. Other days, my body fell into a static posture: my hands on my thighs, my back hunched. I was barely breathing. I felt that my future was hopeless. The present, pointless.

Thankfully, Tashi was gone at that time. My sister cried a great deal in those days, but it took me a long time to understand that she was crying about me. She was begging me to tell her what had happened. You know, I told her. Everyone does. They've known all along and that's why they watch me day and night. That's why they talk about me and laugh, falling silent when I pass by. What do you mean? What do they know about you? she asked. They see who I am. A shattered woman that everyone avoids. An undying ghost trapped among the living.

Then the idea came to me. A shock of wisdom that would surely save me. I would circle the camp monastery, prostrating myself the whole way. Circumambulating the holy place, I would kill my old self and bring a new self to life. One hundred and eight times. I would prostrate around the monastery one hundred and eight times. A sacred number, the number of beads in a rosary. In complete darkness, I walked across the camp to the monastery. Clasping my hands before my chest, I lifted my hands to the sky, then back to my chest. I knelt on the ground, slid my body down. I stretched my hands as far as they could go, clasped them again in prayer, and pressed the ground with my fingertips. Rising, I stepped up to the indent in the earth where my fingers had reached and repeated the steps.

The first circumambulation was quick. I can do this, I thought. I can be reborn. In this single night, I can wash everything away. Return to a pure beam of light, an idea in my mother's womb. All suffering could end with my labor! Voices filled my head, laughing in joy, astounded by my brilliance. All around me, they spun round and round. The rain fell and I spun too, my arms reaching out to the world, to all the stars that came out to witness what I had discovered. Dance, I cried. Let's dance for a minute. The stars danced with me. This must have been the year His Holiness was awarded the Nobel Peace Prize because the monastery was washed in fresh paint. Soon, I thought, I must send a message to His Holiness so that he can tell the Nobel Committee about my discovery.

Even a simple woman in a refugee camp in Nepal could come up with something so important! What a glorious message. An incandescent message that will liberate everyone, even His Holiness, who labors without end for all beings.

When I woke up, shivering naked in bed, I was once again in my sister's house. She had piled every blanket on my body. I could not move, and I didn't have the strength to try either. Outside, the celebrations had already begun. It was as if a great wall of running water divided my world from theirs. The water roared between my ears.

"I should have brought this to you long ago," Acha said.

Standing on the foot of the bed, she reached into the rafters and pulled out a small metal box. I watched with disbelief as she brought the box to the table and pulled out the Nameless Saint. While I asked how this was possible, Acha Lhamo placed the ku's base on my head and said a prayer, in the same way Ama had done long ago. I felt my entire body loosen and surrender.

"Did you feel that?" I whispered.

"Whatever it is, accept it," my sister said.

Something flitted in the light behind Acha Lhamo. It was the sky shifting. Clouds were gathering in the doorway, rumbling for me.

"There's going to be a storm," I said, looking out and smiling. I could sense that my mother was nearby and she would teach me something. She would show me how to weather the storm.

"There's no storm," my sister said, her voice faint behind the wall of water. Past my sister, a golden branch swayed in the wind, covered with radiant leaves. It swung down and shielded me from all the rain and hail that was about to fall. With nothing to fear, with nothing to weigh us down, my sister and I began to rise from our heels, from our hips, up and up off the bed, until our toes wiggled in the air. I looked at the mountains so far away, shining sunlight in the direction of home, and I decided to take us there. I grasped my sister's hand and took her with me toward the silver tips of the mountains. I pulled her north until the peaks were at our feet, and all we needed to do was step over them. From there, we saw our village, our house, our parents. From there, we could see our mother through the kitchen window.

"At last," I whispered, and fell into a deep and yielding sleep.

Over the next two months, I recovered once again under the Nameless Saint's gaze. When I had the strength, my sister took me for short walks through the camp, and we counted the number of ant mounds, just as I had loved to do as a little girl. We sat in the field braiding flowers into crowns, necklaces, and bracelets. We spoke with one or two people at first, before Acha Lhamo slowly brought me into contact with Ashang Migmar, Gen Lobsang, Dawa, Mo Yutok, Hring-hring, and others. My sickness faded, and I began to feel like myself again. But the Saint would remain our secret.

NOW I WONDER: How did Dolma manage such an act of daring? Was she careful and thorough in her actions, or are her fingerprints all over the house?

I wait a long time for the streetcar before I notice, off in the distance, that it's stuck behind a row of cars. Standing around like this gives me ideas, which isn't always good, but today it is good. I should call my sister. I won't mention the part about Dolma stealing the statue. She would wonder where it has been all these years, but I can redirect her thoughts. "A miracle!" she will say. She'll tell the whole camp. There will be three days of prayers, a raucous party with fresh barley beer and buff curry. Maybe the camp will even get some notice from Dharamsala. But no, Acha must not tell anyone. I will explain that to her. I will explain it well and carefully. If anyone can keep a secret, it's my sister. I check the time. It's night in Nepal, but not too late. In any case, the results of Acha Lhamo's visa application might have arrived, so I should call and ask her about it. The interview with the Canadian consulate in Delhi last month had gone well, but we decided to keep the news from Dolma. The previous rejected applications have been hard on her. This time, though, it will be different. Learning from our earlier attempts, we've thoroughly lined up the documentation and financial guarantees. All we need is a sympathetic consulate official. Yes, it's possible. Life can line up once again.

I dial my sister and wait. The tone doubles up on itself—a quiet ring, then a louder one overlapping it. The distance this sound must travel. The distance the Saint has traveled. Could I not keep him somehow? My call rings and rings. But my sister doesn't pick up. Instead, I get an automated message in Nepali: "This number did not get a reply," the woman says. "Please try another time." The woman repeats herself like the dial tone.

"Eat shit," I tell her.

I'll try my sister again tonight. But now, my phone is ringing. It's a local number I don't recognize. "Acha?"

"Gyaltsen la," he says.

What does this man want? If it wasn't for Dolma, I would never have invited him into my home. Now I'm sure he'll drop by for breakfast regularly.

"Did you hear the news?" he asks.

"About the ku?"

"What? No, Tenkyi, another soul has made a fire offering of her body. A nun, this time. Only twenty-two years old."

I lean back against the glass wall of the bus shelter. I've lost count of the fire offerings. "Where?"

"Tawu, eastern Tibet. Third one there. The village is on lockdown. Roads are closed and troops have been deployed. Phone and internet lines are almost all cut off."

"What's happened to her body?"

"The other nuns managed to take her back before the soldiers came. Last I heard, the troops have surrounded the nunnery."

There have been so many self-immolations, we know how this goes by now. If the nuns can hold out, she might get a proper funeral. But if the soldiers seize her body, all hope is lost. And even if the nuns succeed with the funeral, they will be punished afterward. So will her family. The village will face more regulations, more troops, more arrests that make life unbearable. Another protest in fire. And the cycle continues.

"I'm preparing a few words for the hunger strike," Gyaltsen la says. "Will there be a microphone?"

"No . . . a megaphone, I think."

"A megaphone isn't right for this."

"We have a few megaphones," I say, confused.

"What a poor state. Even in India, we never failed to bring a microphone system to any demonstration. You'd think our kind would be better off here—"

"Please, ask Pasang. I'll be there after work."

"What time?"

"Four," I reply and hang up.

Pulling my backpack around, I hold the bundle gently. The Saint is inside, safe in my arms. Opening the zippers ever so slightly, I push back the plastic covers and open the lid of the box.

"Hello," I say quietly. "Did you hear about the nun? She was only twenty-two."

Younger than Dolma. Younger even than I was when I left for Delhi.

The Saint pulls my gaze back down to him. He wants to know: Who is the nun? What is her story? I reach for my phone again and search online. A photograph and a video have already been smuggled out. In the photograph, a beautiful, young red-cheeked girl sits on her bed, hands under her legs, a smile that is faint yet intelligent. In the video, she is a figure wrapped in flames.

She had been a nun for ten years, recently living in a small mud hut on her own. The video shows low, gray buildings and a pillar of fire that contains the nun. Her hands appear to cover her face. Or are they held up in prayer? A few meters away, there's an older woman. A witness to the sacrifice. Her left arm is raised high up in the air. From her fingertips, a white silk scarf hangs suspended. It is her offering to the nun. Across a wide dusty road, a man stands with his child. They are holding hands. Their mouths are open, their faces strained midcry. In another corner of the image, there are two hands, disembodied, clasped in prayer, and blurred in motion—as if prostrating before the nun.

Within the flames, the nun cried out, "I want the Dalai Lama to return. I want freedom for Tibet." Within the safety of the flames, she could say what had been caught in her throat for so many years. I can hear her so clearly. I hear the village—all the words, cries, and prayers circling that pillar of flames. I hear the fire crackling as it eats her body. Peh, peh, peh, I pray. Let her offering liberate all beings. Let it be enough, finally.

But what about the young nun? If she dies soon, will she be reborn as a person? She must. In a life of safety, comfort, and freedom. A life where she can exist without struggle, without any need or desire to protest. Yes, she must be reborn as such a person. She and all the others who have self-immolated this year—some sixty souls so far.

I think about the story of the blind sea turtle. Imagine the whole world is covered in water. In that water, there is a circular wooden yoke. There is also a blind sea turtle swimming alone. Once every hundred years, the sea turtle pokes his head out of the water, hoping to come out in the center of that yoke. Such is the rarity of a human birth, the preciousness of this form. Do they still teach the story today? Is it not a cruel lesson? To say that life, even an unhappy one, is an implausible fluke we must cherish. Blind sea turtles, we are.

The streetcar approaches, screeching like a wounded animal, wobbling side to side. The tram is packed, but I make it inside and wrap my arm around a metal pole. I pull out my phone and take a screenshot of the nun's photographs. In the gallery view, a quilt of flames and charred bodies appears. Sometimes the flames show themselves above me, washing across the Canadian sky. I check to see if anyone else has seen the sight, but no one seems to notice anything. Another monk has burned himself. Another nomad. On and on for the last three years, the flames keep coming to my phone. But when I open the newspapers or turn on the news, the flames never appear. There is almost no mention of the immolations here.

I peer again into the black box nestled in my bag. The Saint returns my gaze. A mirror to my innermost feelings, he wears the expression I cannot show. He always has. Meanwhile, my own face remains placid, dull, and muted like everyone on the tram, calm like my sister and my parents. Is that good? I now wonder. Is it good that my family, our entire camp, consoled ourselves with the Saint's expression while we passed silences on to each other? What did these silences cost us? I should refuse to fix my face. I should make the same expression as the Saint. Burying my face in my bag, I close my eyes, open my mouth, and crunch my cheeks into my temples. Yes. Everything vibrates and a torrent releases between my ears.

4

A T Union Station, I exit the streetcar and head south. This cleaning shift will give me time to think. I also need this job—which I only have thanks to my shift partner, Ruby, and her friendship with the manager. Why else would anyone hire a sixty-year-old to clean rooms? I cross the road, and the wind lashes at my body. My feet work from memory, carrying me south toward the water and the towering hotel. To my left and right, tall men and women rush by in their suits, their eyes skipping over me. How enormous the people of this country are. What do they eat and have they always been so large? Is that why they bump into me as they rush around with clacking heels and heaving bags? I must seem very small to them, like a mailbox or a fire hydrant, not even worth a glance. Except now, I hold my backpack to my chest, the Saint's statue hovering in my arms. If they so much as bump me this time, if they just graze the strap of my bag, I will give them a hard kick. I will kick and kick until every one of these giants falls, and the sidewalk belongs only to the Saint. Now I've made myself laugh.

Ducking into the employee entrance, I hurry to my locker, careful to catch no one's glance. Under a row of basement windows, I try to steady my breathing as I realize where I have brought the Saint. I have moved the precious ku from one underground room to another. This has been my daily ritual. Day and night, when I want to see the sky, I must arch my neck.

"Did you know that you have to be rich to see the sky here?" I ask him. "Until I came to this country, I did not know this either. I didn't even know that people could live underneath the earth . . ."

He looks up at me. Many important things live underground, buried in the earth so they can be safe from the dangers above.

"You're right," I nod. "Most precious things are hidden."

I close the box, zip up my backpack, and tuck the bundle into the shelf of my locker.

WHEN I FIRST came to this country, I was surprised to learn that Palzom worked as a house cleaner. She had not mentioned it on our phone calls, and I had simply assumed that she was still a nurse. Palzom suggested that I come along to clean with her. It was just a temporary situation, I thought, until I could find a teaching job. It was a temporary solution for her too. So we began to take the long journeys north of the city together, to the quiet, leafy suburbs with brick and ivy-covered homes, and sidewalks no one uses. The owners were seldom home, or they just passed in and out like gusts of wind. Though sometimes there were the owners who could not leave their homes at all. One woman, in her eighties, lived in a computerized chair on the ground floor. She had not seen the two upper floors for a decade, Palzom said. While grand on the outside, the house was decrepit, filled with old boxes and stacks of paper. Our job was to clean the toilets and kitchen, the old woman told us. The rest we could not touch.

If my friend was ashamed of her new occupation, she did not show it. Instead, she mocked her employers. In our private tongue, Palzom commented on the smallness of her employers' drawing rooms, the tattered clothes that filled their closets, and the hard plastic penises that sat in their bedside drawers. Sometimes the maid or gardener would join in, and we joked together in piecemeal English. I even got into the habit of memorizing the homeowners' long lectures of instructions and complaints, and I would recite their arrogant and demeaning words while the other workers howled with joy. But these were rare moments. Our hours at work were mostly silent—as though they were not worth acknowledging aloud.

After our shifts, we would return to Palzom's corner apartment. Sitting at the kitchen table with a bottle of red wine, we looked out at the view of the parking lot, wondering what the rest of our lives might hold. Palzom said she had always been artistic. She thought about becoming an airline stewardess or an interior decorator. I had not considered another career, so Palzom brought home brochures and course listings from community colleges, which littered the apartment, collecting dust and tea rings, but were never thrown out.

Life was ours, she insisted, if only we would make the choice to set off and become who we really were. Someday. For now, we were preparing. Waiting like silkworms in their shells. It didn't seem to matter that we were in our late forties already. This was a new country, a new life, Palzom insisted. I was, once again, transfixed by her ability to set the terms of her world.

But who can predict what will break a woman? Palzom and I were used to insults. We had been accused of stealing from the homeowners, cutting corners with our vacuuming, lingering too long in a room, being lazy, being stupid, being blind. When a response was expected, we denied these accusations but said little else. I did not think anything could push us to react. Then one day, the manager of the cleaning company tripped on a broom.

"You left it there," she shouted at Palzom. "You did this on purpose to hurt me."

It was true that my friend detested the manager. But whereas Palzom kept her thoughts quiet in the past, on that day, she shouted back.

"Shut up!" Palzom shouted. "You don't speak like this, okay. I am human being!"

Among a litany of insults, the manager threatened to have my friend deported. I watched Palzom stand there in silence, tears running down her face and neck, some even dropping into her open palms. I put a coat around her, and we walked to the bus stop together, knowing we would not return.

For a while, Palzom talked only about taking the cleaning company to court.

"How can we sue them?" I asked. "We don't have any money."

"What do you mean?" she said. "Aren't there laws here? They can't just push me around!"

Palzom went to visit a place where lawyers help poor people, and she returned with scribbles in her notebook. Then for a long time, there was no news. Months passed and she began to stay home for whole days, then weeks. She stopped washing. She kept the curtains drawn, ate whatever I left in the fridge, or nothing at all. She said it was too difficult to move because the air had thickened like glue. Once, I coaxed her to leave the apartment with me for groceries, but she made a scene as soon as we stepped into the shop, wailing as if someone had beaten her. I had no patience for her. I scolded my friend and said that she should remain home the next time. It would be easier to go alone.

"Easier to go alone!" Palzom repeated over and over, laughing. Her face looked ugly all of a sudden. I hated her with everything in me.

"Why do you say that? Stop it. Stop laughing."

"Did you come to this country all on your own? Was that how it went?" she asked.

I said nothing, hoping she would stop.

"I had a strange dream that I helped you get a visa . . . so strange," she said. "I even dreamt that you flunked your courses and had to withdraw. What a pity."

"I didn't flunk out," I said, quietly. "I needed to leave."

"Right, how could you have failed when you're so smart and capable of doing everything on your own? I must have dreamt it all."

By then there was something animal in her. Whenever I sat across from Palzom at the kitchen table, I would watch my friend spin ideas, her eyes darting from corner to corner, speaking rapidly in monologue. In those moments, I felt as if I were facing a wolf or some other predatory beast that could easily tear my body apart.

I found new work cleaning a mall's food court. It was a mostly solitary job, and I grew used to the long hours spent lost in my thoughts. After my shifts, instead of going home for our usual shared dinner, I began to eat alone at the restaurants on Queen Street, keeping my gaze down to avoid running into Palzom. But I had a feeling that my friend was always near, always watching. At times, I dreaded the possibility of running into her so much that I wrapped a scarf around my head, leaving only a small slit over my eyes. Still, this did not shroud me enough, for we were so close, so permanently linked that we could recognize each other even by the sound of our footsteps. Only once it was night would I return to the apartment and go straight to my bedroom, carefully and silently locking the door from inside.

Palzom would knock on my door, but I was always busy on the phone with Acha Lhamo or my niece, planning for her eventual move to Canada.

"I'm worried about you," Palzom once said from the other side of the door.

Although it was true that I no longer spoke to her as candidly as I used to, I reassured myself that I was not the one who was struggling. But then her words spun in my ears, and my mind felt unfamiliar, even to me. Like it was full of nothing but air because I was becoming so stupid and forgetful, and everyone could see that. The little girl who had impressed her whole camp with her brilliance was long gone, replaced by an old cleaner who, at times, was unable to even remember her own street. Wasn't it possible that I had imagined Palzom's troubles? And if so, it was also possible that I was the one standing outside that room, knocking softly, voicing my worries. But I continued talking on the phone on these occasions, sometimes talking to an imagined Acha Lhamo or Dolma. There were times when I forgot that these telephone conversations had been fictional, and I would—in the next call with my sister or niece—bring up a topic I thought we had already discussed.

Eventually, Palzom did return to India, guided into an airport taxi by a relative who came from New York to take her home. Pliant and frail, she was so sick she could not walk or even lift her head. She returned home. Not to her doting men but to her elderly mother. A year later, I heard that my friend had died, just a few months after landing in Delhi. They said she was pulled to the afterlife by her mother's death.

Something is rotten in my head. If I go down this path much farther, I may end up with a bad energy inside me. It's not Palzom's fault. My mind splintered when I was a child. Every night, an angry woman yelled at me, and me alone. She frightened me so much that as the sun began to set, I would get sick to my stomach. I wet myself for months. There were bright flashes of light in the corners of my eyes, and a ringing sound that seemed to toll from afar at first, then nearer and louder like a train about to drive over my body. Then one day, I awoke and the pain had vanished. Looking up, I saw that my uncle had arranged our altar so that the Nameless Saint could watch over me at all hours, and I felt calm for a long time. From then on, the Saint's ku mostly stayed in our home. Years later, in Delhi, the pain returned and nearly finished me off. These demons may destroy me yet, just as Palzom's demons destroyed her. Is this why the ku came to this distant country?

TWENTY-EIGHT ROOMS. STRIPPED, straightened, vacuumed, dusted, refilled, and dressed. The instant I finish, I pull my cart into the elevator and journey down to the basement. Checking the narrow windows above the lockers, I make sure no one can see my backpack. The Saint is still inside, but I'm afraid of what I must do next. I might no longer be strong enough for this. When I was young, if I set my mind on a task, nothing could push me off course. Now, I'm afraid of my own mind. I do not fully trust my own senses. But no one can help. It is up to me. As this simple fact sinks in, I grow calm. It's as if I had caught a glimpse of my former self—alone but carrying on.

When I check my phone, it's lined with new messages. From Gyaltsen la, Sonam Phuntsok, the volunteer nurse, and Pasang, the volunteer driver. All three are at the hunger strike. They want to know about the megaphone, the flyers, and the exile administration's official statement on the nun's self-immolation. Both the Toronto police and the RCMP are at the Chinese consulate, and they're asking to see our permit. The hunger strike has been going on for three weeks. Why, Pasang asks me, would the authorities want to see a permit now?

They depend on me. They still have faith in me as a useful, reliable member of the community. I see myself through their eyes, and sense the possibility of my old self returning.

"Ok, b there soon," I type and hit send to all three.

I'm strangely buoyant as I head back up to street level.

A CROWD IS gathered across the street from the Chinese consulate, holding placards and chanting prayers. At the front, our hunger strikers, an elderly man from Montreal and a recently arrived monk from India, are seated in folding chairs flanked by Canadian and Tibetan flags. We stage the demonstration from eight until six each day while visa applicants come and go from the two-story brick building. In an hour or so, the two men will return indoors to continue their fast in private, consuming only water. This is the twenty-second day of their demonstration.

Approaching the group, I notice that there are layers upon layers of blankets on the men. Their organs are already under so much stress, what if the blankets press on their chests? Only their gaunt, ashen faces reveal how far they have pushed their bodies in this protest.

"How are they?" I ask Sonam Phuntsok, the volunteer nurse.

"Frail but stable," she says. "And you?"

"Everything is very good!" I reply with a smile, feeling the Saint against my back. Imagine if Sonam knew about it.

"Have you slept?" she asks. "You look like you need rest."

I despise nothing more than pity. "Aren't there too many blankets on them?" I ask.

"We need to keep them warm. They're especially sensitive to the cold right now."

The gates to the consulate open part way to let a staff member out. He ignores us and carries on, walking toward Bloor Street.

"Soldiers have taken the nun's body," Sonam adds. "They won't allow the nun's parents to see her. Those corpse-eating bastards."

"They believe she is their property," I say, "and property doesn't get to decide when its life will cease."

We look over at the lifeless consulate, protected from us by metal gates, a layer of street barricades, and several policemen. A few years ago, during a protest in the lead-up to the Beijing Olympics, two teenage boys from our community had spontaneously scaled that building. With nearly a thousand of us chanting on the ground, they climbed up to the roof of the consulate, and as people watched, stunned and afraid, the boys ripped the Chinese flag from its pole. Then one of the boys pulled a Tibetan flag from his jacket and waved it triumphantly. Many of us in the crowd cheered the boys on, astounded at the sight, the reversal of power—if only for a moment. But very quickly, the crowd grew worried. People wondered what might happen to the boys inside that building, which was considered Chinese territory.

"Tenkyi la," Pasang says, walking up and offering me a hot cup of tea in a disposable cup.

Pasang is one of the most devoted volunteers in our community, showing up to a demonstration or community gathering every weekend. When Pasang isn't cooking at the community kitchen, he's driving the elderly to the hospital or to one of the monasteries in the city. He works at a vegetable warehouse and regularly sneaks old inventory to the poorest in Parkdale. His coat today, I notice, is too thin—just a jean jacket with a T-shirt inside. Perhaps he should go home. Perhaps we should all just pack up the whole thing.

"Is the permit okay?" I ask.

He shrugs and looks down the road, where Gyaltsen la is speaking with a policewoman. I still don't know why the police are so concerned with us today.

"How long should we carry on? Don't you think it's getting dangerous?" I ask.

"Both the old man and the monk are in good spirits," Pasang says. "They will make it."

Make it where? I wonder. On the first day of the hunger strike, Parkdale's member of provincial parliament had visited, announcing that she would make a statement at Queen's Park. This, our community coalition agreed, was an achievement, but is this all we can hope for? I walk over to the hunger strikers. Bending down, I begin to count how many blankets lie on each of them. What if they die here, on this lawn?

The monk says in a near whisper, "I didn't recognize you, Tenkyi la." He wears a faint and kind smile.

"How are you feeling?"

"Not to worry, not to worry. My suffering is nothing."

"And you, Grandfather?"

The elderly man does not hear me at first. I repeat myself, speaking a little louder. He finally detects me in the corner of his vision and nods faintly. That's when I realize that he isn't fully here anymore. His state of deprivation has taken him to a distant place, a place beyond hunger. When a crow swoops down over us, he doesn't even flinch. Nearby, his family stands around with worry on their faces. They traveled from Montreal in hopes of convincing him to end the hunger strike. I nod at his wife and daughters, who somberly hold banners reading *Free Tibet* and *Human Rights in Tibet*.

The consulate, meanwhile, looks deserted. Then I notice a single curtain pulled back on the second floor. Partway down, a hand holds the fabric, but the face is shrouded in darkness. Come on, I think. Show your face. Speak with us. We're asking so nicely, so patiently. Not with rocks or bombs, but with words on paper and fabric, with shrinking bodies and bodies in flames.

But of course, it's not so simple. Almost as soon as I spot the hand, the curtain falls. If you only knew what is in my backpack, I think.

5

THE heavy iron gate is unlocked, but I open it only as far as necessary to slip in. Walking slowly down the curving driveway, I scan the grounds for staff and watch dogs, but it appears there's no one around. Ahead, the house comes into view. Its pointed roofs and brick exterior look vaguely familiar. I might have cleaned this home years ago, but I would need to see the bathrooms and kitchen to be sure. With each step, the black front doors of the house seem to loom larger. Now there's a pleasant tune coming from somewhere, the back garden? Over a strumming guitar, a soft male voice sings in a foreign language, probably European. The wind picks up, and the aroma of sweet bread and grilled meat wafts toward me. Within the house, the lights are on everywhere and the curtains wide open, and still, I see no one around. Yet each step I take is more hesitant than the last, each step smaller and lower, until I am barely shuffling forward. All day I told myself I was delaying coming here in order to prepare. But now that I'm here, it's clear I have no plan. I may be unable to even speak a word of explanation.

How does my niece know such a family? Does she spend her days among such people, and then at night descend the steps to our basement apartment, wishing the entire time she could be back here, surrounded by such luxury? Maybe it's my own fault. I had let her imagine something altogether different about this country before she arrived. I let my sister, my uncle, the whole camp picture my life so differently. This house, this place must be closer to their dreams.

I should ring the doorbell, speak the truth of my niece's mistake, tell them about our whole family history, and beg for mercy. Every line from my childhood, every answer to the question "Who are you?" is ready at my lips. We are asylees. We are refugees. The Chinese government took our land and killed our people, 1.2 million souls. Our documents are flimsy—just laminated scraps of common paper, not embossed leather passports like yours—and considered illegitimate by most nations. Please overlook our present degradation. You should have seen us before the invasion, when our country had kings and gods and an unbroken thread of history from a time before time.

Of course, there's no way of knowing how these Enjis will react if I ring this bell. They could call the police or simply beat me until every bone is shattered. Maybe I could tell a small lie, say that I found the statue. Statue, I'll say, not the Nameless Saint, not the holy ku who saved my mother as a little girl, then Po Dhondup, and then my own life. Yes, I will just hand him over, turn around, and never mention his reappearance to anyone. Not to Ashang, not even to my sister. After today, Dolma and I will resume our lives as if all this had been a dream. We will not wonder where the Saint's statue will go; or who will attend to him, offering fresh water and incense each morning; or if the Enjis know how immeasurably holy he is. No, all those questions will fade away in time, or perhaps, we will carry them into our next lives. Or maybe, I should just leave the ku here at the doorstep, or in the bushes, just barely visible for the gardener to find. I scan the entryway, my eyes traveling up and down the brick exterior. Then I see the black orb high above me. From the corner, it stares directly at me with a glowing red eye. Someone must be watching me.

My legs become untrustworthy, and I hold the railing to keep myself upright. I sense something moving above me, but when I look up, I see nothing. Not a passing crow, not a branch. Just a gray sky, dark with latent rain. Yet I spot a bright patch of sunlight. Though it doesn't break through the clouds, it's still present. Even with my eyes closed, the sun's glow permeates. Its warmth spreads across my cheeks and eyelids. Something taps my forehead. A rough, warm touch, and behind it the heat of two hands. My entire body vibrates.

The world goes silent, and everything becomes clear. All I hear are my footsteps gaining speed. Every step, every turn, all of it has brought me back to the Saint. My heart is buoyant. My pulse races. I gasp for air as I delight in my courage.

THERE WAS A time when I ran just like this. Following Palzom as we laughed in the dark, running through the campus of the nursing school, guided only by the moonlight and the sound of her footsteps. The campus guard was at the front gate, so we ran in the other direction. I felt all fear slip off my skin. I felt as luminous and ageless as the moon.

When we reached the perimeter wall, we climbed over and waited for Palzom's boyfriend in the shadow of a tree. His name was Raj, and he had restaurants in Goa and Orissa. The place in Goa, Palzom explained, was by the ocean. This meant the entire restaurant had to be dismantled during the rainy summer season and rebuilt in the fall every year. Palzom said these things as if she had been to Goa herself. I learned much later that my friend had never even seen the ocean, just as I had not. But standing by the road and listening to her that night, I tried to imagine an infinite body of water without land at its corners, a pool so deep that nothing, not even light, could touch its floor.

A little later, Raj pulled up in a black Ambassador with another man in the passenger seat. This was Kiran. After our introductions, the car sped through the hot city night, taking us to a series of clubs. Kiran was thirty-eight and a musician, who, though he called himself poor, lived in a large colonial flat near India Gate. He would also be the first man I slept with. I was twenty-six at the time. Despite what Acha Lhamo thought, I had never even kissed Tashi. I had nuzzled his nape. He had brushed his hands over my breasts. I had laid my cheek on his chest as he traced the lines of my palms and our bare feet rubbed against each other. But we had not lain together. Tashi was not the lustful brute people thought. He had the heart of a child and maybe the temperament of one too. And yet to be loved by him was wonderful. He gazed at me with an intense sense of discovery, as though he were learning me. In another life, he would have known something of me, and I, him. But I couldn't just remain in the camp and become Tashi's wife.

Kiran did not know he was the first to lie with me. When he asked if I always twist and turn as I sleep, I replied in my poor Hindi that I always fidgeted in bed. It was unclear if this reply convinced Kiran, but he didn't ask any more questions. Instead, he pressed himself against my back, and although we were both fully clothed and had only just collapsed into bed from drinking all night, he sighed as he caressed and squeezed my shoulder, arm, and hips. I thought about how he desired me and smiled irrepressibly. But it was only when he pressed his body onto mine that I felt my own intoxication surface between my legs. He released his grip once he dozed off, and I sat up looking out the small window beside his bed. Whereas Palzom's dormitory faced an alley shaded by blue tarp, the thick wooden shutters in Kiran's apartment presented the city like a vast ocean of tiny lights in the smog. Once again, I was overwhelmed by Delhi's scale, except now, I wasn't merely sensing its vastness from deep within the forest. I could instead see all that life from a distance—teeming, flickering beneath a sickle moon. I climbed onto Kiran one more time. When I left, he was in a second sleep.

Before we separated the previous night, Palzom and I had planned to meet at a restaurant in Majnu-ka-tilla the next morning. I half-expected that she wouldn't show up, as she often tended to do when she saw Raj. So I was relieved when I saw my friend seated in a corner under a peeling poster. But she was in a solemn mood, staring at a poster of a beige house perched precariously over a waterfall. From one of the bottom floors, you could step right into the river. I wondered if the residents sat on the ledge and spent evenings with their feet in the dark water. I wondered if they made love on that ledge and dipped their fingertips in the current, feeling the cool, constant waters during the harried, brief force of their desire.

As if reading my mind, Palzom said, "Forget it. It's not real."

"The house?"

"It's all fake," she said, shaking her head. "For people like us, these houses will never be real."

Grabbing the menu wedged between some plastic flowers and a bottle of chili sauce, I scanned the list. My breasts were sore, so I hollowed my chest. I wondered if I seemed different. But Palzom kept her gaze down, deep in thought, unhappy and still unwilling to share the source of her sorrows. I smiled and decided to try again, asking if Raj had done something wrong. Palzom grumbled but did not look up. Outside our window, there was a rainbow. Only a section of the band was visible between the tin roof of a low hut and a cement balcony, but its colors were especially vivid that day. They almost matched the flowers in the poster. I wondered at the time if Palzom even noticed the rainbow. I wondered if Kiran had woken yet, and if so, could he see the rainbow from his bedroom window?

A young waiter walked over to take our order. He was around twenty years old and, like the other waiters, was solemn, deferential. I noticed his body, lean but muscular. I stared at his dirty fingernails as he filled our water glasses. His hands were hot and left brief mists on the glass. I leaned back in my chair and stretched my legs out beside the table. As he walked away, his calf brushed up against my leg.

I didn't even know his name. We climbed the metal stairs to a storage room with strips of meat drying on string. The floor was covered with white buckets full of fermenting beer. I can't remember his face either. Only the stifling heat of the small windowless room, the smell of flesh and sweet barley, the sight of his mouth hungrily lapping my breasts. As he turned me around and pulled up my skirt, I felt the hairs on his legs brush against mine again, just as they had downstairs. The thought of people sitting under us, eating noodles, drinking tea, without any knowledge of what was happening above them—it was almost too much. In the course of less than twenty-four hours, I slept with not one but two men. Afterward, I went into a small, deserted alley by the river and relieved myself over a mound of garbage. As I crouched, I felt the stream rush out and was deeply satisfied. The heat in the summer months took the moisture out of me so that I could barely urinate once a day. Then I started to laugh, thinking of my strange night and morning.

Things with Kiran ended within a few months. It wrapped up quickly, without much noise. It was as if both of us had entered the relationship the way we would enter a room for a party—knowing exactly where we had left our bags, umbrella, and shoes so we could make a swift exit once we were ready to leave. It was Kiran who set the tone. And I, the pupil, followed his lead.

"How do you feel?" he asked at our last meeting.

I smiled and said that I was fine.

"Fine?" he repeated, appearing surprised.

"Yes." I smoothed down my hair so he would remember me as a pretty girl. Palzom told me it was important to be remembered well. Even the young waiter in the noodle shop should feel a longing for me. And I wondered if Tashi thought of me with fondness.

Now I understand that I was testing something in those days. With Palzom by my side, I felt ready to try on other selves, one after the other. Through the eyes of my lovers, I wanted to see myself. Through their touch, to feel my own flesh. With their tongues, to taste my own skin and sweat. Through their sex, to find the shape of my pleasure. To find the limit. Then to push past that line, my own and theirs, sometimes brutally so.

Even now, without Palzom, I can find my limits. I can cross them. I can laugh as I run.

"SHUMO, SHUMO." IT'S Dolma, walking toward me.

"Oh, there you are."

"I saw you from across the road! I've been looking for you!"

Rainwater has seeped through my shoes. My skin stings from the cold, but my backpack is still dry.

"The ku," I murmur.

"There's something else now. Come on," my niece says, leading me home.

As we walk down the stairs to our apartment, I can feel her eyes on my neck. I take off my wet boots and socks. Toss them aside.

My hands are still red and trembling. "I couldn't return him," I say.

Dolma shakes her head and looks up at me. Her eyes are red. She has been crying.

"Did the police come?" I ask.

"It's Ama. She's in the hospital."

I let out a little laugh. "What?"

"That's all I know. Ani Dawa left a voicemail. She's not picking up. You weren't picking up."

I rifle through my backpack. My phone is dead. I take it to the wall, plug in the cable, and stand very still so I can think. Dawa is Acha Lhamo's oldest friend, her old weaving partner in the camp. Nowadays, she's a big businesswoman in Kathmandu.

The screen flashes on. Three missed calls, two from Dawa. I call her back directly.

"Hello? Tenkyi? Who is it?"

I clear my throat. I didn't expect Dawa to sound so harried. "Yes, it's me. What's the matter?"

"Hold on. Hold on a minute, will you? Ashang Migmar wants to talk to you."

I can hear Dawa running up several flights of stairs, her shoes clacking loudly. In the background, I can hear some men speaking Nepali.

"The only thing bothering my sister is her arthritis," I say, but Dawa gives no reply.

"Dearest?" my uncle says, sounding worried.

"What's wrong?"

"Could you and Dolma come home?" His voice becomes faint as he adds, "Something has happened to Lhamo."

"Please tell me."

"She was praying at home. The roof was rotting, I kept telling her. A beam of wood must have come loose. It fell down. It hit Lhamo's skull."

"What did the doctor say?"

"I don't know. They say she will be fine. Then they say we should prepare for her passing."

I pull my debit card out of my wallet and tuck it into Dolma's hand. I have enough cash for one round-trip ticket. Then I will have to ask the hotel for a cash advance.

"Go to the travel agent," I say. "I'll book my ticket in a few days."

The front door closes, and my mind goes quiet. So quiet that it frightens me, as if my ears are stuffed with cotton. My hands and limbs have gone boneless. I wait for solidity to return. I don't even try to move.

A long while passes, and the apartment is nearly pitch-dark.

Finally, the sound of traffic washes in from the road.

I think of the bags in my closet filled with gifts for my sister. Turtle-necks, loafers, puffy jackets, so many pairs of socks. A hundred hours browsing the stores, holding up each item, trying to predict my sister's reaction. I had dreams of bringing her to this country. I had dreams of returning. Meanwhile, the gifts piled up. Little dabs of self-soothing while I waited for the means to pull her to me.

THE SUN WILL be up soon, and Dolma's plane will take off over the lake and head east. I drink two glasses of lukewarm water from the tap and swallow five spoons of yogurt. I'm still hungry, so I roll up an old piece of flatbread and bite one end, chewing as I put on my work uniform, comb my hair back, and clip the top half of my hair with a gold barrette. Then I turn on the television and flip the channels until it's on the Home Shopping Network. I will come home to people talking. I will not return to a silent apartment.

Slipping on my boots and coat, I head out. As I walk up the basement stairs to street level, I extend my fingers over the grass. The blades push and crackle against my fingertips. On Springhurst, the usual shadows wait for their ride to the bread factory. Except today, one of the shadows waves in my direction.

"Gen Tenkyi!" the slim one says.

A smile breaks across my face. I should not smile or laugh, but I cannot help it. Someone has called me *teacher*. "Who is that?" I ask, going nearer.

"Wangyal Lodoe," he replies, his face coming into view under the streetlamp. "From Boudha."

"Oh yes!" I say, unable to muster any recollection of the man. "You made it here . . . very good."

We embrace, and I feel Wangyal's chest heave against mine. He is weeping. What causes him to cry, I do not know. Could it be the same thing that often causes me to cry? The passage of time, all it does to a person, and the difficulty of telling that story? Or is it because we have found each other again in this life? A life that is, after all, wondrous in these moments. We step back and gaze at each other.

"You're in Canada too, Genla. I'm so happy to know that. My wife and I will cook for you."

I want to tell him that my only sister is fighting for her life. I will not have a happy meal until she is well again.

"We live just up the street, Genla. In the green building. Number twenty-two. Please come by."

"Alright, I will," I say, my voice cracking.

"I'm so happy to see you again. After all these years," he says, letting his tears continue to fall. "Please come by. I want to hear everything about your life."

"Okay," I say with a nod, and some part of me means it.

A plane passes overhead and I peer upward, expecting some vague sign that my niece is inside. But the pale metal bird carries on, slipping between the clouds. In its wake, four thin lines run across the sky. Then I notice, far in the east, a very bright star, shining in the twilight. And for the first time in years, I remember its name.

"See that star to the southeast, just to the left of the moon?" I say, pointing. "That is Venus, and just down a little, there's a second star, not quite as bright. That's part of the Virgo constellation."

"Yes, I see the two stars," Wangyal replies, squinting. "Genla, this reminds me of your lessons in the schoolyard. You could always find the constellations, and I was always in awe of that. It comforts me that you haven't changed."

Smiling, I guide his attention to the sky again. "Now follow the second star and find the box it forms, and the limbs that stretch out from it. Like a person rising up to the sky. See that? Her arms and legs are spread apart, and just below her right knee, there's another bright star. It's very small, nearly at the horizon where the sunlight is faint. That's Saturn."

"Oh, I see Saturn and the constellation," Wangyal says with excitement.

For a moment, I see his face as a little boy and I recognize him. A kind little boy, smaller than the other boys his age. Craning my neck, I search for more to teach him. Leo is directly above us, in the middle of the sky, with her front leg edging up to Mars. And right nearby is Ursa Major, the bear walking through the universe. But the van to the bread factory has pulled up, and Wangyal must soon climb in.

"The stars, they're always there," I say. "Facing us. Our oldest companions. Pay them some attention from time to time."

Sighing, he says, "It's been many years, hasn't it? We've both aged."

"Yes, but we're still young," I say, stepping back as people file into the van. "Be well, Wangyal. Do a good job at work."

"Thank you, Genla. I will try," he says, before ducking inside the vehicle.

Crossing the overpass to the lake, I begin to imagine not returning to my apartment tonight. What if I take a taxi to the airport, and somehow, I'm allowed to get on the next plane heading east? Then another plane and another. Little by little, I would make my way back home. Back to the camp and to my sister.

How many people are doing this right now? Making their way from place to place, countless ants crossing the planet, some on boats in the middle of the ocean, some in mountain passes, others hidden in the kitchens of city restaurants, or tucked inside a dark box. Even Palzom's ashes traveled from the Ganges to the Indian Ocean. All these journeys. Already fated to succeed, no matter how many lifetimes they take. From far away, we may look like we're standing still, but we are all traveling great distances, forging our fates.

AT HOME, MY backpack greets me, slumped on the bed. I open the box containing the Saint. But as I pull him out, something slips and dislodges inside. My hands recoil, and I stare at the wall before me. What have I done? I check my fingers. They are clean. No flecks of mudstone, not even under my nails. Inside the box, he is still whole, still perfect.

Yet something has changed. His expression is new, or I am seeing him with new eyes. Somehow, the pain that I once read on his face is now gone. So is the distant object of his gaze. Instead, he now stares at me, specifically. With an almost playful manner, he speaks, calling on me to hear his story.

Kneeling, I bend to the earth that made him, to the forces that brought us here, and I listen. He wants me to consider the sequence of events that led to this moment. For a fragile mudstone statue to survive the ransacking of a monastery, to be carried away by a man who was ready to die, then brought into exile, hidden by my sister, sold to an Enji family, before finally landing in my hands. Each movement, a step through another portal.

Just as he has watched over so many of us in our journeys, the Saint has also crossed a thousand boundaries. This is his domain, even across the oceans. Free to travel as he wishes. For now, he travels with us. This is his lesson.

Yes, I tell him. I know the distance you've come to reach me. How carefully, how slowly. For I, too, have traveled to reach you—guided by reasons I did not myself comprehend. But now I see it so clearly. Year after year, wandering so far from home, I survived for a reason. I was meant to look after you because I pay attention—to things that others don't notice, to the moments when something glimmers in the night sky or in restless waters. I listen when you speak, because I know I will never reach the end of you.

I hold the Saint high above me, touch the base of the ku on my forehead, my breastbone, my spine. Peh, peh, peh. I hear the sound of the knee-bone horn, cutting through all dimensions. Come, come, come to me. Do not be afraid. Do not feel alone. Just because you can endure the pain, it doesn't mean that you should. Let me take your sorrow. Let me.

PART III

Lovers

LHAMO

Phewa Tal, Pokhara, Nepal

1984

I have just seen a ghost from my past. He stands across the road before a row of souvenir shops. So tall and fair-skinned, clothed in beige pants and polished leather shoes. I would have mistaken him for a foreigner if I hadn't glanced at his face. And although I cannot hear his voice through the traffic, I watch him speak to an old man with earthen skin and blessed threads around his neck—unmistakably one of our kind. Who is that man you're speaking with? And are you who I think you are? I want to cross the road and ask him, but I remain seated under a peepal tree, spellbound, unable to move.

There's a loud thrash followed by a rumbling in the sky behind me. The air is suddenly buoyant and nettled. Some of the laborers sitting beside me on this concrete base peer up through the thick canopy, expecting raindrops, while others turn back toward Phewa Lake. Now, we can hear the fishermen slapping their nets in the water as they retreat for the day.

"If it rains again," says a young boy nearby, "the monsoon has definitely started."

"Chh chh," a priest says, coming around the tree with a red thread in his hands. He will wrap the string dozens of times around the trunk before he's done, so the rest of us jump off the concrete base.

"Rich people always look a little strange, don't they?" an elderly laborer remarks, smoking his cigarette. It appears he's watching Samphel too. "Makes you wonder what they're frowning at all the time."

"You do wonder," I reply.

Once again, after so many years, the world dissolves around him. I stare at Samphel in luxurious secrecy—the light catching on his gold watch, his ink-black hair jostling as he nods—and I'm convinced that if he turns in my direction, his eyes would blind me with their beauty. Even from this distance, I'm barbed with desire.

"Then again," the old man says, "these people are always inventing new problems just to make up for their good fortune. I know. I've worked for their kind since I was a little boy, before I could even speak, which is how they prefer us. It's a fact."

His friend nods. "That's the absolute truth!"

"Not him," I blurt out.

The old man looks at me with surprise, waiting for more.

"I've known him since we were children."

There's a second thrash in the sky, nearer to us this time, and a hot, forceful breeze sets off a shower of leaves and pulls plastic bags down the road. I tuck my bag of woven necklaces and bracelets against my side. If they get wet, I'll never be able to sell them.

"Little Sister, you're telling me that you are good friends with that rich man?" the old man asks.

"Nearly all my life."

"Then why are you standing here in the dust with us? If you're telling the truth, go and say hello. Go on," he says, lifting his chin toward Samphel. When I fail to move, he laughs and nudges his friend. "Come on, Little Sister, I've seen you selling your tourist knickknacks on this street for months. You and your friend. Here she is now. Let's ask her."

"There you are!" Dawa says, walking up with a huge grin across her face. "I just sold three rocks to some yellow-heads from Germany. *Three!* Let's go celebrate at Bina's. I'm buying."

I grab Dawa's wrist. "Look over there."

She squints for a long while. Dawa's vision has deteriorated from all the years we spent weaving in the dark carpet factory with a single bulb dangling above us. "Who, *him*? Don't bother. Probably a UN worker. Won't buy shit."

"No, look carefully . . . it's Samphel." As I say his name aloud for the first time in years, I begin to wonder what he's been doing all this time. He's not the young boy who once held my hand and took me through the capital, nor is he the monk I dreamt of night after night while I lived with Gen Lobsang's mother. It's as if Samphel has, within the slow, unchanging stretch of my life, moved through three lives of his own. Now he's a man. Well-dressed and self-assured, with a broad chest and strong arms. How, I wonder, does his voice sound now?

"I thought he was a monk," Dawa says. "Looks like he's traded the robe for a gold watch. What a clever guy! Well, let's go say hello, then. He'll be happy to see you, that's for sure," she says, smiling as she takes my wrist.

"What are you doing?" I say, nearly losing my sandals as I'm pulled forward.

"Taking you to see him, what else?"

"Dawa, no. Just wait."

"For what? Another twenty years? Let's see if he'll take us to a fancy meal."

I want to say, *I'm thirty-six, married, and my childhood dream is now dust.* Instead, I let Dawa lead me across the road.

Samphel takes a passing glance at us and turns back to his conversation, as though we weren't even there. A new doubt flowers within my chest.

"Wait, Dawa," I whisper, pleadingly. "He doesn't remember us."

He looks again in our direction, frowning this time. This time, our eyes meet and he holds my gaze.

"Tai' Delek!" Dawa says. "Remember us?"

I watch as she shakes hands with him. Even as my feet move toward him, my mind turns into mist.

"Is that you, Lhamo?" Samphel asks. His voice is steady and deep, with a faint, pleasant crackling.

"You remember," I say, unable to hold back a smile.

We step closer, holding hands as we take in each other's faces, sighing and laughing, our hearts overflowing with joy and relief. *All these years, all these years*, we seem to say with our smiles. Then we let go of each other's hands and step back.

He turns abruptly to the man. "I'll see you tomorrow, then."

The man rushes off, and now it's just the three of us on the road.

"You're cold?" Samphel asks, looking down at my bare, reddened arms.

"It's no problem," I say, embarrassed.

"I can see you shaking," he says with a playful laugh.

"When are you coming to the camp?" Dawa asks. "Everyone will want to see you."

"Let's go somewhere and sit for a minute," he says, turning to me. "Can you?"

The wind picks up and sends a chill through my body. My skirt balloons and pushes against my legs, as if to say: *Go. Go with him.*

Samphel leads the way, and I clutch Dawa's arm, grateful for my friend. If she wasn't here, I might still be standing under the peepal tree. We follow Samphel into a dark doorway and through a narrow hall. At the other end, we enter a pretty courtyard within a two-story building. The square courtyard is furnished with white tables, plants, and a small water garden in the center.

"Is this okay?" he asks.

"We could go somewhere else," I say, looking at the fancy tablecloth.

"You don't like it?"

"It's not that," I say.

Two waiters appear and pull back the chairs for us. One of them slaps the table with a cloth that had been resting on his shoulder. The other brings out utensils wrapped in paper napkins. As we take our seats, the sky cracks as if an axe had come down onto a tree, and the rain finally releases itself in full force over the awning, making thick streams from the pointed edges of the roof. But we are comfortable and protected under the large umbrella. Samphel reads the menu for us—he must have guessed that neither Dawa nor I can read English script. I'm amazed as I watch him speak to the waiter, giving orders, seemingly without any concern for the cost. He has done well for himself. He has become someone.

"Whenever it rains like this," he says, leaning forward so we can hear, "I always think of the Jawalakhel camp. Do you remember, Lhamo? The morning we ran around, you and I, bathing under the awnings? We passed a thin bar of soap between us."

"When was this?" I ask, searching my mind.

"It must have been near the end of our time together. Oh and do you remember how many butter lamps we made in the Jawalakhel camp? Our hands were black and numb for weeks."

He speaks with a gentle intelligence. His words are clear and careful; his mannerisms, quiet and sophisticated. He doesn't carry himself like anyone from our camp. To him, Dawa and I must seem loud, clumsy, and childish. Even Gen Lobsang would appear simpleminded beside Samphel.

"Oh, yes . . ." I say, saddened not to have any memory of that day in the rain. "I didn't think you would remember me so well."

He laughs gently, looking down. Turning to Dawa, he says, "When I think back to my youth, my happiest memories are with Lhamo. And we spent what? A month together in all?"

"Was that all?" I ask.

"It's strange, isn't it, how a few slivers of the past seem to swell in the mind while so much else falls away?"

His words sink straight through my skin, lodging in the depths of my organs. Already I know these words will stay inside me for years, like silt settling in a river bed. Scanning the table, I search for something to say. What I wish to reveal, what I wish to give him in return, is my secret: the ku of the Nameless Saint. I want to tell him that I took the ku for him, that I keep it safe and hidden in the rafters of my house, a complete secret.

But I cannot say any of this, not with Dawa beside me. If she found out, she would be shocked by my actions. Worse yet, she would laugh and tease me, as she readily teases others, for acting like a lovestruck teenager. Perhaps Samphel would do the same. If not here, he might laugh at me later, in private—wondering what could have possessed me to take such a bold and reckless action for his sake.

"She went to find you. All the way to the capital," Dawa tells him, to my horror. "But then you had joined a monastery!"

"You came to see me? When?"

I can't even bear to look up when I answer. "It was a long time ago. Over ten years."

"Yes, I was at the monastery then."

"Why didn't you tell us you took off your robe?" Dawa asks, patting his hand. "We wouldn't have judged you."

"I nearly sent a letter informing your camp," he says with a grin, before adding with a tinge of regret in his voice, "I guess, I was primed to become a good monk. I had no family, no worldly attachments to give up. But I've never been alright being told what to do, where to go, when to wake up. So I had to leave and try to make a life on my own terms, even if I died penniless on the road. Maybe I am like my father in that way. When I left, I was almost thirty, but I was also like a child. I didn't know where to go, or how to earn a living."

Samphel took off his robe two years after I married Tashi. I think about how I wished for him to come to the camp in the days leading up to my wedding. The feverish fantasies I spun for myself. Meanwhile, Samphel had been searching for a freedom of his own. If I had only just waited.

"You don't look penniless now. Are you a businessman?" Dawa asks.

"Me?" He chuckles. "No, I just manage the books. Taxi business."

"You should manage our books if you like. We're businesswomen."

"I don't doubt it! What do you trade in?"

Dawa lifts her heavy backpack onto her lap. One by one, she pulls out black fossils and places them on the table. Opening one of the rocks, she reveals the imprint of a coiled animal. "I bought them from a merchant," she explains. "He collects the fossils along the riverbed, up near Mukti-nath. Do you know what they are?"

Samphel shakes his head. "Tell me."

"In the time of the gods, when Vishnu wandered the earth, the seas rose, and the mountains were created. Sea creatures landed at the base of the new mountains, and when they died, their bodies were trapped forever inside these rocks. The Rana kings used to put up signs threatening to cut off the hands of locals who broke the shells apart. But people still did what they wanted, of course. They even fed their ailing relatives with water steeped with these things. Nowadays, foreigners love buying them."

"I've seen these," Samphel says, leaning over the fossil imprints. "What do the Enjis do with these rocks?"

"Who knows?" Dawa says. "But you should see the looks on their faces when I open the stones!"

"You sound like Ashang Migmar," I tell Samphel. "He often wonders why foreigners want to climb a mountain just to turn around and go back down."

"All the old people sound like that," Dawa says, adding in a male voice, "They don't even burn incense or put up prayer flags at the summit. These Enjis just like to stand on top of things, take photographs of snot-nosed village children, and then they're off to another country."

"If you think about it, most of what we do wouldn't make much sense to other people either," Samphel says.

"Like filling seven silver bowls with water and lighting a butter lamp for our deities every morning," I reply.

"And then emptying the bowls at sunset before refilling them the next morning," he adds, smiling at me.

"Don't be ridiculous," Dawa says. "Deities need water like any other person. Lhamo, show him your wares. Go on."

I don't want to display my trinkets to Samphel, but I don't feel like arguing with Dawa in front of him either. Picking up my damp satchel, I pull out my bundle of friendship bracelets, necklaces, and other jewelry set with imitations of semiprecious stones.

"You made these?"

"Yes."

"Did someone teach you how?"

"No, they're nothing. Simpler than weaving carpets, which is how we used to make a living. When the tourists started to come in bigger numbers, Dawa convinced me to try weaving smaller things so I could work for myself like she does." After a moment's hesitation, I add, "I like this work better. I can choose my own patterns and colors, and just let my mind wander as I weave."

"You're exactly as I remember," he says, picking up a red and black friendship bracelet. "Can I buy this one?"

"It's my gift. We are old friends, aren't we?"

"The oldest."

Reaching out, I place the bracelet around his wrist. How smooth and pink his skin is, as if freshly scrubbed. I could admire his hands for hours.

But as I tie the knot, I notice my rough and calloused hands. If only I had my sister's hands, then I could place delicate and feminine fingers on this table, beside Samphel's. Tying the second knot quickly, I pull my hands back to my lap.

The waiters arrive with a tray of little copper bowls filled with water and lemon slices. Samphel dips his entire right hand into the bowl and squeezes the lemon between his fingers. Dawa and I copy him, shooting each other a glance and trying not to burst into laughter. When we're finished with the bowls, one of the waiters takes them away while another begins to serve the chicken curry, rice, fried beef, flatbread, and cucumber salad. Dawa digs in with gusto, but Samphel stares at his plate, moving the food here and there.

"Will you come to the camp today?" I ask. "It's changed a lot since we were children."

He puts down his spoon and looks at me. "Can we go together? To be frank, I was meaning to visit, but I'm a little nervous to go on my own."

"Nervous?" Dawa asks with wide eyes as she gnaws on a drumstick. "What for? We're not fancy people like you. Gosh, this chicken is good! I have got to get rich so I can eat chicken every day."

"Lhamo," he says, leaning toward me. "There's something I need your help with. It's about my father. Before we fled, he buried our valuables in the earth, in three trunks. In one of the trunks, he put a portrait of my mother. I never knew her. She had me out of wedlock and gave me up as soon as I was born."

"Poor thing," Dawa says.

"Every so often, I would see a new woman in our winter village and wonder if she might be my mother. Sometimes I would even hold her gaze, just to see if she'd react in some way to show that I was hers. When I found a woman I thought could be my mother, I would ask my father: Is she the one? Is that her?" Samphel says, laughing quietly to himself.

"Why didn't your father show you the portrait?" I ask, grieved to learn about his sorrow.

"He said I was too young back then to know her. But the night before we fled, as we were burying our things, my father said I could see her portrait when we came back. I had been crying at the thought of leaving, I remember this. But when I heard my father's promise, I became so happy.

Looking up at the night sky with a big smile, I thought: The sky will look just a little different when we return to this spot and dig up my mother's portrait. Back then, we all thought we would return after a little while, maybe a few weeks."

"And your father?" Dawa asks, softly.

"They said he was working in road construction in India when he died. He was hanging off the side of a hill and his rope snapped."

What a terrible death. I say a prayer.

"But it's possible that my mother's still alive. I would like to find her if that's the case. Or at least find out her identity. I know some people have retrieved the things they buried."

I'm reminded of the possessions we buried for safekeeping. Ashang Migmar insists to this day that he knows exactly where to find everything when we return.

Samphel reaches out and holds my hand. "Do you think Po Dhondup knew where my father hid our things? He would have told his own brother, right? And if that's the case, isn't it possible Po Dhondup might have passed on some information to your uncle? Lhamo, would you help me speak to Ashang Migmar? My mother might be alive. The thought of her being in front of me, looking at me . . ."

I don't know how to respond. Even Dawa is silent.

Smiling, Samphel shakes his head. "I've become emotional as I age. No matter how much time passes, I still feel like a child when I think about my mother."

"Lhamo and I are both certain that our parents are dead," Dawa says. "But if we thought one of them could be alive, we might do anything to find them."

"Ashang could know something," I say, putting my hand over his. "Let's go and see him together."

"Okay!" he says, relieved. Taking his first bite, he adds cheerfully, "Let's eat. No more sad stories, come on!"

But I've never been happier. I would do anything to ease his suffering, and now I have something to give him. Imagine the relief on his face when he sees the Saint after so many years. How happy we will be. Samphel back with me, and the Saint back with him. Our lives reinstated. Our separation will come to mean nothing. If I see our lives the way the

Saint does, within his scale of history and his knowledge of our braided fates, the last twenty years have been no more than a breath. Yes, I can see ourselves through the eyes of destiny. Even though my youth has wilted, what we are now is more honest. What we have endured, what we have borne, has prepared us for each other. This time, we won't squander the gift that is our love.

WE roll the taxi windows all the way down, and the driver blasts
the radio so loud that static buzzes alongside the music. Within a
few minutes, we've left Phewa Lake and are speeding through the hills.
The driver honks at everyone we pass—pedestrians, carts, even stray dogs.
Sometimes he just honks to the beat of the radio. Everyone turns their
head to see who is coming up the road, and some wave at us. Dawa sticks
her full arm out the window and waves back. The wind whips through
the taxi, and my hair flies around as my dress puffs up. My whole body
could fly away. Imagine Samphel watching me float above the valley,
drifting toward the mountains. Pushing the fabric down, I steal glances
at his eyes in the rearview mirror. He is staring at the river gorge.

As our taxi approaches the camp, I notice Bhu Tsering working along
the road. He gets up from the clogged ditch he is clearing and squints in
our direction, trying to see inside. Meanwhile, some of the children run
toward us, banging on the taxi, shouting, "A car has come! A car has
come!"

"Stop touching it!" cries the driver, swatting at the tiny hands patting
the shell of his vehicle. "Is this close enough?" he asks us, slowing down.

"Drive right in," Samphel orders.

I grip the headrest of Samphel's seat as the taxi turns onto the main
road while some men seated under the peepal tree stare at us.

"What do you think?" Dawa asks, shouting over the music. "Isn't our
camp looking nice these days?"

"It seems so different," Samphel remarks, gazing at the food and home-ware shops along the road. Looking back from the tea shop, a few people stretch their necks and point their prayer wheels at the taxi.

"Who is it with you?" Pema Lhakpa asks, scratching at his leg, his old bullet wounds still irritating him after all these years.

"Lhamo and Dawa are here with a foreigner," Hring-hring says.

"Looks like a Japanese," Pema Lhakpa adds, before shouting, "Make sure you bring him to the handicraft factory!"

"It's Po Dhondup's nephew," Dawa says, craning her neck out the window. "He's one of us! One of ours has become a real hero!"

Samphel lowers his gaze, as if he's embarrassed by the attention. But now, as he stares impassively at the patchwork mud and stone homes along the road, the fences made of cut-up tin cans and spare lumber, the flea-ridden goats standing in their feces, I'm not so sure. He is a wealthy person, I remind myself. This place must look poor, cramped, and suffocating to someone like him. At least my home is nice. I tidy it every day, and yesterday I placed some marigolds in a bowl of water for their fragrance. Thankfully, I have enough milk in my clay pot to make tea—butter or milk, whichever he prefers.

Of course, we need to visit Ashang's house first. I direct the driver toward the back of the camp. Soon enough, the road is too narrow for the car to continue, so we have to walk between the stone walls. Dawa heads back to her house to get dinner started but promises to come visit later. Then it's just Samphel and me, alone for the first time, and I'm suddenly nervous. He's taller than most of us by at least a head. I glance at him, noticing how his eyes travel over our homes. Whatever he feels, he does not reveal it. But something tells me he's moved, yet saddened. I'm reminded of how Teacher Mark looked at us when he first stepped onto this hill.

We enter Ashang's courtyard. He's not at his usual place under the awning, where he spins wool or recites prayers. Nor is he inside.

"Wait here," I say, before running around back to the small cornfield we planted years ago. Ashang could be somewhere in here, or on the hill overlooking the camp.

Something grazes my arm. It's Samphel—he's trailed me here and now he's trying to tell me something, though I can't hear him over the song of the frogs. I gesture for him to follow me through the stalks, which tower above us and sway here and there in unison.

"Okay, it's a bit quieter here. What were you saying?" I ask, standing close to him.

"Oh, I wanted to check where you were," he says. "The air is so clean up in the hills."

"It is. I've always loved the sweet smell here in the afternoons, when it isn't too hot." Looking for something else to say, I tell Samphel about our new monastery. "It's under construction on the other side of the camp."

"I don't remember the old monastery."

"Oh, that's right. It was built the year after you stayed with us. Our Rinpoche was a great teacher from Ngari. He came here to rebuild his monastery in exile after it was razed by the Gyami. Everyone was so happy to have him with us, and many families sent their youngest boys to become monks. When our Rinpoche passed a few years ago, he remained seated in a meditative pose for three whole days after his last breath. We even saw footprints in his cremated ashes pointing to the direction of his reincarnation. They're still looking for the child. Hopefully, the shrine will be finished by the time we find him again, and then our hearts can rest easy." Laughing, I add, "Ashang Migmar kept remarking that he wished we had a boy in our family so one of us could don the robe."

"I'm glad he didn't send either of you," Samphel says. "Where is your sister, by the way?"

"Tenkyi's in the capital," I say, staring at the ground. "Last year, she came back to the camp for a little while. She wasn't well."

"Was it serious?"

I struggle to find the words, even now, to address my sister's condition.

"Tenkyi has always had hardships, but she is good at hiding them. Sometimes, I think people only want to see her talents. They want her to be proof of our promise. It's a heavy burden for any person to carry, don't you think?"

"Yes, but it doesn't matter what other people want. None of them will help you when it matters. We must fend for ourselves. Each of us has to live our own life."

"Maybe you're right," I say, unsure of his meaning. "Still, I didn't want her to leave the camp again, but you know Tenkyi. She left as soon as she could."

"Is she married?"

"She isn't. But I am." He says nothing. The longer I waited to admit it, the worse I would look. "My husband isn't around these days," I add.

"I'm saddened to hear that."

"Are you? The last time Tashi came home, he drank two bottles of rakshi, ran naked through the camp, and fell asleep wrapped in a grass mat."

"In that case, I should reconsider my words."

In another month, we'll harvest the corn and I'll be thinking of this moment. Even months later, when these stalks are completely dry and tangled on the ground, when our cows come to feed on them, I'll remember how we stood here. I'll remember the sweet smell of the air and how it felt to stand so close. Already, I feel a longing for this day. But he is still here. Why don't I speak to him in frank terms? Why don't I ask if he will stay with me?

"Where do you think Ashang went?" Samphel asks, reminding me of the reason we're in the field.

"Let's check at home again."

When we enter the courtyard, we spot my uncle spreading old rice on the ground for birds. While he and Samphel take their seats on some carpets under the awning, I head inside to prepare a fresh thermos of tea. I want it to be the best cup of tea Samphel has ever had, and it looks promising up until the point when I need to add butter. But as soon as I open the plastic bag, it releases a rancid smell from the dark-yellow block. Ashang is losing his sense of smell, along with his eyesight. So it will be sweet milk tea.

Carefully, I tear open a pack of biscuits, arranging and rearranging them on a plate so they look nice. When I emerge with the tray of sweet tea and biscuits, my uncle is staring at Samphel with red, misty eyes.

"I look at your face," Ashang says, "and I see your uncle. My goodness . . ."

"You were a friend to him," Samphel replies.

"The day he first came to our tent, he looked so tall and impressive. I thought he was one of the Chushi Gangdruk fighters looking for food.

But then, he was all alone, wasn't he? His whole family had died—except for you and your father, anyway. And just as soon as he found you, he died."

"You oversaw his funeral rites. I will never forget that."

"Your uncle always said that we did him a favor by letting him camp with us. The truth is we survived because of him. Lhamo's father was sick and we would have starved without an extra hand. And if it wasn't for the Saint . . . oh dear," Ashang says, looking distressed as he always does when the Saint comes up.

But Samphel has other concerns. "In the time you knew my uncle," he says, "did he ever tell you about the things my father buried?"

"He buried his things, too? What a pity . . ."

"Did my uncle ever mention it?"

"Let me think . . ."

"Anything."

"Your uncle's village was in the east. It was bombed out. Completely flattened by those godless soldiers. He said they used our prayer books for toilet paper . . . Om mani padme hum, what barbarians."

"But I'm speaking of my father's village, not my uncle's. Please try to remember. He must have told you something."

"Even if Po Dhondup—tut-tut, I shouldn't say his name—even if the deceased said something to me, it would be difficult to find buried things without more information. Then there's the matter of the looters too. Bhuchung's father snuck back two years ago to dig up their belongings. He remembered the exact spot, just as I do for our things. Bhuchung's father dug for a week but the ground was completely barren. He thought the looters might have stolen their things. But maybe he did not bury them well. Lhamo's father and I dug very deep into the earth. I'm sure our things are still there . . ." Ashang drifts off, scratching at his head.

Most of the men in the camp have cut their hair over the years, but my uncle still refuses, saying he won't return home with short hair. And because he insists on keeping his long plaits, weaving in a black strip of cloth and coral stones, he cannot wash them enough to keep the lice away.

"What about my uncle's belongings?" Samphel asks. "Perhaps he kept a map?"

"Ask Po Rithar," Ashang Migmar replies, now trying to sound hopeful. "He might know. He worked in the camp office back then."

"I'll take you there," I offer. "I have some tea leaves I wanted to give him anyway."

As I retrieve a brick of tea from inside, Ashang comes in and takes my arm. "Lhamo, I didn't have it in me to tell him that I failed to keep the ku safe. His uncle would never forgive me."

"I'll explain everything," I say.

"It's my fault for not keeping the Saint with us . . . it broke this old man's heart to hear the boy's pleading."

"Don't worry. He'll be alright."

"Be careful with him," Ashang adds, whispering. "There's something not right with him. To be so fixated on a hopeless dream . . . It's not right."

SAMPHEL FOLLOWS ME through the camp's narrow lanes the same way he did years ago, though now, his hair is peppered gray and his skin is so fair it's nearly transparent. And whereas my skin is a solidly deep-brown shade, his is marked with blue veins and gatherings of blood. Each time I close my eyes, I sense his gaze on me and remember how I felt standing before him the first time we met, how my entire body shook as though something inside me needed to be dislodged. Back then, I did not have the words to express my feelings, but I have them now. Though I didn't study for more than a few years, I have heard a hundred love stories from my uncle and seen my share of Indian films. And I have been married to the wrong man. Through that rite of passage, I broke that man and broke myself, and because of this, I know myself as a story in the mouths of others. On this hill, they still speak of my marriage with pity. They utter the phrase "Where is Tashi these days?" at least once a week, but they no longer lament my strangeness. To them, I am settled, spoken for, and thus understood in a way. There are many unhappy pairings in every valley, they say, though thankfully, my husband only bothers me a few times a year. But tonight, another life appears before me, gleaming so brightly. I just need to say the words.

In silence, we walk under a pink and orange sky, which grumbles deep in its belly while the crickets and frogs have begun their night songs. The camp feels empty because most people have retreated indoors for dinner and evening prayers. There's another gentle rumble in the sky, and I hope it rains, just like the day Samphel described from our childhood, when we bathed passing a bar of soap between us. To the low, setting sky, I say, Come on. Let down all the water you've carried to us. Send everyone else inside, then Samphel and I will run through the rain, down into the gorge, and back to the beginning.

But the sky is mute again. Ahead, a single line of cloud disintegrates over our path. This road I walk on every day has never felt so short.

Po Rithar's brick home appears to our right. His granddaughter is outside, stalking a pair of chickens.

"Yangzo, is Popo home?" I ask from the fence.

She looks over, nods, and resumes her pursuit of the chicken. I push past the gate, and we walk up the stone path to an open doorway with a curtain billowing in the breeze. Po Rithar is on the far bed, his forehead covered with a damp, pink washcloth. He has been sick for three years, but the cause is always changing. If it's not jaundice or his kidney stones, it's his stomach.

"Po Rithar, it's Lhamo."

"Yes, there you are," he says, peering up from beneath the cloth. "Did your uncle get some of Datsing's butter? A good batch this round, everyone says. Almost tastes the way it did back home. The last batch cost Datsing badly."

"I'll remind him. I brought you a block of tea," I say, adding, "I also brought Samphel. You remember him? Po Dhondup's nephew."

"Nephew, did you say? Come closer."

Samphel sits on the edge of the bed and lowers his face so Po Rithar can examine it.

"What did your uncle eat?" Po Rithar asks.

"What do you mean?"

"On the walk back to our camp. He must have eaten something rotten. He could not have died otherwise. My son died after that same journey, but he was always so thin."

I decide to intervene. "Samphel has a few questions for you. My uncle says that if anyone knows the answers, it's you."

"Lhamo, there's tea in the thermos," Po Rithar says.

Going into the kitchen, I pull up the cork and swirl the lukewarm tea. The thick broth glistens in the bottle's dark mouth, while stray tea leaves float and stick to its wall.

"There's too much butter in this. How can you swallow it?"

"The young ones don't like butter," he quips.

Taking the thermos to the tap, I add a little water to thin it out, and run the tea through a sieve one more time. It's going to be drinkable but not what I wish to serve. As I work, I look into the main room every so often. The two men are sitting with their heads leaning toward each other, speaking in low voices. When I return with the thermos and pour three cups, Samphel is tracing his fingers on the bed, marking the lines of a river that splits into three tributaries.

I take a glance at the lines he has drawn in the blanket. "Try this," I say, lifting a cup to Po Rithar, then one to Samphel. Po Rithar takes a sip and promptly returns his gaze to the bed and the imaginary river they're discussing. But Samphel gives me a gentle nod after his first sip.

"It's here, between these streams," he says to Po Rithar.

"That can't be. The ground would be too unstable."

"No, I remember it well. There was water flowing all around me," Samphel says.

"He has a remarkable memory," I tell Po Rithar.

"Hmm," he replies, frowning. "Talk to Dhargye in the capital. He has people inside who can get things out. Go to his house, be useful, and earn his trust. Mention my name, but don't ask for anything right away. You remember the directions I gave? He doesn't live among our kind."

"Yes, but what can he know?" Samphel asks.

"About your father's things? Nothing! But if there's still anything back home, he can get it out."

It's dark when we leave Po Rithar. Samphel and I stand by the gate, facing each other's silhouettes as clouds move quickly above us. The moon is full and luminous, lending a pale glow to our bodies.

"Do you have what you need now?" I ask, speaking quietly so no one will hear.

"I don't know if it's even possible to go back, never mind digging around in the earth. Maybe this is just a foolish dream."

"Many people buried their things underground."

"Has anyone ever managed to find them again?"

"Even if they did, perhaps they would not tell anyone."

"Why not?" he asks.

"There are many reasons to keep quiet about something like that,"
I say.

A lone goat walks by, his bell and footsteps providing cover for our
conversation—or what I have to say next.

"I have something of yours."

3

Do you want butter tea or sweet tea?" I ask, pulling out a pot.
He smiles and replies, "You'll turn my blood into tea. Let's try your butter tea."

"It's good. Better than what I could offer you at Ashang's or Po Rithar's," I say. "I promise."

With a drag of the match and a turn of the kerosene lighter, the stove ignites. "It's so easy to start a fire nowadays. Do you remember how hard it used to be?"

Samphel nods, running his hands over my sheets. Tashi's bed is covered with yarn and imitation stones, so Samphel sits on my bed. The room is dark but for the stove and two butter lamps flickering on the altar. And although the moon is bright tonight, I keep the curtains closed. We can hear a couple of men talking outside, and just around the corner a few children are hopping back and forth through a jump rope that slaps the ground in a steady rhythm. If anyone saw him come into my house at this hour, I will hear about it for the next year.

I drop a handful of tea in the bubbling water. The leaves spin in the pot, instantly flooding the room with a sweet aroma.

He's gazing up at the wooden rafters now.

"What is it?" I ask.

"You have flowers looking down at you."

He's right. Two dandelion flowers have dropped through the rusted holes in the tin.

"I'm embarrassed."

"No, it's perfect. I don't keep any flowers where I live."

"What is your home like?"

"Oh, it's nothing special."

"Describe it to me." He must know why I'm asking this. He must know I want to imagine where he sleeps, where he lets his face relax without any self-consciousness.

"It's a two-room flat in Thamel. I'm surrounded by tourists all day. As for the flat itself, everything was already there from the landlords. I just moved in with my clothes. I haven't given it much attention. I don't have the talent for it like you do."

"You're making fun," I say, feeling shy.

Two leaves spin into each other and stick, each seizing the other in the dizzying storm of rich broth.

"It's true! I would have never pictured your place like this specifically, but now that I'm here, it's unmistakably yours. Everything I see here, it's like I'm looking at you." Then he peers up at my roof again.

Of course, I think. Of course, he can sense it. Even if he can't speak to it yet, he knows something is up there. Not just the weeds looking down on us. The Saint is just above Samphel, to his left, sitting in a tin can tucked beneath the rafters. For years, I've known this moment would come. Long before my uncle spoke about offering the ku to a monastery, perhaps even before Samphel and I were separated by my illness.

In secret, I acted. I waited.

"I've always loved the sound of rain on tin roofs," he says.

"Me too. I sleep better in the rainy season because of it, and the mist and wind. Though Ashang's house is even better because you can feel the breeze from the gorge."

After pouring the tea and milk into a long wooden churner, I toss in a dollop of butter and a handful of salt, and begin to push and pull the handle down and up. The work of churning against the resistance of the tea and the air in the container requires my entire body, and my house fills with the sound of tea roaring through a chamber. Beads of sweat run down the sides of my face before long. When I finish, I place the thermos on the ground, raise the churner up to my shoulders, and pour the broth down the small mouth of the thermos. The tea smells perfect. Sweet yet salty. Light and filling at the same time.

"Now the flatbread. Almost done," I say, squatting down again.

He grasps my hand. "No, wait. Just sit here. Tell me what you wanted to show me."

Sitting down, I feel again how much I've longed to be near him all day.

"I wanted to come back here so many times," he says.

"You came at the right time," I say jovially.

His hand is shaking. I put my hand over his, to ease his heart and my own. I want to tell him that there's nothing to hide between us. But words will not be enough to express everything I have to say. No, I will show him.

Standing on Tashi's bed, I reach into the beams, moving my hands along the rough wood until I feel the cool metal. I bring down the dusty tin can, and, after wiping it clean with my sleeve, I pull the cover off. Tucked inside the old powder milk can, the Saint's ku is wrapped in layers of silk khatas.

"This is yours," I tell him, extending my arms.

He receives the tin can and looks inside. Without a word, he places the can on the small table by the bed. As he turns to me, he frowns in confusion. "What is this? My uncle's ku?"

"We kept the ku here after everything happened. Then Ashang wanted to offer it to a monastery far away, but I always knew this belonged with you. On the night of my wedding, I snuck out and took the ku. I knew that someday, you would come back, and I would return the Nameless Saint to you."

He's quiet again as his eyes run over the Saint. "When I first saw this ku, I thought it was ugly. A mistake. This emaciated man with his grotesque expression. I didn't understand why anyone would even make this ku. Or why people in this camp worshipped him."

I'm taken aback by his candor. But it's true. I too was alarmed the first time I saw the Saint. "And now?" I ask.

"Now I've lived a few years. I've seen what life holds. Even in moments of happiness, sorrow is always there. Always. So when I look at this little ku now, I no longer see ugliness. Instead, I see the truth. A being who shows me what it feels like to be alive." He gazes at me and says, "But I can't take this."

"You must," I say, emptying my woolen bag. "Here, you can take the ku in this."

Samphel admires the design on the side of the bag. "The endless knot," he says.

"No beginning and no end."

"Did you weave this bag?" he asks.

"Yes," I say. "So you mustn't turn down my gift."

Staring at the Nameless Saint, he says, "I will take this because it's from you. Because no one has ever cared for me in this way." His voice cracks as he looks away.

"I've upset you," I say. I want to make him smile again, to make him understand that our lives can be different.

"No, no. I'm upset with myself. With my own uselessness. At least when I was young, I could spin new dreams. Once I thought that we would return home together. I saw it. I saw you riding a horse while I churned the cheese."

"You did say that," I recall, a brief sting inside my chest.

"Now all of my dreams look backward. I wouldn't even call them dreams. Just old words, echoing endlessly in my mind. This idea of seeing my mother's face . . ." He laughs again, softly this time. "Isn't that silly? I doubt she's still alive. She would be around your uncle's age. What if she's alone like me?"

"Yes, I think that's possible," I say.

Now an image comes to me. So clear and vivid it seems like a memory. Samphel and I are on a wide flat plain, walking together. Between us, there's a young woman. I don't recognize her, but I feel I know her. To our side, enormous mountains stretch up to a deep blue sky. Our steps are slow, our breathing labored. We are very tired. But we are also relieved, for we have reached the end of a very long journey. Then a sudden gust of wind comes. It lifts me off the ground, up and up.

"What is it?" he asks.

I'm unsure of what to say after such a strange sight. Instead, I take his hand, which is soft and cold, and whisper, "Samphel, there's so much I want to say to you."

"Then tell me all of it," he replies.

Slowly, I place his hand inside the wrap of my dress, just above my chest. He looks up at me, startled. He is defenseless, I think. A man with money and an education. Strong-willed and capable enough to start over again and again. But for now, he is so open, submitting. But not like Tashi with his half-closed eyes, who feels farthest from me when we are in bed. With Samphel, I am startled by my own courage. I stand to undress and then I guide him down onto the bed. I think of the tea leaves, spinning until they lock together. Impossibly, inevitably.

4

Just before daybreak, I rise to meet Dawa by the main road. This is our daily routine for heading to Phewa Lake together. As I walk through the blue-black camp, a few shadows move here and there, tending to their morning tasks. Even though some of the houses have electricity, most of us still prefer to work in the dark at first, reaching for our small jugs of water by touch, starting the stove by memory.

Dawa is standing on a boulder, craning her neck to see if any buses are coming.

"Any luck?" I ask.

"At this hour? After yesterday, you're starting to believe in all kinds of miracles. Where is your hero, anyway?"

I stifle a smile. "Lakeside. He invited me to breakfast at his hotel. Then we'll spend the day together."

"Just like in the films!" she says, sighing. "So you're not chasing tourists with me today?"

"Not today."

We set off on foot as usual. The road is quiet except for the constant drone of the river and an owl hooting somewhere in the hills. Half an hour later, an old villager crosses our path, walking in the opposite direction. He's as thin as a sprig of wild grass, barefoot, and carries a large wicker basket full of bricks on his back.

"Grandfather," Dawa says, "have you seen any buses?"

"Not this morning, Little Sister," he replies, walking uphill at a steady pace. He keeps his head down, trying to stop the basket strap from slipping off his forehead. "Where are you girls going?"

"Phewa Tal," I say, walking backward to stay with him. "You haven't seen any cars heading our way?"

"Maybe one passed me." He stops suddenly by us. "You look like a singer in that blue dress."

My dress is pink. Dawa laughs, and we let the old man walk on in peace. He turns a corner and disappears from view.

Just then, a donkey cart carrying a family comes rattling down the hill. The driver slows so we can hop on. With us on the cart is a father, a tiny grandmother who seems tough enough to live another hundred years, and a teenaged girl dressed in a bridal outfit.

"Ah ha, what a beautiful dress," Dawa says, holding the bride's red skirt and running her fingers over the gold trim.

"Hear that?" the grandmother says to the girl, who keeps her gaze on the horizon. "She cried all morning."

"Poor thing. She will probably just miss you," Dawa says.

The grandmother looks at Dawa. "Course she will miss me. But that's our fate as women. When I arrived at my new home, I cried for days. I even ran away for a little while," she says, glumly.

I admire the girl's ornaments: a large gold nose ring the size of a small fist and a red translucent veil clasped firmly at the crown of her head. Her father, too, is looking at her in silence. Deep lines run in many directions across his face, like a crumpled piece of paper. He stares out at the gorge for the rest of the trip. Meanwhile, the bride is dripping sweat all over her outfit, creating dark patches that spread across her red petticoat.

"Where is your new home?" I ask.

"I don't know," the girl says.

"Not too far," the grandmother replies.

The bride's right earring catches the rising sun, creating such a bright reflection that I turn away. When I turn back, a poor, sweating, morose bride meets my gaze for the first time. Her small body is tossed left and right, back and forth, as she moves slowly away from her childhood home. That glint of gold makes me feel strange. Is this a bad omen?

"What's the matter?" Dawa asks. "You had a strange expression just now."

At the tip of Phewa Tal, Dawa and I hop off, waving at the bride as the cart travels onward. We stop at a few stores along the main road, asking for directions to Mountain View Hotel. Eventually, we reach a new five-story building painted light blue.

"Looks like heaven," Dawa says.

We pass through the gates and stand before the hotel with its beautiful water fountain and garden that edges the lake. This is the kind of hotel where only foreigners can afford to stay. Through a set of double windows, we see a young, yellow-haired boy sitting at a table, his long legs stretched out. He's reading a thick, tattered book. As if he senses people watching him, the young man looks up and notices us on the lawn, staring like village children.

"Oh, he saw us!" I say.

"Yes, he saw us. We're not mosquitoes! What's the matter with you?"

"Well, let's go inside then," I say. "Samphel's waiting."

"Me? Why would I go in there? I'll wait out here."

"I can't go in alone!"

"They're not going to let us *both* in." Even Dawa has lost her nerve before this fancy hotel.

"Alright, hold my bag." I fix my hair and brush the dust off my dress, all the while imagining how the foreigners will stare at me, wondering why this trinket peddler is on the premises. The hotel workers might push me out before I even reach the reception area. What if Samphel shows up just as the workers tell me to leave? He would see me treated like a beggar. He would see me as they do. No, it's impossible for me to go inside.

"Dawa, please go and bring him to me. I'm begging you."

My friend sighs in exasperation but ultimately agrees. I tell her to ask for a guest named Samphel Gyatso. When he comes down, Dawa should tell him to head to the shore where the fishermen dock their boats. We'll meet there, like the couples I've watched over the years. We'll rent a little rowboat and paddle around the lake, dragging our fingertips along the film of the water, splashing each other, and feeling such relief and joy that our fates have finally brought us back together.

I'M ONLY PART way to the docked boats at Phewa Lake when Dawa comes running up behind me, her plaits coming loose.

"He's gone! Lhamo, he's gone!"

"What do you mean?"

"Samphel paid the bill an hour ago and left the hotel. No one knows where he went, or even which direction he turned when he walked out the door."

"He must have gone to the camp," I reason. "Did he mention the camp to the hotel?"

"I didn't ask . . ." Dawa says.

"Why didn't you ask them that?" I ask, looking up the street at an approaching taxi. "I'll take a taxi back to the camp. He's probably on his way there now. How much cash do you have?" I pull out my pouch and start counting the bills.

"Lhamo . . ." Dawa says, giving me a pitying look as if I were missing some obvious fact.

"Never mind, I have enough. I'll see you later."

As I approach the taxi, it slows briefly to get a look at me before carrying on. Two more taxis pass by, taking glances at me before speeding away. I have no choice but to walk to the nearby bus station. When I reach the road before the station, I wait for a momentary lull in traffic.

That's when I spot him, sitting in a lime-green tourist bus. I climb onto a low stone wall to get a better view and see if it's really him. He's reading something, a newspaper. A neutral, almost contented expression on his face. Outside the mostly empty bus, a young ticket seller shouts at the top of his lungs, "Express bus deluxe deluxe! All the way to Kathmandu! Jump on, jump on!"

Two black-haired foreigners run up and board the bus, relief washing over their faces. They select their seats, three rows in front of Samphel, whose face is cut almost perfectly in half by the shadow of a curtain. His lips are lit by sunlight, slightly parted and slack. He said, in the morning. He said, let's meet then.

The engine starts. Suddenly, everything rattles—the bus, the wall beneath my feet, even my teeth.

"Look at me," I say, staring at him. "Look at me."

The bus takes a reckless loop around the station before it comes to the main road and drives away from me. If I run now, I might still be able to catch him. Instead, I hop off the wall and walk slowly, gingerly, into a small alley, as if my bones might break.

The bus moves farther away, and I think I hear someone call my name. I won't look back. Even if he's shouting for me, I won't turn my head. Ghosts play tricks on the weak. Tenkyi used to tell me this. They call people's names and consume the ones who answer. Why? I asked. Because only the weak and stupid reply to the call of a stranger.

"BACK SO SOON?"

Ashang Migmar is in the courtyard, sitting behind my wooden spinner with a large bundle of raw wool. Streaks of sweat line his face and neck as he slowly spins the cloud of wool into a long thread.

"I finished early," I say and pat my uncle's forehead with a towel. Why doesn't he take care of himself? His hair is tangled at the ends, and his white undershirt is stained with a brown ring around the neck.

I sit beside him and begin to reroll a ball of wool that has several loose bits hanging out here and there. Ashang isn't as careful with his work as he used to be.

"Makes it harder for us if these aren't nice and neat," I say.

"Doesn't look so bad, does it? I keep rubbing my eyes to see a little better, ack."

I work quickly at first, unraveling the ball of wool an arm's length at a time. The sun is nearing its peak. Strange that so much has already happened, and it isn't even lunchtime. My head feels warm, though the rest of my body is numb. With hardly any clouds in the sky, the sun is beating down on this hill. I should wash the rice, but not before sorting it for insects and stones. Then I need to pick out ripened cabbage in the back garden, searching for the leaves that haven't been eaten by goats and caterpillars. Ashang has a pile of dirty clothes to wash, as do I. Once the rice is boiling, but before I put the cabbage on, I'll take the clothes to the larger tap in the middle of the camp and soak everything. If the weather holds up, I'll dry the clothes after lunch. Ashang's prayer altar needs cleaning too. The offering bowls are turning black with tarnish. I can shine them with oil after drying the clothes. Then I'll prepare dinner for us and return to my home afterward to wash the dishes Samphel and I used. The tasks are piling up. I feel weary. Rolling the ball of wool, I see that my work is sloppy, worse than my uncle's.

"So you went to see Samphel?" Ashang asks, continuing to spin and pull threads from the wool.

I put my hands on my knees to stop them from shaking. I pretend not to hear my uncle. Then we resume our work in silence. My fingers have lost their grip, and I have to slump against the house to stay upright.

"It's just as well," he says at last. "It's not right to want something that much."

I don't know if my uncle means this for Samphel or for me. It doesn't matter. Samphel must be halfway to Mugling by now. By evening, he'll be back at the capital with the statue of the Saint, then on his way to meet Dhargye, the man who will help him retrieve his mother's portrait. Everything he wanted, he got. All in just one day.

"I'll make cabbage for lunch once we're finished here," I tell my uncle.

"Right, I'll pick up some buffalo meat for dinner. Let's eat outside tonight."

The last time Ashang bought buff was for my wedding. With the help of friends, my uncle had managed to raise enough money to hold a feast for three nights. It's the wedding of my eldest daughter, he said over and over.

I look into my uncle's eyes, wanting him to say something that might relieve my pain. He has a cataract that keeps his right eye almost completely closed, while a constant stream of mucus flows from the inner corner. I need to buy him sunglasses.

"I've got an idea," he says. "I should do something about my hair."

"Don't make me laugh." For nearly twenty-five years, my uncle has kept his long braids. How many mornings have I watched him wrap his braid around his head and tuck the ends into his crown of hair?

"Go get a razor."

"Stop teasing me."

"My hands aren't steady enough for me to shave my own head," he says.

My uncle is serious. I get up slowly, pressing against the wall for support, and gather a razor and comb from inside. When I return, Ashang has folded up the carpet and is sitting on the bare ground. As I stand above him, he releases his plaits. The braids unravel easily, the strands of his thin gray hair slipping apart. I can see bare patches of his scalp between his locks. He pulls out a black sash that was woven into his hair along with two pieces of coral. Then Ashang takes the comb from me and runs it carefully through his hair. He has always combed as gently as he could so he would not lose more hair. Even now, as he is about to shave it all away, he combs just as slowly, rolling the fallen hair into a ball to discard so birds or insects won't mistakenly eat it and choke. Next, Ashang dampens his hair with some water and rubs in a little shampoo, forming a lather on his scalp.

"You really want to do this?" I ask.

He grunts. I lower the blade onto the crown of his head and pull back. The first swipe across the bumpy surface. I keep going. The hair falls easily down my arm, onto the ground as more and more of his scalp comes into view. I'm struck by the paleness of it, so different from the brown skin of his face and body. I realize that this is a part of my uncle no one has seen in many decades. It will be years before his hair grows back, and much longer before he can weave the sash and coral stones into his braids. Why is he doing this? My uncle, who kept his plaits for over thirty years in this country, longer than any other man in the camp. My uncle, who promised he would return to his pastures to die, with his hair long and braided.

Then I nick his scalp. Blood collects in a small pool and rolls down his scalp. Seeing the red stream slip along his right ear and onto the dusty ground, I let myself cry for the first time in this strange day.

5

A few days later, Tashi turns up at my door with a backpack slung around his shoulder. Standing inside our home, he seems ill at ease as he looks for a place to sit. Our beds are separated, and his is covered with weaving tools.

"You can sit on my bed," I motion to him from the door.

"Lhamo," he says, reaching out his hand as he sits. "I know you're wondering where I went."

I remain standing at a distance. "Did you run out of money?"

"No, no, nothing like that. I've been in Namche, talking to some Sherpas about the trekking business."

His pupils are tinged yellow, and his right hand trembles as it rests on his knee. Namche has a few liquor houses and enough strangers passing through to hold his attention for a few months.

"The men I've met are experienced," he says, "not like the jokers from two years ago. These guys have been guides on Annapurna, Everest, Manaslu."

"Not this again," I groan. "It's been six years, Tashi. If you haven't done it by now . . ."

"Lhamo, it's not that simple. It's not like weaving some trinkets and selling them at Phewa Tal. This is much harder. There are permits and relationships with hotels and travel agents to sort through."

"My simple business has kept us going for years—"

"But don't you want more?" he asks, rising to come near to me. "You're thirty-six and I'm nearly forty. We should have a child. Start a family.

I'm more than ready for all of that. I just need to know you still have faith in me."

He waits for me to reply, his dark eyes framed by many new wrinkles. The last few years have been hard on Tashi's body. His high cheeks have sunken in; his skin is sallow and loose on his thin frame. But his eyes are still tender, and his voice reaches into my past. A wave of tenderness rises in me. Even now, I desire him.

"I do have faith in you," I say.

"There. That wasn't so hard, was it?" Tashi smiles, eyes shining with hope.

FOUR MONTHS AFTER my monthly bleeding stops, a letter arrives at the camp administrative building in my name. It's from Samphel. The script is written in formal cursive, which I cannot read. But I admire the lines, which are even more elegant and confident than Tenkyi's penmanship. Despite everything, I cannot help but love the sight of Samphel's handwriting.

With Dawa's assistance, I'm able to decipher parts of the letter. But as its meaning slowly comes into focus, I begin to feel desperate. What we can read is disappointing—formal, distant, far from what I had imagined. He says nothing of our time together, nothing about his sudden departure. But the final words are too difficult to parse, even for Dawa. My only remaining option is to copy the lines on a separate piece of paper to maintain some privacy, and ask Gen Lobsang for his help.

It takes Gen Lobsang no time at all to read the script. He glances at the page and says with a shrug, "It's a typical ending to a letter. A farewell."

"You're sure, Genla?" I ask.

"I ran into Tashi the other day," he says, his gray eyebrows furrowing. "Said he was staying in the center of town, at a tea house behind a movie hall."

"He comes and goes as he pleases. I didn't change the locks on him."

"He didn't seem well. If you want, I can bring him back, have a good talk with him."

"That's not necessary, Genla," I say, slipping on my shoes by the door. "Thank you. I'll leave you now."

I turn and walk through the field, my mind spinning off in many directions at once. The letter is still in the fold of my chupa. Its meaning now so plain and definitive. A final farewell, written in the voice of a stranger. The words we exchanged in my home were meaningless. Yet a part of me thinks he would not have written without cause. That is not how Samphel works. I wonder if he learned that Tashi left again, and maybe this is his way of reopening things between us. It is a small possibility, but like a gem refracting a glow on its admirer, it soothes me. I want to believe that he is seeking me out, in his own way. After all, a letter is a keepsake. A solid thing I can hold, which he also held. It lets me know that we are still in each other's lives. That we can still speak to each other, even if our words are restrained.

But this is, yet again, another fantasy of my own making. Now that I'm having a child, I must live in the reality of my circumstances. I think about Tashi, the only other person who knows of my pregnancy. He caught on when I ran out to the gutter a few weeks ago, nauseated from the smell of sweet milk tea. I had been like that for a month at least. And Tashi and I have not lain together for nearly a year, perhaps two. But instead of questioning me or storming off for another long stretch, Tashi adopted a new stance. For a few nights every week, he stayed elsewhere. I did not ask him where, and he didn't hide it either. It was almost as if he were daring me to ask. Among the gambling men in the camp, Dawa tells me that Tashi now speaks openly of his other women.

Approaching my home, I hear barking. Mo Yutok is at the bottom of the hill, surrounded by a group of dogs. She's feeding them old flatbread and seemingly trying to make sure the smallest dogs get a few bites. Meanwhile, some crows sit along the hill's gentle slope, waiting for their turn. I stare at Mo Yutok's small, hunched frame, her thin wrists, her long gray plaited hair. A strange and intricate sorrow gathers in my chest. She is the closest thing I have to a mother. And I have filled some hole for her as well, all these years after her daughter's passing. When I think back on my life so far, there have been many women who bore terrible losses—Shumo Yangsel, Gen Lobsang's mother—and who sought to care for me as an adopted daughter. In the end, this may be how we survive. Collecting the shards of ourselves and offering them with honesty to someone else. So I walk up to Mo Yutok, take her hand, and tell her about my baby.

I ASK TO give birth without being cut up, but the doctor says no. He will not tell me why, and I am too afraid to ask again. The room is filled with masked people who move quickly around me as they speak words that I don't know. They put their hands on my belly, pressing a few times. I groan in pain and stare at the tops of their heads. Something cold spreads across my stomach and drips between my thighs. A needle shoots into my veins, and something is lowered onto my nose and mouth. It's a mask with flowing air. I pray to Cherensig, but my mind becomes hazy and my limbs grow heavy. I visualize the Nameless Saint watching over me. His protective glow streams onto my body. Then, no part of me can move. Even my eyes are shut. Only sound remains. A machine beeps, and metal things clang against each other. Then silence.

When my eyes open, a fire rages through my torso. Something has reached deep inside me, taken my baby out, and stitched a line up to my belly button. In the room, I see vague forms. I hear coughs and footsteps. It's difficult to breathe or speak, so I moan for help. Dawa and Ashang Migmar come into view, rising from their seats. They begin opening thermoses of food. They say Tashi has stayed away, but he will come around. The baby, I manage to say. The baby girl is fine, Ashang tells me. She's with the nurse. Something comes over me. I cry for my mother.

The next morning, I am still too weak to carry my child, so Dawa takes her while Ashang wheels me to a taxi and lifts me into the back. In the car, I can hold my baby close to me for the first time. She is the only thing that makes me happy. The drive is bumpy and somewhere along the rocky hills, my stitches come apart. Wrenching pain shoots through me as blood soaks my dress. When I see the camp, I cry in relief. But there is a commotion outside the taxi. Mo Yutok takes the baby, and Ashang tells me I should return to the hospital with Dawa. I beg to remain, but no one listens.

Now I sleep in a room with four other patients while yellow fluids are drained from me and clear fluid is pumped into my arm. The hospital machines sing in a rhythm of beeps. I hear them night and day. But there are other sounds at night, when I'm the only patient awake, when the nurses are away. They're faint at first, but grow louder as I pay attention. A ringing hand bell, a low murmur of prayers, and a woman chanting.

Ama sees me across the crowd. She knows that I also need help. Reaching down to her table, she takes her mirror out, places it on the ground, and kicks it. The mirror slides for a long time. It passes over many mountains, desert canyons, and forests. It crosses many years. Then it stops, clinking against the metal leg of my bed. I try to push myself up, but my stomach cannot keep me upright. Lying back, I shuffle my body to the edge of my bed. I reach my arm down and feel around the floor. The plastic tubes pull at my skin, but I cannot stop now. My fingers grasp the mirror and pull it up to me. Moonlight streams through the window, shining on Ama's mirror, making it bright as a second moon. I will see what it reflects back. I will finally know what it has to show me. My hand shakes, but I manage to keep my grip. Tilting the surface, I focus my eyes.

What I see is a girl with wind-burned cheeks and matted hair. Far in the distance, high up in a sheer mountain full of caves, there is a boy. He stands all alone at the mouth of the highest cave. At first I think he's staring into the horizon, but as I focus my eyes, it's clear that he is looking at the girl.

Is this my past or my future? I cannot tell. All I know is that Samphel and I aren't finished with each other.

SAMPHEL

I

Kathmandu, Nepal

2012

IT isn't in my nature to leave things alone. But twenty years ago, on the day I moved into this house, I stood here in the garden before a sickly banana tree and decided to let it stand. Baji, my old gardener, said, "Banana trees are like illnesses. Best to leave them alone or they'll only spread." Over the next year, the garden flourished under Baji's care, and that crooked little tree righted its posture and sprouted several more kin. Now everything in the garden—the rhododendrons, the marigolds, the white and pink rose bushes—has dwindled except for the banana trees.

The wind breaks and chooses a new course, shaking the bushes along the perimeter and releasing a small shower in my direction. Wiping the drops from my face, I take a sip of whiskey. Baji didn't know that the banana tree reminded me of those unhappy months after I ran from the monastery without a word, when I decided that I could not spend my life meditating on metaphysics while ignoring the wretchedness of my existence. Instead, I had wanted to acquire a new place in the world, in the order of things. I wanted meat every day, hot showers, my clothes pressed and washed by someone else. And yet, there I was, eating stolen bananas on the side of the road. Even when I did manage to get a free meal at a temple, they were served on banana leaves. Sitting on the ground in a long line of the devout and destitute, I would watch the rice, daal, and vegetables drop on the wide leaves. Eating quickly to make room for the next helping, I would lap up the sauces before they ran onto the dusty floor. Now, all these years later, even though I'm poorer than I was as a runaway monk, I'm still surrounded by these lazy, yielding leaves.

The wicker chair crackles as I lean back, rest my head, and close my eyes.

"Sir! Sir!" Parvati shouts from somewhere inside the house.

The light flashes on in the stairway, up along three floors of staggered verandas and windows. She must be running up to my room. Sounding the alarms? The French diplomat's residence next door was ransacked last month in the middle of the night. Mine is probably due for a visit. This pale, beautiful house. My most visible achievement. Bought in cash as a surprise for both Sonam and her daughter, Cheche. This quiet, empty house, painted whiter than the moon. Doesn't it beg to be foraged by the poor animals of the city?

What would I do if I caught sight of some robbers slinking through the bushes? When my wife and her child lived in the house, I might have lunged at any intruders. But alone, I would tell them, I'm a kindred spirit. I'm just like you! Then I would sit back and watch, curious to see what they take, what they think is worth stealing.

It all belongs to the bank anyway. The same goes for my two shops, the cars, and a hilly bit of land in the outskirts of the valley. Collateral for a loan that will default in a few months. And even if they take it all, they won't be satisfied. The collective value of my assets will cover only a third of the debt. Will I find another way to eke out a living for myself? How many times can a man start over? There's not much left in me, and I've grown tired of fighting.

"Sir? Are you here?" Parvati comes running barefoot into the garden. Faithful maid. Nine years in my house, a Nepali daughter in all practical terms. We hired Parvati because her family lived in Biratnagar, in the far southeastern corner of the country. Far enough, Sonam reasoned, that Parvati wouldn't leave too often to visit her family.

Nearby, my Tibetan guard, Kunga, sways slightly in his undershirt and navy shorts, drunk as ever. It's Sunday evening, I recall. Kunga's day off. If he returns upright instead of on all fours, it's a good day. The man is just over sixty, a few years my senior, and has wisely never married. On Sunday mornings, he visits his mother, who lives in the Jawalakhel settlement, and gives her a share of his salary. Then he spends the rest of the day amid the alleyway liquor houses. At night, he returns with black plastic bags stretched thin by bottles. Carrying them straight to his room next to the gate, he keeps vigil for the rest of the week. The liquor fills his head with songs and jokes only he knows. All of this makes him an essentially useless guard. At least once a week, Parvati has to come out and open the gates for me because Kunga is asleep in his cot. It's been this way since we hired him. At first, I was angry each time this happened. I told the old man on several occasions that he was on his way out—never mind that he was from the same camp as me. He took this scolding in silence, nodding his head, but changed nothing. His silence was a sign not of his regret or shame but of his resignation. He knew that it was too late for him to change and he would stay as long as I tolerated him. In time, I came to understand that this man's intransigence also made him trustworthy. He seldom spoke to anyone, and his Sundays were like clockwork. He was utterly reliable in his habits, and this is a worthy trait to me.

"Sir," Parvati says.

"What is it?"

"Phone, sir."

She holds out the cordless receiver and waits for me to come to her. The girl has run all through the house, out to the front garden, and now, two meters from me, she decides she's had enough.

"Alright, have it your way," I say and push myself up. But the ground wavers under me. The fresh bottle of Black Label lies in the grass. Somehow, half of it is gone. Sitting down again, I feel the wicker chair sink into the grass. I focus on Parvati's and Kunga's bodies bobbing against the moonlight as if they were little ducks on the surface of a pond.

"Bring it to me."

"Sir."

"What?"

"I will ask her to call back in the morning."

"After all that?" I fan her over.

Parvati's shadow approaches carefully, like a deer. The girl has always been too thin. Is she eating? I've never seen her sit before a plate of food. Is she unhappy? Does she miss her relatives? Whatever happened to her parents? She never mentions them. Then again, I've never asked. Maybe

Sonam did once, although that seems unlikely. Neither my wife nor I tend to ask about the past—our own or that of others. Sonam and I chose each other knowing full well our limitations, understanding that we are two people who move through life while facing backward. When the past holds such power over you, even threatening the present, you must not speak of it. Instead, you leave it alone, tucked within the silences of your mind.

In any case, Sonam is no longer here for me to ask any questions of her. She and Cheche have settled in a town outside Boston, where they rent a basement studio. Sonam works as a seamstress while Cheche attends a high school nearby. Now I'm the one who needs Parvati to stay here.

When I open my eyes, Parvati is still there, waiting with the wireless phone. I lean my ear into the receiver. "Hello?"

"Samphel la? It's Dawa Tsomo. From the Pokhara camp."

Dawa was Lhamo's friend. She always had an interesting face. I try to sit up and clear my throat. "Tashi Delek," I say, speaking slowly and deliberately.

I've seen Dawa many times over the years. She and her husband, Jangchup, own one of the few remaining Tibetan carpet businesses in Kathmandu. Like me, they're members at the Hotel Yak & Yeti spa, as well as at the Hattiban Golf Course. Though I don't attend many parties anymore, I would run into them regularly at various fundraisers and shows. We would acknowledge each other with a handshake or a nod, but we seldom spoke. As a powerful but childless couple, Dawa and Jangchup were subject to scrutiny, and before Sonam left for America, she never failed to keep me apprised of the goings-on in our community. One evening at dinner, Sonam told me that Jangchup had apparently fathered several children with other women, whom he kept in various townhouses at the edges of the city. When I scolded her for repeating the rumors, Sonam replied that Dawa and Jangchup turned their noses at us because of my business, so we owed them nothing. I stayed quiet. Dawa was justified in her coldness toward me. She knows how I behaved with Lhamo.

"Samphel la?"

"Yes, Dawa la. What's the matter?"

"Lhamo has had a bad accident. A part of her roof collapsed and hit her head."

I ask Dawa to repeat herself, to tell me clearly where Lhamo is. I feel numb as I hear myself saying the name I have not said aloud in so many years.

"Lhamo is in the hospital . . . in the ICU. It would be good for you to come see her."

I clear my throat to indicate that I'm still on the line because I can't find the words to make a response.

"Jangchup and I are already here at the hospital," Dawa says. "We're trying to get some answers."

I am grateful that Dawa hasn't cried, and as I listen to her, I notice how gently she reveals each layer of information.

"The doctors weren't telling Ashang Migmar much, but he's a humble old man. I worry they're not giving Lhamo their full attention. You know how it is when they see poor people." Then, with her voice low, as if she might finally be about to cry, Dawa adds, "Lhamo asked for you. She told me she wanted to see you."

"Lhamo said that? Okay, I will be there soon," I manage to say as my voice breaks.

I hang up, and my hands tremble as I raise my glass. Parvati and Kunga stand nearby, watching over me like stone lions. Without them, I have no one. Do they know this? Their livelihoods depend on me. Even their families depend on the monthly wages I produce. But I have no one without them. What else can I sell to keep them here, so I'm not alone? All my life, this question.

A vivid image comes to me of Lhamo at Phewa Lake. She's sitting across the table from me. The rain has just ended and the sun is behind her, revealing the red and brown hues in her hair and the freckles along her cheeks. Her face, her hair, her bright eyes—all are illuminated by the sun. She was so beautiful that day, I became nervous and made up for it with excessive friendliness. She spoke in a girlish way, using the endearing expressions that people of her camp often pepper in their conversations. Then she smiled, and I felt myself break. We were strangers, yet we were as close as two people could be.

"Alright," I say, pushing myself up so I can walk to the house.

The jeep sits in the driveway. I feel around in the dark until I find the bottom rim of the window, then the door handle. I need to sit against something for a moment, rest my head on the steering wheel. I'll sit for a minute with my eyes closed, then I'll go to see Lhamo. Lhamo who cannot wake up right now.

When I open my eyes again, I'm enveloped in the smell of old beer. Kunga's chin hovers above me as he wraps my arm around his shoulders. The guard is breathing heavily, struggling with my weight. Still, he guides me somewhere.

"What are you doing?"

"Taking you to bed. You'll go in the morning," Kunga says as we walk into the foyer.

I grunt in affirmation, finding I can offer no resistance.

We walk into the foyer and climb three flights of stairs, circling up toward the moon, which bounces in the cobwebbed skylight overhead. It was Sonam's idea to knock a hole in the ceiling. Back then, I would have done anything to please her or Cheche. The two of them were new in my life—an instant family, I thought to myself—though they were still mourning the loss of Ling Gesar, Sonam's dead husband and Cheche's father. That wasn't his real name. He was only nicknamed after the great king of Tibet. A lofty moniker for a property hawker. Sonam had met and married him as a teenager. People often said that Cheche looked just like her father. In this, I understood that there could be no impressing myself onto the child, no way that she'd come to resemble me. Meanwhile, I couldn't admit to her or anyone else that I already had a daughter, one who walks around Toronto with my eyes. A girl who is unmistakably mine in a million other ways.

Kunga pauses to catch his breath. Each step has been more labored than the one before.

"I can walk on my own now," I say. "Just stay beside me."

"Yes," he replies. Up close, with his somber, round eyes, Kunga now reminds me of my father. I look away, startled. Has he always resembled my father or have we just aged? Of course, my father could not have been more than forty years old when he died.

As we reach the top floor, the moon looks as though it had broken through the skylight and was now floating across the ceiling. I extend my hand to try and catch it. A wall of color flashes in my mind's eye—a mural that often appears before me without warning, both in my dreams and in my waking life. Vast in scale, it stretches from my feet to a ceiling high enough to disappear into shadow, and extends into darkness on either side of me. Each time the mural appears, I view the same section of it: a collection of hundreds of palm-sized white Buddhas, illuminated by a beam of light coming through a high window somewhere behind me. As I focus my eyes, I see that even though each Buddha sits cross-legged on a lotus, their expressions are idiosyncratic and their hands are placed in different positions. Some touch the ground; others are clasped together or posed in various mudras. Each figure is outlined in gold pigment with the thinnest paint strokes and filled in with a white so smooth and rich, it could be made of ivory. And although I only ever see this one small segment of the mural, I know that there are countless more deities hidden in the darkness around me. I want to reach out and touch the mural, but more than this, I want to taste it. I don't know why. Just the touch of saliva could ruin this fragile section forever. And yet some part of me suspects I want to destroy the mural. Perhaps then I will be free of it.

Above me, the moon in the skylight passes out of view, covered momentarily by some low clouds. Its glow is faint now, almost undetectable. How kind it is that we have the moon. This constant presence hovering in the dark. So close to us, even when it's hidden. Just like Lhamo has been. My life's companion, if only in my mind. And all this—the home, the cars, the success I once thought would always follow me—began with her. She took me to Po Rithar, who then gave me Dhargye's name. What's more, Lhamo gave me the Nameless Saint. Until that night, I had felt nothing for the statue. As a child, I felt a tightness in my chest upon seeing people's reverence for the Saint. I thought of my father, solitary even in death, while this dead thing was never far from a devotee. But when Lhamo told me of how she had hidden the ku for my sake, the Nameless Saint came to mean something else. I was moved by its ragged state. The thin patches of gold pigment, which appeared more delicate than I remembered. I realized the frailty of the object; no matter how holy it was to some, the ku would wear away. The only constant was our dogged hearts: Lhamo's, which compelled her to protect what she believed was mine. And my own, which called on me to find my mother.

I left Pokhara the next morning. Heeding Po Rithar's advice, I set about meeting Dhargye and the other men who would form my team, one by one. Two years later, in 1986, I retrieved the first of my lost treasures. Seven golden offering bowls from the fourteenth century, forgotten in some dusty cabinet in the Taer Temple until a monk had discovered them. But that is another story.

When I reach the door to my bedroom, I feel for the wall and let it guide me to my bed. Tomorrow, I decide. Tomorrow I will go to Lhamo.

2

I N the morning, I pack a small bag, climb into my jeep, and leave for the daylong drive to Pokhara. Outside my gates, the city is in full regalia, whirring with dust, cows, and prayer bells. Vegetable sellers squat on the ground against a high brick wall, as people walk from seller to seller, bargaining for the day's supply of vegetables. I turn onto another road, and the sweet aroma of roasting corn floats in through the windows. A woman sits on the ground fanning a shallow metal basin that was once used to mix cement but is now filled with coal and corn. Lhamo and I once shared an ear of corn by Swayambhunath Stupa. We had five rupees to spend, and the ear of corn was only a few paisa. How content I was, squatting in the dust with her, passing the small treat back and forth as we took turns crunching into the kernels. How free I felt that entire day with so many coins jangling in my pocket.

I drive along winding, narrow streets, making my way to the Ring Road. One moment I notice how heavy the air feels; the next, the low sky booms three times in quick succession before unleashing a downpour. My wipers can't keep up with the torrent, so I have to pull over to the side of the road. All around me, people run here and there, newspapers over their heads, pants raised, as rivers surge down the streets. A heavy bout like this is a relief to the whole city, even if it sends everyone scrambling under awnings. Water—like electricity, like gasoline—is scarce and getting more unreliable each year. Even the wealthy complain of having to dig deeper and deeper into the ground to reach well water. So everyone is happy to sit in silence, watching the curtain of rain wash down from the sky and fill a hundred thousand buckets across the valley. Then I remember that Lhamo is waiting, at the edge of life and death.

Entering the Ring Road, I pass by the lush hill of Swayambhunath, with its white and gold stupa at the top. Before me, two little boys brave the traffic, holding hands as they run through the dust in their pristine school uniforms. Didn't Lhamo and I run in the same way along this road, clinging tightly to each other's hands? I remember the two of us climbing the steps to the temples and eating everything the pilgrims gave us. Bellies full, we fell asleep under a canopy of trees, free as the monkeys surrounding us. In a lifetime of days forgotten, I hold on to this one.

I turn off the highway and take the road out of the city. The descent is slow, with the usual gridlock of buses, trucks, and private cars. On the other side of the road, a similar stream barely moves up the hill. Briefly, there's a lull in the traffic, and I watch a truck driver come uphill with speed, turning his steering wheel with gusto to the rhythm of a Bollywood song while garlands dance in his window. Then a rumbling comes from behind me, and a row of motorcyclists overtakes my jeep, swerving dangerously close to the cliff's edge. They seem unafraid of the drop to the gorge, which is lined with fallen vehicles. Years ago, I also rode a motorcycle, and there were times when I would see a brief break in the traffic, and, as if a switch had flipped within me, I would ride as fast as I could, trying to make it through before the opening closed. Afterward, my hands and legs would shake uncontrollably, and my skin would be damp with cold sweat. And I would walk away from the bike, afraid of the parts of myself I didn't understand.

But I was different then. This was Kathmandu in the nineties—a new era with new demand for portable Tibetan heritage. Our time, it seemed, had come. My friend Jigme Dorjee had started one of the many factories producing traditional Tibetan carpets. He had eight hundred employees and was shipping out a container of rugs a week to clients in Japan, America, and Germany. The designs could not come fast enough. The rugs were trimmed and rolled as soon as they dried. Importers from around the world flew to Nepal—some making exclusive deals as soon as they landed at the airport. Soon, a third of the country's wealth would come from this industry alone. We refugees were becoming barons of industry.

At our blackjack nights at the Everest Casino, Jigme would tell me about the housing he was building for his workers and their families behind the weaving rooms. This way, when the water or power was cut, the workers could take breaks in their own homes. When water or power returned, the workers could walk back to their stations and continue washing, dyeing, weaving, and inspecting the carpets. This keeps them happy too, he proudly added. They can watch their kids run around and be home for lunch. Jigme said he gave his employees generous bonuses for the Nepali New Year and regularly held picnics and dinner parties for the staff. There was, in all of Jigme's swaggering, an underlying delight, as if he could hardly believe his own fate. *No parents, no country*, he would sigh. *But we own houses next to embassies.*

I indulged my friend's self-regard but said little about my own business. By all indications, Jigme didn't really know what I was up to—not then, at least. I had no factory, no laborers, and no picnics with staff. Only a storefront was visible to the public, a relatively small piece of real estate amid the five-story homes that surround the Boudhanath Stupa. In the shade of that ancient white dome, beneath a golden spire and the gaze of Buddha eyes, sat my humble store of imitation antiques. In truth, while thousands of pilgrims passed before me, circling the stupa to earn merit, I was building a one-way tunnel from Tibet. A secret pathway to unearth and retrieve what was ours.

The last of Kathmandu's outskirts slip by. Now I'm driving on a winding road carved into the hillside. Between the trees, the river gorge flashes to my side. These waters will be my companion for the rest of the drive. I cannot let myself think about what awaits me at the end of this journey.

But I have often been wrong about what awaits me. Like Jigme and so many others, I rose quickly, but the decline of my business was slow, stretching through years of heartbreak and glimmers of hope. Yet I can pin the beginning of the end to a single day. The day of the Yumbu Lhakhang operation. Summer of 1993. This was also the day I learned that I had a seven-year-old daughter.

That morning, Tenkyi appeared at my shop like a crow hopping through a front door. I did not recognize her at first. When her name came to me, I shook her hand but failed to mimic her easy mannerisms, her plain happiness. With the exception of a wet, crumpled newspaper dangling from one hand, she was empty-handed. Not even a purse. She explained that Dawa Tsomo had told her about my store. She wondered if I remembered Dawa. I nodded and gestured to the wicker stools, trying to find the words. The sky rumbled and released another burst of rain. I asked my assistant, Bhim, to get some tea from a nearby café.

Meanwhile, I kept glancing at my watch, wondering if my men would call at any moment. On that day, everything was set. The plan had taken nearly a year to finalize, and the operation was being led by a man named Jampa. He had briefly known my father from living in the same camp, and still had contacts in Tibet. Over the years, Jampa had worked on many deals for me, overseeing retrievals, transferring funds to partners on the ground, and ensuring the transport of goods to Guangzhou and then on to dealers in Beijing, Hong Kong, and the West.

For this operation, Jampa had traveled weeks in advance to meet with partners in Lhoka prefecture, finalize the plan, and ensure every detail for the eventual safe transport of the antiquities to Chengdu. The targets were around thirty relics, including a large copper statue of Chenresig and a gilt bronze panel. The men would enter the Yumbu Lhakhang palace in the early hours, before sunlight hit the valley. While one group packed the antiquities, the other would arrange replicas. Every single object had to be instantly replaced so as not to arouse suspicion.

For years, I had hung a photograph of Yumbu Lhakhang above my desk, never imagining that I would one day be so close to holding its treasures in my hands. Over a hundred years before Jesus, a thousand years before written Tibetan records, Nyatri Tsenpo, the first king of Tibet, descended from the sky to this place. Legend said that he had webbed hands and eyes that could close from the bottom lids as well as the top. Yumbu Lhakhang, his solitary white fortress of stone painted with red and gold paint, sat alone in the wide Yarlung Valley, perched on a narrow, isolated hilltop that resembled a deer's hind leg. The palace overlooked the fields of Zortang, fields so treasured that farmers from every corner of Tibet took its soil to sprinkle over their crops.

But because of its prominence, the palace was not a new target. The Chinese had razed and ransacked it, stealing most of the original relics during the Cultural Revolution—including Nyatri Tsenpo's grave. In the

1980s, the local villagers slowly began to rebuild the palace, though they could not know what exactly had been taken or smashed or melted down. What remained at Yumbu Lhakhang were small artifacts, merely the dregs of the original collection, but still enough to set off waves around the world.

As we sat awaiting tea, Tenkyi smiled brightly, scanning the store. She appeared genuinely happy to see me, and after the initial shock, I felt the same. Here we are, I kept saying, after so many years. She looked around, staring at the statues of gods, the wooden tables carved with motifs of lucky symbols, and rugs beaten and torn to seem old. I wondered what she thought of it all. The store contained no true antiques, nothing of any real value. It was populated with relics created in exile to resemble objects that might have survived the journey out. A shop made for tourists, to give them what they expected.

Tenkyi would have been forty that year, a year younger than me, but she still resembled the girl I had met some thirty years earlier. The same strict brows and expressive mouth. I searched for Lhamo's features in her face, and in a way, it was almost like seeing Lhamo again. The almond-shaped eyes, a gently sloping nose. But Tenkyi had a rounder face, and her skin was tinged pink rather than brown. Lhamo was more angular, and her cheeks were the widest part of her face, with her chin gently tapering. Their bodies, too, were dissimilar. Tenkyi had a sturdy and compact frame, while Lhamo was thin, and even with a soft and rounded belly, carried herself with a lightness.

Now you've seen my body. Lhamo had risen from the bed and stood before me naked. When she turned to gather her clothes, I reached out and pulled her back. Folding myself around her, I felt her heartbeat radiate through my chest.

While Bhim served us tea and biscuits, Tenkyi told me that she had taken a post nearby, at Songtsen Gampo High School, where she was the English teacher for classes nine and ten. She spoke about her job with the kind of enthusiasm that would make her a fine teacher indeed. I could picture her pacing past a blackboard, book in hand, reading a verse aloud, which her students would then repeat. Certainty poured out of Tenkyi as she spoke of her students' potential, and also of their laziness. To be an educator, one needed such a quality—not just in her thoughts, but in her voice, her gait, the way she points the ruler at a student. Tenkyi also had the desire to be liked, to be known. She wore the utter vulnerability of a teacher so plainly.

But as Tenkyi carried on, her mannerisms became increasingly harried, as if she expected to be kicked out at any moment. Briefly, I wanted us both to be children again. Perhaps then we could reach across the table and be frank with each other. As casually as I could, I asked about Lhamo. Tenkyi took a sip of her tea, then placed the cup and saucer carefully back on the small table. With practiced deliberateness and clarity, she told me that Lhamo's life had changed a great deal since I last saw her. I took in her words, wondering how much Tenkyi knew about my visit to the camp eight years earlier.

"Lhamo didn't want me to come here initially," Tenkyi said. "But you must know that."

Still in a daze, I mumbled something about disappointing Lhamo once.

"My sister was heartbroken," Tenkyi replied. "She loved you. She still loves you."

"But she's married."

"Tashi left years ago," she says with a grieved smile. "Isn't it better to be alone than tormented in such a marriage?"

I could say nothing. After Lhamo and I slept together, I returned to my lakeside hotel and began imagining our lives together. I even formulated the words I would say to her, how I would ask Lhamo to leave Tashi and come live with me. But in the morning, doubt flooded my mind like sunlight. Why would she leave her marriage? Least of all for someone like me? I just couldn't believe that Lhamo felt deeply for me.

"But there's something else," Tenkyi said, holding my gaze. "Lhamo also has a daughter who deserves better than Tashi. You're her father. You should know that."

Sitting there, I thought about the sequence of Tenkyi's words. Each consecutive word had fallen like a bombardment, so swift and devastating. I felt ashamed—of my fear, of my ignorance. To defend myself, I even considered telling Tenkyi about the letter I had sent Lhamo after my visit to the camp. It had been a respectable letter, so that if someone else had read it, Lhamo's reputation would not be compromised. Yet there was enough there, I told myself, to signal my feelings. Lhamo would be able to read between the lines, and she would write back if she still felt something for me. But now I saw how pitiful that would sound to Tenkyi, when the truth was, I just lacked the courage to be honest with Lhamo. I couldn't bear the risk of embarrassing myself before her.

Still, maybe this was a second chance.

"Does she want to see me?" I asked.

Tenkyi shrugged and replied that Lhamo was unsure. But it was a possibility, she thought. It was possible I might even meet my daughter, Dolma. In a few months, Lhamo would bring her to the capital to register for secondary school. If I wanted, Tenkyi could try and arrange a meeting. "Perhaps," she said, "you could even be a family someday."

I let out a stunned laugh. Without hesitation, I agreed.

Tenkyi rose to leave. As I reached beside her to open the door, something strange happened. Tenkyi winced and froze, as if expecting me to strike her. She turned away slightly and stood perfectly still, her eyes shut in anticipation. Why would she expect this from me? Later, as I sat alone in my office, what surprised me more than her implication that I would hit her was that she had not made any attempt to protect herself. She had only closed her eyes and waited for the blow.

But I also sensed that her fear was not specific to me. Something in her was injured, perhaps a near-fatal wound. The blow that had nearly finished her off still rang inside her, haunting Tenkyi. It was invisible and unknowable to everyone else, but I recognized it. I had felt that terror many times.

The next morning, Jampa called me. He said they had been ready to enter Yumbu Lhakhang. The men were in the jeep. It wasn't even dawn. All of a sudden, a noise came like thunder, but low, as if rising from the earth. It came booming through the valley. Jampa said he could still hear the sound in his dreams. He thought it was the gods of the valley, angered by our actions. I listened to Jampa, but I wasn't all that certain of the old man anymore. He claimed that when they rushed to the palace, they saw shadows run out the doors and into a waiting truck. When they went inside, everything had been stripped clean. Everything. How was that possible?

Because he had failed, I decided to salvage the trip and give him another job. I told Jampa to go to my father's village, or what remained of it, a day's journey by jeep from Lhasa. He was to try, once again, to uncover three wooden crates buried about two meters underground. If he found the right place, he would see a small stream that splits in three before rejoining. There should be a stupa nearby, although it might have been demolished. That's where I stood as my father buried our possessions. Now I felt it was more important than ever to retrieve the trunks. Not only for myself but for Dolma. She should have something from her grandfather. She should know her grandmother's identity.

Jampa said that he had tried this twice already. In that case, I told him, he would be successful this time. If he was persistent, he would find three wooden boxes. I could not remember all that my father had packed, but I did remember a few items: sheep skins, my grandfather's prayer books and silk brocade paintings, my grandmother's wood and silver cups, her serving bowls, our gold and silver statues of gods, and carpets on which generations of my family had slept. But the most important object was an amulet containing a portrait of my mother. She would have come to us, my father said, had it not been for her other family. He said that although people in the village called me a bastard, I must always remember that I'm not motherless.

Could I see her face, just once?

My father was silent for some time. Then he said, *When we return.*

As we walked back home, hand in hand, my father said he would show me the photograph when the troubles were over. He would even take me to visit her, he said. I walked in the dark, guided by his hand, smiling broadly at the night sky. One day soon, I thought.

It never entered my mind that we might never see that land again.

A month after our phone call, Jampa showed up at the store to resign.

"The earth must have shifted," he said.

"Shifted? Did the villagers say there was an earthquake?" I asked, signaling Jampa to sit. But he remained standing.

"Or it was looted."

"Who looted it?"

Jampa pulled out a handkerchief and wiped the sweat off his face. "Does it matter?"

"Of course, it matters."

"I stood in the place you described. I saw the three tributaries spread and reconnect. That place exists, just as you said. But there was no trace of your father's things. I had six men digging for a week. Then we ran out of money and the authorities were asking questions. I spent everything to pay off the local officials."

Jampa paused for a long while before saying, "I won't spend my final years chasing after your father's things. I buried my possessions before fleeing too. I've let go of them. You should too." With that, he left.

He phoned sometime later and corrected my memory. The tributaries did not converge. The rivers curved inward in one place, but they did not rejoin. For the first time, it occurred to me that there might not even be a photo of my mother in the boxes. My father had never opened the amulet in front of me. Maybe the amulet contained sheets of prayers, which was customary. I had always been eager to believe my father, to imagine that my mother's beauty could have somehow warranted a photograph in a time when few were taken. Even now, I have dreams of the three tributaries where our things are buried. I see my mother's photograph waiting in the earth, beating faintly. If I could just lie with my ear upon the right place.

A T a highway rest stop in Mugling, a voicemail message flashes on my phone. It's from Dawa.

"Please come right away to Ashang Migmar's," she says, her voice strained. "Lhamo is back home."

If Lhamo isn't at the hospital, she's either cured or beyond recovery.

"A bottle of water and a bottle of whiskey," I tell the restaurant workers running to my car.

A boy brings me the bottles in a plastic bag that's ready to tear. I'm reminded of Kunga and his Sunday ritual. How long before I resemble the old guard? I twist the metal cap until it cracks free. One long sip, then another. The sting is a relief. I would stay here if I could, in this dust, surrounded by flies. Sometimes, it seems things are building meaningfully—life, business, knowledge. Maybe it's just a residue of the arrogance of my youth, the echoes of the man who raced his motorbike through traffic. Then the failures begin, one after the next. I watched in awe, almost dazzled, as the failures compounded—as if watching a wrathful god intervene in my life, destroying everything I toiled to build. I watched, hoping that something would remain amid the wreckage. Anything. Some part of myself. Even just a memory of the child who once fought for his life, who once loved a girl completely.

After Tenkyi's visit, her words rang in my mind for many weeks. Anything *was* possible. I could begin another life, the one I should have had, with Lhamo and our child. We might even be a family. They would come to the capital in a few months. This meant I would have one last opportunity for a serious acquisition.

By then, the Chinese had launched a manhunt to stop antique dealers. Sherab Wangyal, one of the biggest dealers in Kathmandu, had been arrested while working on a set of Tibetan tombs along the old Silk Road, each tomb brimming with ancient Persian and Roman coins. The sites were spread out along the slopes of the desert region. It was a complex project, made more arduous because the chief of the local precinct had already robbed many of them, making progress slow and unpredictable. Wangyal had traveled to Lhasa hoping to push things along with local authorities, but he was immediately detained and thrown in jail for two years. He now lives in the hills outside Kathmandu, devoting himself to prayer.

I put aside any thought of Wangyal's arrest when two of my men in Chengdu sent word about finding the long-lost stone lions of Songtsen Gampo's tomb. As the first emperor of Tibet, Gampo had built an empire that stretched northeast to the Taklamakan Desert, nearly as far as modern-day Tajikistan, southwest to Yunnan, and all the way up to Gansu in China. Situated among the Valley of Kings, he was buried in the royal necropolis of Tibetan rulers in the Yarlung Valley. Today, the tomb is an ordinary, unmarked site. Just a large mound of earth to the untrained eye, lined with some prayer flags and a modest monastery. It was pillaged over eleven hundred years ago, just after the fall of the Pugyel dynasty. Both the lions and the stele describing Gampo's merits had been looted. But my men had tracked the lions to a budget antique shop in Hong Kong, where they were on sale for a few thousand dollars. If the lions were authentic, they would be among the earliest existing artifacts of the unified Tibetan Empire. They would command enough to secure a comfortable life not only for Lhamo and Dolma but for generations of my family to come.

Henri Giroux, my old friend, had identified the exquisite clue of the lions' age: a tail fixed flat against the body, curving up under the hind leg and along the right side of its torso. This was a style adopted in the early ninth century. I would soon possess the statues that guarded the emperor who launched our inscribed history. The Tibetan Empire began in the time of these lions, from the first known record describing a mission to improve the horse trade between Tibet and China, to the defiantly modern poems of Dhondup Gyal. Songtsen Gampo's body had turned to ash long ago, but the stone guardians of his soul were still here, within my reach. So I became reckless. Although it was risky traveling to Hong Kong, I decided that given the value of the lions, I should ensure their safe passage myself. But as soon as I stepped up to the teenage customs agent in Hong Kong, I was detained for questioning. Compared to Wangyal, I was a relative unknown with no direct linkages to the trade, and after a week in a windowless holding cell somewhere deep in the airport, they deported me.

When I returned to Nepal, I kept my head down and my store closed. At last, the day came for Lhamo and Dolma to arrive. Tenkyi's instructions were precise. I was to meet them on the other side of the stupa at noon, at the Buddha Friendship Tea Shop. I closed my store at eleven thirty and paced outside, taking glances at the tea shop across the stupa's circular road. In my jacket pockets I had two jewelry boxes: a gold necklace with a bell pendant for Dolma, and a diamond bracelet for Lhamo. The boxes danced in my hands as I worried that I had chosen the wrong gifts— were they too much, too revealing of my hopes?

Then I saw her. Lhamo was walking along the stupa's road. Behind her, a little girl held Tenkyi's hand, skipping along. As they approached the tea shop's plastic chairs, a boy walked up to take their order. I watched their heads turn to him all together and imagined myself in his position. The boy ran off into the dark doorway of the kitchen. From a distance, I could only make out the broad outlines of Lhamo's and Dolma's features. Lhamo's hair was long, as it had been years before, while Dolma's hair was cut at the nape like most other schoolchildren.

Tenkyi caught sight of me and signaled to wait. She stood and walked over, taking care to go clockwise around the stupa rather than walking the shorter, more direct way. Ordinarily, I have no patience for these religious rituals. But on that day, I sensed that something was wrong.

"Didn't you get my message?" she asked, sounding harried. "I left it with your shopkeeper, the Nepali guy."

"Bhim isn't in today. What message?"

"I don't think you should meet them. Given the recent incident."

So news of my detention in Hong Kong had reached even the schoolteachers of the valley. I peered over at the tea shop. Dolma hopped off her mother's lap and sat on the ground. She was peering down the brick lane, as though following a line of ants.

"When can I see them?" I asked.

"You should think about what it would do to them, to be associated with someone who deals in holy objects. We may not be wealthy, but we have our name to protect."

I stared at Dolma. Her face was too distant to see clearly. "What does my daughter look like?"

"Like Lhamo. She also reminds me of my mother somehow, though I don't remember her face."

"It would have been better if I hadn't seen them. Why did you bring them here?"

"To circle the stupa and visit the temples," she said, taken aback. "You should give up that business. It's a sin to sell sacred objects."

"You're lucky that you can live with such a clear conscience—even though I was the one who donated money for your school's textbooks."

"A good man finds a way to earn an honorable living."

I considered a dozen possible defenses: how I didn't need to hear a lecture about an honorable living, not when I was born a beggar; how my father died on the side of a dusty road in India, trying to make an honorable rupee; how no one in the world cares about our pure Buddhist intentions. How so much has been stolen from me, from *us*, more than I could ever take back; and so if anyone should sell statues of our gods to survive, it should be us, because it was the gods who abandoned us first. But I knew that I wouldn't be able to convince Tenkyi or anyone else.

"She's my child," I finally said.

"I understand," Tenkyi nodded. "If you want to be a part of Dolma's life, if you want to help her, I know a good school in the valley. It's far too costly for us to manage."

"I will pay."

As Tenkyi turned to leave, I asked if Lhamo knew that I was there, so near to her. Tenkyi shook her head and said that neither Lhamo nor Dolma knew. Then she walked clockwise back to the tea shop.

For the next six years, up until Tenkyi's departure for Toronto, she came to my store twice a year to tell me about Dolma's education and to collect the tuition money. Because my curiosity about Dolma exceeded these perfunctory reports, I arranged for her to receive mentorship from Henri, who would share perceptive accounts of her developing talents and interests. Still, I could not stay away from Lhamo or Dolma. Not long after our thwarted meeting at the tea shop, I foolishly drove to the camp, wanting to explain myself to Lhamo or to simply see her face-to-face. Instead, I found a hilltop besieged by a roaming leopard, and in that chaos, I met our daughter.

THE CAMP IS within sight. I pull up by the road and decide to walk the final fifty meters. Better to enter quietly, without drawing attention. As I walk, I hear the familiar river carrying along its old route and, somewhere nearby, a few chickens clucking. To my right, the Machapuchare mountain is as large as ever, cutting the clouds that pass over its sharp ridges. Our country lies just beyond that beautiful range.

As I turn onto a small road, I see that the camp has changed. There are many more houses, and the new ones are built with cement pillars and bricks, just like in the capital. A few multistory houses rise from the main road, where half a dozen shops sell vegetables and handicrafts. There used to be nothing but a few shacks along this stretch, offering unrestricted views of the valley. Now, there's an unbroken chain of low buildings. The only landmark familiar to me is the wide peepal tree with its circular cement base, where a few older camp dwellers sit, some smoking and others turning prayer wheels. Even the land past the gorge has changed. The valley is now an ocean of rice paddy fields stretching out to the horizon. It's almost as if the camp sits between two skies. Minute by minute, as the clouds pass, the changing sky is reflected in the watery fields below.

Walking deeper into the camp, I find myself disoriented among the crowded collection of homes. Stepping onto the small, muddy paths off the main road, I wonder how I will find Ashang Migmar's place. Then I see Mo Yutok's stone and mortar house ahead, and the rooftop where I first saw Dolma up close. Before that day, she was a child I knew only from a brief, distant glimpse, and through what Tenkyi had told me.

I pass by Mo's house, spotting her old sign in the window, "U.N.: Please Help Tibet." She must be in her nineties by now. Turning the corner, I find myself in the old courtyard between Ashang Migmar's house and Mo Yutok's, though now the space is tiny, cut in half by another one-room dwelling. What a shame, I think, to pack so many homes onto this small plot of land. It's claustrophobic. But where is everybody? All I can hear are the sounds of children laughing nearby and some crows calling out to each other.

Ashang Migmar's door is ajar. I tap my knuckle against the wood. No answer. I peer in and wait for my eyes to adjust to the dark.

There's someone in the corner, on a bed.

"Ashang Migmar?"

The figure doesn't move. They lie on their side, back facing me, pillows propping them up awkwardly. There are blankets draped over them and stacked at their feet.

"Lhamo?"

No answer. No movement either. Could this be her? It looks as though she were sinking slowly into some invisible mouth in the bed. A naked light bulb hangs from the ceiling. I feel against the wall for a light switch and stumble over a stuffed dog on the floor. It must have fallen off this shelf full of children's toys. I dust off the gray dog and put it back on the shelf between a plastic doll and a pair of orange-rimmed children's sunglasses. I try the other wall and trace a thin wire running toward the light switch. I flip it. Nothing. Up and down a few more times. It must be a load-shedding hour.

Outside in the courtyard, there's still no one. Just two crows hopping around some old rice. A pressure cooker sighs forcefully in a house nearby. Somewhere, there's the murmur of conversation, though I can't tell if the voices are coming closer or staying in place. Someone will be here soon, I tell myself as I return inside. They wouldn't leave her alone for long.

The truth is, I'm afraid to go near her. Because this body must be Lhamo and because I must try to speak with her while we're alone. I move slowly toward the bed, my feet shuffling against the ground, barely willing to lift themselves. The side of her face comes into view. Her eyes are sealed. They've been closed for so long that a thin layer of mucus has formed at the seams. Sweat pools on her forehead over deep wrinkles and dark sunspots. Loose skin hangs from her thin arms, leading toward her small, tough hands. *What a hard life you've lived, Lhamo. You've grown old and so have I. All the years I've wasted chasing a ghost when you were always here, within reach. Now there is nothing anyone can do or give or say to change the past. We cannot live our lives again.*

Gathering my sleeve, I gently wipe the mucus from her eyes. She frowns, but is otherwise unmoved. My legs are failing. I find a squat wicker stool under the bed. When I pull it out and sit, I'm suddenly small, lopsided, crouched before her body. I watch the faint rise and fall of her chest.

Open your eyes. I am here.

A single butter lamp crackles in the corner, gaining life from the breeze in the doorway. The lamp's heat rotates a paper lantern propped up with a wire frame and decorated with prayers, casting shadows that disappear and reappear, shifting on the walls, the ceiling, and across Lhamo's face. I touch her hand. It is dry, weightless. A paper bird. The last time we touched was twenty-seven years ago. What if I had waited for her in the morning? What if I had let myself love her without fear?

Her fingers move faintly in my palm. I stand to check her face. Now, under her eyelids, there's movement. She's in a dream. Is she trying to awaken?

"Samphel la."

A thin woman stands at the door. It's Dawa. She, too, has aged a great deal. Before I can respond, Ashang Migmar walks in with Jangchup, Dawa's husband. I stand to greet Ashang Migmar, who must be nearly in his eighties. The tough old nomad.

"Tai' Delek," I say, smiling.

Ashang and Jangchup nod, their faces grim. How stupid of me to smile. I walk over to shake their hands and touch foreheads. Meanwhile, Lhamo's uncle walks to the prayer altar and begins to empty the day's water from the copper bowls.

"How was the drive?" Jangchup asks.

He has always struck me as a kind man, without any wiles. Whatever success the couple enjoyed in the carpet business must have been due to Dawa.

"Your hair looks like mine did for a while," Ashang says, wiping down the altar. "But I grew mine back."

Even after all these years in Nepal, he still braids his long hair, weaving red and black string through the plaits, draping precious stones from his ears. Around his waist he's tied a red silk sash, and on the wall there's a broad-brimmed hat beside a knife dangling in its sheath from a nail. Ashang Migmar could return to Tibet tomorrow, and no one would know that he'd been away, living nearly a lifetime on a subtropical hilltop in another country.

"What did the doctor say?" I ask Jangchup. "What happened?"

"What, what is he asking?" Ashang Migmar says, straining to hear.

"He's asking what happened to Lhamo."

"It fell," Ashang Migmar says. He begins to cough. "We ran. The sky rained bullets. I left my yaks, my whole life. I took one last look at my pastures. My sister and her husband died. I buried her by a river, with my own hands. Under some rocks! We could not even light a candle for them. I said, Sister, I will take care of your family. You can let go. I took the girls. I broke stones every day for twelve years. I said to the girls, we suffered so the two of you won't suffer. Isn't that right? We fled and lived like beggars even though we have a home. Now everyone has gone. Where is my little girl? What's happened to my poor girl? I won't let her die in this country! My poor girl!"

I am stunned by his outburst, and not just because I remember Ashang Migmar as a stoic man who carried my uncle's corpse all the way to Kathmandu. I'm also stunned because it's as though my own father had returned as an aged man, resuming his nightly alcohol-fueled lamentations.

"Come, sit," Dawa says with tears in her eyes, guiding Ashang Migmar to the bed.

Lost in thought, he sinks down quietly beside Lhamo. Meanwhile, Jangchup turns away and wipes his eyes, before staring at the carpet. Calm returns, and Dawa sits down to tell me everything she knows about the accident. Lhamo had been reciting prayers at her house. This is a typical source of income for the elderly in the camp. Meanwhile, there had been three months of constant rain. I know how these camp roofs are. They're fragile, complex. Lined from the inside with plastic, fabric, and newspapers. Hiding what festers above day and night. The wooden supports must have rotted, along with hundreds of smaller pieces of lumber wedged under the tin sheets.

The beam's end licked her head and split her scalp open.

Lhamo walked out into the courtyard with her hair matted in blood. Mo Yutok had been praying outside when Lhamo came to her with blood streaming down her face. She asked for a mirror. She said she wanted to check her head in the sunlight.

4

IT has been a long time since I swam in the river," she says.
"Me as well."

"You have a better excuse." She pauses, then adds, "Your uncle used to swim every chance he had. We called him 'The Fish.'"

"Hmm. My memories here are of you and Tenkyi."

"We had a lot of fun then . . ."

The sun is setting over the valley. In the river below the ridge, two buffalo sit unmoving near a young woman washing some pots. On the shore behind her, long, transparent saris are drying slowly, draped across several boulders.

"Those were the days," I say.

"The good old days. Days of serenity."

"Now you're making fun of me—"

"A sick woman like me? And in your own dream? Never. Besides, are there not rivers like this in Kathmandu?"

"You are different."

"Am I? Let us sit for a minute. Here, this is nice."

"Yes, you are. Maybe this will sound strange, but I feel like you know something about me that even I don't know."

The woman in the river begins singing to herself as she scrapes the bottom of a pan, one arm plunging into the water up to her elbow. The sound of her singing carries faintly over the ridge. Her song is rhythmic, like a prayer.

"And no, there are no rivers like this in the city. The Bagmati is only as deep as a hand, full of garbage, and streaming with sewage . . ."

"It's been a while since I've gone to Kathmandu. I went there to look for you once."

"Yes, Dawa told me that."

"I took a plane there and stayed with Gen Lobsang's mother. I went to your father's house, but another family lived there."

"What year was it?"

"Let's not talk about the past. What have you been doing? You've seen many different countries, right?"

"I was held in the Hong Kong airport once. They nearly sent me to China—"

"I heard you had to pay a great deal of money."

"No, no, I just stayed in the airport holding area for a few days with the other poor black-haired people."

"What was it like?"

"The cell? A windowless room with other rooms fanning out from it, somewhere deep within the airport. There must have been a red flag next to my name. I thought they were finally going to throw me in jail for the antiques. But maybe it was just my Tibetan name, I don't know. On the second day, two very tall men became incredibly angry. They threw chairs down and yelled that they had been there for a month. The men could not afford tickets home because they had expected to get jobs and earn money in Hong Kong."

"Poor men—"

"There were many brown-skinned Asians like us. Mostly, they were quiet and tired looking. I think they were young laborers."

"Some people have no luck. All the young ones in our camp don't have papers. All they can do is sell trinkets, just like their mothers and fathers. It's a shame they could not be office workers."

"We have a daughter. Your sister told me."

She looks down. "I wish you could have known her from the beginning."

"What is she like?"

"Like a boy when she was younger. Always playing ball, like you. Remember when you came to the camp with a busted ball tucked under your arm?"

"My friends Polo and Golok saw it in a nettle bush outside the zoo. I just reached in and pulled it out. My arms were red for days."

"She's coming back any day now. From a country called Canada that I have never seen."

"I came here to see you and Dolma once, many years ago. But there was a commotion in the camp. A leopard was lurking around, and so I went up to the rooftop like everyone else. That's when I met her."

Lhamo's eyes are watery and appear large like a child's. "I wish I had been at the camp that morning." Her voice cracks. I can't bear the sorrow in her voice.

Once the great animal was captured, Dolma had pushed her small body through the crowd, wanting to see the creature—to touch it, she later said. All fear, it seemed, had departed because she wanted to see the rare thing up close. That is when I began to worry about her. Would she turn out like me, fixated on unreachable things? And that is also when I chose to keep my distance.

Someone calls to the woman at the river, someone we can't see from our place on the ridge. She waits to answer, then shouts that she's almost finished. Her voice rings straight up into the darkening sky, where the words echo for a moment.

"When we last spoke, my sister told me Dolma will fly home right away, but Tenkyi won't be able come just yet. She was weeping. I told her not to cry because I feel strong, like I have another ten, fifteen years in me."

"You do," I say, emptied of everything.

"We are still young, aren't we?" She laughs as she says this. "This morning I woke up thinking that phone call with my sister was a dream. But who can tell what is real and what is a dream? My head isn't the same. At least my child will be here soon."

"I will send someone to fetch her at the airport."

"If you could go?"

"I'll stay here with you. But I will send someone. Don't worry."

The woman at the river has resumed her prayer-like song, though she now pauses every so often as if to catch her breath. Bracing herself on a rock, she wipes her eyes.

We watch in silence. Her exposed arms and shoulders gleam in the sun as she stands in the river, working breathlessly. Her long black hair is loose, its ends pulling here and there in the water.

"Is she crying?" I ask.

"It appears she might be."

"I wonder what happened."

"A woman's life is a series of hardships. Looks like it'll rain any minute."

"These clouds move so fast," I say.

"Yes, it's going to rain."

"I want to explain myself. That morning when I left—"

"I thought that was why you brought me here. Tell me."

"I was afraid."

"Of me?"

"No. Maybe. I was afraid you would change your mind, once you saw me clearly. Or maybe I wasn't sure you should leave your husband for me. I thought to myself, why would she give up so much, risk turning her life upside down, just for me? I'm not good enough for that. All I ever did was take. I have never reached the end of my hunger, Lhamo. Even the Saint's ku you gave me, I took it when I shouldn't have."

"The ku belonged with you. It was your uncle's."

"But in the end, I sold it."

"I see."

"I needed the money. For Dolma and for others who rely on me. I sold everything."

"The good thing is, we can be calm now," she says. "Now that we know how things have turned out."

I can say nothing.

"But we had beautiful dreams, didn't we? We said we would return to our villages together. You would churn the cheese. I would ride horses. Remember?" She turns and looks at me.

My eyes are full of tears. I turn away.

"Just like the sun has to set soon, my life is ending now. There's nothing anyone can do about it."

I feel around on the hard ground. It's still warm from the day. I can hold on to this fact.

"Oh," she says, smiling, "did you ever find your father's things?"

"No, I didn't."

"You always wanted to. And to know your mother's face."

"For a long while, I believed I would succeed. In some ways, I drove everything in my life toward that wish."

"But I suppose we must all make peace with the things we cannot have."

"Yes," I say. "Now I just want to sit by this river, beside you."

She gives me a slight nod. "I've always wanted us to sit like this, you and I, speaking openly." After a pause, she says, "I know what I want you to tell Dolma when you meet her."

"Okay."

"Tell her about your life. Tell her about mine. Speak to her without holding anything back. I couldn't do that, no matter how I tried. Something has been lodged in this throat of mine. But I don't want that for my daughter. I want her to speak freely. Do you understand?"

5

W HEN the monks from the monastery tell us it's time, we hold the cremation by the river, a short drive from the camp. Large black birds of prey circle above, dropping down every so often to hop back and forth at the edges of the sun-scorched banks. Nearly everyone from the camp is here, grimacing and shielding their faces from the heat. I stand at the back of the crowd, hoping to be left alone. In the flames, I can make out Lhamo's body on the pyre. I tell myself: Lhamo is burning away in that fire. My Lhamo.

I turn away.

Ashang Migmar walks up to me and directs my gaze to the other side of the pyre. "That's him. Tashi Tamding. My daughter's husband."

A thin, pale man stands in the crowd, expressionless before the fire. It's clear from his gaunt figure that he isn't light skinned from living an easy life. He looks like the kind of man who stays inside dark dwellings, inside himself. I want to hear him speak. I want to know the voice that Lhamo heard for many years, the voice that she chose for her life.

But then Tashi shoots me a glance. Seeing the grim look on his face, I choose to remain at a distance.

"Does he know who I am?" I ask.

"He doesn't know anything," Ashang Migmar says, gesturing at his temple. "Fell one too many times while drunk. Should have come back from prison in better shape, but I guess he found a way to get alcohol there. Anyway, his head is gone."

I stare at the fire. I recognize Tashi's slumped shoulders, the eyes cast permanently down, the hands so limp and jittery, I wonder how they ever held a bottle. I know he's a man staring down a dark well that no one else can see—a well he's always at risk of falling into. Now I feel an unexpected grief for Tashi. And it's not just his condition. What pains me is this new detail from Lhamo's life, this glimpse into the isolation they must have both felt. Lhamo, for being married to a haunted man. Tashi, for being locked within his struggle.

Farther down the riverbank, there's another pyre. This one is much smaller than Lhamo's and is nearly reduced to embers. It must belong to a child. Three young men with shaved heads sit nearby. They look alike and appear to share the same depth of pain. None of them face the pyre. Instead, they stare at the river, each slumped in a different position, smoking in silence. The cremation worker walks in and sweeps up the smoldering ashes. The youngest of the three men pours the fine dust into a copper urn, which they cover with a white cloth and fix with a rubber band. Then, without a word, all three climb onto a motorcycle and drive away.

When I turn my attention back to Lhamo's pyre, the lower half of her body has disintegrated. How can this be? A minute ago, it had seemed as though the fire were burning through her slowly and evenly, layer by layer. But now, it's as if her cremation had sped up, and I feel cheated of the time I need to say goodbye. But of course, there's no way to complain, nowhere to lodge an objection. What power can anyone have over fire? Like death, it takes what it wants.

I glance at my watch. Dolma's plane landed five hours ago. Bhim informed me that he picked her up in my second car, and by now, they must be nearly at the camp. It is said that openly grieving the dead could endanger their swift passage to rebirth, and so Ashang Migmar had thought it would be better to spare Dolma the cremation. She can grieve with the other women of the camp instead.

Now the smoke billows up and begins to spread flecks of ash over the mourners. I open my hands and watch the gray snow fall gently onto my palms. All around me, everything is dusted by Lhamo's ashes—the riverbank, the mourners, even the crows.

Earlier, the pyre had smelled of sandalwood, pine, and incense. But the sources of these sweet smells have burned away, and I am surrounded by smoke. It enters my lungs, and I cough as my eyes sting. People begin to walk away, heading back to the camp for prayers. Before long, Lhamo's pyre is nearly gone, reduced to a mound of smoking gray ash with lumps of charcoal.

"I'll manage the end of this," I say to Ashang Migmar. "Go and rest now."

"The ashes," he replies, holding up a plastic bag with a bronze container inside.

"I'll bring them back to you," I say, taking the urn.

"Good. I should get back for the prayer ceremonies . . ." he trails off, mumbling about the rituals that are now needed to help Lhamo through the in-between.

There are still many weeks remaining in her journey within the bardo. The living must keep a vigil for her, until her karma is fulfilled. But I know that I must do more than light candles and pray for Lhamo.

"Wait," I say, pulling out an envelope from the inner pocket of my jacket.

"What's this?" Ashang Migmar asks.

"Take it. You can open it later."

He feels the envelope and recognizes that it's cash. A smile breaks for the briefest moment, then his face flushes red as he insists that there's no need. I know I should have given it to him in private at the camp, but I won't return there now. Whether the old man knows it or not, this is the last we'll see of each other.

"I can commission a thangka painting and a green Tara statue for Lhamo with this," Ashang Migmar replies brightly.

"That's good," I say and watch as he walks to the road.

"Where should I put the ashes?" asks the man sweeping up.

I hand him Ashang Migmar's bronze container. There's still smoke rising from her remains. The man scoops the ashes into the container, and I'm overcome by a need to leave this place, to drive away as quickly as the three brothers had. For as long as I live, I never want to lay eyes on this riverbank again.

With the full container in my hands, I walk to the river's edge. The ashes look just like the sand here. I twist the lid off, pour the ashes into the plastic bag, and tie it shut. Then I squat down, dig my fingers into the cool, damp soil and fill the bronze container. In a numbed daze, I walk to my jeep holding the container of sand in one hand and the plastic bag of warm ashes in the other. A high crackling sound comes from the horizon as a white car appears on the gravel road along the gorge. It's moving too fast for this rough terrain.

As it nears, I recognize the car as one of mine. So Bhim has brought Dolma here instead of the camp. Although now, it doesn't matter. The cremation is finished, and the child has been spared the sight of her mother burning. I place the bag and container on the seat, shielding my eyes from the sun's glare, as Bhim slams the brakes and stops the car. Before I can say a word, he hops out and runs around back to open the door.

A young woman, small in frame with a messy ponytail and dark circles under her eyes, emerges from the car. She meets my gaze for a moment then turns away abruptly, peering down at the funeral site, where a few charred logs smolder by the riverbank. Even from here, I can see that her eyes are tinged red. Grimacing in the bright sun, she studies the movements of the old man who is tidying the pyre. She is clearly locked in some internal struggle to make herself as stiff and calm as she can. I'm reminded of a brittle branch in a storm.

"Why did you bring her here?" I ask Bhim with a sense of futility after he runs over to me.

"Sir, I drove to the camp first, but she found out about the funeral and insisted . . ." Bhim quiets as he grows unsure of whether it's smart to blame the girl.

"Is it over?" she asks. Her voice is mature and pleasant, though she looks like she could be a teenager.

I nod. "Do you know who I am?"

"My mother's sweetheart," she says.

It's like a knife has grazed the surface of my heart. "Did your Ama tell you that?" I ask, unable to stop myself.

"She never told me anything." There is a hint of bitterness in her voice.

"I've wanted to meet you—" I say, before stopping myself. These are not the words she wants to hear from me.

"When did you get here?" she asks.

"Three days ago, it must have been."

"Is my father here?" she asks wearily, seeming to brace herself for disappointment.

"He's been here the whole time. Now he's with Ashang Migmar helping with the rest of the prayers."

All at once, tears fall from her eyes. She is so plainly Lhamo's child, so plainly mine. Even Bhim must see this. But neither he nor Dolma can know my dizzying bewilderment. It's as if the earth and sky had traded places. The woman whose body succumbed to flames, whose ashes flew above me just a moment ago, has now returned. Her mouth, her small hands, her narrow shoulders. Yes, she is here. Standing within reach, staring at the riverbank where her body turned to ash, weeping for all that has been irretrievably lost. At least now, she is willing to show her anger. I sense that we may even be able to speak in plain and honest terms. But I fear what I might say, and I fear what she might say.

"Take me back to the camp," she tells Bhim, her Nepali faltering.

He turns to me for direction.

"Go," I say. "I'll follow you."

Now that I have seen her, I must stay near. Even if she doesn't need me, I will remain beside her.

PART IV

Self

DOLMA

Pokhara, Nepal

2012

I stand before the padlocked door, holding the keys to Ama's house. Samphel waits behind me. He has been trailing me since I arrived, as if it were his duty.

"I'll take care of her clothes," I say, turning the key. "You can just sit inside."

The door opens and a damp emptiness meets us, followed by the scent of sandalwood, juniper, and butter. The sealed remnants of Ama's last day here. I wish to turn around and close the door immediately, to preserve this sacred air. But already, the wind from the gorge is sweeping in through my limbs, circling within these walls, and carrying my mother's scent into the valley. Did she lock up after the accident, thinking she would return soon? Did she think it would be a quick trip to the hospital?

When Po Migmar handed me the keys in his courtyard, he was surrounded by people and in the middle of an endless procession of tasks for the death rituals. I walked up to him and asked, "Is it true? Is my mother dead?" I knew his heart was broken because he could not answer me. Avoiding my gaze, he asked if I wanted to do something. "Yes," I said, "give me something to do." So Po Migmar told me to go back to Ama's house, sort through all her clothes, and decide who should be given which items. As I listened to him, a few women in the courtyard came to embrace me with wicks and butter lamps in their hands. Someone let

Mo Yutok know that I had arrived. She came toward me, her face furrowed as she took small steps with her cane. As she held my face and wept, Mo Yutok said that I looked just like my mother. I feared those words would break me, but my legs carried me to my mother's house.

All I want is to sit here quietly, alone within these four walls. But I stop myself from sending Samphel away. I have questions for him.

Against the far wall, Ama's single bed sits under a window framed by short plaid curtains. Two blankets are neatly folded at one end. On the opposite end, a single pillow rests with a rosary nearby. My own bed, perpendicular to Ama's, looks much the same as I left it, still dressed with blue floral sheets I chose six or seven years ago. Yet it's as if I had returned to someone's re-creation of our house. This cannot be the room where we lived for so many years. It is too cramped; the ceiling is too low. These four walls could not have contained someone like my mother.

I notice a patch of sunlight on the floor. It shines through the jagged edges of a rotted beam. I stand in the light and peer through the hole, which has been covered by a clear plastic tarp, likely held down by a few bricks on the roof. Ama sat in this spot. Deep in repose one moment, cut open the next. A sharp pain throbs behind my eyes. I have not slept in two, maybe three days at this point. There was only that one moment, just before the plane began its descent into the Kathmandu Valley, when I slipped into a dreamless oblivion. Then, just as suddenly, I was pulled back to consciousness for no apparent reason. Outside my window, gray clouds sped by, dense and endless, giving me the sense that we could plunge for years through that suffocating haze without ever meeting the earth. Then an intense ache radiated from the back of my head, so excruciating that I reached into my hair, but there was no wound, no blood. Instead, my body was overcome by exhaustion. I pulled my hands down and saw that my skin was now as gray and lifeless as the clouds outside. Somehow, I knew that my mother had departed her body.

I turn away from the hole in the roof and face the kitchen counter. A large, empty pot rests on the burner beside a bag of flour and an open jar of sugar. She was making sweet bread. Perhaps a snack for the afternoon, after her prayers were completed. I close the sugar jar and place it on the kitchen shelf beside a fresh block of butter wrapped in plastic. To my side, strips of dried meat hang from a string tied between two nails.

At the end of the shelf, a Mickey Mouse greeting card, yellowed and faded, cheerfully greets 2007—the year I left for Canada. Beside it, there's an old photo of Ama with Shumo Tenkyi. They're both so young, probably in their twenties, and they stand before a painted backdrop of hills and mountains—their whole lives ahead of them. On a lower shelf, three fresh jars of radishes slowly ferment, aging for a meal that my mother will never eat.

"Do you want something to drink?" I ask, turning around.

The man is seated on the edge of Ama's bed. I notice his hands gripping the mattress, and a flash of rage comes through me. I want to shout at him to get off her bed.

"I'm alright," he says, looking oddly meek. "I'd like to help."

I walk over to the metal armoire where Ama kept her clothes. "We'll offer them to the poorest families in the camp first," I say. "After that, whatever remains, we'll give to beggars in town."

"That's good," he says, nodding.

I crank open the stiff metal doors and bring all her clothes to the floor in a pile. Next, I reach under her bed and pull out the suitcases tucked deep beneath. A dozen more musty dresses and blouses join the pile. Sitting beside Samphel, I notice a harsh, almost sweetly pungent scent of smoke. Of course. He watched the cremation. Even he had a chance to say goodbye.

Parsing through her possessions, I work as quickly as I can, handing them to Samphel and instructing him to fold them into various groupings. I had forgotten many of her clothes, but now as I sift through them, they are accompanied by intense and merciless bursts of memory. A lilac silk blouse that Ama wore on my first day of secondary school; gazing up at her that day, I had thought she looked like a heavenly being. A pale-yellow dress with tiny orange flowers that she wore for picnics in the warmer months. The dark green shawl she draped around her shoulders every winter, and which she folded around me on so many nights. And then there are the more recent purchases I do not recognize. Plain and unadorned dresses in various shades of gray and brown. When did my mother become old? How could I have missed these last years with her?

In the end, it is only a modest offering of clothes. The aggregate fabric of my mother's life makes up very little. Four or five shawls. One sweater, piling and stretched thin at the wrists and underarms. A handful of silk and linen blouses. Eight dresses, a few from many years ago. Four patterned matrimonial aprons, which my mother wore every day—even after Tashi was long gone. I could get rid of everything in a day, but what if she returns? Could she still be here, somewhere on this hill?

In the corner, I spot a lone, forgotten dress. It's made of dark wool, so old and thick it could be a rag from another time. I reach for the dress and hold it up. It's cut straight across at the knee with the hem left raw.

"Let me see that," Samphel says, reaching out. I pass it to him and begin tidying the clothes, which he has folded poorly.

"The day I met your mother, she was wearing this dress. It was her mother's."

I'm astonished. Ama never mentioned my grandmother, much less showed me something that belonged to her.

"Back then, your mother would also tie her father's red sash across her waist. And in her hair, she wore a little red ribbon. That's the first thing I saw when I came to this camp. That red ribbon. It kept flashing in the sunlight from a distance. Then she ran down toward us, fearless and open, and she looked me straight in the eyes."

"Were you two close right away?"

He smiles with a sorrow I had not detected before. "Meeting her was like entering a deep, cold river pool."

"Do you have any photos?"

"Of your mother?"

"I found a few pictures of the camp in the 1970s, but none with Ama, my aunt, or Po Migmar."

"Will you show me later?" he asks. "I have no photographs from that time."

We take a break outside, sitting on a couple of plastic buckets, our backs leaning against the house. I pull out a cigarette and offer him the pack. He's curious to try the taste of Canadian smoke and fishes one out for himself. We inhale in silence as faint voices rise and fall on the nearby path. A few crickets signal the coming sunset.

We're finally facing each other. Why keep any secrets now?

"I have something of yours," I say. "Back in Toronto."

"Of mine?"

"The mudstone Mahasiddha you sold. The Nameless Saint."

He blinks rapidly while taking a long drag. "How did you come across it?"

"By an improbable series of happenings my mother would have called 'karma.' I saw him at a rich Enji family's house," I say, pausing to tap away some ash. "I just have one question: How could you do it?"

"I held on to that statue as long as I could."

"But how could you sell it? Not just that ku—all the relics you stole?"

"You consider me a thief."

"What would you call yourself?"

"Dolma, when you get to be my age, you see that the world doesn't run on charity," he says, sounding more assured. "You have to get a hold of something valuable, something others want. That's how you survive. If fortune allows you to avoid that manner of advancement, it means your ancestors took enough before your lifetime."

"I don't believe that. Even if everyone is implicated, that doesn't erase our responsibility for our own actions."

"I'm not saying I'm innocent. But who is?"

"The Saint's ku mattered to our camp. To this day, Po Migmar still talks about it."

"Believe me, I didn't want to sell it. And not because of these fantasies about it disappearing and reappearing over the years, but because it was your mother who gave me that statue."

"Everyone thinks it vanished into thin air, and you're telling me my mother took it?"

"I don't know," he sighs. "What I do know is that survival is an ugly game, and our objects are all the world really values of our people. Our objects and our ideas. But not us, and not our lives. Whether we're here for another two hundred years or wiped off the face of the planet, it doesn't matter to anyone else, not really."

"People find our culture beautiful," I say. "But not our suffering. No one wants to put that in a glass case. Nobody wants to own that."

"You must understand . . . I grieved the loss of the statue along with every item I sold," he says quietly.

"I took the ku from your buyers," I admit. "They don't know this, but I saw the code to the safe."

He turns to me with a serious expression, his eyes searching my face. "Where is it now?"

"With Shumo Tenkyi."

"Did anyone see you take it?"

"No, I went back for the ku during another party. The house was full of people."

"Only your aunt knows about this?"

I nod.

"Were there cameras?"

"If there were, the family's collection manager is in a lot of trouble."

"What? Look, we can still fix this."

"Will you give it back to the buyers?"

Samphel shakes his head. "I will send someone in Toronto to pick it up from your aunt. He'll put the ku in a container and ship it back to Nepal. Nice and slow, quietly through the oceans, back to the camp."

We both laugh, then look down and press our hands to our mouths in shame. If someone walked by, we could never explain this moment.

A rooster hops onto the roof across from us and walks gingerly along the slippery spine. We watch him in a sustained silence, listening as his feet scrape against the tin, wondering if he will make it to the other end. I have spent many afternoons sitting in this exact spot, watching the rain stream down that corrugated roof, observing the sun travel across this patch of sky. I was in this exact spot the day Tashi reappeared after a year-long disappearance.

"I've come to celebrate Losar!" he announced.

Ama came to the door and barely let her eyes rest on him. Instead, she said to me, "Tell your father I went to the camp hall to cook for the festivities." I walked up to him and repeated my mother's words. He laughed and said it had been years since we did Losar properly. Now that he had returned, we would remedy that. So we began our preparations. As he worked on the house, scrubbing the floors and beating the rugs outside, I went to get supplies for our special meal of guthuk. I had memorized his instructions: we would need flour to make balls of dough, paper to write the words hidden inside, beef to make a savory broth, and whatever vegetables were fresh. Walking to the shops, I hoped I would get a good word like *sun* or *moon* in the soup that year, and that my father wouldn't get *coal* as he had that one time. The good-natured fun of guthuk had turned sour as Tashi explained with a bitter smile that coal meant black-hearted. The guthuk had wounded him with an accusation he could not treat as a joke.

When I returned, the grass broom was on the floor beside a bucket of dirty water and sopping wet rags. But Tashi wasn't inside. I put the groceries down and searched around back, finding only a goat and some chickens milling about. I went to the neighbor's house and called out for him along the footpaths of the camp. Back home, the juice from the beef had seeped through the newspaper and pooled on the linoleum floor. In my daze, I threw everything in the freezer and ruined the potatoes and cilantro—something I let my mother believe was Tashi's fault.

Two days passed without any sight of him, and I began to wonder if I had imagined his return. Then, on the third day of Losar, he showed up at the camp hall, his face darkened and greased with sweat. Running onto the stage, he gestured before the painted backdrop of the Potala Palace, and cried out my mother's name, asking if she wanted to go on pilgrimage there. Swaying in place, Tashi pointed at the painting, stared at the stairs leading to the Potala, and said that he had once been there himself, but it looked a little different now. A few of the older kids howled, falling over themselves. I hid behind the door in shame. Then Tashi tripped and nearly pulled the whole painting off the wall. Four men ran up to the stage and led him away while my mother hid in the community kitchen. Back at home, the men told me to lock the doors and get the barley wheat and hot water ready. Then they held Tashi down on the bed and fed him broth while I watched him weep, helpless, on their shoulders.

In the days that followed, he slept for long stretches and woke desperate for alcohol, rummaging through the room, begging me to buy a bottle. While my mother sold her trinkets by Phewa Lake, I watched over him, preparing food, holding him up as he walked to the toilet, wiping his face and limbs with a damp cloth to wash away his sour smell. When he lost the ability to control his bowels, I was the one to clean the floors. As he watched me clean, I felt a kind of pride knowing he could see me, his child all grown up. Throughout my childhood, Tashi had often told me not to call him my father. It was something my mother laughed off as vanity, saying he just couldn't accept that he was aging. But I hoped he wouldn't forget those days. Staying by his side, I did my homework at the window and occasionally studied his face as he lay in fevered sleep. One day, I took my mother's small compact mirror, edged up to him as he slept, and compared our faces. The tip of his nose was similar to my tip, but my bridge looked like my mother's. His hairline came to a point in the middle of his forehead, whereas mine was rounded. His eyes were light brown, almost golden before the sun's rays, and they sloped down at the edges. But my eyes were dark, and they angled up like a cat, something even my mother's didn't do. But the tip of the nose, Tashi and I shared that. I told him this while offering a cup of bone broth. "Pala," I said, "we have the same nose tip. Look." But he just turned away toward the wall and said, "Don't call me that."

Now I sit beside a man whose eyes are dark and angled up like mine, whose gently curving hairline matches my own. A man in whom I finally recognize all the parts of me I never understood.

Samphel notices my gaze and shifts in place uncomfortably. "How is your aunt?" he asks.

"She is herself. Which is to say, she is a mystery to me."

"That's a trait in your family."

"Coming from you, I don't know how to take that," I say, before adding, "You know, I remember you. From the day of the leopard."

"I didn't think you would." He pauses. "I shouldn't have come."

"Why do you say that?" I ask, remembering how angry Ama became when I mentioned his name that night at our store. We never spoke about him again.

"It wasn't my place . . ." he says, trailing off.

"There's something I've always wanted to ask you about that day." It's my turn to pause, waiting for the words to dislodge from my throat. "Did you leave that night because you were unhappy?" He frowns in confusion, and I'm forced to try again. "Were you unhappy with me? Was I not what you hoped for? Is that why you left and never came back?"

He shakes his head, searching for the words. "That question is so far from the truth, Dolma. All my life . . . What I mean to say is that I grew up asking myself the same thing about my mother. She gave me up as an infant because I was born out of wedlock. I have no memory of her. I don't even know her name. A few times, my father spoke lovingly of her. And he was a hard man, so I understood how wonderful my mother must have been for him to speak that way. Because I begged him, my father promised I would see her someday when the battles ended, when peace returned. He said we would find her then. But my father fell to his death building a mountain road in India."

"Did they call you names? Because you were born out of wedlock?"

"When we lived in the Jawalakhel camp, my father would drink every night and talk to the shadows in our hut. In his sleep, he was transported back to the dusty fur market of our village, where people had jeered and called me a bastard while he walked mute and shaking with anger. But in his dreams, my father seemed to speak back, arguing with people from long ago."

Samphel's voice becomes quiet as he adds, "I always thought he was angry with me because I had brought him shame. But when you have a child, you begin to realize what your parents experienced. All I wanted was for you to be spared our suffering. The day your aunt told me that you were pursuing further studies in Canada, I couldn't stop smiling. You must keep going forward with that. Don't worry about the money. There's always a way."

I say nothing. The British School, Henri, Professor Wallace, all the years of grasping after a dream. The years I spent separated from my mother, convinced it would be worth our sacrifices. Was it worth what it cost us?

"The camp has changed a lot," Samphel remarks, seemingly bothered by the silence for the first time.

"It's still just a hilltop of stateless people," I say. "The entire camp envied me before I left. Picture that: hundreds of hearts dreaming their names in place of mine on a visa."

"Dolma, listen," he says. "I have to leave tomorrow to take care of something. But I can come back. Would you like that?"

"Where are you going?"

He looks at me, considering what to say. "I don't want to lie to you."

"Then don't lie. Just tell me."

"I have your mother's ashes. The container I gave your uncle is just full of river sand."

"You took Ama's ashes," I repeat, somehow puzzled that he continues to surprise me. "So, what's your plan?"

"I have to take her home somehow."

"She is home."

"No, she's not."

"I'm coming with you then."

"It's not safe."

"After everything you've taken, if you think I'm going to let you leave with my mother's ashes . . ."

He doesn't protest anymore. "Okay, we leave tomorrow morning."

Another rooster, this one larger, has jumped onto the other end of the roof.

"Now, which way will the first rooster go?" I ask.

"Back the way it came."

"Or it has to find a new path."

2

O UR flight leaves for Jomsom at dawn. We are a strange pair at the airport, related yet without a relationship, standing side by side with nothing to say. Around us, people haul enormous duffel bags and suitcases packed to their limits. They glance at us with curiosity because we've brought only the bags we carry on our backs. Mine holds a couple of days' worth of clothes, and Samphel's contains Ama's ashes. This will be a quick trip, and when we return, we will carry even less. We may even be released from each other. Perhaps, we will never speak again.

At the airline counter, Samphel pulls out a stack of bills for our tickets. "Here," he says, handing me an envelope of cash along with my boarding pass.

"I don't need it."

"Take it. You will."

Looking away, I accept the cash, but the stack slips from my hand and falls to the ground. I also dropped a mug this morning, sending shattered porcelain across the floor. It was another sleepless night, this time staring at my mother's empty bed.

The rickety plane takes off with twelve passengers and a flight attendant who walks the narrow aisle, bracing herself on the headrests while holding out a plastic tray of hard candy. I notice Samphel across the aisle, peering out the window as we glide between the hills. He studies the scene below as if looking for a familiar sight. It's possible he traveled through this region when he fled Tibet. My mother too. Somewhere along these ravines, hidden by the forests. How strange it must be to see it all from this vantage. In less than an hour, we will travel a distance that would have taken weeks or even months to cross on foot some fifty years ago. That such a journey could now be so quick, so forgettable, seems almost cruel. As though all that struggle meant nothing. I think about the last flight I took. How tired I felt as the plane descended into Kathmandu, the pulsing ache in the back of my head. What caused those sensations?

We make a sudden, rough descent into a narrow valley. The plane skids when it lands, swerving side to side as it brakes to a stop. As we wait in the aisle to exit, intense gusts of wind blow in through the airplane door, and an abrupt, urgent need rises in me. I need to see what's outside, I need to see the land. The instant I step outside, my body is pierced by a million needlepoints of icy wind. Enormous mountains appear in every direction, reaching such immense heights I need to look straight up to see their gleaming, snow-covered tips. Closer to me, in the shadows of the mountains, are treeless rock and sand hills that are massive in their own right. I turn left and right on the tarmac, trying to fathom the scale of these peaks. They seem to overwhelm the sky, shining so bright that even the sun seems dull and small. Under their ageless gaze, I feel at once minuscule and contented—as though I were a child again, peering up at my mother. Samphel, meanwhile, shows no interest in the landscape. He stands by the entrance to the airport, waiting for me to catch up.

As we look around Jomsom's main road, it's clear why he was in a hurry. The other passengers from the plane already have their plans in motion. Some quickly file into a row of white jeeps, and others walk off with their waiting family. There's one available driver, but he's willing to take us only to Muktinath, where he had already intended to go and gather some holy water. But he will not take us north. "No real roads that way and I won't drive on the riverbank," he says. Motioning up the desolate valley with its low river, he adds, "Until the snows come, you can walk to Kagbeni and find help there."

"How long will that take?" Samphel asks.

"An hour for us but maybe two or three for you," the driver says, scanning us with curiosity. "What do you want up north?"

"We're visiting someone," Samphel replies curtly before turning to me. "Let's go."

As we leave the corridor of shops and guesthouses, we turn down a dirt road and spot a village on the horizon. A bright patch of green nestled among the gray desert hills. It can't be more than a few kilometers away, I think. But as soon as we reach the exposed footpath, the wind envelopes us, pushing against each step we take. With the sand blowing in every direction, it's impossible for us to raise our heads for more than a few seconds at a time. The walk is slow and earns me a blister almost instantly.

"Are you sure you want to do this?" he shouts, shielding his eyes. "You can wait at the guesthouse here."

"You're the one wearing office shoes. I can manage."

He laughs. After a pause, he says, "My father and I lived here. But he was often gone."

"How long did you live here?" I ask, walking closer so I can hear him.

"A few years. There were two women, sisters, who cared for me when he was away. My father often went back to the border to do things—I never knew what, but I missed him terribly. He was the only person I had in my life. Nearly every day, I asked the sisters: When will my father return? They always said: Tomorrow, tomorrow. So I would search the horizon, hoping to glimpse his return. Sometimes my eyes played tricks on me. I would see him in the distance, walking with a beautiful yak that would give us cheese and milk. Other times, I saw him with my mother." He laughs. "I really believed they would come back together." Samphel falls silent after this, as though surprised by his own words.

Several hours later, we reach the staggered wheat fields of Kagbeni. Hidden among the swaying barley, we spot a few women farming in colorful dresses. Against the stark gray hills, the village is surreal, its unreality heightened by the Tibetan architecture. It is the first time I've ever seen such homes in person. Walking along the narrow stone paths, we see vibrantly painted window frames, roofs stacked with firewood, and prayer flags streaming above us. Ahead, a small stupa towers over the path, and as we pass through it, an inner chamber reveals painted frescoes of deities and Buddhist symbols. We come upon a large ancient mud monastery, washed in red dye. Chatting in the sun, a couple of monks smile at us with friendly nods. I want to go inside, but Samphel presses on, leading me through a labyrinthine complex. This appears to be a crumbling palace, though now it houses goats and laypeople. At every turn, intimately scaled mud walls hem us inside, protecting us from the wind, while ladders carved out of single tree trunks lead into narrow holes. Here and there along the ancient corridors, we see people repairing walls and making homes for themselves in the ruins. A few even greet us in our tongue. I have never been to a village that so closely resembles our country. The world that stretches from here is at once unknown and familiar, dreamlike yet real.

On the other side of the palace, we come across a garage with a jeep and a hand-painted English sign announcing a tour company. There's no one around except for some children huddled together and one of the region's miniature cows that reaches my waist. Coming up to us, a young boy says that someone will be here eventually, so we wait by the office for half an hour. Finally, a man walks up. Speaking in Nepali, he tells us that his name is Tseten and he saw us from his window next door. He wonders if he can help. I sense from his name and features that he might be Tibetan but is perhaps wary of using our language. Henri used to take research trips here, and he heard many unsettling rumors of spies in this border region. Farther up in the Lo Manthang area, nearing Tibet, he said that it's common for Chinese patrols to cross the border into Nepal and question the locals about their activities and allegiances to the Dalai Lama.

"We need to get to Lo Manthang," Samphel tells Tseten, also in Nepali.

"Where are you two from?" the man asks, looking at Samphel's leather loafers and pressed pants. My canvas sneakers, too, are no match for this terrain.

"I'm from Pokhara," I say.

"Pokhara? You look like a foreigner," Tseten says, a smile coming to his face. "The only way to Lo right now is on foot or by horse. Everyone who can drive has gone upriver for a wedding."

"How long is the walk?" I ask.

"You better go on horse. You can ride my horses. It will take three days."

Three days to Lo Manthang. It's a relief to have this time to say goodbye to my mother. But I cannot shake this vague and shapeless sense of dread. It covers everything.

Tseten brings two ponies, each with a saddle made from several layers of wool carpet, ornately carved iron stirrups, and red ribbons braided through their tails. Mine is the smaller of the two, a brown mare with dark legs and shaggy bangs. Tseten says her name is Zema, chosen by his daughter because of her pretty eyes. Zema wears an amulet around her neck to protect her, but her dark, expressive eyes seem to look at me and the world without fear. Samphel is given a pale, mottled pony named Jha because he can fly like a bird.

"I need to make a phone call before we leave," Samphel says.

Leading the horses, Tseten takes us to a storefront in a mud house with a long-distance telephone. I stay near Samphel, listening in.

"Did you hear back from Nawang Dorjee?" he asks the person on the other line.

"Tell him to try again. Give her a few days to calm down, and next time, he should tell her I sent him."

Samphel puts the receiver down and pays for the call. "Nawang used to work for me, but now he lives in Toronto," he says quietly. "He will take care of things."

"You said he should try again. What happened?"

"He visited your aunt, but she wouldn't give him the ku. Said she had no idea what he was talking about."

I'm strangely pleased as I picture my aunt turning the man away.

"Don't worry," Samphel says, "we'll get it back here."

We climb onto the horses and leave for the next village, our bodies jostling slowly as we follow Tseten on foot. The green fields of Kagbeni end, and we travel along the dry riverbed of the Kali Gandaki, which has carved this corridor between the mountains. All around us, the sandstone canyons seem to disintegrate with each gust of wind, eroding and shifting the land. Passing through the towering, crumbling cliffs, I feel myself becoming just as transitory. The river bed fills with water, and we climb onto a narrow footpath carved into the mountainside. Along the way, we pass some men with a herd of around a hundred goats, crowding each other as their bells ring and echo against the hills. The men exchange greetings with Tseten and gaze at us, trying to figure out who we could be. Our faces and skin match theirs, but our clothes and shoes belong to another world entirely. Tseten and Samphel continue on, but I want to tell these men that we're here with my mother's ashes. I want everyone to know of her passing.

At sundown, we zigzag up a craggy hill, sending rocks tumbling down the cliff every so often. My back seizes with pain, and my numb hands clutch the saddle. Although I find myself struggling to stay upright, Zema is steady in her climb. She seems to know how much I need her. The ascent ends, and we reach a village perched at the top of the cliff. Tseten leads us to a family-owned lodge, where we are quickly shown two available rooms. Samphel gives me the main guest room, and he takes a spare bed in the prayer room upstairs. He says his stomach hurts too much to eat, so he heads off to sleep almost as soon as we walk in.

At dinner, the owner of the guesthouse says that she speaks the same language as the people in Bhari, but in the north, in Lo Manthang, the language is different. One of the porters, seemingly drunk, takes issue with her comparison of the Gurung dialect to the language of Bhari. They're completely different, the porter insists. The banter continues long after everyone's plates are cleared, but I head upstairs. Exhausted and covered in dust, I take a bucket shower and go to my room. From my bedroom window, I can see the face of a rocky hill towering above me in the moonlight. Like everything here, the hill seems impossible to traverse. Under its watch, the houses of the village spread out like a paper fan, their flat clay roofs covered with firewood collected for the long winter ahead and hundreds of prayer flags, each line stretching across three or four homes. All the flags are windworn, their dye faded, their ends frayed, and some have dissolved almost completely. I imagine prayer flags can last only a few months here before they're eaten by the wind. As I look around, it seems like a miracle that my mother and aunt could have survived this land as children all those years ago.

I lie back in the narrow wooden bed, pressed down by a heavy stack of musty blankets. I'm desperate for sleep. But I'm also hounded by a rapid stream of thoughts. I need to grow up and help my family. I ought to make lots of money and give up this fantasy of endless studying. While Po Migmar and Shumo are alive, I should give them a comfortable life. Lucrative white-collar careers spring to mind. Without any paper, I scribble some notes on my arm in the dark. My eyelids become heavy as I notice a prickling sensation in my throat. I hope I'm not getting sick, but that would explain why my body hurts so much. The next moment, I wake up under a bright white moon and an indigo sky. I urgently need to pee. Slipping out from under the heavy blankets, I tiptoe to the door and open the latch.

The sight before me is something from a dream. Over a dozen men, including some of the porters from dinner, are asleep on the floor. They've covered nearly every inch of the hallway. In fact, there's no way for me to walk from my room to the toilet without hopping over three bodies lying at my feet. Earlier, as I listened to these men in the kitchen, I hadn't considered where they would all sleep. I had just been envious of their animated discussion.

Closing the door, I return to the bed and stare out the window at the moon illuminating the world below. Pulling up the latch, I push back one of the windows. The opening is just wide enough for me to slip out onto the rooftop. Once I manage to pass through, I find myself standing in a dark blue world, all alone, the wind sending my hair in every direction. Finding a corner free of firewood, I squat down and relieve myself, shivering uncontrollably.

When I get up, the back of my head pulses in pain. A sudden heat washes through me, settling in my chest and fingertips. I'm not alone here. Looking around, I see no one else. Just the silhouette of the mountains and prayer flags. Still, it's clear that someone or something very old is near. I sense their companionship from nowhere and everywhere. And I think of the leopard who paced before our house.

Walking back to the window, I move slowly. With every step, I'm intensely aware of someone's gaze on me. The constant wind picks up as I slide through the opening. It whistles through the cracks of the walls and windows, as if to call me back outside.

3

IN the morning, there's no sign of the men who had been sleeping outside my door. The wooden floor is swept clean, and the corridor is also empty. Downstairs, some of the men are recovering from hangovers with cups of tea; others have already left. Samphel is sitting on his own by the stove, with an untouched plate of eggs and flatbread and a cup of tea. I take a seat beside him as the owner prepares my breakfast. She brings my tea and takes a quick glance at my arm. It's covered in illegible pen marks. I lick my thumb and rub out the ink, trying to remember what I wrote. But last night's apparition hangs inside my eyelids. The wind that sounded like language, the presence of an ageless companion.

"How did you sleep?" Samphel asks, turning toward me.

"Fine and you?" I reply, my voice hoarse as my throat stings again. I may be falling ill after all.

"Fine," he says, eyes bleary. Even his skin looks worse today, wrinkled and sagging from his cheeks. Once again, but for a few bites of bread, his plate of food is untouched. As much as I try, I cannot picture Samphel as a younger man. Even when I think back to the day of the leopard, I find I've replaced him with the man I see today—someone in his early sixties, worn down but also hardened, alone for too many years. It's clear that he's struggling, but he's also resolved to continue on. In a way, this quality in him reminds me of my mother. Maybe this is what drew them together. *And what else, Ama? Now that I sit beside your sweetheart, what else can I learn about you from observing this man?* I stare at Samphel's backpack, her ashes silent inside.

Tseten is eager to resume our journey, so we climb back onto the horses and return to the trail along a steep canyon. The morning takes us over a seemingly endless row of desolate hills until we stop for lunch in a village of two houses that seems to exist solely to feed travelers. Tseten leads us into a kitchen where a group of elderly French trekkers is already seated, mixing tablets into their water bottles and talking jovially in their tongue. In the center, a young girl serves us a simple meal from her hearth.

Around us, the mud walls are decorated with enormous posters of beautiful western homes, a panoramic photograph of the Potala Palace, and several portraits of the Dalai Lama. But the most prized object on display seems to be a shelf with copper and steel cups and plates, brightly polished and carefully arranged. Samphel and I eat quickly in relative silence as the other travelers glance at us. It occurs to me that between the locals who live on this land and the foreigners who trek through here for brief holidays, we make the least sense in this place, belonging neither here nor elsewhere. What's more, although the two of us look alike, we say so little to each other. Between us, there is everything—my bones, my skin, so many of my features that originate from him. And yet, there is also nothing between us.

But we travel together. Even as we finish our plates, we are in sync, slipping away from the strange fishbowl of the kitchen and going out to wash our hands at the taps. The girl who prepared our meals is nearby, feeding Zema and Jha from a pot of leftovers. Hearing us speak in Tibetan, she becomes friendly, animated. Walking over, she tells me her name is Kesang, and she asks where we've come from.

"Pokhara," I say, noticing the mountain behind her house, which rises sharply hundreds of feet into the sky. "Have you always lived here?"

"I was born here," Kesang says. "A while back, this village was even smaller. There was only one house then, my house."

My surprise must be apparent because she laughs and continues. "My mother came here from Tibet, and she chose this place because there's a god on this mountain who visited her one night. When she died, I didn't want to leave the mountain, so I found a husband who would live here."

"My mother just died," I say. It's the first time I've said this to a stranger.

Kesang nods and sets her pot down under the stream of water. "I have a son. He can't walk well like you and me. Being a mother is difficult.

You worry about your child from the moment they're born. It's hard because it isn't just your body that you give to them. Your mind is also theirs."

I struggle to think of something to say in response. My thoughts have become foggy, jumbled in the last few days. "Do you remember anything your mother told you about those early days?" I ask.

"No, it was long ago, so I don't remember. Nothing here lasts for long, not even the past," she replies, looking up at the sky. "It might rain tomorrow."

The sky is a clear and sharp blue, but the wind has picked up. Tseten approaches, asking Samphel and me to get back on our horses. I climb onto Zema and pet the coarse mane along her neck. She carries me forward, up a gentle hill. Soon, we lose sight of the village, but I keep thinking about what Kesang said, about the burdens of a mother and also the gravity a mother commands—calling on a daughter to remain in such isolation.

Along the way, we come upon a young woman in a wool chupa. She's accompanying a black-haired yak. After years of hearing about it, this is my first sighting of the gentle, horned cattle. Po Migmar used to speak fondly about his yaks—each one, he said, had their own personality and unique beauty. The yak before me has been decorated with braids woven into red tassels, a brass bell, and a colorful rug saddle, similar to the ones on our horses.

As we pass each other, the young woman, who could be roughly my age, stares at me with intense curiosity. I turn back and lock eyes with her. She reminds me of my aunt. Perhaps this is how Shumo looked at my age. Now the girl's expression appears vaguely accusatory, as if to ask why I should have my life and not hers.

The accusation doesn't come from the girl with the yak. It comes from within me. All my life I've carried this silent guilt. Throughout my child-hood, Po Migmar would speak of my aunt and her brilliance—a mind like my grandmother's, he said—and I would proudly look at my aunt, the schoolteacher. Everyone said I was like her. But our lives could not have taken more differing paths. In the West, I could become someone new, pursue my supposed promise without true hardship. But Shumo could not. She couldn't direct her identity the way she wished. In truth, all this had made me distrust my own nature, made me question whether I even have a core sense of myself. If I was able to change my speech so quickly to match Henri's, if I could reshape myself to fit into the world of scholars, maybe there was never anything steady within me. Now I watch the sand that flies off these hills, and I recognize that my character is no different. It is fleeting, disappearing. Still, I lust for more. What is this hunger? I wish to be free from myself, to quiet my mind, outrun it.

Eventually, the girl with the yak turns her gaze back and continues on her journey, and I turn away as well. Our shadows move against the hills, slowly separating.

LATE AFTERNOON, WE reach the top of a hill, and yet another valley stretches before us with a horizon of endless mountains. Nearby, a tall pole is covered in prayer flags. There are so many flags on it, the pole curves toward the ground, seemingly ready to break in half. As Zema labors on, her hoofs crunching the desert earth in a slow rhythm, I sense my own weight on her torso. This poor creature, silently bearing such a burden. My chest seizes, as if contracting in size, and my breathing becomes shallow. I fear I might collapse.

"Where are you going?" someone asks.

I dismount from Zema, and, walking past the prayer flags, I come to the edge of the hill and rest my hands on my knees. Dropping my head, I try to take in as much air as my chest will allow. Tears stream down my face, but I keep quiet.

"Sit down for a minute," Samphel says.

I wave him away. He steps back but remains within my sightline. Lowering myself to the ground, I dig my fingers into the soil to keep steady. A few clouds have moved in, casting shadows that range hundreds of miles across the distant mountains. If I should wail anywhere, this would be the place.

"It's going to get dark before we reach Tsarang," Tseten says. "We should go."

"One moment," Samphel replies. He sits down nearby.

"Let's go," I say, rising from the ground and patting my hands against my legs.

"It's alright to rest a little while, you know," he says. "Now or anytime. Nothing will fall apart if you need to catch your breath."

"No, let's keep going. If I stop now, I might not be able to go on."

An hour later, we come upon a row of massive red cliffs that jut straight into the sky and are capped with jagged peaks. Against the surrounding gray mountains, these otherworldly formations look as if they had been washed with red paint. Across the sheer cliff face, a few cave openings are scattered about, some of them impossibly high, while closer to the ground, there's an ancient mud stupa encircled by miniature stupas, and a few homes loosely clustered. When I ask Tseten where we are, he glances at me with surprise.

"Long long ago," he says, "Guru Rinpoche was overseeing the construction of Samye, the first monastery in Tibet. But there was a demon who kept making trouble, undoing the construction each night to stop the dharma from spreading. So Guru Rinpoche started building another monastery here called Lo Gekar. It's nearby. When the demon started dismantling Lo Gekar, Guru Rinpoche had no choice but to kill the demon, tearing the body apart and spreading the remains across this area. He built Lo Gekar over the demon's heart and that stupa was constructed over the head. See that long prayer wall ahead? It was erected on the intestines. And those cliffs were splashed with the demon's blood."

Even if I hadn't learned the story of Guru Rinpoche and the demon, I can sense the battles that scar this land. Struggles that are mythic and humble, sacred and profane. Now that we are so close to the border, we are in the midst of a million small battles. From the Khampa fighters who hid in these caves while taking on an entire army, to countless families who fled on foot while wanting to turn back at each step, to the ones who still wait for the day when they can walk across the mountains once again.

As we pass through the village, Tseten peers up at the cliffs. "They're red even in the winter. Even when this whole area is covered in snow, you can still see the red cliffs."

"There's something strange about this place," Samphel says. "I get the feeling of being watched here. But not by people."

"Of course," Tseten says. "Our gods live in these caves. Some Westerners think we're just telling stories when we say that. They try to climb the mountains or go into the caves. Doesn't matter how much we tell them not to. Inevitably, they fall sick or have other troubles."

"And you?" I ask. "Have you been in the caves?"

"Yes, but not these ones," he says. "Some caves have beautiful paintings of deities and Mahasiddhas. Others are tombs or storerooms for texts. Come along."

We begin another long, sharp ascent. Noticing that our ponies need a rest, Samphel and I hop off to walk beside Tseten, who seems more relaxed around us now.

"What's your last name?" I ask him.

"My last name is Gurung," he replies, speaking in Tibetan for the first time, "but I'm not a Gurung. If the police ask, I tell them I'm a Gurung. If you admit to being a Tibetan, it only brings trouble. That's how it is." After a pause, he asks, "What are you doing in Lo?"

"Just having a look," Samphel says.

Tseten laughs, unconvinced, but he doesn't press us either. He seems to have the same patience as others here. Maybe it's the land that demands it. Things reveal themselves in their own time, or not at all.

The afternoon takes us through deep desert canyons and across layers of sandy mountains. With their eroding edges and endlessly shifting hues under the clouds, these mountains appear to yield silently to every force— even our footsteps that mark their surface over and over. Though the houses are becoming sparse, there are more caves here. Some are carved in precise, geometric lines, hundreds of meters up sheer mountain faces, as though they were made for solitary meditation. Other caves dot the mountains in huge clusters, suggesting that entire villages once lived in sky homes.

At sunset, we come upon the village of Tsarang. It is the most pleasant place yet, protected from the wind in a gentle valley with fields of tall barley and wheat surrounded by groves of poplar trees. In the distance, an old fort sits above a prominent cliff. Horses roam about, drinking from the neatly irrigated stream that has been diverted to run alongside every road, while dogs nap in perfect crevices between stone walls. The mud and stone houses are beautifully kept with painted facades, and at the far end of the village, there sits an imposing monastery washed in white and red paint.

There's one lodge in the village, and we happen to pass its owner. Tseten inquires about rooms for the night, and the owner leads us back to his home. It's a beautiful, two-story Tibetan-style home featuring a courtyard, warm carved-wood details, and a second floor with two empty guest rooms. The first will be mine, the other will be Samphel's, and Tseten will sleep in the kitchen by the stove. An hour later, as we drink tea together, I look out the window and see the group of French trekkers pitching their tents on the grass.

The owner laughs. "These foreigners are better prepared than you. Good thing you got here first."

"That's how their kind ate the world," Samphel replies, to which the owner nods in agreement.

An elderly man walks in, spinning a prayer wheel. He sits beside me, and the owner brings another cup of tea, asking his father if he wants something to eat. The father shakes his head. Speaking in Tibetan, he introduces himself as Pemba and asks us where we're from.

"Bhayul," Samphel says.

"He's from the capital. I'm from Pokhara," I say.

Po Pemba smiles, revealing a gold-plated tooth. "I know the camps in Pokhara."

"Do you know one by the gorge?"

"Of course," he says, beaming. "Way up in the hills? At night, the air is so cold and pure, especially after a storm. Almost like it is here."

My eyes well up at his loving recollection of my camp. "That's where I'm from," I say, nodding.

"It is good to meet someone who knows the same places, isn't it? Almost as if I'm back there now. What are you doing here?"

"My mother died," I say. "We're carrying her ashes."

"I understand," Po Pemba replies, his voice faint and melancholy. "You're doing a good thing."

"You want to go all the way to the border?" Tseten asks, putting down his cup.

"There are patrols," the owner says. "It's too dangerous."

"You better get someone to help you," Po Pemba adds.

"That's what we'll do," Samphel says. "We'll find someone at Lo Manthang."

"My wife used to live on the other side of the border," Tseten says, rearranging the cup before him. "We met when the border was still open, years ago. But then we heard the Chinese were building a fence and putting up an encampment. So my wife left her family and came to live with me on this side. She can never go back now. Once in a while, the authorities allow people to gather at the border for brief periods. That's when she sees her sister for a few hours." Looking over at me, he adds, "I had a feeling when I saw you two from my window. I sensed you wanted to go there, so I came down."

"That's our good fortune," I say, vaguely embarrassed that I assumed Tseten had approached us simply to make some money.

The conversation drifts to a topic of apparent controversy: the new road being built from Jomsom to Lo Manthang. The lodge owner thinks it will be good for getting medical care and supplies without using horses, especially in the winter months. But Po Pemba shakes his head vigorously, calling all of this foolishness.

"We've managed to preserve our way of life for thousands of years," he says. "A road will bring nothing good. Look at the Chinese trucks that keep driving through now. Speaking of which, has there been any news of the nun who self-immolated? Om mani padme hum."

"Pala, please," the lodge owner says, urging his father to lower his voice.

"There have been so many fire sacrifices," Tseten says softly.

Po Pemba turns to me and says, "If I can't speak freely while things are still quiet here, maybe I should dig a hole and speak into the earth."

I WAKE TO the sound of bells and prayers. For a moment, I think I'm back at the camp, and that it's my mother doing her morning rituals nearby. A flinch of dread shakes me out of my reverie. My head is pounding, and my eyes sting with every blink. Long hours of sleep must have passed, but I feel as if I've just closed my eyes. No memories of my dreams, not even the faintest recollections. Heading down the corridor toward the stairs, I pass the prayer room by the landing. Inside, Po Pemba is chanting before an altar while ringing a brass bell intermittently. He senses me at the door and waves me in from his seat before a low table. When I step inside and kneel on the floor beside him, my limbs feel as if they had been deadened to sensation.

"I have something for you," he says. Setting the bell down, he reaches into a slot beneath the table and pulls out a bundle of red threads. "These were blessed by my root guru last year. Take this and tie it around your neck. Once you wear it, the gods will protect you. Let go of all your fear. You have an important job to do."

"Thank you," I say, quietly moved by the care of this old man as I tie one of the threads loosely around my neck.

"Your body has become frail," he says, flipping the page on the prayers before him.

"Is it possible to feel my mother's pain? I have this sharp sensation in the back of my head that comes and goes."

"She is the basis of your body," he says. "But remember: What you're doing here isn't only for your mother. It's also for your own sake."

"I'd better go," I say, somewhat puzzled by his words. Before I leave, he holds my hand and says a prayer for our safe journey and for my long life. Po Pemba and I touch foreheads and say farewell.

WE BEGIN THE gradual ascent out of the Tsarang valley, and before long, we're back in the gray desert terrain, encircled by hills. The next climb is steep and feels suffocating, with the horses' labored movements. Once again, Samphel and I decide to go by foot. When we reach the top of the third hill, Tseten stops in place.

"This is the border of Lo," he says. "We will reach Lo Manthang soon."

He says a prayer and places a rock on the cairn that marks the border. Following his example, I reach down and add a stone to the top of the pile, saying a prayer for our safe passage. Samphel watches me with surprise.

"You know your prayers," he says.

"I've forgotten most of them. Shumo Tenkyi worries that I'm not a good Tibetan."

"And what, exactly, is a good Tibetan?"

"Someone who knows our prayers and speaks our tongue. Someone devout, quiet, feminine. Like the women of her generation, I guess."

"I always wonder where these ideals come from," he says. "To tell you the truth, your mother and aunt never fit into that box. I remember them as tough, sharp, outspoken, and loving, even as children. Anyway, forget that nonsense. Live your life as you wish."

"You're just saying that because you disrobed and became a smuggler."

He laughs. "You're probably right. Don't follow my example, either."

We continue through a flat and colorless terrain that seems endless. The mountains are no longer in view. Instead, we are faced with wall after wall of dust from every direction. The featureless landscape nearly lulls me to sleep several times, but Zema's strenuous movement jerks me back. After a short ascent, we turn the corner and see a wave of prayer flags strung across two boulders.

"We're here," Tseten says.

Below us, a massive valley sits encircled by endless layers of desert mountains. It's Lo Manthang, named the plain of spiritual longing. At its center is a walled city that edges the Kali Gandaki River, the same one that eventually passes before my camp. On the other side of the city, there are terraced barley fields, some trees, and crumbling stone watchtowers high above nearby hills. Footpaths branch out from one corner to the city walls, where people enter and exit through a single gate. Once home to a mighty kingdom controlling trade between Tibet and Nepal, the city now stands like a sturdy but diminished elder, seven hundred years of memories contained within its walls.

"Dolma, look there," Samphel says, pointing to the horizon.

A white band of mountains rises far above the valley, reaching higher than anything we've seen so far. At their peaks, clouds linger as though locked in conversation with the mountains.

"Is that our country?" I ask.

"Yes, in a sense," Tseten says. "All the land in this region is. We've been climbing to the highlands these past four days."

"It still seems far away," I say, unable to hide my disappointment.

"It's very close," Samphel says. He stares intently at the mountains, as if to see beyond the peaks.

I begin to think about Kelsang's prediction of rain. Will the clouds spill over the ridges and reach her village of two families washing her home with the rain of our country? Or do those clouds come from the lowlands, trying like us to enter Tibet?

"I'll be going back now," Tseten says.

"Don't you want to stay for the night?" I ask.

"No, I must return to my family. Someone in Lo will bring you back."

Samphel hands him some bills, which Tseten pockets without counting.

"Be careful," he says, tying the two ponies together. Then he rides off on Jha with Zema in tow, traveling at least twice the pace we rode.

I had expected Lo Manthang to be no different from the other villages we'd passed through: a quiet place where people notice our entry, asking where we're from and where we're going. But the walled city is buzzing with activity. Everyone seems to be rushing about. As we wander through the maze of narrow roads, some just wide enough for us to pass single file, I'm relieved to be enclosed from the wind. Even the sun is obstructed. And all around us, people speak our tongue without fear. It's strange to admit it, but I've never felt so safe, so at ease. Is this how it is to feel to be at home?

We stop at a stationery store and ask the clerk about hiring a driver.

The woman finishes polishing a glass case of pens and says, "Everyone's at the monastery for the school festival. Try asking there."

When we reach the monastery, young monks immediately guide us to sit on the floor inside. The moment we sit, a tall monk places a plastic cup in my hands, while another fills it with tea. A third monk follows, handing out paper plates with heaps of sweet rice mixed with raisins. Meanwhile, at the center of the crowded room, a man is giving a speech while a lone Nepali policeman sitting on the only plastic chair presides above us like a king.

"Nepal is falling apart elsewhere," the man tells the crowd in Tibetan, "because of a lack of Buddha dharma. But then, this community worships monks a little *too* much. You ought to do as much for your children as you do for the monasteries. And to the young monks here, since this gathering is held once a year at eight o'clock, you should all come on time. Not eight thirty, not nine. Eight. Just because you have free food and lodging, doesn't mean you can be slackers, or the monastery will fall into bad shape."

Switching to Nepali, he adds, "And all of you should speak Nepali more and be happy because the local police are here. Thank you, sir."

"I've read about this monastery," I whisper. This must be where Henri's friend worked. He spent over a decade restoring old murals. "Some of the most important murals are here, centuries old . . ." I say, trailing off and looking around.

"Let's go find them," Samphel says.

We slip out a side door and walk into the empty courtyard. Glancing into a few doors, we walk until we reach a two-story building with a roof that's under renovation. We duck through a doorway and enter an almost pitch-black room. Our hesitant footsteps echo in the dark while a draft comes from somewhere we can't see. I sense that the ceilings stretch to the second floor and the walls carry on for many meters. My eyes slowly adjust, and I see that the only source of light is high above us, to the right. Coming from a tiny window, a single line of sunlight streams into the space, illuminating a flash of colors on a wall.

Thousands upon thousands of white Buddhas swim before me. Lined in gold pigment, rendered in vivid hues, each one unique as a fingerprint. My eyes begin to play tricks on me. The lines on the wall appear to ripple like water, and I'm nearly driven back from the room, out into the sunlight.

"I have been here before," Samphel says, walking along the mural.

I cannot see his face in the darkness. I can only hear him. Following the sound of his voice, I listen as he speaks quietly.

"Fifty years ago, I stood here. We lived and died by rumors in those days. *The Americans are coming, their planes will land any day. The Gyami are withdrawing thanks to our fighters in the mountains.* We even heard rumors about sheep wandering to a nearby valley, just waiting to be claimed. But I cared most about the rumor of an oracle who had come to the Lo Valley. She was dressed in a leopard skin and wore a five-pointed crown. She could fly over the mountains and bring people back from the dead. An entire village owed their lives to her. Night after night, I dreamt about finding the oracle. In my dream, I ask for my mother's name and to see her face. My requests are simple, and the oracle smiles. Without hesitation, she bends down and whispers: *Your mother is waiting for you back home. Here is a glimpse of her face. As soon as you can, return to her.*"

He pauses to examine the illuminated section of the mural. Yet his eyes reveal the true object of his gaze. Not the figures before him, but something else, something only he can see. Perhaps something submerged within his mind, forgotten until this moment.

4

I N the morning, we find a tractor leaving for Chhoser, the last village before the border. We hop on for the journey along the rocky mountain path. Samphel stares at the arid expanse while he sits rigidly. He has no plan after Chhoser, that much is clear, but if we can pull this off, what then? I wonder if he even knows what he hopes will happen at the border.

Across from us, an elderly woman smiles broadly in our direction. "Where are you two from?" she asks, raising the familiar question. She has cataracts in both eyes. I wonder how much of our faces she can see.

"Bhayul," Samphel responds.

"Are you a merchant?"

"Yes, Ama la."

"They call me Ama Rinchen. And your daughter?"

"She goes to school abroad, in Canada," he says without hesitation. I briefly catch his gaze, unsure of how to respond to his words, while a flutter of surprise and wonder comes from the tractor's passengers. Canada, they repeat.

"Is that in Europe?" asks the driver, turning back.

"No, it's by Ari," I reply.

The woman nods. "Very good." Smiling brightly as her cataracts catch the light, she adds, "I would've gone to school if I could."

I give her a smile and look back at the low river along the rocky road. Did my mother walk through here as a child? Would she recognize this place now? The tractor turns into a lush valley with trees and irrigated fields. Whitewashed mud homes are scattered across the river, some nestled against a steep mountain into which a monastery is also carved. All of us passengers hop off the tractor, which promptly turns back. As a few of us cross the dry, rocky riverbed, Ama Rinchen grips my arm with her bony hand. Ahead, the monastery looms above the houses, and I notice two monks leaning over the edge of a mud balcony, dousing the walls with buckets of watery red paint.

"My entire family has moved away," Ama Rinchen says. "So I had to ask the neighbors to paint my home for the holiday."

"What holiday?" Samphel asks.

Ama Rinchen looks at him sideways for a moment. "It's Guru Rinpoche day, funny boy! You better go to the monastery now."

I let out a laugh. I wish she would invite us in for tea, but Ama Rinchen seems more concerned with our spiritual welfare. She leads us up the steep, ancient steps of the monastery and onto the veranda where the two monks are working. The younger monk, who must be no more than ten or eleven, gives us a nod and passes a freshly loaded rag to his partner before calling on someone inside. A tall, middle-aged monk emerges from a doorway that's fitted into the mountain. He greets us, inviting us into the shrine room. But as we enter, I'm struck by something else. To the side of the monastery, farther up the mountain, there are at least a dozen openings carved into the cliff face. It looks like a large cave complex.

"Old caves," the monk says, seeing my interest. "Some of the poorest still live there from time to time."

"How old?" I ask. "A thousand years?"

"Some say many more."

"I stayed there for several years with my children after fleeing," Ama Rinchen says. "I know them well."

"Can we go inside?" I ask.

"Yes, I'd like to see it," Samphel says, to my surprise.

Ama Rinchen offers to take us there, and we follow her for the short walk to the caves.

Across the mountain's sheer face, dozens of cave entrances are scattered inconsistently, suggesting that they were carved over many decades, if not centuries. There seem to be at least six levels, though a few openings sit much higher, as though they were the homes of isolated beings. From one of its lowest mouths, there hangs a long, narrow ladder carved from a tree trunk.

"You'll have to climb up," Ama Rinchen says, pointing to a vertical shaft about five meters above our heads. "I'll wait for you here."

Samphel goes first, his heels hanging over the notched levels, his backpack rising above me with each move. As I hoist myself up, the ladder rocks from side to side while the wind seems to lift me. When I reach the top, the opening is much smaller than it had looked from below. I duck inside and find the ceiling is too low for me to stand upright, so I have to shuffle, bent over, toward the first chamber, where the ceiling is slightly higher. In this room, the walls are pale and sun-drenched, with a round cave opening that lets in light. As I get up close, I see the surfaces here are rough and uneven, like a pond in a rainstorm, though there is not a drop of water in these caves. Three more mouths surround me: one on each side, and one above my head. I peek into the chamber on the right where Samphel stands, staring at a corner.

"Seems to be a kitchen. See the mud stove?" he says. "Still mostly intact."

The walls here are coated with black smoke from the waist up. The stove, or what remains of it, is made of pale mud bricks stacked loosely in a half circle. What mortar had kept these bricks in place is now all but gone. How many souls across the centuries have cooked at this hearth? The kitchen leads to another chamber, though I can't see inside because the mouth faces a wall. I turn and look down the other opening toward a series of rooms, each leading to the next. But the hole in the ceiling draws me upward. And I think I hear a faint sound coming through there. Wings flapping or a flag. Maybe there's a bird trapped inside.

"I'm going up," I tell Samphel.

Extending my arms through the opening, I pull myself up. When I stand, I notice my jacket and pants are coated in pale dust. Now the sound of flapping seems nearer. It appears to come from a chamber to my left. The opening to this room is the smallest yet, just a narrow slit, roughly the size of my torso. Sticking one leg in, then my head, I push myself through. Despite its slim entrance, the next chamber is spacious and again has a large opening that lets in light. One corner is piled with shards of broken mud. Another holds a stone slab whose purpose is a mystery to me. I hear the rhythmic sound again.

Following it, I enter another series of rooms, but the sound begins to fade away. A cool breeze circles me and I notice another opening above my head. But I can't muster another vertical climb. My legs have become heavy, my feet ache with each step, and the skin of my palms are scraped and beaten from the last effort. It occurs to me that we haven't eaten all day. I put a hand on my belly and feel a rising hunger twist painfully.

"Dolma, this way."

It's Samphel calling from a dark hallway behind me. He must have taken a different shaft to this level. The corridor ahead has an even lower ceiling and requires us to bend almost in half as we shuffle past a series of lightless rooms.

"I know these caves," Samphel says, leading me toward a light-filled chamber. He presses his fingers against the stone. "Hard pale walls. I would dig my fingers into them, just trying to break off a piece to eat. I was so hungry in those years. Listen," he says, freezing in place.

It's the flapping sound again. So I didn't imagine it. Though now it reminds me of a prayer wheel, but always just beyond our reach.

"This sound was everywhere, even back then," he whispers. "I followed it from room to room, thinking there was a bird I could catch. I came down this corridor, and as I drew closer to the room at the end, the sound grew louder."

"What was inside?" I ask.

"Come," he says.

I follow Samphel into the light-filled room and wait for my eyes to adjust. The space is littered with old dinged-up metal pots but is otherwise empty. On the far side, there's a child-sized opening, through which we can see the sky, the surrounding mountains, and the river in the distance.

"There used to be a huge mound of loose paper in here," he says, motioning. "It was so tall, I couldn't even see the other side of the room. It had been so long since I had seen paper, and never so much at once. I circled that hill with wide eyes. It was covered with a thick coating of dust, some feathers, and bird droppings. As wind blew, the pages crackled and moved together like a sleeping animal. Though I couldn't read, I recognized that the sheets were lined with prayers. But all I kept thinking was that my father and I could live for months on this much paper."

He laughs softly and continues, "Then I began to worry that someone else would find this room. It was only a matter of time. There were at least twenty families camped out along with us. I would ask my father what to do. But first, I needed to eat. Picking up a sheet, I stared at the beautiful lines of holy script. I gave it no more thought. Taking one last look around, I bit down and tore off a piece. Dust filled my mouth and throat. Pushing the paper inside, I stifled a cough and waited for saliva to come and soften the page. But my throat burned and I could not swallow. So I spat it out. The sad, crumpled sheet fell to the ground. I stared at it, my hunger intensifying. I was about to stuff it back in my mouth when I heard a sound.

"In the chamber next to this one, there was a towering figure facing away from me and rapidly turning a hand drum. They wore a five-pointed crown on their head and an animal skin around their shoulders. The next moment, the figure turned to face me. I was so frightened, I thought I had gone blind. All I saw was the white light of my fear. But as my eyes refocused, I saw a woman. She approached me and asked who I was. I remember thinking it was strange that she didn't crouch down or speak gently like a mother. Instead, she spoke with a stern and bold voice that sounded like neither a woman nor a man.

"Then I thought: The rumors are true. The oracle is here. I had searched for her in the old monastery, like a fool, but of course she would be in the caves. Just like the saints and hermits. As she drew near, I backed away. She was capable of setting off a hailstorm upon her enemies. All of time spun in her eyes. She seemed to grow larger as she neared. Her fingers looked like an eagle's talons; her bare, colorless feet were almost transparent on the red floor. Even sunlight lay itself down on her long black hair, wanting nothing but to rest upon her. I dropped to my knees and claimed my place at her feet, pressing my palms together at my forehead.

"'What's this?' she asked, staring at the little paper ball at my feet. 'What a shame,' she said. 'The next people to see this will not leave it here.' I had no idea what she meant. But it sounded like the kind of thing a medium would say, so I told her that I had been searching for her. I told her that my mother and I had been separated. My mother was trapped with a bad husband, but I didn't know her name or face. The oracle turned and gazed out the cave's mouth, down to the desolate valley. She was quiet for a long time, then replied that she could not speak to the gods anymore. With that, she walked to the opening and began to climb down the mountain. I went to the mouth of the cave, kneeled over the edge, and watched her descend the ladder. I begged her to stop and come back to me, but in the wind, my voice barely carried past my nose.

"When she reached the ground, she took off her leopard skin and hat, and headed toward a black nomad tent near the river. Although it was large, there were no animals around it. The oracle has become poor, I thought. Without her ceremonial garb, she appeared just like an ordinary woman. Then I heard a child shout and call her Ama. Two little girls came into view as they ran around a row of boulders. I couldn't believe my eyes. The great oracle was a mother. Then an old envy awoke inside me, dragging itself out. I could not stop staring at the girls. Everything they had was due to their mother, just as everything I lacked was due to my mother abandoning me. I shouted from the cave, 'Did she even want me?' But there was no reply. The smaller girl ran toward her mother, while the older one walked. Just as I was about to turn away, the older girl stopped in place. Then, as if instructed by an invisible power, she looked up, in the direction of the caves, and stared directly at me. I felt something shake within me, reaching a place beyond my hunger. A vast ocean of calm."

Straightening his posture, Samphel walks to the cave opening and gazes out over the surrounding cliffs, then down at the dried-up river we crossed to enter the village. Bracing against the cave wall, he lowers himself and sits on the floor, still facing the opening. I think about the leopard that circled our house.

"Was that my mother outside the caves?" I ask. "And Shumo Tenkyi?"

"I'll tell you the truth," he says, grimacing and shaking his head. "I don't know. There were so many of us here back then. We were all in a daze. Sometimes I think I'm still in a daze."

He closes his eyes. Then a brief smile flashes across his face, as if he could still see them now.

"But it might have been your mother."

★ ★ ★

WHEN SAMPHEL AND I descend from the caves, we find Ama Rinchen sitting on a boulder with her sunglasses on. "Had enough?" she asks.

"We have to go now," Samphel says.

"Already? Where to?"

"To the border," I say, though I know it's reckless to reveal so much to a stranger.

"That's forbidden. No one can go," she replies. "Besides, there are thousands of soldiers stationed there. This place is as good as home. Just think to yourselves," she says, patting her dress, "'I am there.'"

"We must go, Grandmother," I tell her.

"Well then, it is your fate to go."

Placing her sunglasses on her head, Ama Rinchen says a prayer for our safety and for our wishes to be fulfilled. She prays for us to attain freedom from suffering and desire, then she prays the same for all sentient beings. We touch foreheads as we hold hands. I will miss this woman. Though we met only a short while ago, her presence is comforting in ways I cannot describe. Looking into her cataracts, I realize that if something happens at the border, this could be the last kind face I ever see.

5

Now that we're so close, each step is arduous. I have never been this dirty or tired, this desperate for rest and a hot shower. My body has become a burden, something I must push up this rocky mountain. My stomach wrenches in hunger, and a row of blisters sticks against my threadbare socks. I keep thinking that each bend will be the last; that we're about to behold some immense, unquestionable sight that will let us know we've made it. But at each turn, the path continues to rise upward and my initial excitement wanes, as I reconsider our defiant decision to walk to a place so many have warned against.

But Samphel's eyes are focused on his feet, his determination sharp as a spike. I can see him as a child now, from the steady intensity in his gaze, from the way he persists. If his story is true, then my grandmother was an oracle. Yet no one speaks of this. What happened to her? And to my grandfather? If only I could ask my mother. But it's too late for that now. Her knowledge, her memories, all of it has vanished. A wave of grief plunges through my body, hitting me with such force that I must stop to catch my breath.

"What's the matter?" Samphel asks.

I shake my head and say, "Let me carry her."

The backpack is lighter than I expected. I open the zipper and pull out the plastic bag of ashes. It is cold, soft, and loose in my hands. The last of my mother. How little she has become, so humble and tender. Yet all my life, there was no one larger. No one more mysterious. Now I see that what I wanted most was to know my mother—her dreams, her sorrows, the ghosts that lived only in her mind. I hold her against my cheeks, my eyelids, my forehead. I hold her close so she can now say what she couldn't tell me in life.

It is one thing to spend your life circling a place you cannot enter. It is another to be forced to walk away from all you know, launched toward an abyss, onto this rocky earth that breaks apart, dissolving under your feet, as if to say even the earth here is precarious. From where did you get the strength, Ama? And Shumo Tenkyi, Po Migmar, and everyone else who crossed into this strange land?

I think of the Nameless Saint. His promise of continual return. His freedom to move. His frailty. His persistence. That minute but ancient mirror of our humanity. I think of my aunt. How she knelt before the ku, her expression changing as she was transported to a past that was tucked away inside her mind. How she looked around the basement and asked me, *Do you feel that?* I didn't feel anything, but I realized then how little I understood—of my aunt, of the world that made her. A world that still lives within her. How can I tear the Nameless Saint away from her?

"I don't want the Saint's ku to come back to the camp," I say, resuming the climb. "The ku should remain where it is, with Shumo Tenkyi."

"It's not safe, Dolma. Not for you, not for your aunt."

"Shumo will keep the ku hidden. She will care for it."

He glances at me but says nothing for some time. I sense that he's considering whether it's even possible to change my mind.

"Alright," he finally says. "And you? What will you do?"

"I'll stay at the camp for a little while, help Po Migmar with the prayers."

"Then you'll go back to Canada and resume your studies?"

"You'd like that, wouldn't you? For me to go back to the country of promise."

"Of course I want that. Look around, Dolma. This is where we were not long ago—starving, lost, terrified. Your future is in the West."

"If this place holds nothing for us, why have we returned? Why are we carrying Ama back? We should just forget this land, in that case."

Samphel lets out a deep sigh. "You're right," he says. "We can't let go. And this land hasn't let go of us either."

We continue walking in silent, heavy exhaustion. Each step I take sends a puff of dust into the air. Once again, I need to pause. This time, I turn around and see that we have ascended a great distance. We are high above the caves and the village where Ama Rinchen resides.

"Get down," Samphel says, pulling me behind a rock.

There's a small stone house ahead, circled by a low wall. Two Nepali officers stand outside. One is in uniform, washing his clothes at a tall tap. The other is wearing only his undershirt and shorts as he lathers his hair. This must be the last outpost.

"We're close to the border," Samphel whispers.

"They'll never let us pass," I say.

"Once they go back inside, we have to run. Okay?"

I give a nod, and we resume watching the men as they carry out their tasks. It occurs to me that they might not go inside for a long time. We may have to stay here for hours. Then the ground begins to shake. A loud rattling comes up the mountain, heading toward us. First, we see an exhaust pipe, then the rest of a tractor. There's no time to hide, nowhere to seek cover. As the vehicle nears, I spot a monk standing in the back of the tractor. An older monk sits behind a steering wheel, and when he notices us, he doesn't stop the vehicle or react in any way.

"Where are you going?" asks the young monk in the back as the tractor passes.

"We're going up to the border with my mother's ashes," I say. "Will you take us?"

He bangs on the side of the tractor, and it slows slightly. "Hurry," he says, keeping watch.

We climb into the back as quickly as we can while the tractor continues moving.

"We're heading to the border to pick up supplies we ordered," the young monk says. "We get a few minutes there, that's all."

"Thank you," I say.

"Just let my brother do the talking," he says. His delicate features suggest that he's just a teenager. Perhaps no older than fifteen.

When we pull up to the police outpost, the older monk answers the questions. Casually, he tells the officers that Samphel and I are staff from the monastery and that we're collecting supplies at the border.

"We'll bring you some treats," he adds, cheerfully.

"Don't give us that bad whiskey again," says the officer washing his laundry.

"Alright, some Chinese vodka then."

"Is it good?"

"The best, but I've never tasted it."

They all have a good laugh, and the tractor sets off again.

"Be quick," someone shouts from behind us. "I mean it."

We turn a corner, and the station disappears from sight. Standing in the back of the tractor, I keep looking around, eager to see how the landscape will change. But it's the same dry expanse, a slow incline hemmed in by nearby hills. The mountains we saw from Lo Manthang are no longer visible, nor the clouds they held to their peaks. Nothing but wind and dust. The tractor pushes itself upward as loose rocks fall from the roadside.

Then we reach the end of the climb, and the tractor levels. The earth becomes perfectly flat, as if pulled taut. I wonder if we've reached the raised land of our country. Like Samphel, the teenage monk peers into the distance, watching a lone deer grazing amid the tall grass. I wonder if he and his brother have family on the other side, but I'm afraid to ask so close to the border. I think about Tseten's wife. I might be closer to her sister and relatives than she has been in a long time. Am I close to my own lost relatives?

We rattle along the dirt road. Then a brightly painted concrete arch appears like a solitary traffic light in the middle of a field. As we near the arch, Chinese and Nepali script come into view. The young monk reads the text in both languages, and tells us that it announces a friendship between the two nations. What else is there to say? We pass wordlessly under the slim concrete curve.

The tractor slowly turns around the hill. Then we see new terrain. Flat land stretches for hundreds of kilometers in every direction, mirrored by an endless sky. It is a scale that I have never experienced. On one side of the plains, there is a line of enormous snow-covered mountains, rising straight from the earth. No sandstone hills, no layers of smaller peaks. They remind me of the mountain behind Kesang's house. A deity watching the world pass by, beneath her gaze. Yes, the mountains convey a godlike lucidity. A kind of near permanence. After days in a dissolving landscape, this solidity feels like a relief. Then I notice the clouds that are everywhere. They hover just above the mountains, casting wide shadows, while some completely envelop the peaks.

I turn around and see how sharply the land drops behind us. Like a cliff, I think. This is what my family saw. This is what Samphel and his father saw. Wrenched from their homes, stripped of their belongings, they faced a deep and unknown valley, and descended into the lowlands.

So this must be it, this elevated earth. The Land of Snows.

Still, I don't trust my senses. It's hard to believe that I have somehow reached my ancestors' land. All my life, even reaching its very edges seemed impossible. Now I don't feel ready.

"Is this it? Are we there?" I ask, then wonder why I still say *there*.

But no one has heard me. The young monk has his eyes closed and his hands folded in prayer while he chants rapidly. Samphel continues to face the horizon, his eyes straining, as if still trying to see far beyond what is visible. Now I sense some fear in him. Could it be that he is also afraid of going home? Does the prospect of returning, however implausible, fill him with a hard and braided dread?

The tractor lurches to a stop. To the side, there's a waist-high pile of boxes. A collection of stoves, crates of alcohol, mattresses wrapped in plastic—just sitting on the desert earth.

"Do what you need to," the driver monk says as he gets out. "But stay nearby."

Moving quickly, the two monks begin loading the back of the tractor. Samphel and I step down and look around. We're both unsure of what to do, how to behave.

"Can we go a little farther?" I ask the young monk.

He cocks his chin. "Over a thousand soldiers live there, just watching the border."

In the distance, I see a chain-link fence five or six kilometers away. It runs across the horizon, from the mountains on our left to the hills on our right. Somehow, I didn't notice the fence earlier. But now I cannot unsee it. And just beyond the fence, there's a nondescript rectangular building. It would fade into the land, if not for its bright turquoise roof.

"If we're not fast, they'll come and detain us," the young monk adds, before resuming his work.

I feel a mix of fear and defiance in my chest. It all seems so pointless, so petty. Against the mountains, the land, and the sky, this fence and the barracks look puny. Merely the work of humans. I can even see straight through the chain link to the plains that stretch on for hundreds of kilometers. If I were an insect, I could fly back and forth all day.

But perhaps this is the point. After all, what better way is there to demonstrate our lack of power? Yes, this is how you break a heart. With a wire fence that shows everything that cannot be touched. While the wind sweeps the expanse, while the rain clouds roam, free as ever. We get a glimpse and nothing more.

"Okay, let's go," the older monk says, putting the last box in the tractor.

"We just got here," Samphel replies, shaken out of a daze.

"We're done," the monk replies, opening the door.

I want to do something. I want to shout in the direction of the barracks, if only to let them know that we are here, that we have dared to come. But my voice will not carry far in this wind. I look around, searching for a rock. Anything that I can throw, just to get a little closer. But the earth here contains no rocks. A few steps ahead, I spot some fist-sized stones. But when I walk to them, I realize that they're miniature stupas. The remains of cremated bodies, hand molded into conical shapes. Some are still intact, while others are disintegrating into the soil. We are not the first to bring the remains of our loved ones here.

The tractor's gate slams shut. All the boxes are stacked in the rear.

"Okay, let's go," the older monk shouts again as he starts the engine.

"A little longer," I say, pleading.

The young monk climbs into the back and says, "I told you. We can't stay for more than a few minutes each time."

What if I lived nearby? In a lifetime of short visits, could I stitch together a year on this land?

The tractor begins to turn around.

"Come on, Dolma," Samphel says.

He starts to pick at the many knots in the plastic bag. But I'm not ready. My hands shake uncontrollably, unable to even grip the knots.

"Just make a small hole," he says. "Then we can cup the ashes out."

I dig my fingernails into the plastic, but our unsteady hands pull too much and the bag tears. There's no more time. Now, I think. It must be now. We rip the bag and let the ashes fly.

Ama. A momentary pillar in the sky. Ama.

She twists upward and is swept away.

Samphel lowers to his knees. He places his palms on the desert soil. I kneel as well. Side by side, we face the mountains and the land beyond the fence. We bow and touch our foreheads to the soil. All that it contains, all that it holds.

"In another life," he says, "you and I will cross this border. We will go to the places where your grandparents buried their possessions. You will claim your inheritance and you will choose the life you want."

"We'll build our homes there," I say.

"We'll herd animals and churn cheese," he adds, smiling.

"And no one will limit our time, our movements, or our words," I say. "No one will question whether we belong."

"That question will be banished from the earth," he replies, facing the fence again. "People will walk across this land as freely as our ancestors did for thousands of years. And this sight before us, this silly fence, will be a story we tell each other. Just a story about a brief and terrible time in our history."

"But not now," I say, finally accepting the truth.

"Not now," Samphel repeats as his eyes meet mine. Letting his grief pool in his eyes, he adds, "For now, we must leave. But we will continue to circle this land. In this life and the next. That is our sorrow and our hope."

Then he turns his gaze back to the ground and grips the soil in his palms. He folds his fingers inward and presses as hard as he can. Hard enough that his skin could burst open. And lifting his hands to his face, he opens his mouth and takes in the earth.

6

A MA, look down. Do you see us? Don't leave just yet. Stay for a
moment. I am your daughter, from a life you're already forgetting.
Beside me is your sweetheart. See him clutch the soil. See him travel to
his past, to his former self.

This is the border. The mouth of our country. Do you recognize it?
This mythic scale, this haunted beauty? A fence cuts the land, but a fence
cannot stop the dead. The evidence is all around us, in these ashes quietly
released, these final acts of devotion.

But what about the living? For years, I held a dream of a homecoming.
Now that I stand here, I see that I am a stranger, for what do I know of
this place, of what lies beyond this fence? Even my question is mistaken.
Knowledge. Such a puny deity, and I have worshipped at its altar for
years. All the books in the world stacked together would mean nothing
in this vastness.

And yet, standing here at the cleft of two worlds, I feel a kind of
stability. This is a familiar threshold, facing in opposite directions: Toward
a country I cannot truly enter. And back to a world that cannot be my
home. Forward or back, no step makes sense. So I must remain between
two realms. This fence under my feet is a tightrope I can never leave.

Ama, I finally understand why I have struggled. I was born at this
border, and I have lived at this border. At our camp, at my school in
Kathmandu, in the West. All along, I was standing here. On this edge
of becoming. Where the needle trembles yet cannot move.

Do you hear that? An engine rattles in its metal case. Tires press upon the dry earth. They say it's time. They say there's no more time. But I will not listen. I will lie on the ground, cradle my head in my arms, and tuck my legs into my chest. I will feel the ache in my head, my back, my feet. And I will let the pain come and go, like the air in my lungs, like everything in life. The sun will set, stretching the shadows of the mountains. The sky will turn pink and orange, as birds sweep over me in waves. Night will cast its gaze upon the earth, revealing a million stars. Even the far edges of our universe will come into view, tethered to our fate for eternity. The moon will rise, show her face to me, and fall away. The sun will return, warm my skin, and slip away. Walls of rain will bathe my body. Sunlight will darken my skin. Wind will burn my cheeks. And I will endure each day and night because there is nowhere else to go. Because this is my place.

Here, I will cease to wonder about my past or my future because I will see with new eyes. I will see with the Nameless Saint's vision, with endless memory and timeless freedom. Your childhood home. Your pastures. Your parents whom I never met. All of our ancestors. I have finally found a way to hear them. At last, their message is clear. This land will remain. Long after our own brief, flickering lights fade, these mountains, these plains, this wind will persist. And because this land is the source of everything that makes us, we will still be here.

ACKNOWLEDGMENTS

Colonialization, displacement, and exile have many costs, including proximity and access to one's history, culture, and language. But in the decade that I spent writing this novel, some of the greatest joys for me have come from learning about my people, family, and self. For this I am indebted to an entire constellation of formal and informal resources including relatives, friends, writers, scholars, and organizations that helped me piece together, bit by bit, the tapestry of our past and present. Although I borrowed liberally from these teachers, I own any errors as my own. I share my sources here for my fellow Tibetans who are also learning against the silences and erasures of history. Our stories are our survival.

On the topic of the Tibetan oracular tradition, I drew from Hildegard Diemberger's "Female Oracles in Modern Tibet," W. Geoffrey Arnott's "Nechung: A Modern Parallel to the Delphic Oracle," John Vincent Bellezza's *Spirit-mediums, Sacred Mountains and Related Bon Textual Traditions in Upper Tibet*, "The Voice of the Gods in Upper Tibet: The Trance-induced Invocations and Songs of Praise of the Spirit-medium Phowo Srigyal" and "The Liturgies and Oracular Utterances of the Spirit-mediums of Upper Tibet," Réne De Nebesky-Wojkowitz's *Oracles and Demons of Tibet*, Tsering Rithar Sherpa's documentary *The Spirit Doesn't Come Anymore*, Per-arne Berglie's "Spirit-possession in Theory and Practice—Séances with Tibetan Spirit-mediums in Nepal" and "To Tell the Future by Using Threads—And Some Reflections on Tibetan Divination," Katarina Turpeinen's "The Soteriological Context of a Tibetan Oracle," and Homayun Sidky's "The State Oracle of Tibet, Spirit Possession, and Shamanism."

On the conditions of early Tibetan refugees in Nepal in the 1960s, I consulted: "Aid to Tibetan Refugees: An Agricultural Colony in Nepal" by the International Committee of the Red Cross, *The International Review of the Red Cross*, Second Year—No. 20, November 1962 edited by Jean-G. Lossier, "Battle Against Despair" by Peter Larson, "Cultural Survival: The Tibetans in Nepal" and "Exiles from the Land of Snows: Survey of a Tibetan Refugee Community" by Carol Rose, and "Tibetan Settlements in Thangboche and Jawalakhel: Report-I" Refugee Watch. I must also give a special thanks to the Tibet Oral History Project for capturing oral histories of our elders in this precious well of stories. For the history of the early years of occupation and resistance, I consulted the Panchen Lama's *70,000 Character Petition*, as well as *Arrested Histories: Tibet, the CIA, and Histories of a Forgotten War* by Carole McGranahan, and *Forbidden Memory: Tibet During the Cultural Revolution* by Tsering Woeser. I also read "The Tibetan Rebellion of 1959 and China's Changing Relations with India and the Soviet Union" by Chen Jian, and "Tibet and the Chinese People's Republic" by the International Commission of Jurists.

On the subject of the Tibetan antiquities trade, I relied on conversations with friends as well as *The Museum on the Roof of the World: Art, Politics, and the Representation of Tibet* by Clare E. Harris. Two texts were vital for references to Buddhist metaphysics: *Hidden Teachings of Tibet: An Explanation of the Terma Tradition of Tibetan Buddhism* by Tulku Thondup Rinpoche, and the *Bardo Thodol* or *The Tibetan Book of the Dead*. Gloria E. Anzaldúa, Homi K. Bhabha, and Edward Said provided important frameworks for the themes of my novel.

Thank you to my agent, Michelle Brower, who took a chance on me with a partial, helped with many drafts, and found wonderful homes for this book; Rob Arnold, for your kindness and early belief in my project; and Danya Kukafka, for your excellent notes. Thank you to my superb editors Anita Chong and Grace McNamee, for your dedication, care, and impeccable skill in bringing out the best in this book. Grace, after all of our edits, I see how absolutely flawless your instincts are about my work. Anita, you combed through this text and set the highest standard for every line. Gratitude to everyone at Bloomsbury, especially: Lauren Dooley, Paula Dragosh, Akshaya Iyer, Myunghee Kwon, Jonathan Lee, Nancy Miller, Lauren Ollerhead, Valentina Rice, and Ellen Whitaker. Thank you to the McClelland & Stewart team, especially: Tonia Addison, Jared Bland, Jennifer Griffiths, Sarah Howland, and Ruta Liormonas, and Kimberlee Kemp. I must also thank a number of institutions that were critical in the creation of this work. Thank you: Art Omi: Writers; Banff Centre for Arts and Creativity; Catwalk Institute; Columbia University's TOMS Fellowship, Writing Fellowship; and Teaching Fellowship; Hedgebrook; Monson

Arts; PLAYA Summerlake; the Barbara Deming Memorial Fund; the Canada Council for the Arts; the Lillian E. Smith Center; Tin House; Vermont Studio Center; Virginia Center for the Creative Arts, Wildacres; and Willapa Bay AiR.

My early readers and dear friends Tenzin Dickie, Julie Kantor, Dhondup Tashi Rekjong, and Sarah Ulicny gave generously to this manuscript and I will forever be grateful. I have also been fortunate to receive advice, encouragement, and camaraderie from a community of friends while writing this novel, including: Jessamine Chan, Tomomi Chu, Paige Cooper, Padma Dolma, Rinchen Dolma, Christy Jung, Bhutila Karpoche, Yewande Omotoso, Madalina Preda, Alessandro Ricciarelli, Clarisse Baleja Saïdi, Anakana Schofield, Shruti Swamy, Tenzin Nawang Tekan, Xuan Juliana Wang, and David Wu. Thank you to my many teachers over the years, especially: Donald Antrim, Dennis Bock, Jonathan Dee, David Ebershoff, Binnie Kirshenbaum, Hari Kunzru, Victor LaValle, Maureen Medved, Maaza Mengiste, Jay Neugeboren, Barbara Parkin, John Reed, Gary Shteyngart, Rhea Tregebov, and Leni Zumas. I must also thank my fellow Tibetan writers, of past and present, in occupied Tibet and in exile, who have shown me what is possible. There are too many to list, but at the front of my mind, I have found solace and inspiration in the works of Tsering Wangmo Dhompa, Rinchen Lhamo, Jamyang Norbu, Bhuchung D. Sonam, and Tenzin Tsundue. And to my Greenpeace crew, it has been an honor to dream and work toward a better world with you.

Finally, I want to thank my late father, who taught me to love books, laugh loudly, and dream big. Although you cannot hold this book, your love is in every line. To my mother, who has endured so much in this life, and still maintains her impish sense of humor and giant heart: You are my hero. Thank you to my siblings, who never let me feel alone and always let me be the baby, and to our family's true babies, Karma and Dorje, we love you forever and ever. Thank you to all my relatives across the world and in Tibet, I miss you and love you—even if I have never met you. To Barbara and Michael, thank you for raising my fellow. And at last, thank you, Charles, for being an unfailing and devoted reader, editor, and partner in this endeavor for the last eight years. What a privilege it's been to experience this together, our first book.

A NOTE ON THE AUTHOR

Tsering Yangzom Lama holds an MFA from Columbia University and a BA from the University of British Columbia in creative writing and international relations. She has received grants and residencies from the Canada Council for the Arts, Art Omi, Hedgebrook, Tin House, and the Barbara Deming Memorial Fund, among others. Lama was born and raised in Nepal, and has since lived in Vancouver, Toronto, and New York City.